Praise for *Blood Rivalry*

"Fans of legal thrillers with as much bite as Blood Rivalry will not want to put this book down. Attaway has delivered one of the best installments in this genre…. emotionally satisfying, yet morally unsettling, and that's what makes it so intriguing." — 5 Stars

Perfect for fans of Greg Iles' Natchez Burning trilogy
and James Lee Burke's A Private Cathedral.

Reader Views

"Attaway's command of character and finely evoked milieu over eras…fascinates and convinces, keeping the pages turning as this character-driven political thriller builds toward an urgent and satisfying confrontation."

Perfect for fans of Robert Bailey's Legacy of Lies
and John Grisham's The Boys from Biloxi.

BookLife Review

"…a compelling Southern saga that masterfully weaves together themes of power, family legacy, and the pursuit of redemption…. a must-read for fans of Southern Gothic and intricate legal dramas."

"…a sophisticated blend of legal thriller and historical drama…. a must-read for fans of Southern Gothic and intricate legal dramas."

Seattle Book Review

"…a fast-paced, beautifully sophisticated political and family thriller. Very highly recommended."

"…a confident blend of personal mystery and political intrigue…"

Readers' Favorite

A SOUTHERN NOVEL OF POWER, DECEIT, AND REBIRTH

BLOOD RIVALRY

AN ATKINS FAMILY LOW COUNTRY SAGA
BOOK 3

PAUL ATTAWAY

Copyright © 2025 by Paul Attaway

This is a work of fiction. Unless otherwise indicated, all the names, characters, businesses, places, events and incidents in this book are either the product of the author's imagination or used in a fictitious manner. Any resemblance to actual persons, living or dead, or actual events is purely coincidental.

All rights reserved. No part of this publication may be reproduced or transmitted in any form or by any electronic, mechanical, recording, or other means except as allowed under Section 107 or 108 of the 1976 United States Copyright Act, without the prior written permission of the author.

All Bible scriptures are from the English Standard Version. Published by Linksland Publishing

Library of Congress Control Number:

Paperback ISBN: 979-8-89989-083-3
Ebook ISBN: 979-8-89989-082-6

Editing, design, and distribution by Bublish
Printed in the United States of America

This book is dedicated to my children and the family that we are because of them. Their mother and I continue to take joy in watching them navigate this world.

Ecclesiastes 1:2 (2) Vanity of vanities, says the Preacher, vanity of vanities! All is vanity.

PART ONE

Ecclesiastes 1: 13-14 (13) And I applied my heart to seek and to search out by wisdom all that is done under heaven. It is an unhappy business that God has given to the children of man to be busy with. (14) I have seen everything that is done under the sun, and behold, all is vanity and a striving after wind.

Chapter 1

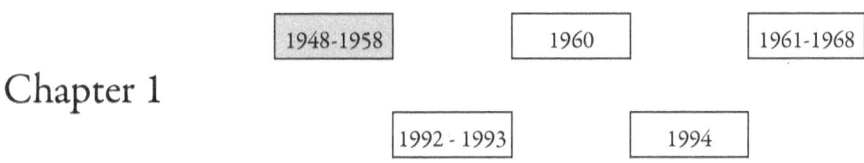

MAY 28, 1948

Colin Dunsmore sat alone at the back of the dining car with a cigarette and cup of coffee, watching the landscape pass by, lost in thought, as the trail of smoke off the end of his Lucky Strike spiraled lazily up and out of the cracked-open window. His attention was drawn back inside by the waiter removing a tin ashtray and the plate holding the remains of his breakfast: scrambled eggs, bacon, and toast. Simple, the way he liked it. Now, all he needed was a new ashtray. As if reading his mind, the waiter, armed with a fresh pot of coffee, both refilled his mug and replaced his ashtray before passing through the car to tend to the other travelers.

Colin believed he knew the story of everyone sitting in the half-full dining car. The salesmen. The young couple in love. The parents taking their children on a trip to see their grandparents. And what did they want? What was Colin so sure of? That they wanted nothing more than to live free of worry. They wanted good-paying jobs, a home, a high school game on Friday night, maybe a Saturday afternoon picnic, barbeque, and church on Sunday. The world was waking up from the hell of the last decade. While there was talk of the growing menace of Communist Russia and another war in Southeast Asia, no one wanted to hear of it. Didn't the bomb render all future wars futile?

He could so easily read everybody else, but what of himself—his own life? What was *his* story? He supposed it was a story with Southern roots stretching back generations. It was a story still being written. He was the eldest son of a powerful South Carolina family, made so by the minor wealth (though substantial in rural South Carolina) accumulated by his father and his father before him and by the power the family wielded in local and state elections through its ironclad grip on the state-wide Democratic Party.

His father Ian had aspirations for Colin, aspirations that included him in the family business and that would place him in the governor's mansion, but no further. That was the story his father was writing for him.

Colin had slept well the night before, rocked to sleep by the train's rhythmic passage. He woke rested and invigorated, knowing he was almost home. Six hours to go. He'd be home in time for Declaration Day, and he was looking forward to barbeque, cold beer, horseshoes, and an afternoon with his family at the country club to which his father belonged. He had been twenty-nine when he was deployed to Europe, leaving his wife Barabra home alone to raise their two twin boys. Today, he was thirty-five years old and ready to get on with his life.

As the countryside passed by outside the window, he thought about much of what he had witnessed and experienced fighting for the Allies. Just months before the war came to an end, he was wounded in the Ardennes region between Belgium and Luxembourg as the Nazis made one last desperate attempt to divide the Allied supply lines and regain command of the Western Front.

Since returning to the States, he had worked for a general at the Pentagon. The general was responsible for advising the House and Senate Committees on Armed Forces and America's delegation to the newly formed United Nations. It was during these times, while recuperating in the hospital and working for the general, that Colin observed real power—power executed by those who *actually* had it, as opposed to those whose ephemeral grip was *illusory* at best.

While healing from his wounds in a hospital bed outside of Paris and waiting to be sent home, Colin read of protests in Manila staged by American troops after Truman announced that the plan to bring the men home would be slowed down to ensure troop levels were high enough to maintain peace in the Far East. The announcement met with large-scale riots, with nearly 20,000 soldiers openly protesting in Manila and Guam—something unheard of in the military. In response, Truman reversed course and kept to the original plan to bring everyone home as fast as possible. This demonstration evidenced genuine power—power executed by the masses.

Working for the general, Colin regularly visited the White House, the offices of numerous congressmen, New York City, and San Francisco. He attended fundraisers for political candidates seeking public office and went on lavish trips with the general and senators on the Armed Forces committee, paid for by wealthy contributors and military contractors hungry for federal dollars to purchase their latest tank, ship, submarine, jet, or weapons system.

From these experiences, Colin drew two conclusions. First, politicians thought they had power—and while some did, it was tenuous and exercised at the whim of the voter. No, the *real* power lied with the moneymen and the kingmakers, the men who picked the winners and who would allow them to stay in office as long as they did as they were told. Second, the voters, when acting en masse, could foil even the efforts of the moneyed class.

Ah, but the man who had the ability to leverage the appetites of the huddled masses, *and* to pick the winners and thus own them—well, that man had *real* power. That man could decide when a nation went to war. That man had it all.

These were the thoughts that occupied Colin, inspired him, animated him, and that would drive him for the rest of his life.

He was six hours from the Union Depot train station in Columbia, South Carolina, and then a forty-minute drive to the family home in the countryside. This weekend, he'd relax. Next week, he would pick up where he had left off six years ago: working for his father, learning the family business, and glad-handing the party faithful. But this time, he was showing up with his plan—a plan larger than anything his father had ever imagined.

This was the story Colin was writing for himself.

Chapter 2

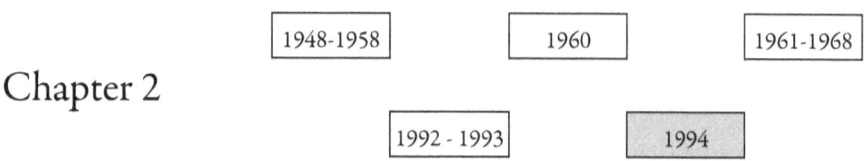

CHARLESTON, SOUTH CAROLINA
SATURDAY, MAY 21, 1994

Walker flinched as the screen door to his home slammed behind him.

"I know, I know!" he began with a groan, shaking his head in frustration. Earlier that day, he'd promised his wife, Isabelle, *again*, that he'd reattach the hydraulic door closer. He sat on the bench on his porch—or as the folks in Charleston called them, his piazza—and hurriedly laced up his shoes, avowing to fix the door the following day. It was already five o'clock and Walker figured she'd be home any minute. He needed to start his run soon before she appeared and asked him what he was thinking. He could hear her now.

"Um, Honey, it's five o'clock. What do you think you're doing? We agreed we'd be ready and out the door tonight by six."

"Yeah, but I really need this run," he'd answer.

But Isabelle wasn't home, so Walker was having this conversation with himself.

She was entertaining the spouses of the two men Walker had played golf with that afternoon. Yep, Walker needed this run to shed the anger and frustration that had been building since lunch. He glanced upward one last time at the broken door as he stood up from the bench.

"Tomorrow, honey. I promise," he said to himself and then set off on a fast pace down Tradd Street.

* * *

Earlier that day in the Men's Grill at the Wappoo Country Club

The activity in the room was typical for a Saturday at the Men's Grill. Golfers who had teed-off in the morning were strolling in for lunch, looking forward to the camaraderie of settled bets, good-natured ribbing about who three-putted which greens, and talk of the baseball season, while those with an afternoon tee time would be just sitting down for lunch. Located throughout the room were televisions, all muted, airing either the golf tournament or a major league baseball game.

Hives of activity could be found across the room, organized largely by age. The younger golfers were seated at the square, mahogany-topped bar in the center of the room. Some were standing. Others were seated, perched on the edge of their barstools, or leaning against the brass railing that ran along the outer edge of the bar top. These men had wives and children waiting for them, and therefore they had some place to be. at the pool, at home, at a birthday party for one of their kid's friends, or possibly a little league game. They had time for a quick beer and then they were off.

Across the room, at a line of card tables, one could find the other end of the spectrum: men who'd settled in for an afternoon of Gin Rummy; men whose children had grown up, and whose wives were happy they had someplace to go.

Walker belonged to the former hive of activity—the younger men, with a wife and kids and other places to be. Today, he was relaxing in a lounge chair enjoying a cold beer and chatting with his good friend, Eddie Wentworth.

"So, you have guests today," stated Eddie, referring to Walker's foursome, which had a tee time right before Eddie's.

"Yep."

"Well, don't hold us up. I have a big match."

"Hardly," Walker said with a chuckle. "Let me guess, you've got—what, ten dollars on the line?"

"Go easy on me. I'm a government employee," Eddie said with a laugh, sipping his beer. "I'm not raking in the big bucks like you. So, who are your guests?"

"Dan Tompkins and I are hosting the CEO and CFO of a large conglomerate out of Atlanta looking to expand their operations in our little corner of the world."

"And Dan—the president of our Chamber of Commerce—thought meeting you could help sway their decision? Is that it, or is there more to it?"

"Well, he needs another member to host two guests for a round of golf, and we're hoping to do a little business with them as well."

"Good for you."

"Thanks," said Walker.

"Will I see you tonight at the reunion?"

"Absolutely. Looking forward to it—but even if I *didn't* want to go, there'd be no way you could keep Izzy away."

Walker's attention was drawn to the group of men entering from the men's locker room—Dan Tompkins, with two other men in tow. Walker and Eddie rose from their seats and nodded towards each other knowingly. Walker set off to meet with his group. Eddie moved to a table to await the arrival of his playing partners.

"Walker, good to see you," said Dan. "Let me introduce you to Steve Eckles and Chris Wright."

"Pleased to meet you, Steve, Chris."

Steve and Chris looked as if they had stepped off the pages of *Golf Digest*. They were dressed in pleated khaki pants, stylish belts fashioned from the skin of some exotic animal, and golf shirts boasting the logo of an exclusive private golf club they either belonged to or had played at as a guest.

Handshakes were exchanged and the four men took a seat at a table overlooking the first tee. While the men exchanged pleasantries, their water glasses were filled, and a waiter appeared to take their drink orders, assuring them he'd return to go over the menu and explain the day's special.

"Excellent, Marcus. Thank you," said Dan, who took the opportunity to focus the table's conversation. "Gentleman, I've really been looking forward to our time together today. First of all, Steve, you mentioned that you were a big fan of Seth Raynor designed golf courses."

Steve nodded as he took a sip of the beer Marcus had just placed in front of him.

"Well, we have a fine Seth Raynor course here at Wappoo Country Club."

Walker leaned back in his chair and listened to Dan go on about the history of the club and Charleston. He'd heard it all before but had to agree with Dan, both the club and especially the city of Charleston were steeped in history. Walker had heard Dan make countless pitches at conferences singing the praises of the Holy City and if Walker was right, any minute now, Dan would deliver one of his favorite lines about the City's history, a line designed to mask the ugliness and reality that the Civil War began here.

"You see, here in Charleston, we celebrate *history*," Dan said, concluding with one of his favorite lines, "but not always *the* history."

Walker hid his smile with a sip of his beer.

"Well, we've certainly heard a great deal about Charleston. It's wonderful to see it rising from the ashes, so to speak, of Hurricane Hugo," said Steve. "What's it been now—five years since it hit?"

"It will be five years this September," answered Walker.

"Walker is one of the folks in town benefitting from our city's latest renaissance. Walker and his lovely wife, Isabelle, bought a charming home on one of our more historic streets at quite a discount. Didn't you?" Dan prompted, turning in his seat towards Walker.

"Well, after you add up all the blood, sweat, tears, and money we spent to repair the house, I'm not sure what we paid was 'quite a discount,'" remarked Walker with a smile. "The owners were old and didn't want to deal with the cleanup. They sold and moved to Arizona where their grandchildren lived. It was a good deal for all of us."

"Oh, and Walker—before we go on, please thank your wife for spending her day with our wives," said Chris. "We understand she has quite a lot planned for them to see."

"I certainly will, and you can trust that they are in good hands. My wife is a wonderful ambassador for our city."

"That she is," said Dan. "In fact, both Isabelle and Walker are. Why, Walker here is one of our community's leaders. He's the younger of the two Atkins's in the law firm of Atkins & Atkins where he has built a fine legal practice in the areas of tax planning, trust and estates work, and general business advice for closely held businesses. He also works with his father and three other gentlemen in a private equity group that invests in real estate and all manner of business interests. I'll let him tell you more about that in a minute, but Walker is also charitable with his time."

Walker sat back in his chair and cast his eyes downward, feigning embarrassment as Dan carried on about his wider role in the city. But as Dan rambled on about Walker's involvement with the Rotary Club, the Chamber of Commerce, St. Michael's Church, and so forth, Walker realized how much he loved the reputation he had worked so hard to build. *Don't forget to mention my work with the Boys & Girl's Club*, he thought.

"Walker is active with Fellowship of Christian Athletes. And Walker, weren't you just elected to serve on the Board of the local Boys & Girls Club?" asked Dan.

Walker nodded and leaned back in his chair as Marcus arrived and placed their lunch orders in front of them.

"I'm exhausted just listening to this," commented Chris.

You should try being me, Walker thought to himself. "Oh, Dan goes on and makes more of it all than he should. None of it would be possible without my wife and a support network."

"You know, I remember you . . ." Steve chimed in at last, his brows furrowed.

Walker gripped his fork and said nothing. His body broke out in a cold sweat, followed by a heavy wave of dread. *No. Please, don't bring it up. Not when this lunch has been going so well, and after all I've had done to make people forget, to replace that one memory with a new one*, he thought.

"From your high school days," Steve added.

Walker closed his eyes for a moment, silently wishing the moment would pass.

"I've never seen a more powerful high school runner than you," Steve went on with a laugh, shaking his head. "Except for maybe your friend and teammate, Eddie Wentworth," he added as he nodded his head towards the table to his right. "That's Eddie, isn't it."

Walker relaxed and smiled. *What a relief.*

"Yes, it is. The most graceful runner I've ever seen. Hey, Eddie!" Walker called out, waving his friend over. "I'd like to introduce you to someone who remembers how you used to kick my ass in cross country back in the day."

Eddie rose from his table, as did Walker, Steve, and Chris. After introductions were made, Eddie pulled up a chair. He, like Walker, made no effort to hide his pleasure as Steve regaled the table with tales of Walker and Eddie's dominance in high school across the Southeast United States in both Track & Field and Cross Country.

"Did either of you compete in college?" asked Steve.

"Eddie did and did quite well running for the University of Georgia. He was an alternate on the 1984 Olympic team for both the five- and ten-thousand-meter races."

"Is that so? And what about you, Walker?" asked Steve.

"I had a very brief career at Georgetown University but pulled my hamstring in my freshmen year and then rushed my return to the track and injured it again. It's never quite been the same."

So engrossed in the conversation was everyone that no one noticed who had walked up and was standing behind Walker.

"Never quite the same, you say?" the new arrival bellowed, inserting himself into the group conversation uninvited. Walker felt himself go rigid. "Why, if you're talkin' about Walker never quite bein' the same... well, my goodness, everyone in these parts knows that story. Ain't that right, Walker? What with you bein' held hostage for pert near a week! Is that about right, Walker?"

Walker felt his heart sink.

There it was—the story, the *memory* he'd been running from.

Slowly, Walker turned in his seat. The blowhard standing behind him was none other than Johnny Dunsmore, the governor of the great state of South Carolina. Dressed for golf, with a drink in his left hand and already reeking of alcohol, Johnny Dunsmore was trailed by three sycophants who Walker knew enjoyed telling anyone who would listen that they played golf with the Governor.

"Dan," the governor said, "aren't you going to introduce me to your guests?"

"Of course. Steve, Chris, allow me to introduce you to Johnny Dunsmore, the governor of South Carolina."

"Please to meet you, boys. Where y'all from?"

"Atlanta," answered Steve, still looking visibly bewildered. His eyes flicked to Walker in a way that made it clear he hadn't forgotten what Johnny had just said about him being kidnapped for "pert near a week" all those years ago.

"Well, that explains the confused look on your face. Y'all not bein' from around here, you don't know the story I'm talkin' about. Everybody 'round here knows how poor little Walker here was tied to a chair by a madman and held prisoner along with his momma up the Santee River. Why, if it hadn't been for his big brother Eli savin' the day, you wouldn't be with us—would ya, Walker?" he asked, resting a hand on Walker's shoulder and looking down at him.

The governor was an imposing figure. Well over six feet tall, broad shoulders. He was good looking and knew it. Nature had smiled upon him. Even his broken nose from his days playing college rugby added to his mystique and rugged appearance. He looked good in a tuxedo too.

Before Walker could answer, the governor continued. "Now, Eli, well . . ." He scoffed in a way that conveyed he was impressed. "*That* boy can play golf. Don't know why you asked Walker here to fill out your foursome when everyone knows Eli coulda gone pro."

Walker had no intention of answering the question and instead turned his head and gazed at the governor's hand resting on his shoulder in an expression of utter disgust.

"Governor, I'd like you to meet Steve Eckles and Chris Wright," said Dan.

Walker hoped Dan's interlude would change the subject of conversation. It did not.

To Walker's chagrin, Chris cleared his throat and said, "You were . . . kidnapped, Walker, and *held hostage?*" He balked. "How did you escape? Well, I guess Governor Dunsmore already answered that question—"

"Yes, yes. His brother, Eli," Johnny said, and Walker braced himself as the governor chose to dive straight into the memory Walker avoided most. The story Walker had been running from ever since that fateful week in 1978.

It was the event most folks in the Charleston area called the "Shootout in the Swamps."

Midway through, Eddie returned to his table where the rest of his foursome was wrapping up lunch and beginning to head out. He mouthed a sympathetic "Sorry!" at Walker. Walker nodded in appreciation. He knew Eddie understood how everyone's memory of that week weighed on him and how hard it'd been for him to distance himself from it.

I could kill Johnny Dunsmore. What an ass! he thought furiously to himself.

"If we want to hit any balls on the driving range before we tee-off, we'd better get going," Walker said as he abruptly rose from the table and started towards the exit.

He looked back and watched Dan and his guests shake the governor's hand.

"So much for an enjoyable afternoon," he mumbled to himself and then stormed off to collect his clubs.

* * *

Walker's collegiate career as a runner may have ended in his freshmen year of college, but his identity as a runner had not.

Walker was a runner. He ran because he enjoyed it. He ran to stay in shape. At times he ran to clear his mind. And sometimes he ran to vent and burn off frustration. And that was why Walker was running now, instead of fixing the door or getting ready for the evening out.

He needed to burn off frustration, to exorcise his demons—the demons from that fateful week in 1978. Demons that others wouldn't let him bury. Demons that had immortalized him as defenseless and weak and in need of a savior.

Walker was running on autopilot, paying little attention to his surroundings. He wasn't jogging or maintaining a controlled pace. He wasn't hoping to end this run on a pleasing runner's high. He was running frantically at near top speed, and he was replaying every patronizing word Governor Johnny Dunsmore had said. It was hard not to agonize over how Johnny's appearance had sabotaged what had been a free flowing and natural conversation amongst the group.

Walker had been looking for the right time to talk to the gentlemen from Atlanta about a parcel of land his investment group had under contract, which they believed was an ideal location for the furniture factory the men planned to build. But after Johnny Dunsmore's appearance, all Steve and Chris wanted to talk about were the events of 1978 and how Walker's brother, Eli, had saved the day.

Walker's lack of control over the situation and his anger at Johnny Dunsmore took him off his golf game. He could never find his tempo, swinging too hard at first and then guiding the club head as he struggled to slow his swing down and get his timing and sequence under control. No rhythm. He was embarrassed by his game, and he was pretty sure Steve and Chris, who shot an 81 and a 79 respectively, were embarrassed for him.

Ugh, and I've been playing so well, he thought.

Walker sprinted up Lockwood and turned right onto Calhoun Street and pushed himself as hard as he could until he reached St. Philips Street, where he took a right and slowed to a jog.

Dripping with sweat, breathing heavily, and exhausted emotionally as well as physically, Walker continued south on St. Philips Street through the College of Charleston campus until he came to the Cistern—the beautiful park in the middle of the campus. He took a seat on a bench and leaned forward, resting his head in his hands.

Walker, face down, mumbled into his hands. "Will I ever escape other people's memory of that week? Will I ever cease to be the poor defenseless child strapped to the chair? Will that forever be how people see me?"

He knew his wife, Isabelle—the best thing to ever happen to him—was sitting at home and likely growing angrier by the minute. He'd left her a note that had said, "Off for a run. Back in a while." He knew he owed her more than that. He knew how excited she was for their high school reunion. He had been too—until Johnny Dunsmore's appearance reminded him that no matter what he accomplished in this town, he would never step outside of his brother's shadow and replace the memory everyone had forged of him. And now he had to spend the evening with classmates who he feared would want to regurgitate it all. But then, there was his wife, Izzy.

Walker lifted his head from his hands. "I'm sorry, honey," he said to himself, knowing he'd needed to say the same thing to her. Standing, he began to jog home.

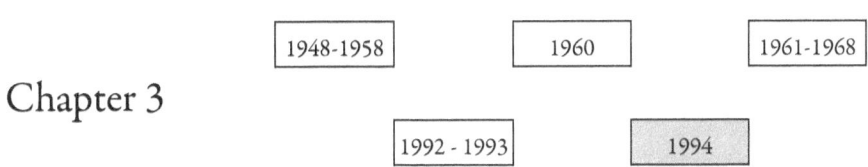

Chapter 3

Charleston, South Carolina
Saturday, May 21, 1994

"I could just scream!" said Isabelle, fists clenched. "If he wasn't the father of my children—" She paused, shaking her head. "I *swear* there are times I want to ring his neck."

"I'm so sorry, Mrs. Atkins. I know how much you were looking forward to tonight."

"Oh, I'm going. With him or without him."

"What would you like me to do with the kids?" Amy asked.

Isabelle looked at Amy, her regular babysitter, and realized that Amy was the same age she was when she'd become friends with the people who would be at her high school reunion tonight. Izzy had been seventeen years old and a junior at a new school when she'd fallen for Walker, and they'd been a couple ever since.

Isabelle took a deep breath, trying to calm herself. She had arrived home shortly after five with plans to take a quick shower and change into clothes more appropriate for the evening. She'd spent the day showing the wives of the two men her husband had played golf with around Charleston. It had been a lovely day, and she had thoroughly enjoyed the women's company, but her mood changed on a dime when she read Walker's cryptic note: "Off for a run. Back in a while." Amy arrived at 5:30, right on time, but there was no sign of Walker.

She sighed. "Let's stick to our plan. I'm sure their father will walk up any minute now, all sweaty and apologetic, so we'll go. We're gonna be late, though!" she said, looking at her watch. "But we'll go. It's such a nice night . . . Why don't you take the kids to White Point Gardens to run around and play before feeding them dinner? You'll find all their favorites in the fridge."

Amy gave Isabelle a shy smile. "Mrs. Atkins, little Peter and Anna asked if I could take them to the Market for ice cream."

"I think that's a fine idea," said Isabelle as she reached for her purse and pulled out a ten dollar bill. "This should cover it."

"Yes, ma'am. Thank you."

Amy left Isabelle in the kitchen and walked into the small backyard where Peter and Anna were both busy coloring at a small, child-sized table under the shade of a crepe myrtle tree. Ten minutes later, they were dressed and out the door, leaving Isabelle with nothing to do but stew and open a bottle of wine. She was looking forward to the reunion, and she knew that Walker was too. So, none of this made sense. Where had he gone—and *why*?

* * *

Walker entered the kitchen from the piazza and saw Isabelle sitting on the screened-in porch on the backside of their home reading a book. He filled a glass with ice and poured it full of water. He noticed that she never looked his way. He was sure she was intentionally ignoring him. He walked onto the porch.

"I'm sorry," he said at once, and he meant it.

Isabelle kept staring at her book. "You should be."

He knew her well enough to know her anger was short-lived; Isabelle had never been one to hold grudges. She wasn't that kind of a person. He loved that about her.

She placed her book in her lap and looked up at him.

"Walker, what's going on? You know how much I wanted to go tonight. We both did. We talked about it. I need a break from the kids. Love them to death, but I could use a night out with friends—good friends, old friends."

"I had a bad day."

"You're kidding. A bad round of golf and you want to blow off our fifteen-year reunion! Are you kidding me?"

"No. It wasn't the golf . . ." He dropped down into the chair next to his wife and hung his head. "It happened again."

"What happened again?"

"The past. That's what. I'm having this great time at the club . . . I really liked the guys from Atlanta—"

"Good, because I liked their wives, too. So, what went wrong?"

"The governor, that's what. That ass rolled into the Men's Grill and for some reason felt that our guests had to hear all about the 'shootout in the swamp.' Poor little Walker, defenseless and needing to be saved by his big brother! I'm. Just. So. Sick of it."

Walker's lament was met with silence. He saw a mixture of concern and exasperation on his wife's face.

"Can't we just stay home tonight?" he asked. "What if everyone wants to remember it all over again? It all went down our senior year, if you don't remember."

"Oh, I remember, all right. But I don't care, Walker, and neither do your friends. And these are *good* friends we're seeing tonight."

"Yea, but we see many of them all the time as it is. Good grief, over half our class never left Charleston."

"Well, I wasn't going to tell you because I wanted it to be a surprise, but Toby and Stella will be there."

"Really?" Walker sat up a bit in his chair and tilted his head to one side, the beginnings of a smile appearing at the corners of his mouth.

"Really. They flew in from New York yesterday. They're staying at the Francis Marion Hotel."

Walker reached for his wife's hand, looked up at her, and smiled. "You're right. A night out with old friends will do us well. I'll be ready in a flash."

Chapter 4

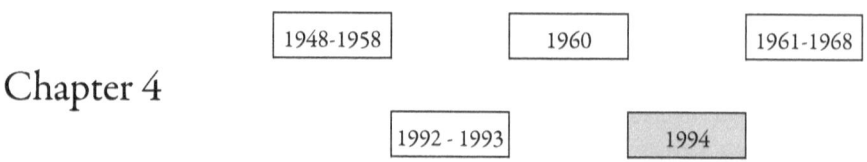

JAMES ISLAND, SOUTH CAROLINA
SATURDAY, MAY 21, 1994

By 6:30 that evening, The Abaco was filled with the sort of bristling nostalgia unique to a high school reunion. The classes of '74 and '79 had gathered to celebrate the fifteen and twenty years that now separated them from the graduation that marked the end of their adolescence.

Name tags were available at the entrance but were worn only by spouses of graduates and by those who had left and never looked back, thus creating a division between those who stayed and those who, in their minds, had moved on. Those who had stayed, naturally, remembered one another. This was a small town, after all. But it was easy to forget anyone who had willingly drifted outside of its circle.

The talk among those who had stayed was centered on the weather, their kids, little league, summer plans—the usual. For those who had traveled for the reunion, the conversations struck a similar tone. "So, how have you been?" "I'd like you to meet my husband." "My wife." "Is Bowens still a hot spot?" "Any children?" "What are you doing these days?"

But after a few beers, it was like old times. The men gathered in groups, remembering their glory days on this or that team, and the women did the same, catching up on each other's lives and exchanging gossip about so-and-so's divorce. And the spouses who had been drug along for the ride found themselves standing outside the circles of reunited cliques or leaning against the bar, occasionally glancing at their watch, wondering how long the evening would last.

The turnout for both classes was strong. Most folks were gathered on the outdoor patio overlooking Ellis Creek enjoying the unseasonably cool May evening. The tide was coming in and pushing the water lazily up the small tributary fed by the Ashley River. A massive oak tree cast its shadow over the patio and the Spanish Moss hung low enough off its branches so that when the wind blew, it fell to the deck in clumps.

Waiters moved through the crowd holding trays of appetizers. It seemed folks couldn't get enough of the conch fritters—the house specialty. Though it was less than fifteen minutes by car from downtown Charleston, the combination of The Abaco's casual atmosphere and the clear evening sky above created the perfect setting whereby, for a few hours, the shared memories of their youth isolated them from the hectic pace of their lives today. Yes, the turnout was strong—but noticeably absent from the Class of '79 was one member in particular: Walker Atkins.

"Hey, Eddie," Toby Robertson began, standing in a group of about eight classmates, "I thought you said Walker would be here."

"I saw him earlier today. He said he'd be here," Eddie informed the group. He shrugged in a way that suggested he'd done everything he could, and whether Walker showed up wasn't up to him.

Toby and Eddie were two of the Three Musketeers, as they had been known in high school, with Walker being the third. They had been the best of friends and the anchors for the school's Cross Country and Track & Field teams—teams which had garnered national attention. Eddie and Walker were the real stars, and their races against each other had been legendary.

Toby looked put out. "Well, the sun is setting soon, and I wanted a few pictures of the old gang back together. Gotta have Walker in the picture. Why isn't he here?"

"Isn't it obvious?" said Venessa, Eddie's wife.

"Isn't *what* obvious?" asked Toby.

"His brother Eli owns this place," Vanessa clarified, voice hushed, gesturing to a sign over the front doorway that read The Abaco.

"Yes, I know that," Toby replied, clearly insulted. "What am I not getting? Walker and Eli get along great with each other, don't they?"

"Yes and no." Eddie stepped in, taking over for his wife. "It's not that Eli owns the place, as much as it's that Eli is more likely to come up in conversation because of it—and Walker avoids all conversation about Eli, because that means rehashing the *Shootout in the Swamp*."

"Oh." Toby's eyes widened. "That still bothers him?"

"It doesn't bother him. He's fine. What bothers him is having it brought up again and again and *again*. Why, it happened today, in fact, at the club," Eddie went on. "Walker was having lunch and getting ready to golf with some prospective new clients when Governor Dunsmore waltzed into the Men's Grill and barged into their conversation. For some reason, Dunsmore thought that was the perfect time to tell Walker's guests about the shootout in the swamp. He described Walker as defenseless, tied to a chair, and needing his older brother to save him . . ."

Toby grimaced, sighing. "Yikes."

"Yeah, exactly." Eddie tipped his beer at Toby. "Those were the governor's exact words when he told the story, too: 'poor little Walker.' You should have seen the look on Walker's face. He was simultaneously crushed and on the verge of strangling the governor. Wouldn't have blamed him, either way."

"Hey, honey, is that the story you were telling me about on the way down here?" asked the wife of a fellow member of the Class of '79 standing on the edge of the group. The look on Eddie's face made it clear he hadn't realized so many people were listening in, and he seemed to regret speaking so openly.

"That's right. But I was only a student here for one year—our senior year. These guys know the story better than anyone else, I'm sure," her husband said, looking around, hoping someone would provide all the gruesome details.

An awkward silence filled the void.

"I'm sorry - but who are you?" Eddie asked, and the guy flinched.

"Oh, excuse me," said their fellow grad in a somewhat embarrassed tone. "I'm Peter. This is my wife, Carol."

There were a few muttered, half-hearted hellos. Then, Toby gave Eddie a look—as if asking for permission to proceed—and Eddie nodded. It was better to clear the air with Peter, Carol, and any other eavesdroppers than to fuel the rumor mill.

Toby cleared his throat. "When we were all in the sixth grade, a girl here in town was found in the woods just off the Savannah Highway. She had been raped and murdered. Pretty gruesome, according to the rumors."

"Kimberly Prestwick. That was the girl's name," added his wife, Stella.

Toby nodded. "Kimberly was dating Eli Atkins, the man who owns this restaurant, and the man who is Walker's older brother."

"How far apart are they in age?" asked Carol.

"They're separated by six years. Kimberly and Eli were seniors in high school at the time. Anyway, when Kimberly's body was found, all evidence pointed to Eli as the most likely suspect. He was arrested and, well . . . this is where the story gets really crazy," said Toby. He looked to Eddie for backup. "I don't even know how to tell it . . ."

Others had now gathered around to hear the story.

Eddie looked about and frowned. "This is part of the problem," he said as he surveyed the growing crowd. "The story gets sensationalized and retold again and again. This happened over fifteen years ago, and it's still what we're talking about *today*—and we're wondering why Walker isn't here?" Turning to his wife, he said, "You're right, honey, it should be obvious to all of us why Walker's not here."

"Don't blame me," said Vanessa. "I was on the planning committee for this weekend, and I pushed to hold the event at the Francis Marion Hotel, but The Abaco is the hottest restaurant in town, and well . . . Eli is Eli. Class of '74 really wanted the event here."

"Perhaps it's worth finishing the story," Toby offered, speaking to Eddie. "Let's just clear the air on all of this. Then, if Walker shows up, people will be less interested in talking about it—we'll get it out of their systems."

Eddie sighed, nodding. "All right, everyone. I'll give you the abridged version. Understand this above all else: Eli did not kill Kimberly—but he *ran*, which made him look guilty. The search for Eli went on for over a month, but no one ever saw him again. Not us, not the police, not a single soul knew where Eli had gone." He paused, staring at his captivated audience for a few seconds. "You can imagine all the rumors that sprouted up. Well, six years later, this madman came to town. Turned out he was a serial killer who had been burying his victims all over the southeastern part of the country for over twenty years. This guy—Rath was his name—kidnapped Walker and his mother and was holding them in a shack on the banks of the Santee River. He contacted Walker's dad and told him where he could find Walker and his wife. Walker's dad, Monty, had something Rath wanted him to bring with him. Like I said, it all gets pretty crazy. The craziest part was that Eli, who had been missing for six years, all of a sudden shows up out of nowhere and finds Rath, kills him, and saves his father, mother, and little brother."

"Unbelievable," said Carol, turning to her husband.

Toby scoffed. "This isn't even the half of it."

Carol and Peter stared at Toby with a look of impatience and anticipation.

"Rath, the crazed killer, was Eli's biological Dad," Toby told them.

Carol's mouth fell open. Peter looked entirely bewildered. *"What?"*

"Yep. Apparently, Rath was married to Walker and Eli's mom back when they were in college together. She left him, met Monty and a few years later, they got married. Walker is their child. Oh, and for the record, Monty Atkins is a great guy. He's been a fantastic father to both Eli and Walker."

Those in the crowd who knew Monty all shook their heads in agreement.

"Where was Eli during those six years?" Peter asked. "And did he ever tell anyone why he ran?"

"The Bahamas," answered Eddie. "And no, he never told anyone why he left. To this day, he never talks about it. Eli and Walker are both successful and good at what they do, but they have different personalities. Eli is quiet and keeps to himself—but it seems like the quieter he is, the larger the myth surrounding his hero status grows. For Walker, it's different. He works harder than anyone I know, and he has a very public personality. Good grief, he's involved in more charities, associations, and business dealings around town than anyone else! But it doesn't matter how hard he works to change the script and how he believes people perceive him, in Walker's world he believes people still see him as the little boy, defenseless and tied to a chair. Walker has done everything in his power to make a name for himself as an adult—a name that separates him from who he was when he was a kid, tied to a chair, held captive by that madman. But the story is like his shadow. No matter how fast he runs, it will always be one step behind him."

Everybody stayed quiet for a moment.

"Walker and Eli aren't enemies," Eddie clarified, "but they don't see each other as much as they probably could. Eli has done nothing to fuel the story or create any animosity between him and Walker. Walker doesn't resent Eli, but he resents the role he has been left to play in this ongoing saga. The whole mess has driven a wedge between him and his brother and I'm afraid it's up to Walker to come around and move on. Well, anyway, that's what I think."

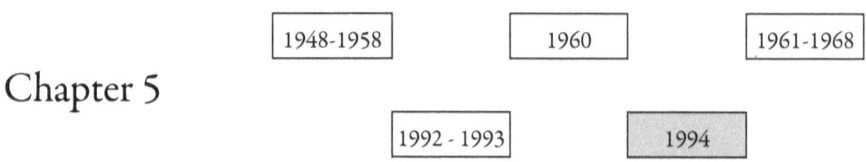

Chapter 5

JAMES ISLAND, SOUTH CAROLINA
SATURDAY, MAY 21, 1994

"Well, look who decided to grace us with his presence. If it isn't the one and only Walker Atkins!"

Walker had climbed the stairs to the rooftop porch at a snail's pace, hoping to go unnoticed, only for Toby to blow his cover. And of course, it would be *Toby* who would blow his cover. Upon seeing Stella, Toby's wife, Isabelle let go of his hand and hurried to give her a big hug. They had been close friends for years.

"It is so good to see you two!" said Isabelle.

"I didn't know you guys would be here," Walker lied, approaching the group.

Toby raised his brows skeptically. "Would it have affected your arrival time if you had?"

"Sure would've," Walker countered. "I wouldn't have shown up at all."

"Yeah, yeah, yeah. Somebody get this man a drink," Toby called out.

Before Walker and Isabelle arrived, Toby and Eddie had finished rehashing the Shootout in the Swamp and had pleaded with those who were listening to not bring it up if Walker and Isabelle made it to the reunion. Everyone agreed, and Walker had no idea he'd been the center of attention just minutes before he had pulled into the parking lot.

Isabelle had been right. They needed a night out. And it was great seeing everybody again.

The time flew by, the sun had set, and the party was beginning to wind down when a woman from the Class of '74 walked up to Walker.

"Walker, do you remember me?" asked the beautiful woman standing before him. "I'm Ella Gaston, Class of '74. Well, Ella Thompson now, but I was Ella Gaston back in high school. This is my husband, Roger."

"Ella, of course, I remember you," said Walker as he flashed a quick glance in Toby's direction. "How could I forget? Roger, nice to meet you," he said as he watched Toby smile and walk towards the bar.

Roger shook Walker's hand. "You too, Walker."

"Ella, where are you living these days?"

"Miami, mostly. But we have a place in Vail, too. It is so good to see you!" she exclaimed. "And I was hoping I would."

"Oh? Why's that?" asked Walker.

"You're a lawyer, right?"

"Yes, I'm a lawyer."

"Well, it's about my parents. They need help. They were hoodwinked into making a bad investment. They stand to lose their home and their life's savings. I don't know if the kind of law you practice is the kind of help they need, but I'd sure appreciate it if you would meet with them. If you're not right for them, maybe you can recommend a lawyer who is."

"I'm sure I can help them, and I'd be happy to," Walker announced. He felt the eyes of others in the vicinity on him and was pleased to be needed.

"Oh, thank you so much. And I want you to send us the bills. We're paying for this," she said with a sharp glance at her husband. "Aren't we, Roger?"

"Of course, honey," Roger said. It was hard to discern if his smile was genuine or expertly artificial. "Walker, here's my card. As Ella said, send me any bills."

"I certainly will, but I'd prefer to call you and discuss the fees after I meet with them. Would that be all right?"

"Yes, that's fine. Say, it's great to meet you. Ella has told me all about the 'shootout in the swamp.' That's a hell of a story," Roger said, changing the subject. As soon as he did, Walker felt heat creeping up his neck. "I was hoping to meet your brother, Eli, while I was here."

"Well, I guess you're just stuck with me," Walker said, with a bit more of an edge than he'd intended. Now it was *his* turn for an artificial smile. Something told him his wasn't as convincing as Roger's, though.

Like the angel she was, Isabelle swooped in, placing an arm around Walker. "Hi, Ella. I'm Isabelle, Walker's wife. I hate to take him away, but there are a few from our class who are saying their goodbyes."

"Oh, but of course," said Ella. "Walker, thank you again for agreeing to meet with my parents. I truly appreciate it."

"My pleasure, Ella. You two have a good night."

Ella and her husband made their exit, and Walker breathed a sigh of relief.

"Thank you," he said to Isabelle in a whisper, squeezing her hand. She smiled and kissed him on the cheek, then turned to look at Toby, who was standing at the bar and laughing with Eddie about something.

"What's gotten into Toby? He hasn't stopped snickering since Ella and her husband introduced themselves to you," said Isabelle.

Doing nothing to conceal the grin spreading across his face, Walker answered, "Well, let's just say that I know Ella better than she remembers."

"What are you talking about?" asked Isabelle, returning his grin.

"Did I ever tell you the story about the first naked girl I ever saw?" asked Walker.

"Sure, the summer at Kiawah Island when you were a kid and riding your bike through the woods. Oh, that's right. Ella Gaston was the girl, wasn't she?"

"Yep. And Toby was there. That was the summer we met. We must have been twelve or thirteen years old. Never forgot her."

"No, I get it. She was beautiful. Still is. Who was the guy she was with?"

"Beau Eastley."

"The quarterback?"

"Yep."

"Now, *I* would have liked to have seen *him*," said Isabelle as she flashed a devilish grin at Walker.

"Would you have?" he asked, raising his brows.

"Sure. We all had a crush on him. Whatever happened to Beau Eastley? I didn't see him here tonight."

"He was recruited by Clemson. Blew his knee out in the fourth quarter of a meaningless game his freshmen year. Clemson had a big lead, and everyone was getting time on the field. He never fully recovered. Real tragedy. A lotta folks thought he could have played on Sundays. Started drinking. Put on about a hundred pounds. I hear he's divorced, so you might still be able to live out all your schoolgirl fantasies with him, if you like."

She squeezed his hand, then gave him a kiss. "Nah. I'm happy with what I got, Walker."

"I love it when you say my name."

And Walker meant it. He was happiest and at his best when he was with Isabelle. Always had been.

"Let's go join the others," said Isabelle.

* * *

By 9:30 p.m., everyone had left except Walker and Isabelle, Toby and Stella, and Eddie and Vanessa—the three Musketeers and their better halves. They had all met and begun dating in high school. They had scattered during college, but returned to Charleston and each other afterwords. That was, except for Toby and Stella. They went north for college and now they split their time between New York City and Zurich. Toby was a private banker.

"So, looks like we're it. I hear everyone is headed to the Touch of Class," said Eddie.

"The Touch of Class? What's that?" asked Stella.

"A jazz club down on Meeting Street. Been here for about ten years now." Eddie gave them a look of disbelief. "Good grief, y'all *have* been gone, haven't you?"

"Seems like forever sometimes," said Toby. "And we miss it."

"Then come home. *We* did," said Isabelle.

"Well, there's not much demand for private bankers in Charleston," said Toby, pressing his lips into a fine line. He glanced at his wife. "Don't get me wrong, though. We talk about it."

"More and more as the kids are getting older," said Stella reassuringly.

"She's right. And things are in the works. I'm hoping to wrap up commitments in Zurich so we can live in New York City full-time. If that happens, we may look into buying a home in Charleston."

"Oh, that would be wonderful," said Vanessa.

"Say, I'm starved. Anybody else hungry?" asked Eddie.

"What?" Toby's wife laughed. "Didn't you eat any of the appetizers they laid out?"

"Yeah, but you can't make a *meal* out of them," Eddie said as he turned towards the bartender. "Excuse me, is the kitchen still open?"

"'Fraid not. Closing early tonight."

"Billy, let's keep it open a little longer for this crew." Billy, the bartender, looked over his shoulder and saw his boss walk up the stairs. "In fact, whatever they want is on me."

"Sure thing, boss."

Eli Atkins, Walker's older brother—rockstar chef, local hero, scratch golfer—approached the group with a smile. He shook hands with Toby and Eddie and hugged their wives. Walker remained seated. As Eli walked around the table toward him, Walker slowly stood, relaxed, and hugged his big brother.

"Good to see you, Eli."

"Good to see you, too, Walkie-Talkie."

They smiled and slapped each other on the back.

"Pull up a chair and join us?" asked Walker.

"Love to."

Chapter 6

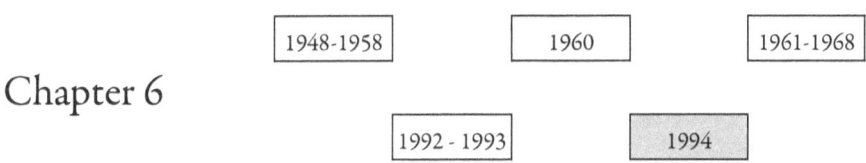

CHARLESTON, SOUTH CAROLINA
THURSDAY, MAY 26, 1994

Walker started the coffee maker, walked outside, sat in a rocking chair on the piazza alongside his home, and bent over to lace up his Nike Tailwinds.

He had always been an unrepentant shoe-dog. He experimented with every innovation and had a collection of running shoes dating back to his high school days. Whenever Izzy asked why he needed so many shoes, he'd point his eyes at her side of the closet and shrug as if to say, "Need I say more?" The Tailwinds were his favorites. Like old friends. He had good and bad days running, but never because of the Tailwinds.

The sun would be rising soon. He had time for a short run. A long weekend was on the horizon, and he was looking forward to it. In fact, he, Izzy, and the kids would be driving out to the family home on Kiawah Island later that day. He just needed a couple of hours at the office, and then he would shut it down after lunch and they could hit the road.

He looked at his watch—6:05 a.m. Right on track.

The route he had in mind would place him on the Battery in time to see the sunrise over the Harbor. After a bit of stretching, he was off. He headed west on Tradd Street—a street with more pre-revolutionary homes than any other in Charleston. By God's grace, homes built on this street in the first half of the 18th Century had survived the Revolutionary War, the Civil War, an earthquake, hurricanes, and more fires than one could count. The road turned south at the end of Tradd Street, and his route took him along Murray Boulevard. The Ashley River was to his right, and it flowed into the Harbor. As he approached the end of Murray Boulevard, the road turned north onto East Bay Street, and he could see Fort Sumter, where the first shots of the Civil War were fired. Good grief. Living in Charleston was like living in a museum but one that was alive and vibrant.

As he neared the end of his run, Walker picked up his pace and finished accelerating past his home. He knew he wasn't training for cross country anymore, but that competitive edge remained. So, as he neared the end of his runs, he always sprinted.

He slowed to a walk as he passed his house and meandered in a circle in the middle of the street until his breathing settled. He then walked up onto his piazza, picked up the *Post & Courier*, walked into the house, and grabbed a glass of water before heading to the screened-in porch in the back to cool down and scan the day's headlines. Forty-five minutes later, he was showered and out the door with a cup of coffee in hand. Walker's office was on State Street, just north of Broad Street—a ten-minute walk, at most. He was looking forward to a few quiet hours in the office. He had one meeting on his calendar: the meeting with Ella Gaston's parents.

Though Ella was adamant at the class reunion that her parents needed and wanted his help, he did not expect to hear from them. To his surprise, they called. But when Mrs. Beasly, his administrative assistant, inquired about the reason for the meeting, they said they preferred to speak with Mr. Atkins in his office. Consequently, Walker would be going into the meeting blind without knowing why they wanted an attorney's counsel. He was confident that whatever problems they had, he could help. He just hoped he could put the image of their daughter out of his head. Having a photographic memory has its advantages. Walker smiled as he walked up Church Street.

But even if he had known why they needed an attorney, he never could have foreseen the extent to which the trajectory of so many lives would be forever altered by this half-hour meeting.

* * *

Walker looked up, his attention broken in response to the soft knocking on his door. He'd been reading the final draft of an article his father,

Monty, had written on new banking regulations—grinning all the while at his father's continued commitment to both the firm and the legal practice, even though he was slowing down and gradually preparing to retire.

"Yes, Mrs. Beasley?"

"Mr. Atkins, the Gastons are here. I put them in the small conference room."

"Thank you, but I prefer to meet them in my office," he said, setting the article aside and extracting a new legal pad from the top right drawer of his desk. "Could you show them back?"

"Of course. Can I bring you a cup of coffee?"

"No, thank you."

"Very well."

Walker had tried to get Mrs. Beasley to take the formality down a notch and had asked her, time and time again, to call him Walker, but she insisted on calling him Mr. Atkins. She was close to sixty and very traditional. She had attended secretarial school years ago, before women were offered many options in the working world, and she'd never veered from her upbringing. Walker felt awkward calling her by her first name, Catherine, when she was so formal, so they stuck with last names. At times, Walker wished he had a younger secretary, one more relaxed around the office, but Mrs. Beasley was excellent at her job, and she protected and took care of Walker like he was her son.

A minute later, an elderly couple entered his office, and Walker stood, walked around his desk, and greeted his guests.

"Mr. and Mrs. Gaston, it's a pleasure to meet you."

They shook hands, and Walker asked them to take a seat. Walker's office was large enough for his desk and a seating area with a small sofa and two chairs around a coffee table. He motioned them towards the couch, and as everyone was getting comfortable, Mrs. Beasley returned and placed two cups of coffee, a pitcher of water, and three glasses on the coffee table.

"So, Mr. and Mrs. Gaston, what can I do for you today?" asked Walker.

"Please call us Hugh and Loraine," said Mrs. Gaston. "We're simple folks."

"Of course, and please call me Walker."

Walker sat across from them, assuming he did not have to ask the question again and that, eventually, one of them would explain why they wished to speak with an attorney. Walker saw a beaten man sitting across from him; Hugh was slumped in his chair, head down, holding his well-worn trucker's hat with both hands in his lap. *He's embarrassed,* Walker thought. *He won't look me in the eye.*

Walker's patience was rewarded. Loraine shifted to the front of her chair and sat at an angle so she could face her husband. She gently took her husband's hand, smiled at him, and then turned towards Walker. "Mr. Atkins, we need your help. We're about to lose our home and everything we've worked for."

Walker looked at Hugh, who remained silent, nodding at Loraine to continue.

Loraine reached into her purse and pulled out a notice of default from the lender holding the mortgage on their home. "We received this in the mail a little over a week ago. Ella and her husband Roger dropped by for a visit before heading to their reunion where she ran into you. Ella could tell we were upset. I was crying, and Hugh was fit to be tied. So, we showed her the notice. That's how come she knew to ask you about helping us."

Walker gave Lorraine a neutral, non-judgmental nod. He'd learned that was an important aspect of being a lawyer—receiving sensitive information without judgment.

"Understood," he said, and then turned to Hugh. "So, Hugh, your wife says you were fit to be tied. I assume you weren't expecting the notice. Is that right?"

Hugh looked like he'd rather be anywhere else on the planet than sitting in Walker's office, discussing this subject. "That's right," he grumbled. "We'd signed a piece of paper when we bought the house so that the bank could take the money we owed them each month right out of our bank account."

"So, I'm guessing there wasn't enough money in the account to cover the payment."

"We received this notice in the mail the same day," said Loraine as she pulled another envelope from her purse. Walker leaned forward to take it from her. He removed a single sheet of paper from the envelope.

"An overdraft notice," he announced.

Hugh mumbled something in response.

"Excuse me, I'm sorry, but I couldn't make out what you said . . ."

Hugh sat up straight in his chair and Walker was sure this was the first time the man had looked him in the eye. "I said that I've never been overdrawn in my life."

"Understood," replied Walker.

"We pay our bills. Those bastards *stole* our money!"

Loraine patted Hugh's hand. "He's talking about the bank, Coastal S&L."

"I'm talkin' bout *all* of them. Coastal, the folks who sold us the home, and those bastards who put us in the loan in the first place. Bunch of crooks—the whole lot of 'em. I apologize for my cursin', but not for bein' angry. They stole our money."

"Apology not necessary, sir. Let's see if I can't help you folks get on top of this. But first, I'm going to need some more information. Why don't you tell me how you came to own the house located at 72 Crestline Road in Pawleys Island," he said as he read the address off the Default Notice.

* * *

September 1992

"Oh, Hugh, this is wonderful. I'm having such a grand time!"

"You deserve it, sweetheart. We both do."

Earlier that day, Hugh and Loraine had checked into the Crescent Hotel at Surfside Beach just south of Myrtle Beach for a long overdue vacation. Since finishing high school, Hugh Gaston had worked nonstop. He and his wife had saved for the future, never splurging while raising their kids. But now they were grandparents and were looking forward to a slower pace, and Hugh had just sold his machine shop, so they had money in the bank to support a comfortable retirement.

"What shall we do, honey? I know you'll want to do a little fishing while we're here."

"I've got it all planned. You're right, I'd like to do some fishing, and in two days I will—we *both* will. I chartered a captain for the entire day. I figure the rest of the time we can just relax and do nothing. Sleep in. Read a book by the pool. Take walks on the beach."

Which they did. The weather was perfect, and they hated seeing the trip end, so they added a couple of days to their vacation. One afternoon, they took a drive, wanting to explore the area, and they saw a sign just off the coastal highway advertising a new community: The Grand Ocean Pavilions. They turned off the exit and followed the road until they reached a dead end at a parking lot with a doublewide trailer and another sign that read, "Grand Ocean Pavilions Sales Office."

Hugh and Loraine entered the trailer and were met by an attractive young couple named Rick and Stacy, who couldn't have been happier to meet them. Hugh was drawn to a table in the center of the trailer where he stood looking enviously at a model of an upcoming real estate development.

"I'm sure you've seen your fair share of these," commented Rick. "Let me tell you what we've got going here. Over here is where the clubhouse will be. In fact, construction has already begun, and everyone is psyched for the Grand Opening."

"So psyched," Stacy added as she bounced up and down on the balls of her feet. "The clubhouse will have a fitness center complete with Nautilus weights and rooms for jazzercise classes. I'm also a certified power aerobics instructor and will be teaching classes there. We have some big news that we're about to announce." Pausing, she looked at Rick. "Rick, I know it's not official yet, but do you think I can tell them about the good news?"

"I don't see why not. But don't you two tell anyone," he said as he winked at Hugh and Loraine.

"Well, as soon as the Clubhouse opens, we'll be announcing our Celebrity Showcase Series. Suzanne Somers and Jake, the star of the hit TV show, *Body by Jake*, have agreed to instruct private classes for exclusive clientele three times a year."

"Rumor has it that Suzanne has her eye on one of the development's premier ocean-view lots," added Rick.

Rick and Stacey came at Hugh and Loraine like an experienced tag team. Rick pointed out the four construction development phases while Stacy described the various designer packages available.

"Let me tell you about Phase One. Next to the clubhouse, we're building two dozen townhomes, each with a garage. Stacy, why don't you show Loraine what our interior designer came up with?" said Rick. "She's from Virginia Beach. You're going to love her."

Hugh was mesmerized by the map. It looked like one of those model train layouts at a hobby expo, but instead of trains, tiny Monopoly homes dotted the map. Rick explained that the little green flags on the lots indicated which lots had been sold.

"What are these over here?" asked Hugh.

"You have a good eye, Hugh. You like to fish?"

"I sure do."

"Then those are the lots for you. They are on an inlet coming off the ocean, and each lot has its own dock. The inlet flows back to our private, exclusive pier, complete with a tackle shop, bar, and restaurant."

Rick then looked over his shoulder and leaned in close to Hugh as if he were sharing a state secret, even though no one else was in the trailer with them. "A lot of folks go for the glitz and glamor of the ocean views, but the smart money is taking a hard look at these inlet lots. That's where the *real* value is," said Rick as he winked at Hugh.

Ten minutes later, Hugh and Loraine were getting a tour of the property in an open-air jeep with Rick and Stacy. Hugh was in the front passenger seat, and Loraine was in the back with Stacy.

"And over there—*that's* where the first tee will be. We'll break ground next week. Hope to complete the first nine holes by year end. Do you play golf, Hugh?" asked Rick.

"No, I don't, but I been thinkin' it's about time I gave it a shot."

And so it went. Hugh and Loraine tried to contain their excitement and play it cool, but they weren't fooling Rick and Stacy. Back at the trailer, the hard sell began. Retreat, advance, retreat, advance. They were a well-oiled machine. After a while, Rick read the room and called for a break.

"Say, we've been goin' on quite a spell here. I think you two need a few minutes together. Stacy and I will step back into our office. Why don't y'all have a seat on the sofa and mull things over? Hugh, you look like you could use a beer."

Rick returned with a cold beer and Stacy handed Loraine a stack of folders about the Grand Ocean Pavilions.

"Stacy and I will be in the back. Now you two take all the time you need and just knock on the door in the back when you're ready to talk."

Hugh and Loraine, still sitting on the sofa, remained quiet until they were alone. Loraine was sitting up straight on the edge of the sofa positioned at an angle towards her husband who was resting comfortably leaning back on the sofa.

"So, sweetheart, what do you think?" Loraine said as she placed the folders Stacy had given her on the coffee table. She fully expected Hugh to poo-poo the idea of buying a home here, him being the practical one, so you could have blown her over when she heard his answer.

"I could get used to this," he confessed with a grin, and Loraine clapped her hands over her mouth in excitement.

"You mean it, Hugh? You really do?"

"What have we been savin' for all these years if it wasn't for somethin' like this? I worked myself to the bone, by God, and we done good, honey. The kids are all out of the house and doin' well. It's our turn."

And just like that, Hugh and Loraine, who had never made an impetuous decision in their lives, decided now was the time.

"But can we afford it?" asked Loraine.

"Well, let's find out," he said, pushing himself up from the sofa. He placed the half-drunk beer on the table and walked purposefully to the back of the trailer.

* * *

"Can you *afford* it?" Rick asked rhetorically, giving them his best salesmen smile. "Hugh and Loraine, you can't afford *not* to! I know the prices seem steep, but we work with some very creative lenders—experts at financial engineering. Let's put you in touch with our preferred lender and see what they can come up with."

Hugh didn't know what *financial engineering* was, but he didn't want to look naive, so he agreed that meeting their preferred lender was a swell idea. At about that time, Stacy and her substantial bust came bouncing into the room.

"You'll never guess who I just got off the phone with," she said, pausing for dramatic effect. *"Gretchen Caldwell."*

Hugh and Loraine glanced at each other, wondering if that name should mean something to them.

"Can she meet us?" asked Rick.

"She can."

Rick turned to Hugh and Loraine. "Well, this is your lucky day. Gretchen is the best in the business. She works for Palmetto Lending, and they love our property. They know value when they see it. Hugh, you're going to like working with them—you're similar that way."

Thirty minutes later, the four of them were sitting in a booth at the Pirate's Cove—a seafood restaurant currently serving Happy Hour—awaiting the arrival of Gretchen Caldwell, the "best in the business." Rick and Stacy were sitting across from Hugh and Loraine, enraptured by Loraine's stories about their children and grandchildren, when their attention was drawn to a ball of energy moving towards them with a large purse draped over her left shoulder and impossibly high heels clicking off the wood floor.

"Gretchen, I would like you to meet Hugh and Loraine Gaston," said Rick.

Hugh stood to greet Gretchen and was met by a firm handshake. Gretchen was a slender, incredibly tan woman trapped between three-inch heels and a pile of blow-dried blond curls.

"The pleasure is mine," she said as she quickly placed her purse on the table, pulled up a chair, and sat at the end of the booth. Before the approaching waitress could get words out of her mouth, Gretchen ordered a bottle of Perrier and a glass of ice.

"Gretchen, thank you for squeezing us in on such short notice," said Stacy. "Rick and I have just spent a wonderful afternoon with Hugh and Loraine touring the Grand Ocean Pavilions and they are interested in learning about your financing options."

"Anything in particular?" asked Gretchen.

"One of the inlet lots," said Rick.

Gretchen nodded, as if in admiration of their excellent taste, and pulled a pen and notebook from her purse.

"Well, we're just *looking* right now," Hugh reiterated. "Long way to go before we could make any real decisions."

"Okay," said Gretchen, placating him with a smile. "I understand. Smart. Consider all your options." She turned back to Rick. "Any parcel in particular?"

"Yes, one of the Sunset Townhomes," answered Rick.

Gretchen nodded again, letting everyone know she was impressed. "So, we're talking about the homes going for $185,000."

Hugh and Loraine looked at each other, alarmed.

Loraine cleared her throat. "We were told they were going for $149,500," she said softly.

"That's right, they are," said Rick, looking a bit embarrassed.

"So, you haven't instituted the price hikes yet," said Gretchen as she looked at Rick and Stacy's side of the booth.

"No, not yet. Not till the end of the month," said Rick, looking across the table at Hugh and Loraine. Then, shrugging, he added, "No one is supposed to know about that."

"Looks like you two have a real incentive to get that lot under contract before those prices go up," said Gretchen. "If only my code of conduct didn't prevent me from acting on all the info I hear early, I'd be buying up every lot I could get my hands on—but that doesn't stop you two," she said as she looked at Hugh and Loraine's side of the table. "So, let's see what kind of loan we can fix you up with. I'll need a little information about your finances. Hugh, are you still working?"

"No, recently retired."

"What did you do?"

"I owned a machine shop, and I just sold it."

"Good for you. Okay, I'll need the address of your current home, the details on the mortgage you have on your home, if you have one, a list of any other real estate holdings, twelve months of credit card bills, the details of the sale of your machine shop, copies of your last three tax returns, and twelve months of bank statements and brokerage account statements. That should get me started."

Gretchen looked up, and Hugh and Loraine's total look of dismay seemed to tell her everything she needed to know. "Stupid me. Why am I asking you all of this? Here I am, telling you what you already know. Why don't you put me in touch with your CPA and estate planning attorney and they can send it all over to me in one neat package?"

Hugh cleared his throat nervously. "Um, that won't be necessary," said Hugh. "I can answer your questions and send you what you need."

"Smart," said Rick. "Why pay someone to do what you can do better?"

After twenty minutes of questions, answers, head-nodding, and note-taking, Gretchen held her hand up, signaling to all to be as still and quiet as possible while she deliberated. Head bent over, she furiously pecked away at her TI-30 calculator, occasionally writing something down, and then more calculating until she appeared to be both done and pleased with herself. Putting her pen on the table, she leaned back in her chair, smiled, and then sat up quick as a flash and extended her hand towards Hugh once more to be shaken.

"Hugh and Loraine, it's as good as done. I can put you in that house."

Rick and Stacy smiled at Hugh and Loraine, who didn't know quite what to do—so they smiled back, and Hugh shook Gretchen's still suspended hand.

Hugh and Loraine looked at each other and breathed a small sigh of relief.

By the end of the week, after exchanging a mountain of paperwork and signing releases, guarantees, disclosure statements, loan documents, assignments, acknowledgments, and a whole host of other documents, they were owners of an inlet lot in Grand Ocean Pavilions. Construction was to begin soon, and their current house would be listed for sale within the week. They couldn't wait to tell their children and grandchildren.

* * *

Hugh and Loraine filled Walker in over the course of an hour. He took detailed notes, wrapped up the meeting, and told the Gastons he'd be in touch with them the following week. Mrs. Beasley showed the Gastons out as Walker threw his legal pad into his briefcase.

He was late and he knew it.

Mrs. Beasley stepped back into Walker's office and stood there while he finished tiding up his desk. He saw her fiddle with her glasses with one hand and clutch her notepad to her chest with the other. He knew the signals. She had something to say.

"Mrs. Beasley, something on your mind?"

"Yes." She paused. "Are you going to be able to help them?"

"Why do you ask? Do you know them?"

"Yes. And I know a little about the trouble they're in. We attend the same church. I hope you can help them. They're good people. He's a veteran . . . Korea. He came home and married Loraine. He took over his father-in-law's machine shop and did well. A common story amongst my generation. She's a wonderful wife and mother. They raised a fine family. Like I said, I hope you can help them, Mr. Atkins."

Walker knew that if what the Gastons had told him turned out to be true that they had indeed been wronged. That didn't guarantee that a lawyer could help them, but Walker was determined to try.

"Mrs. Beasley, I'll do everything in my power to save them from the mess they're in."

"Oh, thank you, sir. Thank you," she said as she beamed back at him, this time holding her notepad tightly against her chest with both arms.

* * *

Twenty minutes later, Walker was behind the wheel of the family station wagon, and they were on the road.

"Good meeting?" asked Izzy.

"Yeah . . . but curious."

"How so?"

"Well, if the Gastons are telling me the truth, then there's a lender in town and a few other companies working together in what couldn't be anything other than a criminal enterprise."

Chapter 7

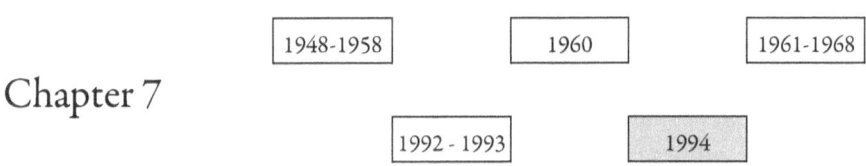

KIAWAH ISLAND, SOUTH CAROLINA
THURSDAY, MAY 26, 1994

While it never took longer than an hour to drive from downtown Charleston to the family home on Kiawah Island, it always felt like entering another world. Walker loved the time he spent on the island and always had. Beginning when he was six years old, his father had rented a house each summer for a couple of weeks—longer when he could afford it—until he eventually purchased a home on the island. It was at this home that Walker and Izzy would be spending Memorial Day weekend.

When Walker pulled up the driveway, the first thing he saw was his father sitting on the porch with a book in hand, reading. The sound of the tires rolling across the shell-covered tabby driveway grabbed Monty's attention, and he put the book aside, stood, and started down the stairs.

"Papa! Papa!" Walker's kids cried, running toward their grandfather. They met him halfway up the driveway and gave him a big hug.

"Will you take us fishing, Papa?" asked Peter. "Please, Papa, please!"

"You betcha. But let me help your dad unpack the car first, and then we'll go."

"Dad, go. I got it," said Walker. "You go."

"Thanks, son."

"Is Emmylou inside?"

"No. She ran to the store for a few items she said we needed for dinner. Should be back soon, though. Sure you don't need any help?"

"None whatsoever. Now go."

Monty smiled and turned towards his two grandchildren: Peter and Anna, twins, age four and a half. "All right, you two. Let's head to the garage and grab our gear. I got us a great spot picked out."

"Don't be late for dinner!" cried Walker. "We're cookin' steaks tonight."

"We won't," said Monty over his shoulder as each child grabbed one of his hands and ran toward the garage, pulling him along.

* * *

Spring in the Lowcountry had passed, and the summer season—no longer hovering impatiently across the horizon—had arrived. Gone was the scent of the jasmine and the gardenias had yet to bloom. But one constant on the island was the aroma of the damp salt air.

The sun would be setting soon. Walker smiled. That had always been the clock he and Eli abided by when they were kids. He moved from a chair outside to a sofa on the screened-in porch to escape the dreaded no-see-ums, which so often accompanied dusk this time of year.

"Can we join you?" asked Emmylou.

"Of course."

"It's just you looked so deep in thought."

"No, no. Not at all. Just enjoying a few moments of quiet."

Isabelle handed Walker a beer. "Figured you were due for another one."

He smiled and took the beer from her hand.

Emmylou placed two wine glasses on a small glass-topped table and took a seat in the wicker chair across from Walker. Isabelle filled the two glasses with a California Chardonnay and then sat beside him.

"You know, Walker," Emmylou began, "when your father and I first started dating, we would come here just for the quiet. That took some getting used to for me. I was always the one who wanted to travel. That had been my modus operandi. Travel here and there. Always on the go. But it was your father who taught me to slow down and relax. It's nice. I've grown to love this place."

Walker smiled and nodded his head slowly. "I'm happy to hear that. Dad worked so hard when he was a younger man. I'm glad he still harbors fond memories of his time in this house, and I'm even happier he met you."

Walker saw his wife nod in agreement. "Emmylou, you were a Godsend. Walker, you weren't here long in the immediate aftermath of . . . everything that happened," she said, skirting over the topic, "but as you know, while you were away at college, I saw more of your father during that time than you did. I'd come home from USC for the weekends from time to time and I'd drop by just to check in on him. He was so lonely, and he avoided people when at all possible."

Walker cast his eyes outside at nothing in particular, thinking to himself how much Isabelle's intuition never ceased to amaze him. He knew she was right, and he also knew that while he was at college, he was clueless as to how lost his father was. Frankly, had he been aware, it still wouldn't have made sense to him at the time. He knew that being married to his mother, Rose, had been no picnic.

Walker sensed his wife looking at him. He turned his eyes towards hers.

"Sweetheart, as for your mother," she went on, as if having read his mind, "Monty *loved* her, and towards the end they had rebuilt their marriage. His heart broke when she died. After that, work was all he had. Which again, Emmylou, was why you were such a Godsend. With you, he realized he could start living again."

Walker nodded his head slowly, smiled to himself, and before speaking, silently thanked the Lord for the blessing of having Isabelle in his life.

"That you did," said Walker. "And it's wonderful. We're all looking forward to your tenth wedding anniversary in September. Does Dad know about the party?"

"Yes, he knows." Emmylou waved a hand dismissively. "He grumbled about it, but I know he's looking forward to it. What he *doesn't* know is that the day after, we're jetting off to Europe."

"Where are you going?" asked Isabelle.

"Where *aren't* we going? We're starting in London, but the after that we're heading to Paris, Rome, Venice, Vienna, Budapest, the coast of France, Morocco, and I forget where else. We're also going to Scotland, and I have secured a tee time at the Old Course at St. Andrews."

"Oh, he will love it," said Isabelle.

"True, but he'll be missing a big chunk of the college football season," said Walker in a faux-serious voice.

Isabelle swatted Walker's arm playfully.

"Don't I know it," Emmylou said with a laugh and a sigh. "And that's why we'll be back in time for the Bama-LSU game. It's in Baton Rouge this year, and our mutual friend—the man who introduced me to your father, Laz Fontenot—has lined up seats for us on the fifty-yard line."

"I do hope the tickets are on the Alabama side of the field," said Walker, smiling.

Suddenly, the sound of children's laughter filled the air, along with the sound of his dad's voice. The kids ran onto the porch, excited to tell everyone about the fish they had caught.

"Well, are we going to have them for dinner?" asked Grandma Lou.

"No, Papa says it's best we put 'em back in the ocean so they can get bigger, then we can catch them next summer and have a real big dinner!" said Anna.

"That's right. A regular feast is what we'll have," said Monty as he walked onto the porch with a beer he'd grabbed from the refrigerator.

"Okay, kids. Let's go change your clothes," said Isabelle as she rose from her seat. "We'll have dinner shortly."

"Okay, Mom," they replied in unison.

"Home by sundown. Right on time," Walker joked, looking at his dad. It was funny to think how the tables had turned. Monty laughed and sat in the chair on the other side of the glass-topped table across from Emmylou.

"You have a good time with the kids, Pop?" Walker asked.

"The best." Monty shook his head, grinning. "I can't tell you the joy they bring me."

Walker stood. "You two just relax. I'll go start the grill."

"Sounds great, son," Monty said. He winked at Isabelle and tipped his beer at Walker as he walked into the backyard, the screen door bouncing shut behind him.

* * *

"That was a fine meal. Thank you, everyone," said Monty, shoving away his empty plate. They sat together at the same solid-oak table they had for years—*decades*, now, Walker realized—which was stationed beside the dining room's largest window. Outside, the sun had set fully, with moonlight reaching across the sky like a thin, cotton shawl.

"It's good to see you haven't lost your world-famous appetite." Walker nodded at his dad's empty plate and grinned.

"It's a crime. That man can eat anything, and he never puts on a pound," said Emmylou.

This was true for Walker as well. He and his father both ran on the slim side, regardless of their legendary appetites. Monty, in particular, could eat whatever he wanted and never seemed to put on any weight.

Walker grinned at his dad, then turned his gaze to the dining room window, where he caught a glimpse of his own reflection. He and his dad clearly had a lot more in common than just their infamous appetites. They had the same thin hair—Monty being bald, and Walker on his way—and long, angular faces that they tended to cock to one side for almost any reason, whether perturbed, interested, or in deep concentration, or when they were just listening to what someone else had to say.

"Guilty as charged," said Monty as he cleared the table, drawing Walker's attention again.

"Monty, don't worry about that. Emmylou and I can clean up. Why don't you and Walker sit out back and enjoy the night air?" Izzy suggested.

"Thank you, sweetheart," said Walker. "Dad, can I grab you a beer?"

"Yep. I'll see you out back."

When Walker joined his father in the backyard, Monty was stoking the flames in the backyard firepit. Walker added sage and some mint leaves he kept close by to keep the bugs away, a trick he had learned from a dear family friend, Mrs. Babcock, who had passed away some time ago.

"Hey, Dad. Do you have a minute to talk about some prospective clients I visited with today?"

"Sure. Love to."

"At my high school reunion last week, a girl from the class of '74, Ella Gaston, approached me about her parents, Loraine and Hugh, needing help. I met them this afternoon. They're good people, and it sounds like they may be victims of a rather complicated scam."

"What kind of scam?" asked Monty.

"Lending. Banking. Securities. Like I said, it's complicated."

"On the surface, it might seem complicated, but in my experience, once you start pulling the thread, complicated plans unravel," said Monty. "You'll find they're all pretty much the same thing—just variations of an old scam. So, what string should we start pulling?"

"I think it may all begin with a little company selling folks on a dream," said Walker.

"It often does."

Walker began telling Monty the Gastons' story. Monty mostly listened, asking only the occasional question. After a while, Monty seemed to look for a reason to slow Walker down, knowing how worked up he could get when he saw someone being taken advantage of.

"Walker, from where I'm sitting, it sounds like the Gastons were victims of some slick salesmanship, but nothing that was illegal, at least not that you could prove in court. Are you sure this is something the firm wants to get involved with?"

"The salesmanship was just part of it. The real crimes occurred when the Gastons were maneuvered into a loan they couldn't repay."

Walker noticed his father looked doubtful. "Are you familiar with Palmetto Lending Tree?"

"No, I don't believe so. I might have seen some ads on TV. Don't they make high-interest auto title loans to low-income people?"

"You're thinking of Palmetto Quick Cash," said Walker, "and yes, they make auto title loans. I think Palmetto Quick Cash and Palmetto Lending Tree are related somehow, and I also think they're working closely with Coastal Savings & Loan, who I know you're familiar with."

"Well, yeah, sure." Monty shrugged. "I knew the founders—the Hutchinson family. They started the bank in the '60s and then sold it in the late 80s. I did some work for them back then."

"Do you know who they sold it to?"

"I didn't work on the sale, but I believe the Dunsmores are minority owners."

Walker raised his brows. "Johnny Dunsmore's family?"

"Yeah. You'd be surprised how deep their involvement in this state runs."

Walker took a swig of his beer and stared off into the evening.

"But again, son, where's the criminal behavior in all of this?"

Walker started up, more determined than ever to convince his father something was amiss, and shared with him the rest of the story he'd heard from Hugh and Loraine Gaston earlier that day.

* * *

September 1992

"Hugh and Loraine, it's as good as done," said Gretchen. I can put you in that house. This is how I see it. Palmetto Lending Tree can put you in a 30-year mortgage at 9.5%. If you open a High-Yield Checking Account at Coastal S&L with a minimum of $100,000, we can get you a loan with only 3% down, and we can add that 3% into the loan amount so at closing, you'll get your downpayment back."

"I'm confused," said Loraine. "Do you work for Palmetto Lending Tree or Coastal Savings & Loan?"

"Perfectly understandable question," she said. "Palmetto Lending Tree originates the loan and sells it to Coastal S&L, and they service the loan. I work for Palmetto Lending Tree."

Assuming that her explanation was satisfactory, she continued.

"Your monthly payment will be around $1,700, but we'll put the $100k in your high-yield account to work buying bonds that are paying 9.5% a year. By my calculations, the monthly payments you receive from the man who purchased your machine shop will make up the difference. Then, you sell your current home. That's what you said, right? That you'd look at selling your current home?"

Hugh and Loraine nodded and said they couldn't afford two homes.

"And you paid off the mortgage last year, so when you sell that house, you'll likely pocket $80k."

"If we put $100,000 into a bank account, can we spend it?" asked Loraine.

"No, that money will have to be used to pay the mortgage, but here's the best part: the federal government will ensure your bank account up to $100,000. They recently raised the amount of FDIC insurance, so you can never lose that money, and it just keeps earning money buying high-interest CDs."

"But where are we supposed to get $100k and still have enough money to live on if we haven't sold our current home?" asked Loraine.

"How short are you, do you think?"

Hugh, who had been silent this whole time, piped up. "'Bout $50k."

"No problem at all. Palmetto Lending Tree can loan you $50k, and when you sell your home, you can pay it back. We can loan it to you on a short-term basis at 5% if you give Palmetto Realty, a sister company, the listing on the house. Good grief, you'll make almost *twice* that much in the High Yield Account at Coastal Savings and Loan."

Again, Hugh and Loraine looked at each other as if each were asking the other whether this was too good to be true. But they both wanted it to be true, and Gretchen was certainly confident that the math worked.

No, they deserved this. It was time to invest in their own future.

Kiawah Island, South Carolina
Thursday, May 26, 1994

Monty stood up and stoked the fire. "Well, right out of the gate, there are a few obvious problems," he said with a sigh. "For one, while a pure checking account is federally insured up to $100,000, investments are *not* insured. That Charlie Keating character in Scottsdale got sent to jail for selling junk bonds through his S&L—Lincoln Savings and Loan, I believe it was called—and then telling the folks who opened accounts with him that their money was safe because the federal government insured it. Secondly, you can add closing fees and points to a mortgage, but not the downpayment! That's absurd. But Walker, you know all this."

Walker said nothing.

"Son, what's this all about?" Cocking his head to one side, Monty continued, "You know, you can't save everyone that comes across your doorstep."

"I know, but my gut tells me that I'm onto something big. It's just a hunch, but I believe that Palmetto Lending Tree and Coastal S&L and possibly Palmetto Quick Cash are all related in some way—through mutual ownership, that is," said Walker.

"So?"

Walker turned his back to the fire and stared out at the darkness. He stood silently as he picked at the label on his beer bottle. "Pop, they have *nothing*, certainly not enough to pay us, but in the same week they received a Notice of Default on their mortgage, they received a Notice of Overdraft on a bank account that they thought had a balance of close to $100,000. They were lied to and were told the balance was insured by the federal government."

"That may very well be, but if so, unravelling it all will require extensive litigation. That's not the kind of work we do, Walker. When was the last time you were in a courtroom other than to probate a will?"

Walker turned toward his father. "I can do this. I'm not saying I've decided to take the case. I want to do a little homework first, but ... I can do this. I can help them."

Monty peered back at his son across the fire pit, through the smoke rising from the embers. and wondered how long his son would carry his cross. "Okay," he said. "It's your firm now. So, what's your first move?"

"To look behind the curtains for loose ends and start pulling."

Chapter 8

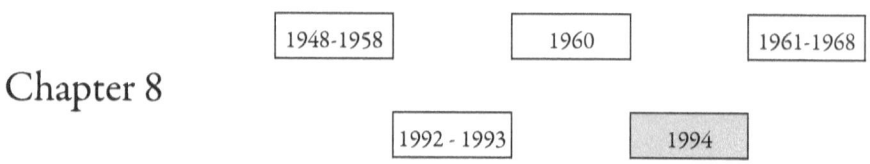

Charleston, South Carolina
Wednesday, June 1, 1994

It was 6:30 in the morning when Walker unlocked the front door to his office, flicked the lobby lights on, and made his way to the break room to start the coffee. The long Memorial Day weekend had been a wonderful reprieve from his hectic schedule, but now he was back in Charleston and ready to get to work. The day before, he'd called his office and asked one the paralegals to drive to the Secretary of State's office in Columbia and make copies of various organizational documents and annual filings for Palmetto Lending Tree and the other companies that had sunk their tentacles into the Gastons.

As he waited for the coffee to brew, Walker stood in the break room and reflected on his conversation with his father. He kept coming back to one thought that had occurred to him after their conversation: What happened to the Gastons *couldn't* have been a one-off. If it had happened to them, it must have happened to others. The Gastons' story could be the proverbial "tip of the iceberg." This case could bring him national attention. This could be *huge*.

Walker stared impatiently at the coffee maker, willing it to brew faster.

A few minutes later, armed with a fresh cup of coffee, he took a seat behind his desk and opened the folder the paralegal had left him. He thumbed through the pages in the folder and found copies of incorporation documents, organizational documents, articles, bylaws, and required annual filings for Grand Ocean Pavilions No.1, LLC, as well as several other numerically named limited liability companies. Each one appeared to be for a different phase of construction at the beachside project the Gastons had bought into, as well as the requisite organizational documents and required annual filings for Palmetto Lending Tree, Palmetto Quick Cash, and Coastal Savings & Loan. *Perfect. Just what I asked for. Yep, this could be huge. Let's look for some loose ends and start pulling.*

* * *

Two hours later, Walker stood and frantically walked about his office. Knowing he was onto something, he returned to his desk and looked at his work product: a diagram of the ownership structure of each corporation, partnership, and limited liability company.

He continued to stare at the web of generically named legal entities. Each company was registered in one of several Caribbean islands, and each one was owned by another group of faceless companies that were *also* registered in one of several Caribbean islands. Someone had gone to a great deal of trouble building this maze of corporations.

Someone doesn't want the world to know who owns these companies.
Someone has something to hide.
Walker just smiled. *Yep, I'm onto something big.*
He punched the speaker button on his phone. "Mrs. Beasley, please call Eddie Wentworth in the AG's office and see if he can meet me this Friday morning for a run."

"Of course, Mr. Atkins."

Walker continued to walk about his office, more slowly now, running his left hand across his scalp and stopping occasionally to glance back at his notes. He was looking for patterns and for things in common. He was asking questions. *Who sits at the top of all this? There must be someone. Someone, somewhere, is filing all these reports. Someone manages the money. And that someone will know who the real owners are. But who is that person and how do I find them?*

Walker's eyes scanned his diagram and notes. Was there a preference for registering in one island over another? A pattern was taking shape. *Yes. The Bahamas. Nassau, specifically.* And he had found only one name in all the records he'd searched and that man lived in Nassau—

Anthony Ferguson.

Mr. Anthony Ferguson, it may be time for me to pay you a visit.

But first, Walker had some good old fashioned legwork to do.

* * *

Walker was dressed and at his kitchen table the following morning before the sun was up with a copy of the Yellow Pages and a AAA map, plotting his route for the day. He planned to visit the offices of Palmetto Lending Tree, Palmetto Quick Cash, Palmetto Prefab Homes, and Coastal Savings & Loan, and to do so by posing as a prospective customer of each. He noticed that Palmetto Lending Tree, Palmetto Quick Cash, and Palmetto Prefab Homes, the contractor hired to build Hugh and Loraine Gaston's dream home in the Grand Ocean Pavilions, each had dozens of offices across the state and often shared the same address.

However, to play the role, he realized he could not pull this off driving his 1985 Saab 900 Turbo. In his time in Europe after law school, he fell in love with European craftsmanship and purchased this car while living there. No, Walker needed something less conspicuous. He looked at his watch; it wasn't too early to call the restaurant.

Eli picked up on the third ring.

"Eli here."

"I figured I could catch you at your office. What's the special going to be tonight?" Walker knew that most mornings, Eli, along with other local chefs planning the day's menu, met commercial fishermen at Shem Creek, bringing in the catch from the night before.

"We'll have plenty of tilefish but based on a couple of beauties I'm looking at, Redfish will be the special tonight. Want me to save you one?"

"Make it two. Izzy got us a sitter."

"You got it. So, what's up?" Eli paused, the sound of the kitchen chatter in the background filling the void. "I know you didn't call to discuss the menu."

"Eli, can I borrow your pickup truck?"

* * *

Walker's first stop was an office for Palmetto Prefab Homes located in Walterboro, a little over an hour's drive west on State Highway 64. On the way, he decided to use the alias "Walker Bristol"—using his real first name and his mother's maiden name.

Walker pulled into town around 9:15 and passed the turnoff for the Walterboro Army Airfield, where our nation housed German POWs during World War II. Up ahead, he could see the County Courthouse, which had been designed by Robert Mills from Charleston, America's first natively born and trained architect and the architect for the Washington Monument and a host of noteworthy buildings.

Following the directions he'd mapped out that morning, he continued north on Highway 64 through town. As he approached the outer edge of the other side of town, he saw a gravel parking lot on the right-hand side of the road populated by half a dozen or so mobile homes draped with bunting. Beside them was a sign that read, "Palmetto Prefab Homes." He turned off the highway, onto the poorly paved road, and parked in front of the Sales Office.

When he entered, he was greeted by an elderly gentleman wearing blue jeans and a dark green shirt with a Palmetto Tree logo stitched to the breast.

"Welcome to Palmetto Prefab Homes, makers of the finest custom premanufactured homes and trailers. My name is Butch—says so right *here*, in case you forget." The man laughed and pointed at his name embroidered in cursive on his shirt. "What can I do you for today?"

"Well, I'm Walker Bristol," he lied. "I'm new to town and trying to get my bearings. I'm not sure where me and the misses are gonna live. I saw your sign drivin' by and thought I'd check you out."

"You did a smart thing. Let me tell you what we got."

For the next fifteen minutes, Butch talked about the various mobile homes they sold, as well as the mobile home parks in the area Walker should visit. Walker asked questions about features and options offered by the different models, and which of the mobile home parks Butch would pick if it were up to him. They went back and forth. Walker was surprised at how easy it was to carry on a conversation that had no basis in fact.

"Personally, I'd be happy in a mobile home, but I can't say the same for the little woman," said Walker, chuckling. "What can you tell me about your premanufactured homes? Where in town might we find a lot for sale?"

Butch was a font of information. He had been building houses since he was sixteen years old and knew all there was to know about construction, and for his money, you couldn't get a better, more modern home for the dollar than you could with a Palmetto Premanufactured home.

"And the best part is, we build them fast," Butch went on. "The pieces are shipped from our factory and one of our trained installers will have you and the little woman living in your very own home in just a few weeks."

"That sounds great. So, let's talk. What's all this going to cost me?"

"Not as much as you'd think, but it gets even better. We work closely with the best lenders in the game, and I can just about guarantee that they can get you whatever money you need to buy one of our fine homes," explained Butch.

"What lender is that? You see, my wife and I are here because we need to, well, how do I say this . . . We need to start over a bit."

Good grief, thought Walker. *This is kind of fun.*

"Trust me, it won't be a problem. Palmetto Lending Tree," Butch proudly announced, as if that would answer any questions Walker might have. "That's the lender we use."

Walker bit his upper lip to hide the smile forming at the corners of his mouth.

"Palmetto Lending Tree?" he repeated. It was hard to pretend he'd never heard of the company, but it seemed Butch wasn't the wiser.

"Here she comes now," said Butch, nodding to the open window.

Butch stepped around Walker to open the door, and a young, attractive girl walked up the three metal steps inside the trailer holding a cardboard tray with two drinks in it and a bag of food from Hardees. She was wearing a khaki skirt and a shirt like Butch's. Above the pocket was her name, embroidered in cursive: *Lynette*.

Butch took the tray and bag from her. "Thank you, sweetheart. Lynette, let me introduce you to Mr. Bristol. He's interested in buying our Model SFR2000 Prefab Home and wants to know how much of the purchase price you can get for him."

"Pert near all of it," she said as she smiled at Walker and cocked her head. "Have a seat in my office." She nodded to the desk on the other side of the trailer. "I've got just a few questions to ask you and then I'll be able to answer Butch's."

"Say, I'm a little confused," said Walker. "Are y'all the same company?"

"We might be," said Butch as he smiled at Lynette. "I know it looks that way, but we don't really know."

Lynette shrugged her shoulders and took a seat behind her small metal desk. "Even if we did, I'm sure I wouldn't understand any of it."

"Ain't that the truth. All I know is that I answer to my boss, and she answers to hers. Mine's in Greenville and hers lives in Columbia. I guess those two folks could have the same boss."

Lynette nodded in agreement and then waved Walker over with her left hand. "Have a seat, honey."

Walker took a seat, answered her questions, and filled out one sheet of paper with his fake name and actual phone number and thought to himself that he'd have to give Izzy a ring and get her to play along in case they call the number.

Thirty minutes later, Lynette approved him for a loan for 97% of the purchase price of a model SFR2000 Prefab Home and she said they could kick back the 3% downpayment by adding it to the purchase price if he signed the contract by close of business the next day. The terms were monthly payments for fifteen years at an annual interest rate of 12.5%.

"Of course, I'll have to make a call or two and verify this information," she said as she tapped the brightly painted fingernails of her left hand on the application.

"That sounds great. My wife gets here tomorrow. I'm picking her up at the bus station in the morning. We'll come right over. She'll need to see it, of course."

* * *

The rest of the day played out in a similar fashion. Walker visited a Palmetto Prefab Homes office in another small town and had a nearly identical experience as that in Walterboro. On his way back to Charleston, he stopped into a Palmetto Quick Cash office in a strip mall sandwiched between a coin laundry mat and a Chinese restaurant and was told they could make same-day loans secured by the title to his car, or an assignment of disability payments, or even child-support payments. He skimmed a standard loan agreement while the salesmen extolled the features of their flexible repayment plans.

"Yes, sir. You work with us, and we'll work with you. Interest free for the first four years? No problem. Need more time to pay off the loan? No problem."

Walker nodded his head like it all sounded grand to him as he remembered the sage advice from one of his law school professors: *The large print giveth and the small print taketh away*. Sure enough, the small print in the loan agreement Walker was reviewing provided stiff penalties and exorbitantly high interest rates if you were a day late. In other words, anyone who took out one of these loans would be paying it back for years to come. They owned you.

On a whim, Walker stopped into a rundown used car sales lot and found, to no surprise, that Palmetto Quick Cash had an office on site.

His final stop was at a Coastal Savings & Loan branch. From his research, he found that they had six locations across the state: Myrtle Beach, Columbia, Greenville, Beaufort, Summerville, and James Island, which was the branch he stopped into as he made his way home.

The James Island branch was located off the Maybank Highway in a standalone building complete with a drive-through teller at one end of a brand-new, upscale commercial development. The décor inside the bank was smart and professional and gave off an air of competence, stability, and security. Upon entering, Walker was led to a comfortable seating area and asked if he preferred coffee, still or sparkling water, or tea while he waited for the next available private banker. While he drank his coffee, he perused the magazines on the table before him: *Fortune*, *Forbes*, *Golf Digest*, and several high-gloss real estate publications touting luxury beachside destinations.

The bank's layout was identical to every other bank he had visited: a wall of tellers on one side, with the other three sides lined with single-occupant offices separated from the main lobby by a door and a floor-to-ceiling glass window. Walker watched as a man in one office stood from his desk and walked smartly out to where Walker was sitting.

"Mr. Atkins? I'm Harvey Bishop. It's a pleasure to meet you. Please, follow me to my office."

Walker had decided to use his real name, seeing as this was a federally- and state-regulated lending institution—unlike the renegade, loosely regulated operations he'd seen that morning. He predicted they might ask for a business card or some proof of ID if he talked about opening an account and decided to cover his bases.

"So, what brings you into our bank today?" asked Mr. Bishop.

Walker had rehearsed his spiel on the drive. "I'm here both in a professional and personal capacity. I'm a trust and estate attorney in town with a clientele that comes to me for tax and estate planning advice. On occasion, they'll ask me for general investment and financial guidance. Given our wonderful climate in the Lowcountry, many of my clients have been retiring here from someplace else and are trying to get a lay of the land. So, they'll often ask me which banks I prefer, etc. I am somewhat familiar with your bank—you've had a presence in the state for some time—but you have grown quickly over the last few years, and I got to thinking that I needed to learn more about what you have to offer."

"Well, thank you for dropping in. I'd be happy to help educate you. And yes, we have grown quickly over the last few years. The bank was founded in 1959 by the Hutchinson family. Fine folks. They operated the bank out of a single branch for years, not too far from here. The bank was purchased in 1979 by an investment group with some local and regional financial support, and they have grown the bank very aggressively since then."

"If the bank was a mutual bank, owned by its depositors, how did they take on the new investors required to grow the bank?" asked Walker.

"Now, I'm way out over my skis on this one, because I don't understand all the legal mumbo-jumbo," he said as he innocently shrugged his shoulders, "but they executed something called a demutualization. The best I can gather, the previous owners, which included all the depositors, received a one-time buyout from the folks buying the bank, and then these new owners converted the bank to a company that could sell stock to people who weren't depositors. I've told you all I know or could possibly understand," said Harvey, chuckling. "But you're the lawyer—I'll bet you know more about that stuff than I do."

And you'd be right, thought Walker. *Dad helped draft the language in the state statutes allowing for these types of conversions.*

"I'm afraid banking law is not my expertise, but I get what you're talking about. So, what kind of products do you have?" Pointing to a brochure on Harvey's desk, Walker added, "What can you tell me about these High Yield Accounts you're advertising?"

"Love to. This account is very popular. You open a checking account with us and the money you deposit is used to purchase high-yield bonds. Those bonds pay you 9.5% interest. Now, you can write checks on this checking account for up to one-half of what you deposit if you wish. Since what you deposit into the account is invested in these Bonds, we charge you interest on the amount you withdraw. Still, the rate is only 10%, so you're really only paying a half percent interest."

"So, it's like a line of credit," said Walker.

"Exactly. And the best part is that the FDIC insures bank deposits up to $100,000. You can't lose," he said with a grin. Walker tried to hide his reaction by furrowing his brow and nodding his head, remembering his conversation with his dad about Charlie Keating and how checking accounts were federally insured up to $100,000, but investments were *not*.

"Wow, that's fantastic," he said. "I can see why these accounts are so popular. Say, do you have any printed information on these accounts I can take with me?"

"Absolutely."

Ten minutes later, Walker was back in his car with a dozen brochures touting the features and benefits of the Palmetto High-Yield Accounts. As he pulled out of the parking lot, he wondered if Harvey knew he was breaking the law. *Someone* did, and Walker was going to find out who.

Chapter 9

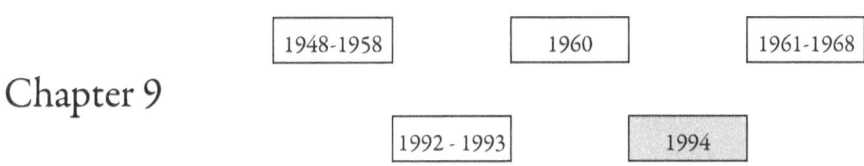

CHARLESTON, SOUTH CAROLINA
FRIDAY, JUNE 3, 1994

Early Friday morning, Walker jogged to Burbages at the corner of Savage and Broad Street for his run with Mr. Eddie Wentworth—which Mrs. Beasley had scheduled—and arrived right on time at precisely 6:30 a.m.

Already there waiting for him was Eddie: childhood friend, high school cross country rival, and all-around good guy. The last time they had seen each other in person was at their high school reunion nearly two weeks ago.

Eddie was sitting on the bench in front of the store, reading the morning paper, oblivious at first to Walker's approach. Though Burbages would not open for another couple of hours, Al Burb, the family-run grocery's second-generation owner and friend to all, could be seen through the shop's broad picture window. The man was forever hard at work. Today, he was inside stocking the shelves.

Walker gently rapped on the front window and waved; Al returned the gesture. This exchange grabbed Eddie's attention. He folded his newspaper and set it down on the bench, standing to greet Walker with a bright smile.

"You ready?" Eddie asked.
"Sure. What are we thinking?"
"Five miles or so work for you?"
"Sure, follow me."

Eddie and Walker had been running and competing together since ninth grade. Hailed as two of the top runners in the Southeast coming out of high school, their duels were legendary, and their styles could not have been more different. Walker was the planner, never leaving anything to chance, always aware of his splits and his pace, and consumed by the latest shoes, running gear, and diet crazes for distance runners. Eddie, on the other hand, ate what he wanted, wore holes in his shoes before buying another pair, and didn't even wear a watch while running. He employed a different philosophy: keep up with who was in first and then run faster than him at the end of the race. Throughout it all, they had become good friends—and now, almost twenty years later, they were *great* friends.

After a few minutes, they had settled into a comfortable pace and were able to carry on a conversation.

"I know you're fond of asking the faithful-and-always-reliable Mrs. Beasley to make all of your appointments," Eddie began, teasing, "but I'd like to remind you that you *do* have my phone number and can call me yourself whenever you'd like. Or are you too important for that?"

"Way too important. I thought you knew that by now." Walker smiled and caught a glimpse of his old friend doing the same.

Eddie had worked for South Carolina's Attorney General's Office for the last several years. Eddie and Walker went their separate ways after high school—Walker to Georgetown University and Eddie to the University of Georgia. They were reunited in law school when Walker joined Eddie in Athens, Georgia, and they both graduated from UGA's law school in 1986. Eddie's plan was to get as much courtroom experience as fast as possible and then join a white-collar firm in Atlanta and begin a career in commercial litigation. During his summers in law school, he interned for the office of the public defender in Athens. His first job out of law school was with the Charleston County Prosecutors Office. He logged more time in a court room in his first two years than the top-ranked students in his law school class who joined the big firms did in their first five.

Eddie never made it to Atlanta, though. Why? *Love.* He fell in love with Charleston all over again, and upon his return, he fell in love with his high school sweetheart, Vanessa Rhett. They were married at St. Philips on Church Street—the church her family had attended for generations. In short order, he caught the political bug and was lured away to join the Attorney General's Office, where he rose quickly through the ranks.

For the first mile or so, they caught up with each other, each asking about the other's kids. Updates were hardly necessary. Their wives were the best of friends and spoke to each other almost daily. The elephant in the room whenever the four of them were together was whether Eddie would stay with the AG's office. To keep advancing in the department—or, as some speculated, eventually run for the top position as the attorney general—they would have to move to Columbia.

Eventually they got around to the reason Mrs. Beasley set up this meeting.

"So, what do you need from the AG's office?"

Without revealing their identities, Walker told Eddie about his new clients and about everything he had learned over the past two days concerning what he was calling the "Palmetto Enterprise"—that being Palmetto Prefab Homes, Palmetto Lending Tree, and Palmetto Quick Cash. He added that he suspected that Coastal Savings & Loan was involved as well.

Eddie stayed quiet throughout, never asking a single question.

Walker had led the two of them north on Ashley Boulevard, east on Calhoun, and down East Bay to the Battery. They were now heading up Rutledge and would be back in front of Burbages in a couple of minutes. They stopped talking with maybe a quarter mile to go and couldn't help themselves—they sprinted up to the corner, Eddie edging Walker out by a stride.

As they were catching their breath, Al exited his store and brought each of them a bottle of water. "You two are nuts, you know that?"

"Thanks, Al," they responded in unison.

"Don't thank me. I put it on your tab," he said as he walked back inside.

Eddie and Walker tipped their water bottles towards each other as if to toast. "To Burbages, the best neighborhood grocery store in the business," said Eddie. "You know, I remember walking here as a kid and buying push-pops from Al's dad."

"To Burbages," replied Walker.

Eddie gathered himself as his breathing and heart rate returned to a normal resting rate. He stood with one hand on his waist, his head tipped back as he drained the water bottle. Eddie was of average height but longer in the legs than most. His hair was still best described as sandy blond and tussled, but what set him apart from others—in looks, that was—were his eyes: one was green and the other blue. The effect fed his easy-going manner. Nothing ever seemed to upset Eddie, and he was everyone's friend.

"Walker, some of what you told me today is news to me, but not everything. Our office has received complaints about the trio of Palmetto companies, ranging from defective workmanship on the prefab houses to predatory lending. We've also suspected a nexus with Costal S&L but can't prove anything. Could you drop by our office this afternoon, say around 3:30? I have a standing meeting with the boss every Friday afternoon, and I'd like him to hear what you have to say."

"Love to. See you this afternoon."

Eddie took off jogging back to his house on Legare Street and Walker towards his on Tradd.

* * *

Eddie and Joshua were already hard at work when Walker was shown to Eddie's office at 3:30 that afternoon, as scheduled. Walker and Joshua weren't strangers, so introductions were skipped. After hands were shaken, Walker took a seat in a chair next to Joshua, across the desk from Eddie.

Joshua wasted no time. "Walker," he said, brusquely, "Eddie was just filling me in on your new client and the legwork you did this week. Wanna tell me what you've learned?"

"*Prospective* new client," corrected Walker, "but yes, I'd be happy to."

"Prospective?" asked Joshua as he looked at Eddie. "Am I missing something here?"

"No," said Walker. "Let me explain. I will in all likelihood take them on. It's just that there's one more thing I want to check out first before doing so. And, since we haven't signed an engagement letter, technically, I can't call them my clients."

Eddie looked at his boss. "You good?" Joshua nodded that he was, and Eddie turned back towards Walker.

"What have you covered so far?" asked Walker.

"I told him about your visits to the various Palmetto enterprises and was about to tell him what you found at the Secretary of State's office when you walked in. Why don't you pick up there?"

"Sounds good," said Walker. "Can I use the whiteboard on the wall over there?"

Eddie handed Walker a few dry-erase markers and turned his seat towards the whiteboard. Walker spent the next few minutes drawing a multilevel organizational chart of every partnership and corporate entity he had uncovered, including their places of domicile, with lines connecting the legal entities together in a way that made the entire architecture resemble an electric circuit board. While he was doing this, he occasionally glanced over his shoulder and couldn't help but notice that Joshua was looking on in disbelief.

"So, it's true, what they say about you," said Joshua. "You have a photographic memory."

"That's probably an exaggeration, but concerning my work product, yes, my recall is pretty good."

The AG was clearly impressed.

"You mind telling me your next step?" asked Joshua.

"No, not at all. First, in representing my client, if they become my clients, that is, I'll wait until the lender files the suit to foreclose on their home. It's my hope that between now and then, I'll uncover grounds for a counter-suit and damages in favor of my client."

"Is a bankruptcy filing in their future?"

"I hope not, but it may come to that if I can't convince a judge to forestall the foreclosure sale of their home."

"Understood. Then what?"

"Answering that question, sir, is partly why I approached Eddie. I still have work to do before I can formulate the basis for a suit, but I expect to find the basis for complaints against the developer and the lender. That will start the discovery process and given what I learned about the domicile of the dozens of partnerships and corporate entities shielding the identity of the people running this operation, I anticipate a lengthy, cantankerous, and expensive discovery process. I know it shouldn't matter, but since I'm taking this case pro bono, the reality of the expenses I will incur means that, at some point, it *will* matter. No doubt the defendants will sniff this out, and time will then become their ally—and delay, their weapon."

Walker looked to Eddie and then back to Joshua. "I understand that your office has received complaints from others about these companies," said Walker as he pointed at the whiteboard. "I'm wondering if your office has enough to bring criminal charges. Doing so would certainly help my client's case."

Joshua stood from his chair and started pacing before saying anything. He looked out the window and began speaking with his back to the room. "Walker, this office may be able to muster resources you don't have, but at the same time, we don't have the resources to root out *every* criminal in the state. On top of that, you have certain advantages we don't have."

Walker and Eddie exchanged curious glances, and then Joshua turned around, facing them again as he said, "I'm going to let you in on something. We've been investigating some of these predatory lenders around the state. The problem is there are no usury laws on the books, so we can't prosecute someone for charging some poor schmuck a ridiculously higher interest rate because traditional banks won't lend the guy a dime. So, we're left with pursuing these lenders on the grounds of fraud—which is very hard to prove. So, the answer to your question is: no, we don't have enough to bring criminal charges. Now, if we can find a connection to Coastal S&L . . . well, that's a game changer."

"I understand, but what did you mean when you said I have advantages you don't have?" Walker asked.

"You're not us. Bad guys can smell cops and prosecutors a mile away. Look at what you've learned already. And you're smart. We've got some real talent in our office, but it's spread too thin." He paused, scratching his chin for a moment. "This is what I'd like to do," he went on, looking at Walker directly. "I want to hire you as a consultant. You share what you find with us, and we share what we find with you. Once we have enough to call a grand jury, we will, and if we issue an indictment, we can bring the weight of the State down on these guys. What do you say?"

Walker could hardly contain his excitement, but Joshua continued selling the idea before Walker could speak up.

"Eddie will be your contact. There'd be some paperwork for you to sign, and we can't pay you the same hourly rate you're used to, but it might help you carry this pro bono matter to a just end for your clients."

Walker was ready to go all in, but as he said earlier, he had a little more due diligence to conduct. Joshua seemed to read his mind. "You said there was one more thing you wanted to run down before deciding whether to take on the couple you mentioned as new clients. Mind if I ask what that's all about?"

Pointing at the diagram on the whiteboard, Walker answered the question. "In all my research to date, I've only found one name associated with any of these companies—a registered agent in the Bahamas named Anthony Ferguson."

"And you're going to track this guy down?" asked Joshua.

"Exactly."

Chapter 10

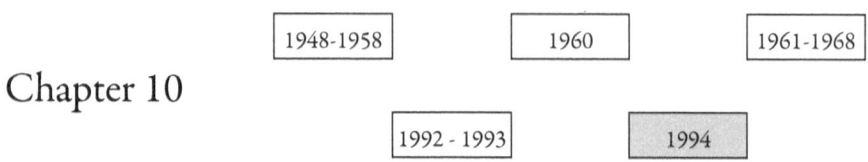

Charleston, South Carolina
Friday, June 3, 1994

Walker sat on the screened-in porch with his feet up, enjoying a drink and reading John Grisham's latest novel, *The Client*, while he waited for Isabelle to get ready.

They had a sitter, and Eli had promised to save them two specials that night, but dinner wasn't for another couple of hours. The AG's office had been Walker's last appointment for the day, so he strolled into the house around 4:30, which gave him some time to play with Anna and Peter in the backyard before the sitter arrived. She had already left and taken the kids to the park across the street from Colonial Lake to play with some other children.

Isabelle walked onto the porch wearing a simple yellow sundress and flat sandals. She had her mother's dark, thick, lustrous hair and her father's green eyes. She usually wore her hair shoulder length but had cut it recently in anticipation of another hot summer. Walker had fallen in love with Isabelle the first time he saw her when she was working as a waitress at Wappoo Country Club all those years ago. She had spilled an entire pitcher of water across the table. Mortified and in tears, she shrank away to hide in the kitchen, but Walker was mesmerized; and he still was today. They were sixteen when they met.

"Honey, you want to play some dominoes before dinner? We've got plenty of time."

"You think your fragile male ego can stand another ass-kicking?" she asked, winking.

"Baby Doll, I let you win last time. We both know that."

"Ha! Sure, set 'em up. I'm going to pour myself a glass of wine and be right back."

Walker followed her back into the house and freshened his drink. "How was your meeting with the City today?"

Isabelle worked for the Charleston Historical Preservation Society. This foundation was one of several in town dedicated to preserving the history of Charleston. They were most closely associated with ensuring that the historic homes across the peninsula were preserved, maintained, and not replaced. However, their charter extended far beyond the physical preservation of the city's beautiful buildings and homes. The organization saw themselves as preservationist for the soul of Charleston and of the memories of the people who had lived and died in the Holy City. This meant preserving and, where appropriate, honoring the good, the bad, and the ugly of a city with stories and memories echoing back to the Colonial Era.

Isabelle had double-majored at the College of Charleston, earning one degree in American History and another in Historic Preservation and Community Planning. After she'd completed her four years of college, she received a doctorate in history. She wrote her thesis on the impact the migration of the Loyalists who fled the Southern Colonies during the Revolutionary War era had on life in the Bahamas. Isabelle was proud of her work but shied away from the pretense of calling herself a doctor. "Doctors save lives," she'd say. Nevertheless, at her employer's insistence, her business card read "Dr. Atkins."

"Good. They're going to let us use the old Ryan Slave Market on Chalmers Street for our photography exhibit later this fall."

"That's great news. So how is it shaping up?"

"We have a lot of work to do between now and then, but I'm hopeful and excited. Nailing down the location for the exhibit is a big step in the right direction."

The Historical Preservation Society would be working with the Charleston Library Society to host an exhibit that would bring together underrepresented photographers from around the South. The exhibit would take place in October during the annual Fall home and garden tour, a time when many of the exceptional homes on the peninsula were opened to the public.

"How long has that building been empty?" asked Walker.

"About five years now. The city has plans to build a museum on the site, one that would explore and discuss the history of slavery in this country, but it's still a couple of years out."

"Good for you. I look forward to seeing what y'all put together. Okay, you ready to play?"

"Born ready," she said as they each turned over a domino.

Walker turned over the higher-numbered tile and would go first. After they had each selected their seven dominoes, Walker began by downing the double six, a spinner out of the gate. Isabelle surveyed her hand, and having only one six, surmised that Walker was long in that suit. Not liking her play but having no choice, she played the 6-0 domino, which drew Walker's play as if he'd known it was coming. The 0-3 gave Walker 15 points. He smiled smugly and moved his peg three spots on the cribbage board, which was how they kept score.

As play continued over the next thirty minutes, Walker filled Izzy in on the Gastons, his investigations earlier that week, and his meeting with the AG. Walker had rounded the corner and had a commanding lead until late in the game. On the next round, Izzy played to her long suits by capping each row in a suit in which Walker was void, sending him to the boneyard. He pulled six dominoes before landing on one he could play. Izzy went out and took all the points Walker held, giving her a slight lead.

"So, you'd be working with Eddie?"

"Yep."

Izzy's silence rang in Walker's ears.

"What? Do you see a problem with that?"

"The Boys & Girls Club. Your work with the church. All the other charities you're involved with . . . Then there's your professional organizations and your regular legal practice. Oh, and let's not forget me and the kids." Her voice was rising. "And now you're going to become a crime fighter, too?"

Walker shut his eyes tight. He could feel his frustration level rising. This was important to him. Why didn't she see that?

Walker felt Izzy's hand on his and opened his eyes to find her leaning over the game table and staring at him with a mixed look of love and concern. "Honey, I know you. You'll go all in on this. Is this going to conflict with your representation of the Gastons? I mean, are you going to focus too much on helping Eddie jail every crooked businessman in the state and forget that your first job is to help the Gastons out of their mess?"

"I haven't decided to take them on as clients yet."

"Yes, you have. You're simply doing all this extra work to fool yourself into thinking you're making an informed decision, but you've already made up your mind. Haven't you?"

Walker stared into his hands and mumbled quietly, "Yep."

"And you're going to take up the AG on his offer, too."

"Yep."

"I hope you find the peace you're looking for. I do. I really do. Not just for you, but for our marriage. These kids don't raise themselves and all too often you're here in body but not in spirit."

The silence returned.

"They need a father. They need *you*."

Walker slowly nodded his head. "Just support me in this and when it's done, I'll slow down. I promise."

Izzy cocked her head to the side and gently swept a loose strand of hair behind her ear. "I'm going to hold you to that."

They each relaxed.

"Okay. Shall we finish this game or just head out to dinner?" asked Isabelle.

"We're finishing, Baby Doll. I'm about to win."

"Watch it, big boy, or that'll be the last time you get lucky tonight," she said, smiling right back at him.

* * *

Walker and Izzy had a wonderful dinner at The Abaco. They stayed late, and as the crowd dwindled, Eli and his wife, Rachel, joined them.

While the wives caught up with each other and talked about their kids and their work, Walker and Eli talked about the mess Major League Baseball had turned into, with league realignment taking shape and the looming strike. The Braves had won the last three National League Division titles and were due to win a world series. The timing of the strike was awful if you were a Braves fan. The stars had aligned; their pitching rotation was one for the ages. It would be a shame if they couldn't capitalize on it. But after talking baseball, Walker turned to Eli to talk to him about what really interested him: a trip to Nassau.

"What's in Nassau for you?" asked Eli.

"I'm not sure. Answers, I hope."

"Answers? To what kind of questions?"

"I have some new clients. Not my usual trust and estate work, but they need help and I can help them. Well, the little work I have done so far has turned up what may be a criminal enterprise involving offshore companies and partnerships, many of them domiciled in the Bahamas. I've found the name of a lawyer in Nassau, who I want to track down." He leaned in a little closer, lowering his voice. "I can't tell you much right now, but I met with Eddie in the AG's office, and they're interested in what I may learn."

"Then let *them* go," Eli counseled, narrowing his eyes. "If it's a criminal enterprise, I don't think it's a good idea for you to be looking into them. We have a state department for this type of work, Walker."

Walker recoiled slightly, taken aback by his brother's resistance. "Look, Eli, I've been in this business for a long time—"

"Then you should know better and stay out of this," Eli countered, sipping his beer.

"I don't need you protecting me." It was an effort not to raise his voice. Who the hell did Eli think he was? Walker glanced at Izzy and Rachel to confirm they weren't listening in and gave his brother a pointed look. "I know what I'm doing. This is white-collar crime stuff. It's nothing violent or dangerous."

"Oh, little brother—"

"Don't give me that *little brother* crap," Walker blurted, angrily peeling the label off the beer in his hands. "I'm no kid. I know how to conduct myself."

To his chagrin, Eli shrugged, clearly not taking him seriously. "In my experience, folks get violent when you start messing with their money, and if they're hiding behind banking secrecy laws, then they are hiding more than just money."

"I'll be all right. I'm going to visit an office or two and see what I can learn, that's all. I'm just wondering if you still have any contacts in Nassau, what with all you went through there," said Walker.

Eli sat quietly and stared at Walker. "Trying to save the world, are you?" he said eventually, voice neutral. Walker couldn't tell if he was being genuine or mocking him. "Always looking out for the little guy."

Walker shrugged. "They need help. I can help them."

Eli remained silent for a little longer, looking at Walker in a way that was impossible for him to decrypt.

"I'll make a call."

Chapter 11

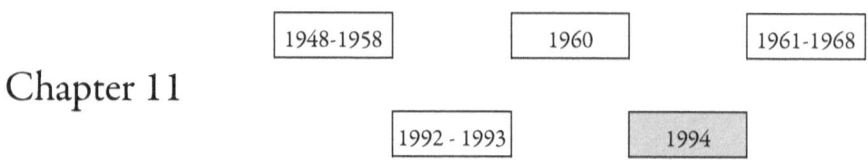

Nassau, The Bahamas
Tuesday, June 7, 1994

The pilot announced that they were beginning their descent and would arrive in Nassau at the Lynden Pindling International Airport within fifteen minutes, touching down at 10:30 a.m. Walker looked out the window at the impossibly blue ocean and remembered the phone conversation he'd had with Eli the day after they'd had dinner together.

"Are you still determined to go to Nassau?"

"Yep."

There was a pause before Eli continued. "Okay. I made a call this morning to a man named Nigel Pinder. He'll take care of you. He'll make hotel arrangements, have someone meet you at the airport, and he'll join you for dinner on your first night there. Just give me your flight information and the rest will be taken care of."

"Look, I don't need anyone to take care of me. I just need someone—"

Eli cut him off before he could finish. "You asked for my help. This is the help you're gonna get."

When Eli fled Charleston to avoid standing trial for a murder he did not commit, he'd ran to the Bahamas. He had help escaping, establishing a new identity, and figuring out life outside of the United States, and Nigel Pinder was one of the people who helped.

"Walker, Nigel is a good man and resourceful. Don't let his appearance fool you. If you find yourself in any kind of trouble while you're there, you couldn't have a better friend in the Islands than Nigel. I'd put my life in his hands. Walker, *I did* put my life in his hands."

The sound and feel of the tires bouncing along the runway as the plane touched down brought Walker back to the present. Ten minutes later, he was passing through customs, and he saw a man holding up a sign with his name on it. The man was elderly and wore long blue pants, a yellow short-sleeved shirt with palm trees and green fronds splashed across it, and a tan, wide-brim Panama hat.

"Good morning! I'm who you're looking for, I believe," said Walker. He had a leather satchel hanging off his shoulder and an overnight bag in his hand but still managed to shake hands with the man waiting for him.

"Ah, yes, Mr. Atkins. Good to meet you, mon. My name is Deaven, and I will be your driver while you are here."

"My driver?"

"Yeah, mon. Mr. Nigel Pinder sent me."

Deavan took Walker's bag from him, led him to an old British Land Rover, and held the passenger-side door open for him.

"First time to the Bahamas, Mr. Atkins?" he asked.

"Yes, it is."

"Well, I know you're only here for a short stay, but I'm here to drive you anywhere you want, mon."

"Thank you. I may take you up on that."

The car lacked air conditioning, so they drove with the windows down on West Bay Street towards downtown Nassau. By the time Walker reached the hotel, his shirt was sticking to his back; the humidity was possibly even worse here in the Bahamas than in Charleston. He entered the Graycliff Hotel and was immediately struck by a blast of cold air and the elegant, old-world charm of the hotel's architecture and décor. He walked to the front desk and was met by a beautiful young woman behind the desk.

"Welcome to the Bahamas. May I help you?"

"Yes, I have a room reservation for two nights under the name Walker Atkins."

"Oh, yes, Mr. Atkins, we have been expecting you. We are upgrading your room, courtesy of Mr. Pinder."

"Well, that was nice of him, but it's just me, so I don't really need a bigger room."

"Mr. Pinder insists."

"Well, if Mr. Pinder insists . . ." Who *was* this Mr. Pinder, really?

As if reading Walker's mind, the woman behind the counter remarked, "Mr. Pinder is a dear friend of our hotel's owner. As I understand, the friendship between their respective families stretches back several generations. We're happy to take care of his associates."

"Would you accept a traveler's check?" he asked, trying to keep his tone neutral. The truth was that he was growing a bit concerned about the cost of this place.

"Yes, we would, Mr. Atkins, but the charges have been taken care of," the front desk agent said with a professional smile. This definitely wasn't the first time she'd done this; it was almost as if she was reciting a well-memorized script. "Again, you are Mr. Pinder's guest. Now, Antoine will show you to your room. If there is anything you need, please just ring the front desk, and we will be happy to help."

Walker thanked the young woman and then spoke to Deavan. "Can we meet back here in about twenty minutes for a tour of the island.?"

"Yeah, mon."

Swept along by gracious forces he could not explain, Walker began to relax and followed Antoine to his beautiful deluxe suite room with a view of the patio gardens below. In his room, he found a bottle of white wine waiting for him in a bucket of ice and a note in an envelope addressed to him in perfectly handwritten cursive.

> *"Walker, I do hope you enjoy the accommodations. Sir Winston Churchill once occupied the room you are staying in. I am so looking forward to meeting you. Eli told me you were coming and asked that I lend a hand where I could. Your brother is someone I will never forget. We shall dine tonight at 7:00 in the restaurant in your hotel. If you are in the mood for a cocktail before dinner, I'll be in the bar. Cheers."*

Walker sat at the end of the bed taking in the opulence of his surroundings. What was going on? He'd come to the Bahamas to track down a lawyer named Anthony Ferguson in the hopes of learning more about his involvement with the Palmetto companies back in South Carolina. But admittedly, he had no real plan. How was he going to get the guy to talk? And now here he was, the fawned-over guest of one Nigel Pinder. Who was this guy? All he knew about him was what his brother had told him: "I'd put my life in his hands. Walker, *I did* put my life in his hands."

Well, all right then. If Eli can trust him with his life, I guess I can trust him with my plans, such as they are. Looking at his watch, he realized that he had the rest of the afternoon free to explore the area before meeting the mysterious Nigel Pinder for a drink and dinner. *All right Deavan, time to explore.*

* * *

Walker met Deaven in the hotel bar, where he said he would be waiting, and the two of them came up with a game plan. First stop, lunch. They climbed back in the Range Rover and headed down the hill toward the harbor.

"So, Deaven, where are we and where are we going?"

"We're in downtown Nassau."

"And what about all those large buildings over there?" asked Walker as he pointed out the driver's side window.

"That's Paradise Island, mon. Tall grass over there."

"Tall grass? I don't understand."

"Tall grass means *big money*. Lots and lots of money over there."

"Got it."

"My wife works in one of the big hotels over there. She has a good job. But you're staying at the most elegant hotel on the island, the Greycliff. I wanted you to see our downtown before heading to lunch. But now I'll take you to the Fish Fry on Arawak Cay."

"Fish Fry, is that the name of a restaurant?" asked Walker.

"Not one restaurant, but many," answered Deavan. "It's called Arawak Cay but it's a lot of restaurants and bars that the locals call the Fish Fry. Very good food."

"Excellent. I'm starving." Walker sat in the back seat on the passenger side with his arm hanging out the open window and watched the sand and the surf pass by. *I've never seen water like this. So, Eli spent five years here… How bad could it have been?*

Ten minutes later, they pulled into a packed parking lot. Walker was happy to be with a local because the crowds from the recently disembarked cruise ship were overwhelming; it looked like every outdoor seat was taken.

"Stick with me, mon," said Deaven as he led Walker through the crowds, weaving this way and that. They walked into the back of a restaurant and up to the small bar. Deaven and the elderly woman behind the bar spoke quickly in a heavy island dialect that Walker could not follow. He did understand his name when Deaven mentioned it to the woman, and then he was pretty sure he heard Deavan say "Nigel Pinder" and "Eli's little brother." The woman smiled at Walker and nodded her head.

"Would you like a beer, Mr. Atkins?" she asked.

"Yes, and please, call me Walker."

"Okay, Walker, it is," she said, smiling as she handed him a Kalik beer.

A couple of minutes later, the woman led them to a table for two, where they enjoyed a wonderful lunch of conch fritters, grilled snapper, and dirty rice. She returned with the check as they were finishing their lunch. Walker sensed she wanted to say something, so while he was fishing through his wallet for an American Express check, he paused and looked up at her expectantly.

"So, you're Eli's brother."

"Yes, ma'am."

"Mmmhmmm. How I miss that boy. He arrived on the island all quiet like, but when he left it was like fireworks all across Nassau. You tell him that you ate here and that we all say our hellos to him. You do that, now."

"I sure will. Thank you. And the food was wonderful."

"Of course, it was. You're in paradise now."

* * * *

Walker sat quietly in the back of the car, reflecting on what the woman had said. What had happened to Eli while he was here? Walker knew the basics: Eli lived in Nassau for five years waiting for the right time to return to Charleston and clear his name. While here, he held odd jobs, learned the game of golf, became an accomplished chef, got tangled up with a high-stakes gambler and professional criminal who kidnapped Rachel—the woman Eli would later marry—and finally participated in a sting operation that both brought down the man's international money-laundering scheme and freed Rachel from his clutches. Or at least that was what most people thought had happened. It was so hard to separate the rumors from the truth. And on this front, Eli was of no help. Walker couldn't help but think that Eli stayed quiet intentionally in order to feed the myth that he had become.

"Deavan, do you know where Adelaide Village is?"

"Of course, mon. Everyone knows where Adelaide is."

"Could you drive me there? My brother Eli lived there for five years. I assume you knew my brother too and know all about what happened here," Walker said in a somewhat resigned tone.

"No, mon. Before my time here. I just arrived a few years ago, but I've heard the stories. I'll take you there."

"Thank you. And you said that everyone knows where it is. Is that because it's where Eli lived?"

Deaven chuckled. "No, mon. It's been famous for a long time."

"Famous? How so?"

"In 1831, the British Navy stopped a Portuguese sailing ship and rescued 157 people who the Portuguese boat captain had purchased from slave traders in West Africa. The British captain brought them here, to the Bahamas, and the governor, Sir James Carmichael Smith, gave them land to live on—British land. They named the settlement Adelaide Village."

"The British did this? I thought the British were heavily involved in the slave trade."

"They were, they were, but times change. Attitudes too. In 1807, Great Britain ended the slave trade, at least in the Atlantic where they had influence."

Walker knew none of this and was fascinated by the story. What he *did* know was that his brother had lived in a thatched-roof hut on a beach in Adelaide Village during the five years he hid on the island.

"Here we are, mon. Do you want to get out and walk about?"

"Yeah. Can you wait here?

"Sure, mon."

Walker made his way to the beach and picked a direction to head. He tried to imagine Eli living here, in one of the simple huts that lined the beach. In Charleston, before the events that changed both his life and Eli's forever, Eli had been preparing for a career as a major league baseball player. He'd already been drafted and was going to be playing for the Charleston Pirates, a single-A team in the Pittsburg Pirates farm system. And then disaster struck.

What were you going through, Eli? The rumors that surrounded the truth about his time here highlighted and romanticized the adventure of it all, but Walker was beginning to see things from a different perspective. *You must have been awfully lonely here, Eli. You must have wondered what would become of your hopes and dreams. I know how much you still love baseball . . . and you never got to play.*

Walker turned and made his way back to the car.

* * *

Walker entered the bar at 6:40, looking for someone who looked like a man named Nigel. Eli had described him, and sitting at the corner of the bar chatting up the lovely bartender sat a man who fit the description. He wore gray pants, loafers without socks, a white shirt, and a blue blazer. As Walker approached, Nigel broke away from his conversation and glanced Walker's way. He must have concluded that he looked like someone named Walker, for he stood and took several steps in Walker's direction.

"Nigel Pinder?" asked Walker.

"I am, indeed," the man said in a stiff British accent. He reeked of wealth. Even his tone of voice and curated smile felt foreign—*royal*, even. "And that makes you Walker Atkins. It is my great pleasure to make your acquaintance. Care for a drink before dinner?"

"Sure." Walker smiled, following him back to his seat. "What are you having?"

"Oh, my usual."

The bartender, who was casually cleaning a glass, filled in the rest: "Three measures of Gordon's, one of vodka, half a measure of Kina Lillet, stirred and *not* shaken, with a thin slice of lemon peel. That's what makes it *his* usual." The bartender gave Nigel an affectionate sort of look that revealed they had likely known each other for quite a while. "Everyone else orders the same drink—but they order it shaken and *not* stirred."

"This is true, I must say. For years, I, too, ordered the drink shaken and not stirred. I was set straight by a beautiful, beguiling young woman. She believed that if shaken, the drink lost its texture, and she was adamant that martinis were never intended to have ice shards floating on top. This woman," he went on, voice like the rolling purr of an expensive engine, "is a relation of yours, in fact."

"Of mine? What do you mean?" asked Walker.

"The woman I am speaking of is your sister-in-law, Rachel. Quite a remarkable woman. She sure whipped your brother into shape. Now what about you? What can this lovely lady pour for you?"

"Do you have any whiskey?"

"Scottish or American?" she asked.

"American."

"Bring him some George Dickel bourbon, neat," said Nigel.

Turning back to Walker, he asked about his day, and Walker shared the details with him. They exchanged small talk for the next fifteen minutes until the maître d' approached and led them to a table for two in the corner of the restaurant, far from the kitchen and slightly removed from the rest of the restaurant's guests.

"Your usual table, sir."

"Thank you, Edward," said Nigel as they took their seats.

The dinner was fabulous, as was the wine which Nigel took the pleasure of selecting, doing so without looking at the menu. Walker was beginning to realize he had entered a world about which he knew nothing. He found Nigel to be a natural conversationalist and a font of information about the islands, their history, and their customs.

Walker had come to the islands to investigate Anthony Ferguson but now recognized that he had an excellent opportunity to learn more about his brother Eli's time here, as well. "So, you know my sister-in-law, Rachel," he began.

"I do, indeed."

He was hoping Nigel would take the subject and run with it, but he was met with silence instead. For a moment, they just stared at each other.

Then, Nigel said, "You were hoping I would pull back the curtain and tell you everything you wanted to know about your brother's time here. Am I right?" He cleaned the corners of his mouth with his napkin before neatly returning it to his lap.

Walker reached for his wine glass only to find it empty and quickly set it back down, avoiding eye contact with Nigel.

"I must respect your brother's wishes," Nigel clarified. "Rachel's too. You know they wish everyone would just forget all about it and pretend it had never happened."

Walker peered over his right shoulder, distracted by the waiter who appeared out of nowhere to refill his glass. *They wish everyone would just forget, my ass,* he thought. The more cloak-and-dagger they were, the more attention they got—and they *loved* the attention. How could they not? They were the heroes of every story in Charleston.

"If only that were possible," he mumbled without realizing it.

"Excuse me, dear boy. I don't believe I heard you."

Walker sighed and took a sip of his wine. "I was just saying that on that subject, I agree. I wish folks would just stop talking about it."

"Very good. Then we shall. Let's turn our attention to what brought you to our lovely corner of the world. I understand from my conversation with Eli that you are interested in learning about a lawyer in Nassau. Am I correct?" asked Nigel.

"Yes, that's true. The man's name is Anthony Ferguson."

"I'm not familiar with that name but it shouldn't be a problem learning more about him."

"Can you help me find him? Because all I have for him is a PO Box address."

"Quite sure of it," Nigel answered confidently with a smile.

"Well, that's a start, but in a more general way, I'd like to learn about the world of private bankers and offshore banking."

"It would be my pleasure, but I might suggest that we continue this conversation in the cigar room over an after-dinner drink."

Five minutes later, they were sitting in the corner of the cigar room, respectfully tucked away in a private nook, each with a cigar and a fresh drink—another Dickel whiskey for Walker, and a small glass of port for Nigel. Walker smoked the occasional cigar while playing golf but had never smoked Cubans.

Eventually, Nigel cut to the chase. "Before I explain the world of private banking to you, can you tell me the name of the bank you are interested in and why?"

Walker puffed his Cuban, very much feeling the buzz of the evening—the drinks, the cigar, the wonderful food, and the glamor of it all. "I don't know the name of any offshore banks yet. I just suspect. You see, I may have uncovered a web of companies in South Carolina that prey on the unsuspecting with predatory loans they have no chance of ever repaying—loans that facilitate questionable purchases. These companies are all domiciled in the Caribbean. I figure the money is moved around quite a bit but eventually it makes its way into the hands of the actual owners of the companies."

"These owners, the people whose identity is hidden behind these companies, are who we call the 'beneficial owners,'" explained Nigel. "Now, let me guess, when you investigated the ownership and organizational structure of this *web of companies*, as you say, you found a wall of faceless companies and partnerships, each one seemingly owned by the other and all domiciled in the Bahamas or other Caribbean countries. Am I right?"

"Yep, that's it."

"Very good. But of all the islands these companies call home, why did you pick the Bahamas to visit?"

"I figured that somewhere at the top there's someone who knows what's going on. Someone is filing annual reports with the South Carolina Secretary of State. Someone is moving the money. Well, the only name I could find is that of this guy named Anthony Ferguson and his PO Box address is in Nassau. So, here I am."

"And so you are. A reasonable assumption. Well, let me give you some background information on offshore banking. You see, we British invented offshore banking. The first offshore banks were located off our shore in the English Channel, namely the Bailiwick of Jersey and Guernsey. Today, while you find many offshore banks in the Caribbean, they do not have to be on an island. Many banks in Switzerland are described as 'offshore.' People seek our services for many reasons, but the major one is a desire for privacy, which means they want to avoid prying eyes in the country in which they live, so they bank in another country; in other words, they bank offshore. These other countries will often establish themselves as tax havens as well. This is the second reason people will set up businesses and bank accounts in other countries, so they can avoid onerous taxes in their own. The third major force at work is that of criminals."

"How so?" asked Walker.

"When criminals commit securities fraud, banking fraud, and other so-called white-collar crimes, attention-seeking politicians respond by passing more laws instead of more effectively enforcing the laws that already exist. These onerous regulations do two things. First, they drive up the cost of doing business and lower returns, thus forcing honest businesspeople to do business offshore. Secondly, they give criminals a road map and show them what they must do to avoid getting caught, but such laws hardly deter criminal activity because the chances of getting caught are still rather low, especially if they seek refuge through offshore banking."

"Nigel, I don't mean to be rude, but it's beginning to sound like all offshore banking is a front for criminals. I know that can't be true because Eli speaks so highly of you."

"No offense taken. I understand. I could go on for days about the history of secrecy laws and the proper role of private banking, but it is true that the criminals who avail themselves of our services have sullied the reputation of our noble profession. So, as is the case in every profession, there are good guys, and there are bad guys. I pick my clients carefully. My family has done so for over two hundred years now, so we like to think of ourselves as the good guys, but let's get back to your case, for it sounds like you have uprooted some bad guys. I may have an idea of what your next step should be. Let me make a few phone calls, and let's meet tomorrow for breakfast. Shall we say half past nine? I'll need some time to make those calls."

* * *

Wednesday, June 8, 1994

Walker was up and out the door at seven, having not slept well due to drinking too much the night before with Nigel. He decided a run was in order to shake the cobwebs loose and maybe a dip in the ocean, too.

He studied a map the day before and figured the run to Saunders Beach and back was just under five miles. *Perfect. Run, jump in the ocean, and run back.*

By 9:20 a.m., Walker was showered and heading downstairs to meet Nigel for breakfast, ready to take on the day. Nigel was seated at a table—again, in the corner with no other nearby tables—reading a copy of the city's local newspaper, *The Guardian*.

"Ah, there you are. Sleep well?"

"Yes," lied Walker, wondering how Nigel looked as chipper as he did, knowing that he'd had much more to drink the night before than Walker had. "In fact, I got up early this morning for a run and a dip in the ocean."

"How . . . *lovely*," Nigel said, speaking as one who views exercise as a pastime for others, not for themselves. "Well, let's jump right in. I made a few phone calls this morning. Let me tell you what I've learned about the lawyer whose name you uncovered in your investigations back home: Mr. Anthony Ferguson."

"Excellent," Walker said, sighing with relief. This was going better than he'd hoped. If his suspicions were correct, Anthony Ferguson was a big player in this game.

"Your address for him is a PO Box. Not much help," Nigel went on. "I called a dear friend who is a member of the local bar and inquired about Mr. Ferguson. He had an actual physical address for him, as is required by the local bar, but I'm afraid my friend did not have . . . *kind* things to say about Mr. Ferguson."

"Is that so?"

"His clientele, it is believed, runs the gamut," Nigel said, sitting back in his chair. He eyed Walker for a breath before adding, "He consorts with those who seek private bankers for all the wrong reasons. This development dovetails nicely with your current suspicions."

"Yes, it does."

"Anyway, as to the address—I know the building and more importantly, the owner of the building. Good fellow. He described Anthony Ferguson as a fine tenant, meaning he pays his rent on time and never calls the landlord. But here's something that may be of use to us: the rent checks are drawn on a bank in Miami from an account known as ICC Ltd."

"So, what now?" asked Walker.

"Do you like James Bond movies? I know your brother does."

"Sure, who doesn't?"

"Then I think it's time to do some sleuthing. Let's stir things up, make a little mischief, create some chaos, and see what happens."

Create some chaos? Was this guy joking?

"How do you suggest we do that?" asked Walker.

"Do what you came here to do. Question the man. Walk into Anthony Ferguson's office and ask him about all those companies operating in South Carolina. Tell him you represent clients who have been seriously injured by their business practices and that in research for your lawsuit, you learned that the owners are hiding behind a veil of banking secrecy laws designed to protect drug dealers and third-world tyrants."

"You're kidding, right? He's not going to answer my questions."

"Then why are you here, if not to question the man?"

"Well..." Walker didn't have an answer. "Well, I thought I could question others about him first before I just barge in. I'd love to flip him so that he would give us a road map. To do that, I'll need leverage. I'll need to learn more about him."

Walker began to hear Eli's voice in his head from the previous Friday night warning him about this trip: *"In my experience, folks get violent when you start messing with their money, and if they're hiding behind banking secrecy laws, then they are hiding more than just money."*

"Honestly, Nigel, how do you see this playing out?" he went on. "It's not like I'm going in there armed with a Walther PPK and a bulletproof vest."

"Neither will be necessary. And it's good to know you're not packing," Nigel went on. "We have strict gun control laws here. No, as I said, we want to create a *little* chaos and see how he reacts. Does he leave the office? If so, who does he go to see? Does he make a call? If so, to whom?"

"Okay, that makes sense, but how are we going to know who he sees if he leaves the office, or who he's calling?"

"You leave that to me, dear boy."

* * *

Later that morning, Walker entered the law office of Anthony Ferguson on West Bay Street, posing as himself. The lobby was empty except for two metal folding chairs, a small coffee table, and a desk for someone to sit behind. After a moment, Walker called out, "Hello, anyone here?"

A man of average height wearing tan-colored gabardine pants, a blue Hawaiian shirt, flip flops, and a three-day beard stepped into the room. He had the largest ears Walker had ever seen.

"Are you Anthony Ferguson?" Walker asked.

"Yeah," he answered somewhat hesitantly. "What can I do for you?"

"I represent some business interests in the States that are looking for local representation. We want to set up one or two businesses in the Bahamas," he said, spouting off the script he'd had approved by Nigel earlier, "and you come *highly* recommended."

Anthony's attitude changed on a dime, and he smiled invitingly. "Of course, happy to help. Please excuse the office conditions today. I wasn't expecting any clients, so I gave my girl the day off. I was going to catch up on some paperwork, but I'm always happy to make the acquaintance of a new client."

Walker followed Anthony into his office who took a seat behind a cheap particle board desk arranged at the room's center and motioned for Walker to take the seat on the other side. Walker, try as he might, couldn't keep his eyes from glancing left or right at the man's enormous ears. *Truly incredible.* He forced himself to look the man in the eye and returned to his rehearsed script.

"Mr. Ferguson—"

Anthony held up a hand. "Please, call me Tony."

Walker started up again. "*Tony*, I am here representing clients in South Carolina who have been seriously injured by the coordinated business practices of a collection of companies that all have several things in common. First, they are all owned by a network of partnerships, companies, and trusts domiciled in the Bahamas and other Caribbean nations. Secondly, they all use the services of local registered agents, such as yourself—and in fact, you are the registered agent for half a dozen or more of these shell companies that, in turn, own companies like Palmetto Lending Tree and Coastal Savings & Loan to name a few. The laws these companies hide behind are the very same laws that drug dealers and other criminals hide behind. I intend to file a suit and, in the process, pull the curtain back and expose the dirty operation and everyone involved—and that includes you. I'm here to give you a chance to save yourself and help me. Become an informant, and I'll help you get the immunity you need. Tell me who the real owners are. Tell me who is behind all this."

Walker was done. He had been watching for a reaction of some sort—anything, anything at all—but Tony surprisingly revealed nothing. That was, until Walker mentioned Coastal S&L, at which point Tony sat up and nervously moved a legal pad from one side of the desk to another and looked as if he were waiting for a break in Walker's monologue to speak.

"Mr. Atkins, I have no idea who you are or what you are doing here, but you confuse me with someone else. I run an honest business for people looking for legal representation in the Bahamas. Now," he said, standing abruptly, "I am very busy today, so I must ask you to leave."

Walker remained seated.

Anthony Ferguson's nostrils flared. "I mean it. Leave—*now!*"

Walker stood as well and, out of habit, extended his hand to shake—a meaningless gesture at this point, and one Anthony ignored. This was *exactly* the way Walker had thought all this would unfold and as he turned, walking away, he started to think that at least the bulletproof vest would have been a good idea. *What was Nigel thinking? Now this guy knows who I am! How am I ever going to learn anything?*

Anthony followed him all the way to the front lobby, where a beautiful young woman wearing a tasteful-yet-revealing dress was waiting. Her presence broke the concentration of both men, and as Walker tried to think of one last parting shot, Anthony Ferguson beat him to it.

"We'll have those papers drawn up for you by the end of the week, Mr. Atkins," he said, shooing Walker out the front door. "Always a pleasure."

As Walker exited the office, he glanced back over his shoulder and saw Tony turn his attention to the beautiful young woman.

* * *

Nigel was waiting at a corner table on the second floor of the Café Abaco, overlooking Bay Street and talking with the waiter, when Walker arrived. It seemed that everywhere he went, Nigel was a treasured regular, perpetually taken care of by management. Shortly after Walker was seated, a cold Kalik beer was placed before him.

"Cheers, my good man. I want to hear all about your morning—but first, do you know anything about this restaurant I have invited you to?" asked Nigel.

Walker couldn't disguise his frustration. *What difference does it make? What could be more important right now than what he'd just experienced with Ferguson?* He sighed. "Yeah, I believe so. This is the restaurant where Eli worked when he lived here."

"Quite right. One of several places Eli worked, but other than caddying at the golf course, this was his favorite place of employment, where he honed his skills in the kitchen. From what I am told, he has become quite the chef."

"Yes, he has, and this place was the inspiration for his restaurant in Charleston—in name and in the style of cooking."

"Excellent. Now, how did things go with the learned Anthony Ferguson?"

Walker told him all that had happened, and as he was wrapping things up, his attention was drawn to a woman walking their way. While he was still talking, Nigel stood and greeted the woman, holding both of her hands in his and kissing her on each cheek.

"You're the woman who was waiting in the lobby this morning," said Walker in disbelief.

"Walker, allow me to introduce you to Melissa Bastian. Her family owns this restaurant."

"Hello, Mr. Atkins. It's a pleasure to meet you. I knew your brother Eli when he was here. My Uncle Francesco helped him escape from Charleston. Uncle Francesco was married to Amy Babcock and lived in South Carolina then."

"Of course," said Walker, happy to be learning something about Eli that he already knew for a change. "Your uncle, Uncle Francesco, was married to Mrs. Babcock's daughter."

"True, true, and they still are, but they moved to Beaufort, South Carolina," she said.

"I didn't know him," Walker admitted, "but everyone knew Mrs. Babcock. She became a minor celebrity around town when everyone learned what she did to help Eli. Well, it's nice to meet you, Melissa." Turning to Nigel, he added, with a smile, "Is this what you meant this morning when you said you'd take care of learning about how Ferguson reacted to my sneak attack?"

"It is indeed. Now, Melissa, do tell. How did he react?"

"Walker, immediately after you left, he disappeared into his office for almost fifteen minutes with the door shut while he made a call. I stood close to the door and listened as best I could. The conversation seemed rather heated. I don't know who Mr. Ferguson was talking to—he never mentioned him by name—but the man on the other end must have been his boss and he must have just kept asking him questions, because the only words I heard from Ferguson's mouth were, 'Yes, sir' and 'I don't know, sir.' When he hung up, I hurried back to my chair."

"Did he seem harried when he came back out?" asked Walker.

"A bit, but when he returned, his hair was combed, and his shirt was tucked in. He seemed more interested in making my acquaintance."

"Yes, you have that effect on men. Then what?" asked Nigel.

"I asked him if he handled divorces. He doesn't, by the way, but the man down the hall does, which is where he directed me. I left in the direction of the lawyer to whom he had just referred me, but then kept going and exited the building. My cousin, Teo, was sitting on his motor scooter across the street. He told me that he saw Mr. Ferguson lock up his office and hurriedly walk a few blocks. He eventually entered Continental Bank."

Walker turned to Nigel. "Continental Bank. Does that mean anything to you?"

"Yes. They are considered a reputable bank, which means they represent enough standup citizens to make up for their less reputable clients. Above all else, they guard the identity of their clients zealously."

"I wish we knew who he called," said Walker.

"We don't yet, but we will soon," said Nigel.

* * *

After lunch, Nigel excused himself to make a few calls, and left Walker to his own devices until six o'clock that evening, when they would meet at Nigel's home for a drink before heading to dinner. Deavan was sitting at the bar when lunch was over and at Nigel's suggestion, Deaven drove Walker to the Lyford Cay Golf Club, where Eli had caddied, and according to Nigel, played some inspired golf.

While the story of how Eli had returned from the Bahamas to save Walker from the madman was well known around Charleston, Eli's exploits in the Bahamas were not well known, and that was because those who knew the truth had been asked by Eli and Rachel not to speak about it. It was *their* story, and they did not wish to see Eli's exploits mythologized in any way. Not even Walker knew the whole truth. But he was gaining a new perspective with each day he spent in Nassau.

Nigel had called the Club ahead of time, which meant that Deaven was waived through the heavily guarded gates without question. They were greeted by the General Manager, Mr. Brooks, and escorted through the clubhouse.

Word had apparently spread that *Eli's little brother* was on the premises. As Walker toured the grounds, he felt like a celebrity that people recognized but did not want to bother. Their reaction felt respectful—like those in the presence of a war hero, rather than a rockstar—which only fueled Walker's ongoing curiosity about Eli's true history here.

What had his brother really done? Who had he really been?

Walker knew a little. He knew that it was at this course that Eli had learned to play golf, and that his mentor, Lach McGregor, had died just a few years ago. Attending the funeral had been the only time Eli and Rachel had returned to the Bahamas since 1978.

As Walker and the Club's general manager finished the tour, Mr. Brooks explained that there was one last thing he wanted Walker to see as they entered the bar overlooking the eighteenth green.

"Mr. Atkins, I was not employed here when your brother Eli won the Cup, but I know all about it. Everyone here does. I want to show you something," he said as he led Walker to the corner of the bar and pointed out a brass plate secured to the bar top with four screws.

Walker leaned over and read the inscription out loud:

Drama in the Bahamas
Travis McCoy vs. Eli Atkins
1978
Strict Rules of Golf

"I know Travis," said Walker. "He's a friend of Eli's who occasionally pops into town."

"No doubt. It's my understanding they became fast friends. Mr. McCoy is a member here, though I don't believe he is on the island right now."

"What does 'Strict Rules of Golf' mean?" asked Walker.

Mr. Brooks just smiled but didn't answer the question.

Walker stood quietly at the bar and stared out the window at the eighteenth green and then patted his hand on the bar next to the brass plaque and turned to Mr. Brooks. "It's strange that you'd show me this plaque, only to refuse to explain the significance of it. You said that everyone here knows the story. Well, I don't, and Eli won't talk about his time here."

"You say you know Mr. Travis McCoy."

"I do."

"Ask him the next time you see him. As I understand it, he *loves* to tell the story."

"Thank you," he said, somewhat unconvincingly. "This has been . . . enlightening."

"It was my pleasure. On your next trip to the Bahamas, if you have time for a round of golf, please know that you are always welcome. You would play as a guest of the Club."

"That's very kind. Thank you."

Deaven was waiting for Walker when he exited the clubhouse.

"Back to the hotel, mon?"

"Yes, Deaven. Back to the hotel."

Walker sighed and watched the landscape pass by his window as they drove off.

All these years, Walker had focused on how the shootout in the swamp had negatively affected him, assuming all along that it had not negatively affected Eli. And why would it? Eli was the hero in the story! But after just a few days here, he was gaining a new perspective.

He didn't know all that had happened over the five years Eli lived here, but clearly quite a lot had. What he wanted to know was what happened and why Eli made such a big secret of it all. In fact, Walker realized that he'd begun to feel less curious about what had happened, and more curious about what Eli might be hiding.

* * *

That evening, Deaven picked Walker up outside the Greycliff Hotel and drove him to Nigel's house at Lyford Cay on the western end of the Island. Nigel met them in the circular driveway and showed Walker into the foyer, where he introduced him to his wife, Audrey.

"What a beautiful home," said Walker, shaking Nigel's wife's hand.

"Thank you, Walker. It's so nice to meet you. The way Nigel has been going on these last few days, I feel like I know you. Now, I know you have work to do and then dinner, so I'll be off. Bridge night with the girls at the Club, you see. Do say hello to Eli for me."

"I certainly will."

Nigel gave his wife a quick kiss and then led Walker to a small office overlooking a pool in the courtyard on the back side of the house. Nigel poured himself a drink from his bar and asked Walker what he preferred.

"Whatever you're having will be fine, I'm sure."

As Nigel turned his back to pour Walker's drink, he asked, "So, Walker, what did you think of the Club earlier today?"

"I came down here to learn what I could about Anthony Ferguson—but what I'm doing is learning more about my brother, Eli. Is that why Eli gave me your name? So you could show me that there's so much more about his life that he *could* brag about but doesn't? Am I supposed to be impressed by his humility? Has this whole thing been one big set up?" Walker asked, making no effort to hide his anger.

Nigel handed Walker his drink and sat in the chair across from him. He was wearing khaki pants, topsiders without socks, and a light blue golf shirt. In his right hand, he twirled his drink, considering his answer.

"When Eli arrived on the island, he was just a boy—eighteen years old," Nigel divulged in slow, measured speech. He was choosing his words carefully, Walker realized. "Physically mature, no doubt, but a boy all the same. Five years later, you would not have recognized him. But Walker, although I observed these changes and was, in many respects, his guardian—"

"His guardian?" Walker hadn't realized they were *that* close.

"Yes, I was responsible for him in the eyes of our government, since I sponsored him for his work visa," Nigel clarified. He cleared his throat, refocused. "Anyway, the point I'm trying to make is this: Yes, Eli wanted you to get a glimpse of what his life was like here, but not the whole story, for that is his to tell. Eli knows that he could brag incessantly about what happened here, about what he did here. But he doesn't. And he doesn't as much for your sake as for his own."

Walker was silent, looking away from Nigel, trying to take it all in. And then Nigel leaned forward, and Walker felt drawn towards him, unable to avoid making eye contact.

"You know, Walker, Eli never wanted to be the hero in your story."

Walker nodded, took a deep breath, and leaned back in his chair.

"But know this," Nigel continued. "While here, he behaved selfishly, recklessly, and even violently at times. Still, it all pales in comparison to the selfless, courageous, and chivalrous manner in which he carried himself when it mattered most. So, do you see things differently now?"

"Yeah, I believe I do. But while he may not have intended to become the hero in my story, the secrecy surrounding his time here only elevates him in everyone's eyes."

"An unintended consequence, I can assure you."

"But, Nigel, I'm glad I made the trip and I'm happy to have met you."

Nigel nodded in recognition and held his glass forward in a manner that Walker took as returning the compliment.

"Eli said he put his life in your hands. If that's so, then thank you for taking care of him."

"But of course," Nigel said triumphantly. "But there is still the matter of the sticky wicket your clients in South Carolina find themselves in. So, let us see what we can do about that. There's a man I'd like you to meet—by phone, mind you, but a man who may be able to help us."

Nigel stood and picked up a phone from his desk. He placed the phone on the small table separating the chairs in which he and Walker were seated. He dialed the number and pushed the speaker button. After a few rings, the call was answered.

"Nash here," said the man on the other end.

"Hello, Nash. Nigel here. Thank you for taking our call. I hope this evening finds you with a drink in your hand and a fine meal in your future."

"Not quite, Nigel, or should I say, not yet. You have me on speaker. Anyone else with you?"

"Yes, indeed. Walker Atkins is sitting here with me. I thought you two should meet."

"Walker Atkins. Eli's little brother."

"Yes, sir," said Walker. "And since you know Eli, that makes you another mysterious person from his life I'm meeting for the first time. Nash, it's nice to meet you. Do you have a last name, sir?"

"I do, but Nash will do for now."

"Walker, I called Nash earlier today after your encounter with Anthony Ferguson. I have also spoken to him about the matters brewing in South Carolina that brought you to our corner of the world. I did so because I knew he could help us discover who Ferguson called after you left his office. Nash, why don't you take over from here?" said Nigel.

"Nigel is correct," said Nash. "I can determine where calls are made, at least to the number to which a call is placed, and then we can identify to whom a phone number has been assigned. Under normal circumstances, this is not a service I perform, but for Nigel I make exceptions from time to time. And for Eli, too, because I owe him. So, when you see him, tell him that Nash said we're even. He'll understand."

Walker just shook his head in disbelief. Whenever he thought he had a clearer glimpse into his brother's time here, it got murkier and crazier.

"So, Nash, what did you learn?" asked Nigel.

"The call was placed to the Miami, Florida satellite office of a large international law firm headquartered in Panama City, Panama. They provide corporate and financial services to companies and people across the globe. Ten years ago, they were a small player in this field, but they have grown greatly in the last decade, and they are attracting the attention of several branches of the US federal government because of the company they keep."

"And what company would that be?" asked Nigel.

"The usual sort—drug dealers, arms dealers, and run-of-the-mill, white-collar criminals. But we have reason to believe they are carving out a niche in the world of politics. They cozy up to politicians who would steal, take bribes, and commit old-fashioned graft if they only knew how to get away with it and hide the money. They teach these politicians how to do exactly that and, in the process, they buy politicians who can later help them if they ever come under the scrutiny of one or more of a government's various law enforcement branches."

"So, what are you saying?" asked Walker.

"Palmetto Lending Tree and Palmetto Quik Cash, or whatever they're called, seem like pretty small-time operations to need the services of one of the fastest-growing law firms in the world. Doesn't add up, and I'm in the *we need to take a deeper look when it doesn't add up* business," said Nash.

"Makes sense, I guess, though I don't know what business you're in, but I gotta good idea," said Walker.

"Walker, I've helped you with this—and as I said, I owed it to Eli. And now, I must ask something of you in return." Before Walker could reply, he said, "Please share what you find with Nigel. He'll know how to get the info to me. Can you do that?"

Walker, again, wasn't sure what business this man was in, or why he'd want to know more about any of his personal findings, but he wasn't in a position to ask. "Yes, absolutely."

"Very good," Nash said.

"Nash, don't hang up," said Nigel. "You haven't given us the chap's name."

"The firm is called Sanchez & Sanchez. The first Sanchez is Gilberto Sanchez. He is the firm's founder. The second Sanchez is Luis Sanchez, Gilberto's oldest son. He is the one responsible for the firm's extraordinary growth in the last decade. He's well-educated, charming, and, according to our female sources, incredibly good-looking. A real lady's man. Luis Sanchez has houses all over the world but calls Miami his home."

"So, you believe Luis Sanchez was who Anthony called earlier today?" asked Walker.

"Don't know for a fact, but quite possibly."

"Nash, old boy, can't thank you enough," said Nigel.

"You're welcome. And Walker?"

"Yes."

"Be careful. One man you don't want to underestimate is Luis Sanchez."

Chapter 12

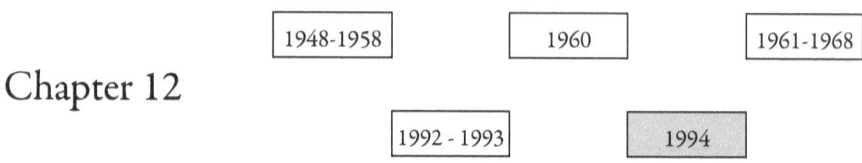

CHARLESTON, SOUTH CAROLINA
FRIDAY, JUNE 10, 1994

Walker was sitting on the screened-in porch waiting for Izzy to get ready. Amy, the babysitter, had taken Anna and Peter out for pizza. Earlier in the day, he'd flown back from the Bahamas and managed to sequester himself behind a closed door at his office, where he caught up a bit from having been out of town. He hadn't had time to talk with his wife, and he badly wanted to; he wanted to share with her all he had learned and experienced on his short trip to Nassau and his changing perspective of his brother's time there. On top of that, what he really wanted to do was stay at home, have dinner, and spend time with the kids—but that would have to wait.

Tonight, at Izzy's insistence, they were heading to a black-tie political event disguised as a charity event at the Hibernian Hall on Meeting Street. The charity they were raising money for had something to do with saving the coastal wetlands. He didn't oppose environmental conservation; he was all for it. What he *was* hostile towards were charitable events designed to focus everyone's attention on the event organizers more so than the cause. That was what Walker called a "Look at me! Aren't I wonderful?" charity.

Walker heard his wife walk into the kitchen and open the refrigerator. Without looking around, he called out, "Honey, who's sponsoring the event tonight?"

"The Dunsmore Family Foundation."

"Ugh. You're kidding!"

"Nope."

"And what cause are we celebrating—other than the Dunsmores, of course?"

"The event is entitled the 'Lowcountry Coastal Habitat: Preserving a Future for our Children,'" she said. "Oh, and you're going to love this, Randal Dunsmore is the keynote speaker."

"Perfect," Walker responded sarcastically.

Randal Dunsmore was the President of the Dunsmore Family Foundation, ne'er-do-well son of Barbara and Colin Dunsmore and Governor Johnny Dunsmore's twin brother.

"I just hope his brother doesn't make an appearance," said Walker. "I can't stand—"

As Walker was trying to finish his thought, his wife walked onto the porch and began to refill his wine glass.

"Wow!" he said, taking in the sight of his wife. "You are stunning!"

And she was. Wearing a black, full-length backless dress and a simple diamond necklace, Izzy smiled and twirled gracefully.

"Well, since I have to go to tonight, I'm consoled knowing that I will be escorted by the most beautiful woman in attendance."

"Your escort!" Izzy said in mock indignation. "You have it backwards, bucko. You're *my* escort tonight," she said as she leaned over and kissed him.

"Suits me," he said. "Now, tell me again, why are we going?"

"As much as I detest it, I must play the game, and the game is shmoozing. Along with the mayor and the governor, big donors will be in attendance, both current and prospective. You know that I'm always in fundraising mode when it comes to the Historical Preservation Society, and we're still looking for a lead underwriter for the Photography Exhibit next fall. So, you be good. Just stand there and look gorgeous for me. Can you do that?" she asked, smiling coyly.

"For you? Absolutely. And I love Mayor Joe. Always happy to see him."

Walker and Isabelle made the short walk to Hibernian Hall. They climbed the steps, and after entering, an old friend immediately cornered Isabelle—which was Walker's cue to set off for the bar. As he waited behind a few men, he glanced around the room and saw all the usual suspects, the same crowd that gathered for every good cause. The only change from year to year was the new young faces, the next lineage of the old families that had graced Charleston high society for generations.

Armed with a glass of red wine in one hand and a glass of white in the other, Walker weaved through the crowd towards Izzy, who was in a deep conspiratorial conversation with Eddie Wentworth's wife, Vanessa, about someone or something they had spied across the room.

"What are you two gabbing about?" asked Walker as he handed Izzy her drink.

"Good thing you're here, Walker. Your wife is a bit taken by that tall, dark drink of water talking to our governor," said Vanessa.

"Good grief, it's not just him. Check out the woman he's with. Looks like she stepped off a Paris runway," said Isabelle. Eddie walked up and joined the three of them just as she finished asking, "Does anyone know who they are?"

"Who? Who we talkin' about?" asked Eddie.

"The couple standing next to the governor and his wife," answered Isabelle.

"Oh, them," said Eddie. "You know how our governor is planning a run for president. That couple you are gawking at is what they call a 'power couple' in Washington, DC, and that man is one of Johnny D's most influential political advisers."

"Does he have a name?" asked Vanessa.

"Sure," said Eddie. "Luis Sanchez."

PART TWO

Ecclesiastes 1: 3-4 (3) What does man gain by all the toil at which he toils under the sun? (4) A generation goes, and a generation comes, but the earth remains forever.

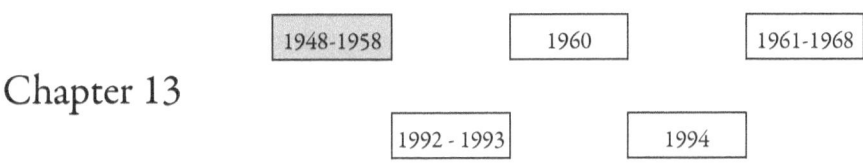

Chapter 13

COLUMBIA, SOUTH CAROLINA
1958

Since stepping off the train in 1948, Colin Dunsmore had slowly and methodically executed his dream of rising to the national stage. The first step had been to learn and grow the family business, which he had. America's post-war years were booming. Times were good, and the Dunsmores rode the wave of economic prosperity.

Colin's grandfather had laid a foundation for the family by capitalizing on the growth in the post–Civil War textile industry in the South—a foundation Colin's father built upon. Colin jumped on the automobile bandwagon and acquired the General Motors dealership rights for Clinton and Laurens, South Carolina. He joined the board of the local bank his father had co-founded and ultimately would become one of its largest shareholders. While Colin's father enjoyed playing a role in seeing people's dreams of home ownership come to fruition, Colin enjoyed the power he wielded more than the joy a loan recipient experienced. Consequently, Colin took more joy from saying "no" to a loan application than from saying "yes."

Colin was also a silent partner in a private lending company, making extremely profitable loans to businesses his bank would not lend to. Through this private lender, he loaned money to liquor stores serving the poorest neighborhoods and people buying used cars. This lender would foreclose at the slightest provocation, unless the borrower came up with loan extension fees or accepted a loan refinance at ever higher interest rates in exchange for additional collateral—one's home, for instance. He financed furniture layaway plans whereby the finance company could take the furniture from the home if the homeowner made 59 of 60 payments but missed the sixtieth payment. Colin's father knew nothing about this side business. Colin also quietly purchased raw land on the outskirts of town, low-rent track homes, and tenement buildings and storefronts in low-income neighborhoods where there was no competition pressuring him to maintain his properties.

To the casual observer, Colin was a chip off the old block, cut from the same cloth as his father, Ian. They may have been cut from the same cloth, but they weathered differently. Ian was a God-fearing man; Colin preferred to be the one who was feared. Ian loved his country; Colin loved that he could harness patriotic sentiments held by others in ways that benefitted him. Ian attended church because he enjoyed it and loved God because God loved him first. Colin's name could be found in the membership roll of the local Baptist church, but his backside rarely graced its pews.

Was there a central defining characteristic or personality trait that explained the differences between the two men? If there was, how did it come to be? Ian was a Rotarian and had been since the local chapter opened and had served as their first president. He didn't just repeat the organization's four-way test at each weekly meeting—he *lived* it. Was it the truth? Was it fair to all concerned? Would it build goodwill and better friendships? Would it be beneficial to all concerned? Ian saw local businesses and statewide public service as foundational to the Rotarian ethic. He believed that politicians could and should serve their fellow man.

Colin admired his father and grandfather but saw them as antiquated, naïve, outdated relics, holding onto idyllic notions about public service while remaining ignorant of how the real world worked. He was not content to amass the power that accompanied wealth. No, he saw the ultimate power as the power over people's lives and choices available to them, the power that arose from defining right and wrong—and in this world, that power lied with those who held public office and those who put them there. For Colin, the notion that holding public office was a public *service* was a sham. Contrary to his father's quixotic ideals, no politician of consequence that he had ever met sought to be in anyone's service. Quite the opposite—they saw everyone as being in *their* service.

So, Colin set about building a family dynasty, and not just within the state of South Carolina, but one with an heir who would one day walk the halls of the White House.

This begged the question: Whose footsteps would walk the halls? His own? No, he was not of the right temperament. His disdain for others was too hard to hide, and he knew it. He also knew he lacked the "it" factor, that elusive charm, the bigger-than-life persona necessary to carry one to the top. He needed someone with charisma, a particular animal magnetism; the kind of man who could talk a woman out of her clothes; the kind of man other men wanted to share a beer with; the kind of man who, in a crowded room, could make you feel like the only person present.

But men like that typically lacked basic human qualities, such as empathy for others, and were dangerous and difficult to control. Colin would have to nurture and mold such a man himself, and for this, he would need a son.

He already had two, Jonathan and Randal, but only one would do.

Chapter 14

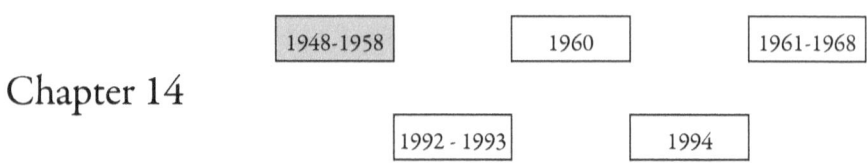

Columbia, South Carolina
July 4, 1954

"Isn't that Charlotte LeMar over there talking with Barbara Dunsmore?" asked one of the country club wives. "And look—isn't that her boy, Johnny, standing there like such the gentlemen?"

A gaggle of wives were gathered under the canopy seeking refuge from the summer heat. Their husbands had all played golf that morning and were beginning to make their way from the Men's Grill towards the pool where families would assemble for the beginning of the sports activities and contests planned for the day.

"I believe you're right. How gracious of Charlotte to grace us with her presence," replied one of the women with an exaggerated eyeroll.

"I didn't think we'd be seeing her 'round here till sometime in October. That's when she usually returns from her time in Europe."

"Do you know how you can tell where she's been in Europe?" asked one of the women.

"No. How?"

"She tells you."

Suppressed laughter ensued, all around.

"Well, I'm guessing she's back for just a short spell. My husband tells me that her husband, Mathias, is receiving some kind of leadership award from the governor next week for his contributions to South Carolina's economy. He must have insisted she be here for that."

"I guess his mistress wasn't available."

More suppressed laughter.

"What do they do with their daughter while she's in Europe? Everyone knows Mathias is married to his work. And what is that poor girl's name?"

"Her name is Dixie, and she's raised by nannies."

"You never see her with any friends."

"Her parents don't know what to do with her," a woman added, and the other wives looked at her in a way that questioned how she would know such a thing. "My nanny and her nanny talk. Oh, the things I hear. They shower her with gifts from wherever they've travelled to but that's all. No love in that household—from what I hear, at least."

The women all shook their heads.

"She's a loner, for sure. It doesn't help that she's a bit of a tomboy."

"Well, I doubt she'll be a loner for long. I overheard my son and a few of his friends in the backyard last week talking about her. Apparently, she's the first in her class to need a bra."

"Speak of the devil. I believe that's her," one of the women commented as she tilted her head towards the entrance. "Oh, my. I see what you mean."

The other women all nodded in agreement. They watched as Dixie LeMar ignored her mother's pleadings to stop and say hello to Mrs. Dunsmore and Johnny, instead shuffling over to a grassy area under a tree away from the crowds. She plopped herself down next to a boy who was sitting there all alone.

"Yes, indeed. She's an awkward one."

"Looks like she's got a least one friend," said one of the wives.

"Who's she sitting with?"

"I believe that's the Dunsmore's other boy—Johnny's twin brother, Randal."

"I don't know if Dixie and Randal make an odd pair or a *perfect* pair..."

"Perfectly odd, if you ask me."

"It's hard to believe that Randal and Johnny are brothers. *Twins*, no less. They couldn't be more different than night and day."

"My little girl has such a crush on Johnny. He's all she ever talks about. Johnny this and Johnny that."

"I swear, my son does too. Pert near idolizes him."

"Some folks win the gene pool, and some don't. Makes you wonder..."

"What's that supposed to mean? Randal and Johnny have the same genes."

"Oh, don't get her started. She read an article last month in *Readers Digest* about 'nature vs. nurture' and won't stop goin' on about it."

"Well, I found it interesting. That's all. It could be nature that explains the differences between those two boys, or it could be nurture. Have you ever heard how Colin and Barabara will go on about all of Johnny's accomplishments, but they can't come up with a single nice thing to say about Randal? And Johnny's reaction to it all is all so weird. Instead of being embarrassed by it all, he just eats it up."

"And what about Randal? How does he react to it all?"

"It's sad. Poor boy doesn't know what to do."

* * *

"Folks, that concludes the swim races. Let's all head over to the first hole for the rest of the day's activities. I want to thank everyone for participating," said Bob Riggins, the Club Pro who every year acted as the master of ceremonies for the Fourth of July games and contests.

"Mom, Dad!" Johnny cried out as he made his way across the pool deck, smiling proudly and waving a fist full of blue ribbons.

"Well done, son."

"We're so proud of you," his mother added.

Colin saw Randal slowly walking up behind Johnny with a few of the dreaded green and purple ribbons balled up in his left hand. "Hey, we better get moving if we want a good seat close to the finish line," said Colin as he winked at his son Johnny. "Randal, grab the lounge chairs."

* * *

The crowd made their way to the first hole, where families set up their chairs and placed blankets on the ground to watch the three-legged races, sack races, apple bobbing, and the like. Every summer, though, there were races from the edge of the tee box to a line drawn on the fairway some distance away—that distance varying in length according to the age of the runners. It was the one serious race of the holiday. Johnny, now fourteen years old, had never lost. The distance of the race was 100 yards, and any boy fourteen or younger could compete.

The children were growing excited about the big races coming up. The six-year-olds were lining up for their race, which was twenty-five yards in distance. Randal saw Johnny coming out of the bathroom and walking towards the starting area—probably to prep for the race. Randal noticed that Johnny had spotted him sitting with Dixie on a bench close to the caddie shack and away from the crowd and that he was headed their way.

"Well, if it isn't Grundle and Dixie D-Cup," said Johnny. He'd started calling her Dixie D-Cup instead of just Dixie Cup, as he had when they were younger, ever since her sizeable breasts appeared, which, in that she was only twelve, was another reality that made her an oddity.

"Leave her alone, Johnny," said Randal.

Johnny scoffed, shoving Randal off the bench. "I don't think so," he said as he approached Dixie. "Show us your tits, Dixie-D."

"I said stop it!" Randal shouted as he lifted himself off the ground.

"What are you gonna do about it?" demanded Johnny.

Randal positioned himself between his brother and his best friend—his *only* friend. "Leave us alone!"

"Grundle, it's hard to believe we have the same parents. Are you sure you're not adopted?"

Grundle had been Johnny's demeaning nickname for Randal since he'd learned the word in his eighth-grade science class while studying human anatomy.

"Now, Dixie D-Cup, I mean it. Show me what you got."

"Leave her alone," Randal said again, getting into his brother's face. For a split second, Randal's audacity seemed to take his brother aback. They stared at each other for a few fast heartbeats—Randal's eyes blinking up at his brother's—and Randal wondered if he should brace himself for a sucker punch.

But to his surprise, Johnny only said, "Okay, *Grundle*." He stepped back. "I will, but only if you enter the race."

"Why?" asked Dixie.

"So everyone can see him come in dead last," said Johnny, never taking his eyes off Randal's.

Randal's hands balled into fists. He was shaking, and to his horror, he had tears welling up in his eyes. He'd been ready to take a sucker punch for Dixie here in private, but to fail in front of *everybody,* once again—

Everybody he knew, his mom and dad, and everybody *they* knew . . .

Tell him you'll do it, he thought furiously to himself, but he just stood there. Frozen.

Johnny laughed. "Thought so. You're nothin' but a coward. Now, Dixie-D, I'm gonna win this race, and as my prize, you're gonna lift that shirt of yours and let me take a good long look. And if you don't, well, you think I've been mean to Grundle up till now? You ain't seen nothin'."

Johnny turned and jogged towards the race area, leaving Dixie on the bench sitting next to Randal, tears rolling down his face.

* * *

"Next up, folks, is our fourteen-and-under group. They will be running the 100-yard dash," announced Bob Riggins.

Boys began to take their places, and as they did, they cleared room for Johnny, who made a point of walking in front of the group of boys to take his place in the middle of the pack. A total of sixteen boys were lined up, waiting for the gun to fire. A small murmur began to spread, and some voices grew quieter as a lone girl walked to the front and squeezed into the line of competitors right next to Johnny.

"What are *you* doin' here?" asked Johnny.

Dixie didn't say anything. She glared at Johnny, and then looked past him at Randal, who had joined the spectators. With a devout smile, she nodded to him, as if to say, *This one's for you.*

Steve—one of the parents serving as the starter—looked at Bob Riggins, as if asking what he should do about the girl who'd wandered into the race. Bob was visibly at a loss. Eventually, he figured that he should do nothing and picked up his megaphone. "All right folks, looks like we're gonna have ourselves quite a race. It's all yours, Steve!"

"On your marks, get set . . ."

The starter fired the gun, and the runners were off. Very quickly, the slowest runners fell away, and at the midway point, it was clear that the winner would come from a group of about four kids—a group that included Johnny and Dixie.

Randal stood on the sidelines, not believing what was happening. As the race progressed, it narrowed to two runners: Dixie and Johnny. The crowd was going wild. Randal eased up on his tiptoes to get a better view and couldn't believe what he saw.

Dixie raced down the track like a gazelle, her hair whipping in the wind like a superhero's cape, as she strode neck-and-neck with his brother. Johnny glanced sideways at her with a look of sheer disbelief that Randal observed with an overwhelming sense of satisfaction. Suddenly, he heard himself scream, "Go, Dixie, go!"

And as if fueled by his words, he saw her strides quicken. The finish line was in sight.

His brother barreled faster and faster, but it wasn't enough.

Dixie won.

For the rest of the summer, Johnny was kind to Randal. Even at the age of fourteen, Johnny was savvy enough to understand that if he publicly belittled his brother after losing a race to a girl who was Randal's best friend—Randal's *only* friend—it would reflect poorly on him.

So, Johnny rose above it and included Randal and Dixie in everything he did for the remainder of the summer. The parents around the Club remarked on what a good sport Johnny was, and before too long, Randal and Dixie had again slipped to the back of everyone's minds. Johnny, again, was front and center.

* * *

As Colin looked around, he was generally pleased with the state of his world. Business was good and the Dunsmore family's control over the Democratic Party in South Carolina was stronger than ever. The first phase of the plan he hatched on the train ride home six years ago was now complete. Now was the time to initiate phase two: going national. To put his son Johnny in the White House, he'd have to grow the family's reputation beyond the state's borders.

Colin recognized that much of his family's fortune was due to good timing and providence. He observed that the truly wealthy seemed to know what would happen before it happened. They spent time together, joined the same clubs, dined at the same restaurants, and attended the same schools. This was the future he saw for his son Johnny—one of privilege, lived amongst those who were also privileged. He was bound and determined to launch his son on the right path, and as he saw it, that began with attending school in the Northeast.

So, when that summer of 1954 ended and fall rolled around, while Randal attended the local public school, Johnny began the ninth grade at Philips Academy in Andover, Massachusetts, the nation's oldest prep school. Colin managed to pry open the doors of Philips Academy for his son by calling on the general he worked for at the Pentagon after coming home from Europe. The general was a proud alumnus of Philips Academy.

Upon graduating from this very toney prep school in 1958, Johnny matriculated onto Georgetown University. The night before he was to check into his freshman dorm, he had dinner with his father.

"Son, at Georgetown, you will meet the sons and daughters of ambassadors, senators, congressmen, and the moneyed class that can put you in these positions. During your time here, doors will be opened to you, and you will walk through them, and then *you'll* be on the inside. This is our family's destiny—the power to rule the lives of others, the power to change the course of history. The generations of men that have come before you have made this possible. Me, my father, his father, and his father before him—we worked hard and placed others before ourselves so that we could place *you* in the White House, above all others. And you won't be the last. The Dunsmores will become a dynasty like the family dynasties of old. The fools in this country think they live in a republic. They think they cast off the yoke of monarchial rule when they rebelled against the British. If they only knew. They've simply replaced one type of monarchy with another. We are the new elite. Johnny, my son, don't let anything stop you."

"What could possibly stop me?"

Chapter 15

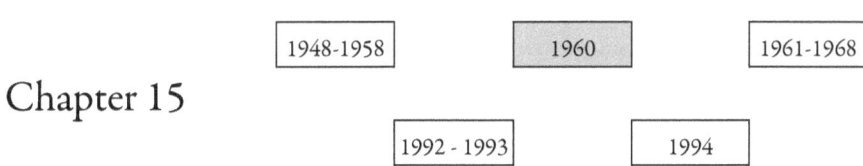

ST. THOMAS, VIRGIN ISLANDS
THURSDAY, APRIL 8, 1960

The sound of seagulls echoed off the surface of the clear blue water, and everywhere Johnny looked, he saw one gleaming white ship after another. He was walking behind his good friend Luis Sanchez with a duffle bag in one hand and a backpack draped over his shoulders. It was clear to Johnny that Luis knew where he was going; to Johnny, Luis looked perfectly at home amongst these monster-sized boats. Up ahead, Luis stopped at the foot of a set of stairs leading up to the deck of the most impressive ship Johnny had ever laid eyes on. He slowed as he approached the end of the dock, and he shook his head in disbelief as it fully dawned on him how he would be spending his spring break. "*This* is your family's boat? You're kidding!"

"A *yacht*—not a boat," said Luis Sanchez. "That twenty-foot dinghy suspended from the stern is a boat. And yes, it's my family's yacht. We've owned it for about ten years. I've spent many wonderful days and nights on this yacht and on the islands we'll visit."

Luis and Johnny's friends were headed to Florida for spring break—if they were going anywhere at all. A few weren't. For Johnny, it felt glamorous to be spending the next week or so casually sailing around the British Virgin Islands.

"Mr. Sanchez, we've been anxiously awaiting your arrival."

Luis and Johnny looked up to see a man at the top of the stairs.

Luis began to climb the stairs. Johnny followed. "Alphonse. Good to see you. Are we ready to launch?"

"Yes, sir."

"Excellent. But first, I must introduce you to our special guest this week—my good friend, Johnny Dunsmore. And Johnny, this is Captain Alphonse Rosado. He has been in my family's employment since the day we purchased this magnificent yacht, and he knows every inch of her."

"I do, indeed. Mr. Dunsmore, I am happy to make your acquaintance, and I can see from the look on your face that she impresses you."

"She?" asked Johnny.

"Yes, *she*—this majestic yacht, that is. Ships are like women; they are full of beauty and grace and require nurturing and delicate handling," explained the captain. "This beauty is the *Peristeria*, a 187-foot-long, triple-mast sailing yacht."

"My grandmother named her the *Peristeria* after the national flower of Panama," said Luis.

"Before we launch, let me introduce you to the rest of the crew—seven men and women —all handpicked by me. I assure you, this is the finest crew in the Islands."

While Captain Rosado made the introductions, Johnny could not keep his eyes off the girl at the end of the line.

"And finally, I'd like to introduce you to the newest member of our crew, Nadia Rymer. Mr. Sanchez, Mr. Dunsmore, we are at your disposal."

"Very good, Alphonse," said Luis. "That will be all for now. So, if there's nothing else, let's cast off."

The crew scattered to their posts, leaving Johnny and Luis standing at the bow. As Johnny looked around, he thought he had died and gone to heaven.

"You're going to have a hard time getting me to leave when this trip is over," said Johnny as he removed his Ray-Bans and looked from one end of the yacht to the other. "And that girl! I think her name is Nadia. She's smokin'!"

"Would you like to meet her? I mean, really meet her?"

"You bet. Who wouldn't?"

"Shouldn't be a problem. She's most likely a local. An islander. They're always looking to meet a rich guy who can take them away. Maybe you can be her prince charming and whisk her away to America?"

"Yeah, right. I was just hoping to fool around a little on break."

"What about your girlfriend back home, Caroline?" asked Luis.

"Who?"

"That's my boy," said Luis as he slapped Johnny good-naturedly on the back. "Let's change. We've got about a three-hour sail ahead of us before we reach the BVIs. We should be there in time for some snorkeling before sunset."

* * *

With an hour to go before sunset, Captain Rosado dropped anchor in a cove off the coast of Norman Island, one of the small islands south of Tortola, known as the little sisters and the inspiration for Robert Louis Stevenson's novel, Treasure Island. After a swim, Johnny and Luis broke out the backgammon board and enjoyed a local drink of rum, fresh fruit juice, and nutmeg. All the while, the crew was busy setting a table for the two of them and preparing their dinner.

Luis handed Johnny a beer. "Johnny, I selected this beer for our trip with you in mind."

Johnny reached for the beer and held it up to read the label.

"*Presidente*," said Johnny.

"That's right. It's brewed in the Dominican Republic and was named after their current president, Rafael Trujillo. He's a friend of the family. In fact, he wouldn't have stayed in office as long as he has if my father hadn't arranged for generous loans and financed construction projects on his island over the years. His nickname is El Jefe."

"El Jefe, huh? I like that. That's a cool nickname."

"It means 'the boss.' Do you remember one of the first nights we hung out together during our freshman year? We stumbled out of one of the bars on M Street and made our way down to the Washington Monument. Do you remember what you told me?" asked Luis.

Johnny nodded quietly. He remembered.

"You told me you were going to be president of the United States someday," Luis reminded him with a sly grin. "Is that still your dream?"

Johnny pulled his knees close to his chest, folding his arms around them. It was the perfect start to a perfect trip, and there was something that felt magical about the moment—especially as he turned to face Luis again and said, "*Abso-f'ing-lutely*."

Luis raised his beer and the two of them clinked their bottles together.

"To you," he said, nodding to Johnny. "*El Jefe*."

Johnny smiled, took a swig of his beer, turned toward his good friend, and nodded in agreement.

"I like that. El Jefe," he repeated.

* * *

Dinner consisted of spiny lobster, mango, rice, and a dish Johnny had never had before—curried vegetables and meat wrapped in paper-thin dough called roti. Throughout the meal, the crew appeared and disappeared with plates, glassware, and utensils as if they were in a five-star restaurant. Each time someone appeared, Johnny would stop talking and lean back in his chair to make room for the staff to do their jobs. Only after they had stepped away from the table would he start backup. Johnny noticed, however, that Luis hardly acknowledged their existence and continued eating and talking as if they weren't even there. By the time desert was served, Johnny had picked up on Luis's nonchalant attitude towards the staff and tried to emulate it. But there was one member of the crew who repeatedly broke his concentration—the newest and youngest member of the crew, Nadia Rymer.

"More wine, sir?" she asked.

Luis merely nodded at his glass on the table, never looking at or speaking to her.

Nadia then turned toward Johnny and waited for his direction, holding the bottom of the bottle in her right hand with the neck resting on a white napkin in her left.

"Oh, yes. More wine. Thank you," Johnny finally answered.

Nadia stepped forward, poured the wine, and smiled, her eyes still cast downward.

"Thank you."

Before leaving, she raised her eyes to meet his and smiled again. It was like looking at the start of a new day—a perfect sunrise. "Of course, Mr. Dunsmore," she said, and Johnny could barely disguise the heat rising in his cheeks. He was practically salivating.

"Oh, you can call me Johnny," he managed to tell her.

Before she could say anything, Luis spoke up. "That will be all," he said brusquely.

Nadia quickly exited.

When she had disappeared below deck, Luis turned to his friend. "So, you like her."

"Are you kidding me?" Johnny said, scoffing. "She's beautiful."

"You're from South Carolina. I'll bet you've never been with a Black woman."

"Black, White, purple, whatever. Her body is killer, and that smile! Besides, I'm on a private boat—excuse me, private *yacht*—anchored in a cove off a small island in the middle of the Caribbean. Who's gonna know?"

Luis smiled mischievously and plunged his fork into the spice cake in front of him. "So, you'd like some time alone with her, I'm guessing."

"Don't know how that's going to happen with crew members everywhere. I mean, she has a job to do, right?"

"Don't go anywhere," said Luis as he rose from his chair and placed his napkin in his seat.

Johnny shrugged his shoulders as if to say, *Where would I go?*

Ten minutes later, Luis returned with a bucket of ice filled with bottles of beer and an arm full of towels.

"This way, sir," he said to Johnny, giving him a devilish grin.

Johnny rose and followed him to the stern, where he began to lower the small boat into the water. Nadia, barefoot and wearing a simple sundress, was waiting for them.

"What's going on?" whispered Johnny, turning towards his friend and away from the girl.

"You said you wanted some alone time with Nadia," Luis whispered back. "Well, here you go. Just motor this boat over to the cove, and you'll have the entire island to yourself."

"Luis, it's dark, and I'm not sure about driving this boat at night in waters I don't know."

"Johnny, it's cool. It's almost a full moon. Besides, *she'll* drive the boat. She grew up on the island of Tortola and has probably been sailing and diving these waters since she was old enough to walk. Now go. I'll see you in the morning."

Nadia was standing with her feet together and hands clasped behind her back. She smiled and nodded encouragingly, as if to confirm Luis's claims. And *wow*, was she gorgeous! And those beers were on ice. They had blankets... He could envision everything that awaited him that night. All they had to do was get the boat to the shore. How hard could that be?

He sighed and broke into a smile. "Okay. You convinced me," he told Luis, proceeding to climb down the ladder into the boat. Luis handed him the bucket of beers, and Nadia climbed gracefully down the ladder, her backside swishing rhythmically as she descended into the boat. Yep, Johnny was sure he had died and gone to heaven.

Nadia started up the boat as Luis cast the lines down to Johnny, and they were off. But Nadia didn't motor to the beach closest to where the yacht was anchored. No, she motored out around the edge of the inlet. A few minutes later, they were entering another small cove, and Nadia skillfully killed the motor and rode the surf onto the beach. Before Johnny could react, Nadia jumped out and grabbed the line, pulling the boat out of the water enough to ensure it would not go anywhere.

Johnny stood up in the boat and almost fell out. Nadia giggled and stepped forward to balance the boat. He then got out and reached back to grab the towels. Feeling helpless, he figured he needed some way to gain control of the situation and prove he was a man and in charge. Before he could come up with anything to say or do, she grabbed him by the hand and led him onto the beach where she laid out the towels halfway between the surf line and the shadows formed by the moonlight against the palm trees.

"A fire would be nice," she said.

Johnny thought a fire was a great idea and when she took a seat on the towels, he concluded that she expected him to build it. So, he began collecting twigs, branches, and driftwood and built a pyramid with the fuel he gathered. When he was sure he'd constructed the makings of a fine fire, he stood with his hands on his hips, admiring his work.

Nadia began to giggle again, and Johnny suddenly understood why. He had nothing with which to start the fire. Nadia walked to the boat and returned with a pack of matches. She was about to start the fire and thought better of it, handing the matches to Johnny, who took them and kneeled to light the fire. Nadia sat across from him and leaned back, resting on her hands with her legs extended, one ankle over the other. Her dress had ridden up a bit, and Johnny was more than distracted. He struggled; the wind kept blowing out the matches. Nadia rose, sauntered over, and, kneeling next to him, leaned forward and slightly into Johnny, using him for balance as she cupped her hands to shield the flame from the wind as he struck another match. This time, the match stayed lit, the kindling was set aflame, and with the next two matches, the fire was underway. Nadia sat back on the towel, and Johnny did too, feeling good about the fire he had started.

Nadia made herself comfortable on one of the towels she'd laid out. She leaned back, resting on her elbows, and then patted her hand on the towel next to her. Johnny sat down as close to her as he dared, crossed his legs and turned to look at her. He was mesmerized. Her skin was the color of cinnamon, her eyes like that of honey, and her long brown hair danced in the gentle breeze across her shoulders. He longed to kiss her full lips. He feared if he said anything it would kill what he believed the mood was shaping up to be, so he said nothing and instead leaned in for a kiss. Nadia leaned backwards and gently placed a hand on his chest.

"Tell me, what's it like being Johnny Dunsmore?"

He had never been asked such a poignant question by anyone. "I don't know how to answer that," he managed to say. "What's it like being Nadia Rymer?"

And with those simple questions and the answers that followed, worlds neither of them knew a thing about were opened before them.

* * *

From then on, Johnny and Nadia were inseparable. At Luis's request, Captain Rosado relieved her of any duties on the ship. Nadia had a friend named Maya from the community college she was attending, and along with Luis, the four of them spent the next week exploring the islands, fishing, and snorkeling. By the end of most evenings, Luis and Maya were drunk, with Maya laughing and falling all over Luis, who, at least by appearance, knew how to handle his alcohol.

They had a good time, but both knew Luis would never attempt to stay in touch or ever think of Maya again after this trip. It seemed she expected nothing less. The envelope of cash he gave her at the end of the week—money for her tuition at the community college—was appreciated. She was studying to become a nurse, she'd said.

The chemistry between Johnny and Nadia was different. He was falling for her. The nightly excursions to the beach they visited their first evening together were now a regular part of their day. On their third night together, he learned of her fascinating ancestry.

"Nadia, I want to learn more about you and the Caribbean. Where do you come from? I mean, has your family always been from the Caribbean?"

"No. Like most Caribbeans today, my ancestry is mixed. On my father's side, his ancestors were captured in Angola by a neighboring tribe when Angola was a Portuguese colony and sold to British slave traders. They were shipped to Barbados in 1665, where they worked, as did their descendants, on sugar cane plantations."

"And your mom . . . ," he asked tentatively. "Were her ancestors slaves too?"

"Almost. In 1815, her ancestors were taken from a small village along the Gambia River and put on a slave ship—but on their way to Hispaniola in the Greater Antilles, to be put to work on a sugar cane plantation, they were saved by the British Navy."

"Yeah, that's right. I'm remembering some of my history. Great Britain and America ended the Transatlantic Slave Trade in the early 1800s. So, what happened to her after the British Navy saved her?" asked Johnny.

"The British took them to Sierra Leone—a colony the British established for freed West African slaves. Somewhere along the way my mother's ancestors met European missionaries and were exposed to Western values and traditions. One of her ancestors became a Methodist minister and joined a mission travelling to the Caribbean and that's how her family arrived here."

"So, your family is from West Africa."

"Yes, but it's not that simple anymore. In my family, you'll also find Spanish and British blood, as well as traces of the nearly extinct Carib Indians. Eventually, ancestors from both my momma's and pappa's side of the family made it to Tortola." She smiled, looking at him. "And you, Johnny—where are your ancestors from?"

He remained silent.

"Johnny, why so quiet? Don't you know where you're from?"

He still said nothing.

"Ah, I bet I know. Let me guess, your ancestors are from Great Britain. Am I right?"

"Nadia, you're gonna hate me."

"No, I won't."

"Yeah, you will."

"Johnny Dunsmore, you're from South Carolina. This much you have told me. You have a twin brother, Randal, and your parents were born in the South. It's easy to guess that your family is wealthy, and you told me they have been in politics for generations. What you don't want to tell me is that your family at one time owned slaves."

Johnny sat silently.

"Yes, I'm right. Johnny, it is of no consequence to me. That ended over one hundred years ago. We've moved on. Our country is poor, and we're a small island, which means we'll never be anything other than poor. But we're happy and healthy, and our people know God."

Johnny sighed, relenting. "Well, Scottish blood, technically—my family came from the Lowlands in Scotland. We've worked hard to bury our past as slave owners, and we're proud Democrats. In our country, it's our party that helps the poor and the workingman. Someday, I'll hold elected office. I'll be a US senator, and then governor of South Carolina, and then, well, who knows from there. Helping people. Helping the disadvantaged. This is the legacy I want to build."

"You sound boring."

"What do you mean, boring? I'm serious."

Laughing, she continued, "You sound like every politician. *Blah, blah, blah*. I want to hear from the *real* Johnny, not the one who hopes he can count on my vote. I want to hear from the Johnny I'm falling in love with."

That did it. He looked at her and was held captive by her beautiful eyes. Her perfect lips lifted into a smile, as though she'd just sprung a trap on him—and it'd worked. He was ensnared, fully and completely, and he didn't know what to do.

He'd been afraid of this moment—afraid she would say exactly this—and what scared him most was that he might say it right back to her. Johnny Dunsmore was in love with an island girl. He fell asleep every night thinking of her and woke each morning doing the same. Because of the confines of the yacht, they had not slept together, not even during their nightly beach excursions. It's not that Johnny didn't want to. The kissing had been passionate, but she made it clear she was not ready, words Johnny had not heard from a girl he'd set his sights on in a long time. And for the first time ever, those words hadn't caused him to dump her and move on.

"Nadia, I . . . " He was at a loss for words.

"Shush," she said, placing her finger on his lips. Johnny realized, abruptly, that she was on the verge of tears. "Johnny, in a few days we'll celebrate Good Friday. Come to church with me."

"Luis and I are heading home tomorrow," he said softly.

Nadia held his hands and his gaze. "Then change your plans. I know you will leave but I want you to see where I live and *how* I live. Please, this is important to me."

* * *

So, they changed their plans and extended their stay and by more than just a few days.

Johnny emerged from down below and walked onto the deck with a cup of coffee in his hands and found Luis already there enjoying the morning and reading a book.

"Where are the girls?" asked Johnny.

"They went ashore for a couple of hours," answered Luis as he nodded towards the harbor in Road Town, Tortola, where they had dropped anchor the previous day. "Nadia said she wanted to do some shopping for her family's big meal this Friday night, and Maya decided to go with her. Sounds like you're the guest of honor."

Luis cocked his head towards Johnny and raised his Ray-Ban sunglasses as he gave his friend a curious look.

"What's come over you, man?" asked Luis. "I've never seen you like this."

Johnny was sitting on the edge of a deck chair, bent at the waist and staring into his cup of coffee, a mixed look of confusion and contemplation plastered on his face. "I don't know? She's not like any girl I've ever known. I know this might sound crazy, but I think she really likes me."

"Of course she does, but so does about every girl on campus. You haven't exactly been the sultan of loyalty to Caroline."

"Those other girls were different. They *didn't* really like me. They liked the idea of me and of being with a big man on campus."

"You're only a sophomore," said Luis with a bemused expression. "I'm not sure you can call yourself a *big man on campus*."

Johnny stood up, staring down at Luis who was still sitting on his deck chair. "But I am, and you know it. At school, at home, wherever—I get what I want. Always have. If a girl sleeps with me, it just makes others want to even more. It's crazy. And it's true with guys too."

"I don't think guys want to sleep with you," Luis responded, chuckling.

Johnny walked to the edge of the ship and placed his hands on the railing. "That's not what I mean. I mean they comply. They follow. They kiss my ass." He turned and leaned back against the railing. "Have you ever noticed I can be a real asshole?"

"Yep."

"But you don't care, do you?"

"No."

Johnny turned and leaned forward, resting his forearms against the railing. He thought back to how he'd treated his brother during their childhood together. "It's like I can't help it," he said. "It's who I've been groomed to be."

"What? An asshole?"

"No . . . someone who will do whatever it takes to get what I've been told is rightfully mine. Being an asshole is just a byproduct." Johnny reclaimed his seat in the deck chair and absentmindedly picked up an empty *Presidente* beer bottle from the table beside it. It appeared to have been left over from the evening before. He began picking at the label. "*You* don't fall in line and buy my bullshit, though. Probably why I like you. And Nadia doesn't buy it, either."

"Is that why you are so taken with her?"

"In part. But she hasn't met the real Johnny—the Johnny who is the big man on campus."

"What do you think she would do if she did?" asked Luis.

"I don't think she'd like him very much."

"Heavy stuff. So what happens now?"

"Spring break ends in a few days, and I never see Nadia again," Johnny said as his head dipped forward.

"And Caroline will be none the wiser, I presume."

Johnny gave Luis a pointed look. "That's right. She's my golden ticket to the White House."

"Her family has that kind of pull?" asked Luis.

"That's what everyone says."

"And you'll go back to being an asshole."

Johnny said nothing and continued to peel the label off the empty beer bottle.

* * *

A few days later, Luis and Maya and Johnny and Nadia enjoyed their last night together on the Peristeria. After the meal, Luis and Maya broke out the backgammon board, and Nadia and Johnny snuck away on the dingy, returning to the cove they had first visited.

This time, with the sounds of the surf gently caressing the beach, she removed her dress, slid off her bikini bottoms, and laid next to Johnny under an ocean of stars scattered across the sky above, running endlessly in every direction.

Chapter 16

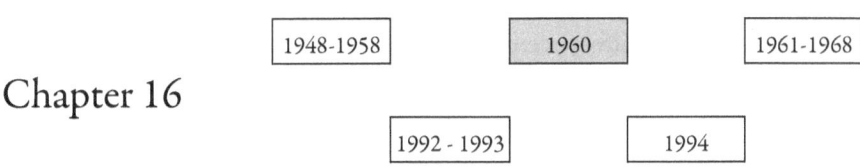

COLUMBIA, SOUTH CAROLINA
SEPTEMBER 4, 1960—LABOR DAY WEEKEND

Johnny and Caroline stood together under the shade of an oak tree, enjoying a sweet iced tea and a few minutes of peace away from the crowds and out of the sun's blistering heat.

"So, this is the life you want, Johnny?" Caroline asked. "Kissing babies, shaking hands ..."

"And making a difference," he added.

Growing up in South Carolina, Johnny's parents never missed a chance to point out the poverty that permeated the state. They would be driving somewhere, and his father would point out sharecroppers working alongside the road with a look of disgust on his face. "'Bout the only thing they own is the shirt on their back and if they're lucky, the hoe in their hands. And one thing they surely don't have is a voice. That's going to be you, son. *You're* going to be their voice. *You're* going to make a difference in their lives."

But for all his father's sermonizing, Johnny could never tell whether the look of disgust was aimed at the poverty or the sharecroppers themselves. Johnny knew his father couldn't have given two hoots about poor people. The only thing they had in common with rich folks was that they all had a vote, and his father was determined to *own* their votes—while still leaving them with nothing but the shirt on their back and, if they were lucky, the hoe in their hands. He would do this without losing any sleep. As Johnny surveyed the crowd gathered there that day, what he was coming to understand was that owning votes meant owning power.

The question remained: How would he choose to use that power?

"Yes, making a difference in their lives," echoed Caroline. "You can be that person for them."

"*We* can be those people, you and me," he intoned. "We've talked about this, Caroline."

He turned towards her and took her hands in his after setting his sweet tea on the ground at their feet, nestled in a cushion of grass. Caroline's eyes dazzled back at his. And for a moment, the pair of them stood beneath the oak tree, envisioning their futures.

"We can make a difference in this world," he went on. "Our generation, that is. But, yeah, as to your question—this *is* what I want," he said definitively. He knelt down, grabbed his tea, and took a swig as he looked to the horizon, his chin lifted slightly.

"It suits you," she said with a smile, admiring his profile.

Caroline Thistle, his girlfriend—whom he met the second week of his freshman year—was visiting him and his family for Labor Day weekend before they each headed back to DC for their junior year of college. It was an election year, which meant both the Dunsmore and Thistle clans would be knee-deep in political theater—the Dunsmores in South Carolina and the Thistles in Virginia and Washington, DC

In South Carolina, five US House of Representatives seats were up for grabs, each seat held by a Democrat and each representative running unopposed for reelection. The outcome was a foregone conclusion. This was South Carolina, after all, where the Party of Lincoln was still about as welcome as the plague.

Johnny and Caroline were attending a fundraiser for the candidates that frankly more closely resembled an early victory celebration. The event was a Labor Day fair, paid for by the Democratic Party of South Carolina, to which all were invited. It was complete with horseshoe-throwing competitions, a petting zoo, face-painting for the children, a dunking booth—at which the governor promised to appear—all the barbeque you could eat, and a concert and dance once the sun set.

"There you are," said Johnny's father. The young couple's reprieve from the heat under the oak tree was ending. "What are y'all doin' hiding over here? There're still folks we want to introduce you to—and Johnny, everybody's askin' about ya. Now, come on."

"Just takin' a break, Dad."

"There'll be plenty of time for that later. Now, come on."

Johnny and Caroline, hand in hand, strolled out from around the tree—all smiles while on display. His parents made no effort to disguise how thrilled they were that Caroline was visiting for the weekend, and they wasted no time introducing the young couple to everyone of consequence.

"Judge Gates, I'd like to introduce you to Caroline Thistle. Of course, you know our son, Johnny. Caroline and Johnny are about to begin their junior year at Georgetown University. Johnny spent his summer interning in our nation's capital for Senator Olin Johnston, and Caroline worked on Kennedy's campaign," boasted Johnny's father, Colin.

Judge Gates was dressed in a white shirt and seersucker pants held up by red, white, and blue suspenders. He was waving his pork pie hat back and forth in a failing attempt to keep cool. "Have you? Say, Johnny, now if you two have hitched your wagon to Senator Johnston and what folks are callin' Camelot, you might want to steer clear of our other senator from this fine state. I saw him across the field pitching horseshoes, and he ain't too keen on young JFK."

Johnny was about to say something when his father piped up. "No need to worry about Strom Thurmond. His days are numbered, as are his kind. It's a new day in South Carolina and the dawn of a new age. There's no future for segregationists," said Colin. Colin stood between Johnny and Carolina with an arm draped over each of their shoulders. "The future lies with our youth—people like my son Johnny and his girlfriend Caroline, here. Ain't that right, Judge?"

The judge was clearly losing his battle against the heat as sweat collected on the ends of what hair strands he had left before driveling down the side of his face. "I hope you're right. Well, anyway, our party is in for quite a ride. We're in for a fight for our soul, I do believe if we are to embrace the young and these new attitudes, as you say. We're gonna have to pretend that a whole lot of what happened in our party never happened. But let's not sully the afternoon with talk of such things. Now, Caroline, my dear, you wouldn't be related to Terrance and Elizabeth Thistle, would you?"

"Yes, Your Honor. They're my parents."

The judge looked at Colin and then at Johnny with a conspiratorial grin. "Well done, my young man, well done," he said as he patted Johnny on the back. The judge then waddled off and took a seat at the first table he came to. This scene, or something similar, was repeated continuously throughout the afternoon and into the evening.

As the sun was setting, folks made their way to the buffet, where a line formed on each side of three picnic tables laid end-to-end. As people exited the line, their paper plates piled high with barbequed pork, ears of corn, potato salad, baked beans smothered in molasses and servings of pecan or banana cream pie, they scurried off to find a seat amongst the round tables that now dotted the fairgrounds. At the center of each table stood two pitchers, one of water and the other of iced sweet tea. The bluegrass band that had been playing took a break and joined the dinner crowd but only after promising everyone they'd return to the stage once supper was done.

Those in the know tried to maneuver their way to the Dunsmores' table, but Colin and Barbara were too savvy to grant their company to just anyone. Those lucky enough to be seated at their table included the chairman of the Democratic Party of South Carolina, Mr. Ernest Talmidge; Judge Gates, a rumored prospect for the next open seat to the South Carolina Supreme Court; Governor Fritz Hollings; and lastly, their respective wives.

"Johnny, I saw you earlier today at the table where the Young Democrats were signing up recruits," said the governor as he dabbed at the corners of his mouth with a plaid-colored napkin.

"Yes, sir. Just doing my part. I was a member in high school and still am," said Johnny.

"That's fine. Just fine. You know, it's important we set people on the right path early in life, and education is the first step in breeding responsible citizens. Education has been a major focus of my administration," expounded the governor.

"You're doing fine work, sir," Johnny's father chimed in.

The governor, who was termed out from running for office again and therefore no longer obliged to hide his utter disgust for Colin Dunsmore, managed to smile, nod, and heap another spoonful of banana cream pudding into his mouth all at the same time.

"Johnny spent his summer interning with Senator Johnston, and Caroline worked for the Kennedy campaign," said Colin.

"Yes, you told me." Turning to the young couple, the governor asked, "Will you two continue in these roles once school starts up again? I imagine the rigors of a Georgetown education place a great demand on your time."

Before Johnny could respond, the normally demur Caroline spoke up. "I most certainly will, and I know Johnny wants to, but I fear he has too much on his plate already. He was elected freshman and sophomore class representative to the Yard—that's our student government body—and this year he will run for president, unprecedented for a junior. He's on the debate team and writes for the school paper. He kept a 3.8 GPA last year. And most importantly," she added with a coquettish flutter of her eyelashes, "he mustn't forget me."

There were laughs and smiles all around.

"Well, Johnny, that's quite a sterling resume you've built for yourself," said Mr. Talmadge. "And Caroline, dear, I must impress upon you, from great men, great things are expected, and we expect great things from young Johnny. That means that if you're along for the ride, you must make sacrifices as well."

"What are we talkin' about here? These two love birds are barely old enough to vote, and you've got them married and running for my office, by God!" exclaimed the governor.

More laughs and smiles. As for Colin and Barbara—they were eating it up. So was Johnny. Caroline, too.

Chapter 17

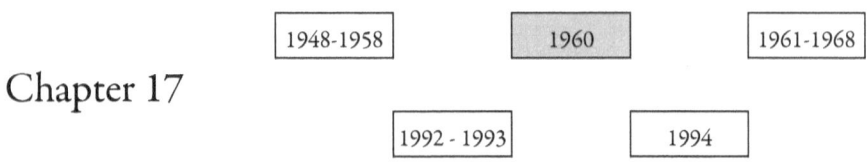

Georgetown, Washington, DC
Friday, September 9, 1960

Less than a week later, Johnny and Caroline were back at Georgetown University to begin their junior year. Caroline would be living with three girlfriends on 34th Street. On this warm Friday afternoon, just a few blocks away, Johnny and Luis were moving the last of Johnny's stuff into their home on Prospect Street when a delivery from Dixie Liquor arrived.

Roscoe, who looked to be about 160 years old, had been making deliveries for Dixie Liquor as long as anyone could remember. He pulled his 1940 Ford pickup truck over to the side of the road and slid out while he left the engine running. He shuffled to the back of the truck, lowered the gate, and lifted one of two boxes of liquor out of the back while Johnny grabbed the other box and placed it on the case of beer.

"Perfect timing, Roscoe," said Johnny.

Roscoe had been a boxer in his youth and was stronger than his age indicated. He affixed a ramp onto the back of the truck and rolled a keg down onto the pavement. Johnny and Luis took over from there and maneuvered it up the steps and onto their Georgetown townhome's once beautiful wood floor.

"This all for just the two of ya?" asked Roscoe as he pocketed the tip Johnny handed him.

"Naw. Got a few friends coming by tonight."

"A few ladies, I hope."

"You can count on it."

Roscoe laughed, but then the coughing took over, and before he could stop, he lit another Marlborough. "See y'all next Friday, then," he said, puffing his cigarette to life. He didn't exactly leave, though, as was his habit.

Taking the hint, Johnny removed a beer from the packaging and handed it to Roscoe.

"Thank you, gladly. Roscoe appreciates ya."

"And *we* appreciate Roscoe," said Johnny and Luis in unison.

And he was off to make his next delivery. Same drill every week.

It was not uncommon for Georgetown students to live off campus after their freshman year. While Johnny had continued to live in a dorm throughout his sophomore year and into this last summer, Luis had been sharing a place off campus with three others—a dump, really—and was ready to move out. Luis and Johnny had agreed to live together, and Luis took responsibility for finding a rental, which he did: a two-bedroom townhome on Prospect Street just a block north of M Street. It had become available just a few weeks ago when the landlord's summer tenants, Yale law school students working in DC, returned to New Haven for their last year.

Luis had moved in immediately, but Johnny was seeing the place for the first time, as he'd been traveling for the last few weeks—first to visit Caroline and her family at her home, and then to South Carolina over Labor Day weekend where Caroline visited him and his family.

Luis and Johnny walked inside, and while Johnny filled the fridge with beer, Luis pulled mail out of the drawer that had accumulated over the past couple of weeks and started going through it. Eventually, he stopped and held up a letter, examining the postmark. Turning towards Johnny, he waved the letter in the air as if he were talking to a jury while holding the incriminating evidence.

"Well, well, well . . . What do we have here?" he said.

Johnny recognized the handwriting even from a distance and walked over to snatch the envelope from Luis's hand. Luis quickly yanked his hand away, and Johnny stood back, hands on his hips, before lunging again for the envelope. Chuckling, Luis yanked his hand away again, and after a short pause, he handed the letter to Johnny. Johnny said nothing, shoved it into his back pocket, and returned to loading the fridge.

"Aren't you going to read it?" asked Luis.

Johnny forced himself to shrug nonchalantly. "It can wait," he claimed, though the envelope was already burning a hole in his pocket. He couldn't *wait* to see what Nadia had written.

"So, how did she find you?" Luis cut straight to the chase. "How does she know where you live?"

Johnny placed the last few beers in the fridge, shut the door, and sighed. "She didn't find me. We've been writing to each other since spring break. Before I left, I gave her my dorm address, and when we lined up this place, I gave her this address."

Luis shook his head in disbelief. "Let me get this straight. You're dating Caroline Thistle—a well-connected beauty with *huge* trust funds, and the daughter from the kind of family that can help put you in the White House—and you're still maintaining a relationship through the mail with some random girl you boinked *once*." As if that weren't enough, he added, "An *island* girl you'll never see again. Do I have this right?"

Johnny said nothing while he retrieved a beer from the fridge and opened it.

"So, tell me, where is this going?" Luis pressed. "Let's say Caroline finds out. What are you going to tell her? That this island girl is just a pen pal?"

Johnny gave him a hard look. "Caroline *won't* find out."

"How can you be so sure? What if Island Girl mails you another—"

"Nadia. Her name is *Nadia*," said Johnny with a degree of force that surprised even him.

"*Ooookay*," said Luis as he reached into the fridge for a beer. "*Nadia* mails you another letter, and Caroline is here waiting for you when the mail arrives. What then?"

Johnny shook his head, as if to say, *Won't happen*.

"Stranger things, my friend." Luis sighed. "I gotta say, though, you got balls. You're risking a lot for a pen pal—arguably *everything*."

Johnny took a swig of his beer, contemplating his next move. "Caroline will never find out because I'm gonna end it."

"You're gonna end it?" Luis said, laughing skeptically. "With which one?"

Johnny hesitated before answering. "Island Girl." And then, with a slight grin and before one last swig of his beer, he added, "Can't forget those huge trust funds."

Johnny and Luis clinked their beers, toasting Johnny's decision. As they did, Luis looked over Johnny's shoulder and out the front window and scoffed. "Speak of the devil."

* * *

Before Luis could open the door to let Caroline in, Johnny fled to his bedroom and shoved Nadia's letter into the back of the top drawer of his bedside table. From where he stood, he could hear the conversation from the front room.

"Hi Luis, this is my friend Marcy. Is Johnny here?"

"Nice to meet you, Marcy. Come on in. And yes, Johnny is here."

Luis hollered Johnny's name, and Johnny took that as his cue. He walked in and, feeling guilty before a jury of one, kissed Caroline.

The night started off slowly, but before too long, their small house filled up and the party was well on its way. It broke up around midnight as people filtered out and headed to other house parties and bars on M or Wisconsin Street. Caroline's friend Marcy took off with Luis, leaving Johnny and Caroline alone.

* * *

With a trashcan in his left hand, Johnny walked around the living room, picking up empty cups and beer cans. Caroline had placed The Drifter's Greatest Hits album on the turntable and was sitting on the sofa, giving Johnny a come-hither look. The two of them had started having sex earlier that summer, and Johnny had been her first. When she asked about his prior experience, he made vague references to a girl in high school but never, of course, mentioned any of his other conquests—though Caroline had to have been aware of his reputation. Most of all, of course, he never mentioned Nadia.

Sex between the two of them had been awkward from the beginning, owing initially to Caroline's lack of experience—but to Johnny, there was something else amiss. Caroline was trying so hard to be cool about it all, as if having sex evidenced her maturity. But to him, her cool attitude seemed forced, as if she were covering for something—and frankly, it was void of much passion, especially when compared to what he had experienced with Nadia that one time.

Johnny liked Caroline, that was for sure, and they were compatible. They both came from the kind of families that people described as "good families," and they both shared Johnny's ambition—a life in politics. For both, the top prize was the White House. They were a good team; everyone said so. Neither of them had said the L word, though. They were just nineteen years old.

They fooled around on the sofa and then made their way to Johnny's bedroom, where Caroline waited until he turned the lights off before getting undressed. After sex, Caroline liked to fall asleep in Johnny's arms the way people pretended to in the movies, waking the following day in the same position—but who *really* did that? So, after a few minutes and before his arm fell asleep, Johnny rolled over, his head inches from the bedside table and Nadia's unopened letter.

* * *

Caroline was the first to rise the next morning, earlier than Johnny cared for. But she said she had a busy day ahead of her at Kennedy election headquarters; the first debate with Nixon was just over two weeks away, and there was still so much to do. She was heading up the efforts to place as many 'Kennedy for President' signs in the front lawns of Alexandria, Virginia, as possible.

They were standing in the kitchen, making plans to meet later that day on Copley Lawn. It was orientation weekend for the incoming freshman class, and Johnny would be staffing the table for Student Government later that afternoon.

As soon as Luis heard the front door open and close, he stumbled out of his bedroom—as did an embarrassed Marcy. On her way out, she told Johnny, "You didn't see me!" Johnny smiled and waved a friendly goodbye as she walked through a barely open front door, trying to look smaller or possibly invisible, he guessed.

"She didn't have to leave on my account," said Johnny to Luis.

"She didn't. She's headed to Mass. Speaking of guilty consciences, how did things go last night with Ms. Trust Funds—I mean, *Caroline?* Have you thought about how you're going to break things off with Island Girl?"

Johnny hadn't read the letter yet but was dying to—and no, he hadn't a clue how to break things off with Nadia. "I don't know. I guess I'll write her a letter. Like you said, when will we ever see each other again?"

And then Luis, looking over Johnny's shoulder, brought the conversation to an end.

"Speak of the devil."

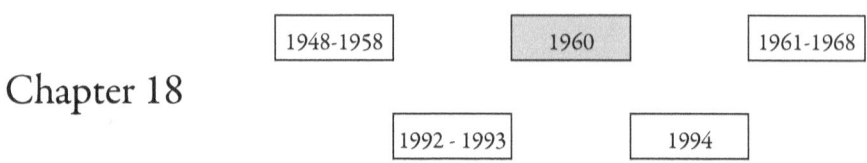

Chapter 18

Luis opened the door and stepped to the side and out of the way, framing Nadia at the bottom of the steps, beaming with joy and barely able to contain herself. Johnny just stood there—inside and a few steps removed from the doorway entrance—frozen, unsure of what was happening.

"Nadia? Oh, my gosh. It's you!"

"Yes!" Her grin wilted a bit. "You seem surprised. Didn't you get my letter?"

Johnny's mind raced back to the unopened letter in his bedside table drawer. What was in that letter? Why hadn't he read it? What would she say if she found it unopened?

"Yes, I got your letter—but you never—well, um, never mind. Come on in."

Nadia sheepishly entered and acknowledged Luis for the first time. "Hi Luis."

"Nadia, what a surprise," he replied, visibly struggling to keep himself from bursting into laughter at Johnny's misfortune.

"Sure seems that way," she said, her smile flatlining. "I've got to admit... this isn't the reunion I was expecting."

Johnny turned to face her. For the first time, his panic and shock were overshadowed by the sight of Nadia standing before him. She was lovelier than ever—and visibly hurt over his reaction. Before thinking twice, he rushed to her, drawing her into his arms. "What sort of reunion were you expecting, exactly?" he asked with a wink.

Luis nearly choked on his own spit.

But Nadia wasn't convinced. "Johnny, you really didn't get my last letter?"

He blinked. "Well, I—"

"I told you I was moving here," she blurted out and everybody went silent. This was more than a spontaneous visit. Significantly more. "I mailed my letter over two weeks ago."

"I guess it doesn't matter that I didn't get your letter," Johnny decided, squeezing her tighter against his body.

Finally, she smiled. "Well, here I am," she said, and looking up at Johnny, she cocked her head slightly, and her eyes—the color of honey, beautiful and pleading for a response—drew him in deeper and deeper, and in that moment, Johnny knew everything had changed.

* * *

"I'll leave you two lovebirds alone," said Luis as he grabbed his wallet and Wayfarer glasses and headed out the door.

When Nadia heard the door close, she threw her arms around Johnny, shrieking with joy.

Though still reeling, Johnny found himself passionately kissing Nadia—forgetting that just ten minutes earlier, he had kissed Caroline goodbye and made plans to meet her later in the day. Forty-five minutes later, they were in the shower together, enjoying the gentle intimacy of washing the sex off each other.

"Johnny, I have to be at work by three o'clock. It's our orientation and then they put us right to work. What shall we do between now and then?"

Johnny figured he had time to take her to lunch before he had to be on campus, but he was calculating the odds of being seen by anyone. "Where are you working?"

"At the Hay Adams Hotel. It's also where I'm staying."

"Pretty swanky!" he said, more than a little surprised.

"No, no. Not like that. I'm an intern at the hotel and I get to stay there for free. When the internship ends, I'll have to find a place to stay. Maybe we can find a place together," she suggested as she slowly washed his chest with the washcloth.

"Yeah, so . . . you said you're moving here. Wow, that's great." Johnny hoped she didn't hear the fear and anxiety in his voice over this revelation.

"Yeah . . . I'm so excited, Johnny, but I'm not moving here permanently—not right away, that is. When the internship is over, I'll go home to finish up school, but that should only take one more semester and then I'll move back—hopefully with a job lined up at the hotel."

She threw her arms around Johnny's neck and squeezed him tight. She then pushed away and looked up at him. He saw a few tears break free and mix with the water from the shower head above.

"Johnny, I'm so *happy*." She burrowed her face into his chest.

Johnny's head was spinning. *Okay, she lives downtown. That's good—that'll make it easier to conceal her from Caroline, and well, everyone else.* And her move wasn't permanent. Not yet, at least. That was good, too. Or was it? He wasn't sure of anything right now. The ground beneath his feet had shifted. Through it all though, he couldn't deny one thing—he was glad to see her.

"Lunch it is. I know a place close to your hotel. We'll take my car. But then I'll have to come back here. I have stuff to do on campus this afternoon."

"Lunch sounds perfect." She smiled at him and kissed him passionately. Then she turned so he could wash her back.

"What time do you get off work tonight?" he asked.

"Not till eleven. Is that too late?" she asked as she looked over her shoulder.

Johnny shook his head. "You said you have a room at the hotel where you work?"

"Room 160. Come see me tonight?" she asked as she turned towards him and pressed her body against his.

"I'll be there."

* * *

And so, it began. For the next two months, Johnny juggled Caroline and Nadia, school, working for Senator Johnson, the debate team, writing for the school paper, the responsibilities of serving as student body class president, and working alongside other young, idealistic voters trying to get JFK elected. The pace was his saving grace, for he was always somewhere, hiding his tracks from both Caroline and Nadia.

Keeping them apart was easier than he'd expected. Nadia never came to campus, and Caroline had no reason to ever cross paths with Nadia—and even if they had, neither was aware of the other. But Johnny wasn't just juggling two girls—he was juggling two *lives*, because the time he spent with each of them couldn't have been more different. And he too was a different person with each of them.

* * *

"Johnny, this weekend my parents are in town. We're having dinner with them Friday night at 1789. The chairman of the Democratic National Party and his wife will be joining us," said Caroline. "Johnny, are you listening to me? Johnny?"

"Uh, yeah. Of course. What time?"

"The reservation is at eight, but my parents want to meet us for a drink before dinner. They're staying at the Hotel Monticello."

Johnny's heart stopped at the word "hotel" as he feared the next words out of her mouth would be "Hay-Adams," the hotel where Nadia worked. Thankfully, he'd dodged a bullet.

"I'll be coming straight from election headquarters. You'll be at the senator's office that afternoon," she said, staring at her calendar. Looking up, her eyes cast ahead of her, she continued, "Oh, have you seen the latest polling? We're closing the gap on Nixon in Virginia. The latest commercial buy on Sunday night TV paid big dividends. Johnny? Johnny, are you listening to me?"

* * *

Johnny was sitting on a blanket across from Nadia, enjoying a hot dog he'd purchased from one of the vendors on the Mall. It was a beautiful fall afternoon, and from where they were sitting, they could see the Washington Monument, the Capitol, and the Lincoln Memorial in the distance.

"What are you reading now?" Johnny asked between bites as he nodded at the book resting on top of her backpack.

One of the first things Nadia did when she arrived in DC was get a library card at a public library branch within walking distance of the Hay-Adams Hotel. She was a voracious reader and teased Johnny because he never read anything other than his textbook assignments and newspapers.

She held up her book for Johnny to see before putting it down so she could take a bite of her hotdog.

"*Pride and Prejudice,*" he said.

"It's wonderful. Have you read it?"

"No. I went to an all-boys school. We wouldn't have read Jane Austen."

"What about college? You could read it now."

"I'm in the business school, so I don't take as many English Lit classes. But in my freshmen year at Georgetown, I read *Heart of Darkness.*"

"And what do you remember about it?"

Johnny paused to think about what she had asked him. "It's been a while since I've done a book report, Nadia."

"I'm not asking for a book report. I like talking about books and ideas and such. Just tell me what you remember."

"Are you sure you're not an English major? I thought you were getting a degree in hotel management."

"So, what if I am? Can't I still read? I come from a tiny island in the Caribbean, Johnny, but I'm interested in the whole world, and since I can't afford to travel it, I let books be my guide. So, Johnny Dunsmore, prep school graduate and current Georgetown student, tell me what you remember about *Heart of Darkness.*"

"The author is critical of imperialism and how White Europeans treated Africans as they profited from the ivory trade, or something like that."

"I would give you a C+ if that was the extent of your answer. Yes, the story was about one man's search for an employee of a British ivory trading company who had gone mad, but there's more. Go on."

"In a minute. First, tell me about *Pride and Prejudice* and how it is that you—a descendant of a people enslaved by the British—are such a fan of nineteenth century British literature. Weren't you reading Jane Eyre just last week?"

"No, no. There will be time for that later. What else can we take away from reading *Heart of Darkness*?" Nadia pressed.

Johnny sighed. "That the line between civilization and savagery is thin and people who think they are civilized and there to help others will justify virtually any actions to further what they believe are just goals."

"Better. You're up to a A-," said Nadia. "And Johnny, when you become the President of these United States, remember that."

* * *

Johnny looked at his watch as he walked through his front door. He was due at Hotel Monticello at seven o'clock. After spending the afternoon on the Mall and visiting the National Archives Museum, he escorted Nadia back to Room 160 and they made love. She was working that night, so Johnny had an excuse to leave and make it back for his dinner date with Caroline and her parents. Time for a quick shower. He would just make it.

Twenty minutes later, he was sitting at the hotel bar with Caroline's parents, Mr. and Mrs. Terrance Thistle, dressed in khaki pants, a blue blazer, a white oxford shirt, a tie decorated with American flags, and penny loafers—the standard uniform for any Georgetown student working on the Hill. Caroline was late, as usual.

"There you are, darling. We were starting to worry about you," said Mrs. Thistle as her daughter breezed in and, all in one swoop, removed her coat and leaned in towards Johnny, who had quickly risen from his seat for a peck on the cheek.

"Hello, cupcake," said Mr. Thistle as he stood to greet his daughter—his only daughter and the apple of his eye. "Busy day at headquarters?"

"Oh, Father, you wouldn't believe all the goings on. Senator Johnson was in the office earlier this week. Everyone thinks he is a vile man, but he brings twenty-four electors with him from Texas, so as a VP, it makes sense. It really is something, headquarters, the election, Camelot! So exciting."

Her father, having taken his seat, leaned back in his chair, and, holding his drink in both hands, smiled and nodded at her as if he knew only so well. Terrance shifted in his seat and eyed Johnny—the young man he hoped to call his son-in-law one day. "And you, Johnny, before our perpetually late daughter graced us with her presence—"

"Oh, Father. Really."

"That's all right, sweetie. We men spend a lifetime waiting on our women. Don't we, Johnny? But as I was saying, Johnny, I want to hear what's happening with you. Exciting things, I imagine. Now, go on."

Johnny proceeded to tell them about the interview he had secured with Robert Kennedy for the school newspaper, *The Hoya*, and how he believed this feather in his cap would secure his victory as both the President of the Yard the following year and Editor of *The Hoya*—a first in Georgetown history.

"And after graduation, what then for you two?" asked Mrs. Thistle with a scandalous smile on her face. To Johnny, it seemed clear she was insinuating marriage, but Caroline bubbled over about all the exciting opportunities that would become available for young people once JFK and Jackie were in the White House. There was talk of building a worldwide service organization, a corp of volunteers that would go into the poorest parts of the world and help them.

"Fine idea. Lord knows they can use our help, even if they don't know it," said Terrance.

The conversation continued in this banal manner throughout dinner, and Johnny's mind wandered back to his afternoon with Nadia.

* * *

"Oh, Johnny, I love this building so. Can you believe it? We saw the Declaration of Independence, the Constitution, and the Bill of Rights. What treasures!"

"Why do you love our country so much?" asked Johnny.

"What? Don't you?"

"Of course, but I asked about *you*."

"I love Tortola. I love my family. I miss them. But America is the land of freedom and hope and possibilities. I love the promise of your country—and it is my dream that America will become my country, too."

"I love our country too, but we've made a lot of mistakes along the way. I'm happy to be in a position to help undo those mistakes and build a better America."

"Such big shoulders you have!" said Nadia as she giggled and continued walking down the corridors of the National Archives Building.

"Hey, what gives? Are you making fun of me?" asked Johnny as he caught up to her.

"Yes, a little. Remember what I said earlier, Johnny. I fear there's a little Colonel Kurtz inside all men like you." And then she kissed him. "And I love you anyway."

* * *

Johnny was brought back to the moment by Mr. Thistle clinking his spoon on his wine glass and calling for a toast. He took his wife's hand in his and raised his glass. "As I look around this table, I'm comforted knowing our country is in good hands. Cheers!"

The four of them toasted themselves and then Caroline's mother, Eleanor, reminded Johnny and Caroline of their duties the next day. "Now, you two, don't stay out too late. We're having brunch at eleven with the Robinsons. They're big donors. The kind of folks you'll need to know."

"We won't, Mother."

"Thank you again for dinner, Mr. Thistle."

"Our pleasure, Johnny. You'll walk my baby girl home now, won't you?"

"Yes, sir." Johnny managed to glance at his watch. It was just after ten o'clock. Nadia got off at eleven.

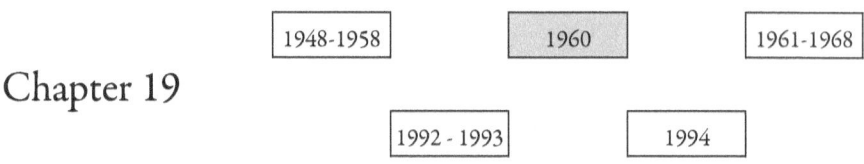

Chapter 19

HAY ADAMS HOTEL LOBBY
WEDNESDAY, NOVEMBER 14, 1960

Nadia was working behind the front desk this morning when she looked up and saw the hotel manager walking towards her.

"Nadia, can I speak to you?" he asked.

"Yes, sir. Is anything wrong?"

"No, not at all. Quite the opposite. I want to let you know that you're doing wonderfully. In fact, earlier this week, I was speaking with the HR department and letting them know that when your internship is over, I anticipate offering you a full-time job here at the Hay-Adams."

Nadia couldn't hide her excitement over the news as she bounced up and down on her toes, struggling to react professionally.

"From your reaction, can I assume that this is good news, Nadia?" asked the manager with a reassuring smile.

"Oh, sir, you have no idea. Thank you, sir. Thank you!"

"Well, I just wanted to let you know. You're doing a great job. So, keep it up."

"I will. You can count on it."

The manager turned and walked back through the lobby towards his office. Nadia stole a look at the clock on the wall. *Only two hours left in my shift. I can't wait to tell Johnny.*

* * *

After her shift ended, she ran to her room to change. She didn't have plans to meet Johnny that day. He'd said something vague about a deadline at school and that he'd be spending the afternoon at the library. Perfect, she thought. I'll show up and surprise him.

Thirty minutes later, she hopped off the bus at the 37th and O Street station just outside the gates of the university. Johnny always said he didn't understand why she took the bus everywhere and not the taxis. "You get where you're going so much faster," he'd remark. "You don't understand what it means to pinch pennies," she'd reply.

It was a beautiful November day. Not a cloud above. Though the leaves were gone, the fall season was hanging on as the temperatures hovered in the mid-sixties.

Healy Hall stood majestically before her, enveloped by the rich blue sky on all sides. The community college she attended in Tortola was a far cry from where she was standing, but it had landed her here. As she looked about, she saw students going in this direction and that, to and from class, she presumed. Scattered across the lawn, she saw boys and girls her age, sitting cross-legged in the grass, some in pairs, some in small groups. What were they talking about? Books they were reading? Something they had discussed in class earlier that day? Their favorite professor?

Nadia had never felt so alive, and her future had never seemed so bright. She couldn't wait to share everything with Johnny. She turned her head slowly, looking for the library and taking in the beauty of the old stone buildings. Not too far inside the front gates she saw a sign directing her to the Riggs Library and she set off in that direction, excited and anxious. She'd never been on campus before. In fact, since the day she'd first surprised Johnny standing on the steps of his townhome, she'd never been anywhere close to campus. He always wanted to eat at a restaurant downtown, close to the hotel. Other than Luis, she'd never met a single one of his friends.

She did know one thing: the nickname for the ground floor of the library was the Fishbowl, because from outside you could see everything going on inside. "Not much work gets done in the Fishbowl," Johnny had told her once. "Most people go there just to be seen."

Nadia slowed as she approached the large floor-to-ceiling windows, and she began to look for Johnny. Would he be in the Fishbowl or would she have to search the upper floors? Would he be alone? She let her eyes roam as she looked for Johnny. Students were gathered in clusters around carrels or the lounge chairs in the center of the great hall. But there was no sign of Johnny. And then she saw him, in the corner, alone and working diligently in a carrel. Her heart leaped. She stood there, just looking at him. *He's beautiful, so handsome.*

She noticed that his concentration was broken. He looked up and away from the window. And then a girl approached and leaned over the carrel. She was smiling at him. Was he smiling back? What were they talking about?

Nadia's heart began to thunder in her chest. *Wait—what's she doing?* She had stepped into the carrel and was kissing him. And he was kissing her back. Nadia felt a tear break free. She wiped it away, turned, and walked back to the bus stop.

* * *

Room 160 at the Hay-Adams Hotel
Monday, November 21, 1960

Nadia was pacing her room, nervously awaiting Johnny's arrival. It was the Monday before Thanksgiving and she had the day off. She *always* had Monday afternoons off—which meant that Johnny would be knocking on her door any minute now. What she didn't know was that for the last two months, he told anyone who asked where he went during the week when his classes had ended that you could find him at Senator Johnson's office. If anyone became curious and called the senator's office looking for him, if Johnny wasn't there, the receptionist knew to tell them that Johnny was working on a research project at the Library of Congress. The flowers Johnny regularly delivered to the receptionist ensured her cooperation.

Nadia knew Johnny was looking forward to whatever she had planned for the afternoon—a trip to a museum, an afternoon on the National Mall reading and talking to each other—and then an early dinner followed by a roll in the hay. Nadia was not familiar with the phrase "a roll in the hay," but she remembered how clever Johnny thought he was when he pointed out that they often took place in the *Hay*-Adams hotel. She remembered thinking at the time he was very clever, too. Today, not so much.

Nadia had decided over the weekend to confront Johnny with what she'd witnessed the Wednesday before standing outside the library. Johnny had told her that he was flying home to South Carolina for Thanksgiving. She couldn't wait until he returned. She was a wreck. She had to know now where all this was going.

The knock on the door startled Nadia even though she was waiting for it. She opened the door and Johnny stepped in quickly and attempted to pull her in for a kiss, but she turned away abruptly, walked back to the bed, and took a seat. Johnny stood motionless and Nadia saw a look of confusion on his face.

"Are you ashamed of me, Johnny?"

"What?" he asked, shocked. "*Ashamed* of you? What are you talking about? Of course not!"

"Then what am I to you?"

She stared up at him as he dragged his left hand through his hair, hoping he'd pass her test. *My God, he doesn't know!*

"You're my girlfriend."

"Then how come I have never met any of your friends? How come you've never taken me back to your place? We always make love here or at the condo Luis's father owns. There are plenty of restaurants and bars in Georgetown, but we never go there. Why Johnny?"

Johnny was speechless. He'd known this day may come but was still unprepared for it. She was right. He'd never taken her to his place or a campus party. How could he?

The silence would have continued until Johnny told her the truth or a lie, but the silence had gone on long enough.

"It's because I'm not your *only* girlfriend, am I? You have another girlfriend, don't you, Johnny?" asked Nadia, breaking the silence.

"Another girlfriend? Of course not!"

"Liar!" she screamed as she bolted upright from the end of the bed. Staring up at him, his eyes were closed shut and his face was contorted by an expression of . . . *something*, but of what, she couldn't be sure. Was it a look of sorrow or defeat?

"Last Wednesday, I went to see you. I had good news I wanted to share with you, so I decided to surprise you by visiting you on campus. Imagine my surprise when I saw you making out with a girl in a carrel in the Fishbowl."

"Nadia," he breathed, "I can explain. It's not how it looked."

"Really! It's not how it looked? She was grabbing your crotch, Johnny, and you had your hand up her shirt. Or is that how you greet every girl you meet?"

"I can explain!" he pleaded.

"You had your chance. You lied instead. And you want to explain now, but only because you've been caught lying. It's too late, Johnny. You failed and now I can't trust anything that comes out of your mouth." She nodded to the door, tears pooling in her eyes. "Goodbye, Johnny."

Chapter 20

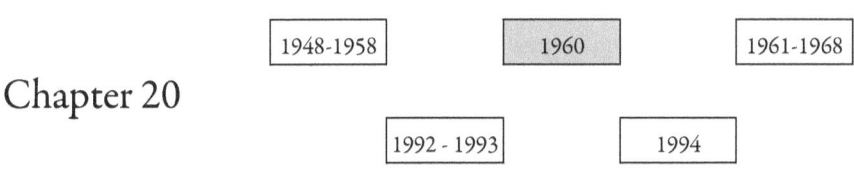

ON A STATE HIGHWAY IN VIRGINIA
WEDNESDAY, NOVEMBER 23, 1960

Johnny must have called the hotel and left a dozen messages for Nadia. Not one call was returned. He stopped calling late Tuesday because he wasn't going to South Carolina to visit his family for Thanksgiving, as he had told Nadia. If he had been, he could have kept calling her from his home there, but that had all been a lie. Where he was *really* going was to the 500-acre horse ranch located in Shenandoah Valley, where he'd be spending Thanksgiving with Caroline's family.

"Johnny, is everything all right? You've hardly said a thing since we left DC," Caroline said.

No, everything is not all right! he wanted to shout.

"Yeah, everything's fine. Just a little hungover," he answered. "A few of the guys came over after we shut down the Tombs."

"Well, you be sure to shape up by the time we get to our family ranch," she said as she wagged her finger at him. "A lot of very important people will be there."

Besides, you talk enough for both of us, he added mentally.

"Of course, sweetheart," he said. "You know you can count on me."

Johnny stole a glance at Caroline sitting in the passenger seat and saw her smile triumphantly and repeat, "*Very* important people."

Forty-five minutes later, Johnny was told to slow down and to take the next right. "Oh, Johnny, I can't wait to show you around. This place is magnificent."

"Well, your beach house where I visited you last summer wasn't too shabby."

"No, it wasn't," she said confidently. "But this place is *special*."

As Johnny drove down a long tree-lined driveway, Caroline pointed across his chest and announced, "Over there, you can make out the barn, and—oh, look! That rider in the distance, I believe that's mother. I'd know her horse's gait anywhere."

Caroline was still talking as Johnny slowed and parked his car in front of what she had told him was one of the nation's finest examples of late eighteenth century Georgia architecture. As he was walking around his car to open the door for Caroline, her father stepped out onto the expansive porch, arms open wide for his little girl to run into. And so began Johnny's weekend with his girlfriend—a weekend during which he couldn't stop thinking about his ex-girlfriend.

* * *

Over the weekend, Johnny secured an internship in New York City for the summer.

"Getting to know the moneyed class in the Big Apple is an important step in your career," Caroline's father told him. "It will be important that they grow comfortable with you."

"But Mr. Thistle, won't working on Wall Street hurt me in the eyes of our constituents who live on Main Street? It's the republicans who are the party of the wealthy," said Johnny.

Mr. Thistle smiled and looked curiously at Johnny. There was something strange about his expression that made him feel like Mr. Thistle, in this moment, considered him to be a naive young man—but also, as if there were something in him he recognized, but something in him that had died a long time ago.

Caroline would be working as an intern in the city, too.

"The UN and the Peace Corp—it's a natural marriage—will be collaborating on efforts to help all those poor people in the rest of the world who need us," boasted Caroline.

And so it went. Thanksgiving with the Thistles was like a Norman Rockwell painting come to life. Every detail was perfect. The food was terrific: turkey and dressing, sweet potatoes, squash casserole, cornbread, green beans, vegetables grown right on site, and pumpkin pie for dessert. The rest of the weekend was spent horseback riding, playing Gin Rummy and bridge, and following along with the college football games. Other guests who had been invited for the weekend included a senator, a judge, a dependable donor, a Wall Street heavyweight, and a tenth-generation Virginian with a last name Johnny believed he remembered from an American history class along the way. It had been perfect, and Johnny couldn't wait for it to end.

Traffic was light Sunday, and they were back in the nation's capital before they knew it. Johnny pulled up in front of Caroline's place and parked the car, leaving the engine running. He stepped out and retrieved her suitcase from the trunk and walked it up the stairs to her front door. She opened the door and picked up the mail on the floor before turning to give him a goodbye kiss. He thought he recognized the handwriting on one of the envelopes, but before he could think about it any further, Caroline said, "I've got so much to do, what with finals coming up. Meet me tomorrow night at nine outside the library?"

"Sure. Maybe we can grab a late dinner at the Tombs."

Caroline smiled and waved goodbye as Johnny walked back to his car. On his way back to his place, all he could think about was giving Nadia a call and hoping she picked up this time.

Chapter 21

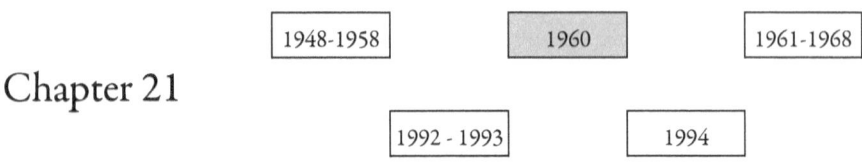

Georgetown
Sunday, November 27, 1960

When Johnny walked back into his place, the phone was ringing. "Johnny D here."

"You pathetic loser. You lying sack of shit. How could you? How dare you!"

"Caroline, what's going on?" he asked though he feared he knew exactly what was going on. She knew. But how?

"Stop it. Don't say another word. Your *girlfriend* wrote me the most interesting letter."

Johnny dropped the receiver to his side wondering what else could possibly happen. He didn't return it to his ear until he could hear Caroline screaming his name. "Johnny. JOHNNY. ANSWER ME."

Not knowing what to do, Johnny did what he'd become accustomed to doing. He lied. "Look, we met on spring break, but nothing happened. She must have followed me here."

"Liar!" she screamed. "I'm holding a Polaroid of you two sitting together on the Mall with the Washington Monument in the background."

"Okay, okay. So, we met a few times. She's new to town and wanted me to show her around town but nothing happened. I swear."

"Then how does she know about the birthmark just above your pecker?"

Johnny's silence was all the confirmation Caroline needed.

"Fuck you, Johnny Dunsmore."

Johnny was still holding the receiver to his ear when he heard Caroline slam the one in her hand down, ending the call—ending their relationship. And possibly ending his father's hopes for the White House.

* * *

Johnny thought the tongue-lashing Caroline had given him was the worst possible, but that was before his father called later that evening and chewed him out.

"Are you out of your mind?"

"Dad, what are you calling about?"

"I just got off the phone with Terrance Thistle. Do you want to know why he called?"

"Oh, good God," he said with a groan.

"He called to uninvite your mother and I from the Presidential Inauguration next January."

A second groan.

"That's right—you pathetic, ungrateful, poor excuse for a son! He told us about you cheating on his daughter with some colored girl you met on spring break. I guess you two have shacked up together. After all we've done for you, *this* is how you repay us? Your mother hasn't stopped crying since we got off the call. She was going to meet Jackie! She'd already told all her friends about it. Do you have any idea how this is going to make us look?"

Johnny was at a complete loss for words, torn between a desire to apologize and grovel and a desire to crawl through the phone and kick his father's ass.

"Now let me tell you what you're going to do, you little shit. You're going to win her back. You're going to do whatever it takes to get her to take you back."

Colin's demands were met with silence.

"And just to make sure we understand each other, tuition for your second semester is due before you return to campus after the Christmas break so you either repair things with the Thistle girl or you make other arrangements regarding your future. DO YOU UNDERSTAND?"

Johnny's desire to kick his father's ass had been replaced with fear.

"I understand."

* * *

Caroline wouldn't answer his calls. They had walked past each other on campus several times, and even then, she ignored him. How could he apologize and win her back if she wouldn't even talk to him? Finally, after a week, he saw her walking across Healy Lawn with a group of friends and decided he had to say something.

"Caroline, please. Just talk to me for a second."

The weather had turned cold since Thanksgiving break, and she was wearing riding boots and a camel-colored overcoat that stopped above her knees and was tied around her waist with a belt. She stopped and said something to her friends, who quietly continued on their way. She then stood her ground and waited for Johnny to approach.

"Caroline, I don't know what to say, but I'm sorry."

Her hands were encased in black leather gloves and wrapped around textbooks pressed against her body. She looked away from Johnny nonchalantly. "There's nothing you can say. You blew it."

"Please don't say that. Just give me another chance. I've broken everything off with her."

"Liar," she said as her head snaped back and she looked at him.

"No, really, I have."

"No, you haven't. She dumped you. She said so in her letter. She said she decided to write me the letter so I'd know what kind of a man I'm mixed up with."

Johnny's head dropped, and he audibly groaned.

"Busted. Again. You know I met her, right?"

"You what? When?" asked Johnny.

"Just the other day. I wanted to. She's beautiful and quite intelligent. But what were you thinking? My family could have taken you places. You and me, we could have gone places together. The White House. It's what we've talked about."

Johnny saw an opening, and he took it. "It's still possible. But it would mean nothing without you."

She was hesitating. Thinking. Maybe reconsidering.

"Johnny Dunsmore, I will never trust you again."

And she walked away.

So much for an opening. He'd blown it.

Nadia had dumped him, and now Caroline had too. And everyone on campus knew. Would this be his college legacy? School body president, editor of the school paper, captain of the Debate Team, aide to Senator Johnston ... and the *idiot* who lost Caroline Thistle, trust funds and all.

According to his father, he had to win her back. But Johnny was torn. Truth was, he didn't know if he *wanted* her back. He didn't know if he wanted a life in politics. But did he want a life with Nadia? Could a life with her be any more different than a life with Caroline and the life he'd been told was his destiny? The only thing Johnny knew for sure was that he didn't know what he wanted.

* * *

"So what are you going to do?" asked Luis.

Luis and Johnny were sitting at the far end of the bar at Old Ebbits Grill. Luis had suggested they go out, but Johnny was afraid of being seen by anyone he knew from campus, so that ruled out the Georgetown bars.

Johnny had just brought Luis up to speed on his run in with Caroline earlier that day and more importantly, he told Luis about his phone call with his father and his father's threats.

"I've just got to win her back."

"Well, that's a given. The question is ... how?'

"I don't know," answered Johnny as he stared at the wall of bottles neatly stacked behind the bar.

"Thinking on this requires another round of drinks," said Luis as he signaled the bar tender with a wave of his hand. "We need to figure out what Caroline wants and needs and see if by getting back together with you, she can meet those needs. So, what does Caroline Thistle need?"

"Nothing. She's good looking and has lots of money," answered Johnny.

"Okay, but did she lose something when she dumped you? Because if she did, then maybe she can regain it by getting back together with you," said Johnny.

"She lost *me* when she dumped me, but that was her goal, so I don't know what you're getting at."

"Then what did she *gain* when she dumped you? Maybe we can take that away."

The bartender placed two frosty mugs on the counter in front of them. Johnny picked up his beer and took a swig. "I guess she avoided the embarrassment of everyone finding out I was cheating on her by dumping me first."

Luis perked up and turned toward his drinking buddy. "Go on."

"I guess she feared everyone would eventually find out about Nadia and she'd be embarrassed, so she got out in front of it by dumping me."

"Okay. So, she has everything, but she craves attention and the right sort of attention. She's Caroline Thistle, heir to a great tobacco fortune. She can't stand the idea of being embarrassed. Can you imagine the shame she'd have felt if the world had learned you chose an inconsequential girl from the islands over her?"

"She's not inconsequential," Johnny barked.

Luis shifted on his bar stool and looked at his friend's profile. "Okay. Understood. But we're onto something. Hear me out."

Johnny shrugged and nodded, taking a sip of his beer.

"You can't win Caroline back so maybe the best thing to do is to win Nadia back and give Nadia what she wants—a front row seat to your life. You'll flaunt her all over campus. Take her to every party. Hold her hand and kiss her in public. It'll drive Caroline crazy. There's no way she'll take a backseat to Island Girl, regardless of how consequential she is. She'll become so jealous that she'll be begging you to take her back."

Johnny sat up a little straighter and cocked his head towards Luis.

"I've got your attention, don't I?" said Luis.

"Yea, you do, but I can't do that to Nadia."

"Then I guess I'd better start looking for a new roommate for next semester."

His friend's blunt response put everything into perspective.

* * *

After three days of calling and leaving messages, Nadia finally called Johnny back.

"Hey, Luis, could you get the phone? I just got out of the shower."

Thirty seconds later, Luis stuck his head around the doorframe and peered into Johnny's room. "It's for you, lover boy. It's Nadia."

The phone call was short. Johnny walked from the kitchen into the living room, where Luis was sitting.

"She's agreed to see me," said Johnny.

"Excellent," replied Luis. "Operation 'Make Caroline Jealous' is underway."

* * *

Johnny was sitting in a booth at Old Ebbitt Grill when Nadia walked in. He slid out of the booth and waved his hand over his head until she saw him. As she walked his way, Johnny looked for a positive sign, a smile, anything. He saw nothing. She took a seat on the side of the booth across from where he had been sitting. A waiter approached the table.

"Can I get you anything?" he asked.

"I'll have a Blatz," said Johnny.

"Nothing for me," answered Nadia.

The silence between Nadia and Johnny continued until the waiter reached the bar with his order. Nadia waited patiently. Johnny broke the silence.

"Nadia, I don't know what to say. I've been awful, just awful. You are such a wonderful person. So genuine and beautiful. I don't know what I was thinking. I was acting selfishly—and stupidly. I was so surprised that day you showed up at my place back in September. I should have told you then, but I didn't know how to, and before you knew it, we were seeing each other. I know you may not believe me, but it's *you* I love. I'd been meaning to break it off with Caroline, but I didn't want to hurt her. You see, I meant well. I was just waiting for the right moment. I was thinking of doing it right before Christmas break, so she'd have time alone and away from everyone on campus to get over it. You know, so it wouldn't be so embarrassing for her. You see, we were quite the couple on campus, very high profile. It would have been devastating for her. I'm not such a bad guy. I was only thinking of her, but now I know that I should have been thinking of you. Well, that was my plan for breaking it off with her. I thought you should know, and then it would have been just you and me. The two of us. That was my plan, Nadia. I just wished it had worked out so you would have been spared this heartache. Because, Nadia, I love you. I really do."

Johnny had finished his speech—a speech he had rehearsed in the shower and with Luis and on the way over. They had debated the use of the L word. Johnny wasn't so sure, but Luis felt it would close the deal. Johnny finally agreed to use it and frankly the speech was as close to the truth as Johnny had been in some time. And now he was waiting for Nadia to say something. Anything.

This time, she broke the silence.

"Johnny, I'm pregnant."

* * *

"Luis, what am I going to do?" asked Johnny two hours later, still at the bar, and still sitting in the same booth—but now with Luis sitting across from him instead of Nadia.

After Nadia had dropped the bombshell news that he was going to be a father, he'd excused himself and went to the men's room, where he'd paced, splashed water on his face, threw up, splashed more water on his face, and tried to calm himself before returning to the booth where Nadia was still sitting. She left shortly thereafter. Johnny had then called Luis, asking him to come as quickly as he could.

"Sounds like you two are going to be setting up housekeeping. Will it be a large wedding or a small intimate affair?" asked Luis jokingly, much to Johnny's chagrin.

"I'm serious here! This isn't funny."

"I know. Just going for some gallows humor to lighten the mood. So, she's determined to have the baby?"

"Of course," he answered in a tone that questioned why one would ask a question for which there was only one answer and then remembered who he was talking to—Luis. "Besides, abortions are illegal," he added in a whisper.

"Not necessarily. In DC, if a doctor will agree that the mother's life is at stake, an abortion can be performed."

"And where are we going to find a doctor who will say that?" asked Johnny.

"There are doctors. There are places you can go."

"Not happening. She's very religious. And how do you know about all this stuff, anyway?"

Luis didn't answer and instead returned to the bigger question at hand: "So, what are you going to do?"

"Luis, my dad said he wouldn't pay next semester's tuition if I can't win back Caroline and secure his invitation to the inauguration. What do you think he's going to do when he finds out I got Island Girl pregnant?"

"Yes, I see your conundrum."

"I don't think you're taking this seriously enough. It's not just that my political career will be over. *Everything* will be over. I'll be back at college in Columbia with my dimwitted twin brother doing God knows what when I graduate because daddy ain't payin' for law school! And then, of course, it's over with Caroline *for sure*."

"Such beautiful trust funds, too. But then, I can only imagine. So, again, what are you going to do?"

"I don't know," answered Johnny. "I just wish this whole mess would go away."

Chapter 22

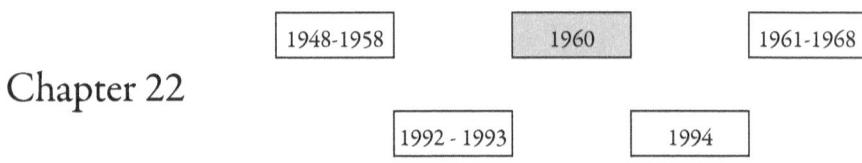

RUSSELL SENATE OFFICE BUILDING IN WASHINGTON, DC
FRIDAY, DECEMBER 16, 1960

The senator was throwing a Christmas party for the office, and the growing crowd congregating in the conference room spilled into the lobby. Theirs was not the only office doing so, and before too long, the Russell Building would be full of interns, aides, secretaries, and of course, their bosses wandering from office party to office party.

On the fifth ring, the receptionist finally made her way to her desk and picked up. "Senator Johnston's office. May I help you?" She paused. "Of course. Please hold," she said, lowering the receiver. "Johnny, it's for you!"

"All right. I'll take it at my desk." Johnny walked down the hall to a small office he shared with another intern and picked up the phone. "Johnny Dunsmore speaking."

"Johnny, Luis here. We still on for tonight?"

"Oh, I don't know. I still feel like a circus freak when I'm on campus. I think I'm gonna hang here for a while, probably hit a bar or two with folks from the office and then head home."

"No, you're not. I got big plans," said Luis, and Johnny could hear the smirk in his friend's voice as he spoke. "You're going to dinner with me and my old man. He promised to take me to a late dinner tonight at Rive Gauche."

"All right. Fine. You convinced me. Should I just meet you at dinner?"

"No. Dad wants to meet us at his place for a drink before dinner. That way, in case his flight is delayed, we're not stuck waiting at the restaurant. He'll be coming straight from the airport, so just shower at my dad's pad. You have enough clothes there for a whole separate wardrobe, anyway."

"Yeah, about that . . . I've meant to clear that out, you know, now that things are over with Nadia."

After Nadia told him she was pregnant, he'd seen her a few times, but was unable to go through with Operation Make Caroline Jealous. When they last saw each other, she'd told him she was returning to Tortola. "Will you return to the States when you finish school and take the job at the hotel?" he'd asked her, only to receive a sharp look. "And just how do you think I'd be able to manage that as a single mom?" she'd responded. "At home, I have family to help with the baby. So, it's home I'm going."

"No rush. Dad's cool with it," said Luis.

"He knows?"

"Yeah. I told him. He laughed. Thought it was great," said Luis. "I believe you went up in his estimation when he heard about it. That's the culture he comes from. Though Panamanian, he's still very European. So, head to his place around seven and be ready by eight. He'll go there directly from the airport to get cleaned up."

"Okay. I'll meet you there."

"Wonderful. We'll have a drink at his condo and then head to dinner. After that, you and I are going to Clyde's to celebrate the end of the semester. I have it on good authority that Caroline will be there."

"Oh, great," he said, his voice dripping with sarcasm.

"Don't worry. My sources tell me she's thawing. It ain't over yet, El Jefe."

"Okay," he said smiling and knowing that it had been sometime since his friend had used that nickname for him. "Gotta split. See you tonight."

* * *

A little over two hours later, Johnny was in a taxi on his way to the condo Luis's father, Gilberto Sanchez, owned, and where many of his secret rendezvous with Nadia had occurred. The driver pulled up to the curb, and Johnny, after paying, stepped onto the curve and was met by the doorman he had come to know.

"Good evening, Mr. Dunsmore. Good to see you again."

"You too, Lucius."

"Did you forget something?" he asked.

Johnny glanced curiously at Lucius, not registering his comment. He chalked it up to the alcohol he'd consumed, or perhaps Lucius's advancing years, and made his way into the elevator without a second thought. When Johnny and Nadia first began crashing at the Sanchez place, he had felt awkward calling a man nearly twice his age by his first name, while this same man called him "Mr. Dunsmore."

He exited the elevator onto the penthouse floor and stumbled down the hall to the Sanchezes' condominium. He reached for the keys Luis gave him back in September and let himself in. Before heading for the shower, he helped himself to a drink at the bar, put Elvis's new record on the turntable, and sashayed towards the bedroom, singing "Stuck on You" along with the King.

Between the drinks at the Christmas party and the one he'd just poured himself, Johnny was already feeling better. *So, Caroline is thawing. Well, well, well, maybe there's hope yet.*

He turned the corner and headed down the hall to the room where he'd shower and dress. It was silent in the apartment, outside of the music he was playing, and he knew that he had the place to himself—which was why it was so jarring for him to walk into the bedroom and see somebody else there.

A figure in the darkness, lying on the bed.

He flipped on the lights.

The glass of bourbon fell from his hands, and he stood like a deer in headlights for a few heart-stopping seconds. The sight before him was horrifying—Nadia's body, limp, hanging in all the wrong ways, like a broken doll. Her face was bloated and puce, eyes bulging and swollen, and there was a thick lacquer of drool glossing her lips, mouth, and chin. And it seemed as if her head was attached to her body by the tie wrapped tightly around her throat—

One of *Johnny's* ties.

He staggered closer to her, determined to shake her back to life. The world spun. Dizzy and sick, he dropped to his knees, vomiting violently—

Then, he felt two strong hands pick him up, carrying him away.

Without saying a word, Luis led Johnny into the bathroom. He turned on the faucet and ran cold water over a towel before handing it to Johnny, who used it to wash his face and the back of his neck.

"When did you get here?" Johnny managed to ask.

"Sometime after you. The more pressing question is when did *you* get here?"

Johnny looked at Luis and, understanding how this must have looked, dropped back to the floor, this time clutching the toilet, and threw up again. Sitting on the floor, sobered by the situation he found himself in, Johnny looked up at Luis. "I didn't kill her. She was here when I got here!"

"Did she have a key?"

Johnny shook his head.

"No? So, did the doorman let her in? The same doorman who knows you by name?"

Johnny's mind shot back to the doorman's comment when he entered the building: *Did you forget something?*

The dots were lining up, and it was easy for anyone to connect. The verdict was clear.

"You have to believe me, Luis! She was like that when I got here!" said Johnny in a frightened voice as he nodded toward the bedroom.

"I do, Johnny, I do. But I'm not your problem."

Johnny and Luis both turned their heads towards the sound of the front door opening. The look on Johnny's face was sheer panic. He stepped into the bedroom and saw the shadow of whoever had just walked in cross the threshold of the bedroom door before he saw the man's face, and then, standing in the doorway, stood Gilberto Sanchez.

Johnny collapsed to his knees, crying uncontrollably and pleading. "I didn't do it! I didn't do it! You must believe me!"

Gilberto looked at Nadia on the bed without registering shock or remorse and walked slowly towards Johnny, who was still on his knees. Gilberto looked down upon Johnny, placed one hand under his chin, and turned Johnny's tear-stained face up towards him.

"It's okay, Johnny. We can make this whole mess go away."

PART THREE

Ecclesiastes 1: 15 (15) What is crooked cannot be made straight, and what is lacking cannot be counted.

Chapter 23

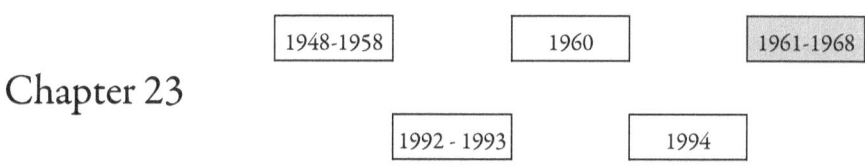

THE PRE-INAUGURAL BALL IN WASHINGTON, DC
TUESDAY, JANUARY 19, 1961

Barbara and Colin stepped out of the back of their limousine, and Barbara grabbed her husband's arm, pulled herself up to his ear, and whispered, "Oh, honey, *look*. It's Tony Curtis and Janet Leigh. And I believe that's Gene Kelly and Nat King Cole, over there."

And so it was. In addition to the inauguration, Eleanor and Terrance Thistle had invited Barbara and Colin Dunsmore to attend the Pre-Inaugural Ball. Rows and rows of red carpets extended from the curb to the entrance to accommodate the arriving limousines and to ensure that the elect pulling up in their chariots would not step in the accumulating snow, ice, and slush. The falling snow had not dampened attendance, and a crowd of 10,000 loyal subjects were pouring into the DC Armory for a glimpse at Camelot and their court.

Colin and Barbara were still standing on the sidewalk when a stretch limo pulled up to the curb, from which their son, Johnny, and Caroline Thistle exited, followed by Caroline's parents. The six of them greeted each other, and Barabara and Colin acted as if they attended functions like this all the time. But once they entered the great hall, they could not hide their amazement. The spectacle and the elegance of the crowd—men in tuxedos and women dressed to impress the other women—was exhilarating. Caroline and her mother were both wearing dresses designed by Oleg Cassini.

Waiters wearing white dinner jackets and gloves were passing through the crowd with trays of champagne-filled flutes held shoulder-high. Seeing the Dunsmores and Thistles in need, a waiter stopped and gracefully lowered his tray, extending his arm into the center of their circle, balancing the sparkling wine before them. The size of the crowd made it difficult to hear, so the six of them stood in a tight circle and silently toasted each other by raising their glasses.

Other guests passing by greeted the Thistles, and Colin noticed how relaxed their daughter Caroline was in this setting: it fit her like a glove. With her arm threaded through Johnny's, she introduced him to everyone that stopped to say hello. Johnny smiled, shook hands, and bowed his head ever so silently.

Colin felt a strong hand on his shoulder, and he turned to see his host, Terrance Thistle. "Colin, I was hoping to speak with you before the festivities began, but Eleanor and I have hardly had a moment of calm since the new year. May I have a word with you?"

"Of course," said Colin.

Terrance turned and took a few steps away from their group and Colin followed suit.

Before Terrance could say what Colin suspected he had to say, Colin figured he'd preempt the man. "Terrance, Barbara and I don't know how to thank you—"

He was silenced by Terrance lifting his hand like a school crossing guard.

"Quite an unfortunate affair, what happened to the girl your son was seeing," said Terrance. "I assume you know all about it."

"Well, the story didn't appear in our papers, of course, but Johnny told us her body was found in the back of an alley."

"The colored girl your son was screwing was a junkie. The police said she was the victim of a drug deal gone bad," said Terrance, his eyes fixed on Colin's.

Colin cast his eyes downward and shook his head in an expression of mock disbelief and sorrow about the state of world.

"I must be honest with you," Terrance went on. "I have a list of donors as long as my arm—*big* donors, who would have given their right nut to be here tonight—but my wife and daughter insisted that we invite you. My daughter tells me the whole affair really shook your boy up. I guess she felt sorry for him and decided to give him another chance. She swears to me that he's changed. I want to know what you think."

"He has. No doubt about it. Barabara and I noticed a difference over the Christmas break. He wasn't running around with old high school friends like he had on previous breaks. No, he's more serious now, about everything."

"Now don't get me wrong. I understand youthful indiscretion. I was no choir boy myself at his age, but let's hope that's all it was—*youthful indiscretion*. It's no secret in this town that Joe Kennedy over there has had his hands full with his boy," he said as he nodded towards the front of the ballroom. "So, let me make myself perfectly clear—the Thistles will not be embarrassed."

Colin was losing his patience with this man but knew he couldn't afford to anger him.

"Terrance, Barbara and I understand that Johnny visited your horse ranch on his way back to Georgetown before second semester classes began. We hope that time together gave you an opportunity to get to know the *real* Johnny Dunsmore."

"Yes, he did visit and frankly, it's why you're here tonight. I wasn't there but I heard all about it from my wife. He made quite an impression on her. She said he was the perfect gentleman and did whatever Caroline asked of him. So, I'll ask you—can you promise me your son is back in line?"

"Yes. He is. You have my word. You can count on him."

"Very good," Terrance said as he smiled. "So, it's off to law school for Johnny while Caroline busies herself with charities and the family's political activities and then the march to the White House begins."

"That's right. And we'll start with the 74th district seat in the South Carolina House of Representatives," said Colin, happy to be back on his ground.

"Excellent. It's all coming together, Colin," Terrance said as a smile spread across his face. "You know, Eleanor and I are quite fond of your son—have been since the day we met him at Georgetown. And our daughter . . . Oh my, is she ever taken with him. So, yes, it's all coming together."

"That's wonderful to hear, Terrance, because my wife and I feel the same way about Caroline. She's delightful and she brings out the best in our son."

The two men toasted their glasses and then both stole a look at the young couple who were speaking with the chairman of the Democratic National Party.

"Colin, tomorrow this nation is going to swear in a young man as president who will be accompanied by a beautiful woman. Voters are ready to trust the youth of this country with its future. There's no reason why one day you and I won't be watching someone swearing in that son of yours with my daughter standing by his side."

Colin beamed and shook his head triumphantly.

"So, I'll make one last comment and then we'll never speak of your son's sorted affair again."

"And what's that, Terrance?"

"If you have any other skeletons in the closet or any other baggage that you need to get rid of, then do it. And that stands not just for Johnny, but for you and your wife and that other son of yours."

"Of course. Not to worry," Colin said as he raised his flute to his lips, took a sip, and swallowed nervously.

Chapter 24

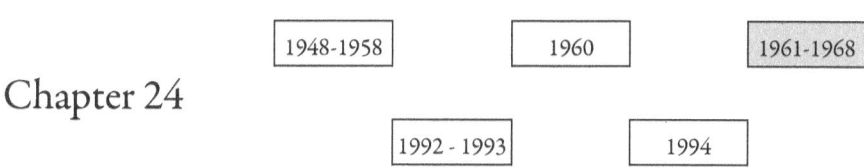

The Dunsmore Residence in Columbia, South Carolina
Saturday, April 8, 1962

Colin, still dressed for the round of golf he'd completed earlier in the afternoon—tan polyester Sansabelt slacks and a red Munsingwear golf shirt—turned on the television and found the channel he wanted to watch. He walked to the wet bar, poured himself a Tom Collins, and picked up the newspaper resting on the mantle above the fireplace before dropping himself comfortably into his recliner.

Barbara was in the kitchen preparing dinner when she heard her husband descend the stairs and take his seat. She stepped into the living room wearing an apron and drying her hands on a dish towel. "Sweetheart, don't get too comfortable now. Our bridge group will be here in less than an hour and you need to shower and start the grill."

"Just give me a minute to watch some local news, will ya?" he grumbled.

She shrugged and returned to the kitchen. A few minutes later, she jumped when she heard Colin bark some unintelligible obscenity at the television. She shook her head and returned to her slicing and dicing. But then came more hollering from her husband.

"Barbara, get in here! You're not gonna believe what that *moron* has done now."

"Who? What moron?" she asked as she scooted into the living room.

"Randal, that's who."

Barbara turned up the volume, sat on the sofa, and along with her husband listened to the local news reporter.

"I'm here on the campus of the University of South Carolina reporting to you live where a group of students calling themselves the Young Communist League of America are staging a protest. Earlier this week, the university announced that the commencement speaker at the graduation proceedings next month will be Robert Caldwell, a graduate of the university and the CEO of Greenrock Mills, one of South Carolina's leading textile manufacturers. From what we've learned, this group of students opposes what he stands for and plans to disrupt the proceedings."

"Is that Randal on the stage with the microphone?" asked Barbara, who was now sitting upright and on the edge of the sofa.

"It certainly looks like him. Just wait till I get my hands on that ungrateful little puke."

"Shush. I want to hear what the reporter says."

"Now, let's move closer to the stage. It looks like the group's leader is going to speak."

"We will not stand for the continued deprivation of our country's working men and women. Capitalism is, by its nature, exploitive, allowing owners who add nothing of value to take the profit from the labor of workers, and without fair compensation. It's time for us, the downtrodden, to cast off the shackles that have held us down and to claim what is rightfully ours!"

"Oh, honey. This isn't good!" exclaimed Barbara. "Tom and Suzie Reynolds had to cancel tonight. The Caldwells are taking their place!"

"I'm gonna kill the little shit."

* * *

Standing behind Randal on the stage were a dozen, scruffy-looking kids attending college on their parents' dime, dressed in bell-bottom jeans and tie-dyed shirts. What the television camera failed to capture was that the crowd Randal was speaking to was less than thirty people strong and consisted mostly of bored fellow students who were looking on in dismay. This was the South, not Haight-Asbury.

When Randal ran out of things to say and began to chant, "Down with capitalism! Down with America!" the crowd, instead of reacting violently, much to the reporter's disappointment, simply laughed and walked away.

Dixie was standing off to the side with her friend Cindy watching from a distance. Cindy and Dixie had known each other in high school and had become friends in college. Randal had begged Dixie and Cindy to come to the rally.

"It's going to be big. The press will be there," he'd said.

"We'll try, Randal, but I have a planning meeting that afternoon—our trip to Washington, DC is in a week, and we still have so much to do. I can't promise that Cindy will be there, but I'll try to make it."

"Wonderful. Afterwords, we're all heading back to my pad. We'll order pizza, drink some brews, and after everyone else is gone, maybe you can spend the night again," he said with a sly smile.

"We'll see," Dixie replied.

"But you'll be there, right?" asked Randal desperately.

"I'll try. I really will."

After the lone reporter left, Randal and the others behind him on the stage stopped chanting. The crowd dispersed, leaving Cindy and Dixie standing together under the shade of a tree.

"Are you going to see Johnny next week when we're in DC?" Cindy asked.

"*Thinking* about it," she replied, as she watched Randal hug his comrades on stage.

"He's going places and he's dreamy," replied Cindy.

Dixie said nothing but didn't disagree.

Randal hopped down from the stage and was heading their way—more like prancing.

"Thanks for coming, you guys! Wasn't that far out?" And then, looking at Dixie, he added, "I bet Johnny doesn't draw crowds like that at his Young Democrats of America meetings." He pronounced *Young Democrats* like he was trying to keep from swallowing rat poison.

Dixie remained silent but looked up at Randal with an expression that he interpreted as one of shared victimhood. Had he the capacity to see the world through any lens other than one that framed him as a martyr, he'd have understood her expression as one of pity instead.

"You two ready to split and head to my pad? It's going to be a scene."

"I can't make it," said Cindy.

Randal looked at Dixie expectantly.

"I'll meet you there, okay, Randal?" answered Dixie.

"Far out." He pushed a strand of hair that had come loose from his ponytail behind his ear. "But don't be late," he added as he turned and caught up with his fellow young communists.

"It's hard to believe Johnny and Randal are brothers," Cindy said.

"Yes, it is," replied Dixie, remembering from years ago when Johnny had made the same observation.

* * *

Senator Olin Johnson's Office
April 14, 1962

"Senator Johnson's office. How may I help you?"

"May I please speak with Johnny Dunsmore?" she asked.

Johnny was walking back from the breakroom with a fresh cup of coffee when the receptionist called out to him. "Johnny, I'm not your answering service. It's another one of your bimbos on the phone. Do you want to take the call?"

"Of course, I'm always happy to talk to a bim—I mean, a constituent. Patch her through."

She connected the call while making a dramatic show of rolling her eyes, but then smiled at Johnny as he gave her a thumbs-up and a conspiratorial grin.

"Johnny Dunsmore. How can I help you?"

"Johnny, it's me, Dixie LeMar. I'm in town for the weekend."

* * *

It was a beautiful spring day in the Nation's capital. Everything was in full bloom, but it was the cherry trees that had captured Dixie's attention. There was a hint of humidity in the air and a gentle cool breeze that couldn't help but put one in a good mood. It certainly had for Dixie.

She was sitting on the steps of the Lincoln Memorial looking out over the Reflecting Pool and admiring the Washington Monument in the distance while waiting for Johnny to arrive. Her conference was over, and she had the afternoon off. She'd arrived early at the agreed upon meeting spot. It gave her time to . . . reflect.

Growing up she had despised Johnny because of the way he'd treated Randal. The image of Randal's humiliation the night she'd beaten him in that Fourth of July race all those summers ago had been burned into her memory. But with all things, the passage of time brought forth new perspectives.

The summer of the fateful race between Dixie and Johnny had been the summer before he left for boarding school. From then on and throughout college, Dixie had only seen Johnny when he came home for short stretches around Thanksgiving and Christmas, or for a week or two during the summer. He was spending his time on school-sponsored internships or at the summer home of one of his friends—at places with names like Montauk, Nantucket, and Martha's Vineyard, and more and more lately at his girlfriend's ranch.

Dixie noticed that sometime while in college, Johnny had changed. The brash cockiness of his youth had vanished and was replaced by an attitude of cool indifference. Was this simply a more mature form of the same cockiness? Was this simply how confident, successful men acted?

One thing she did know was that Johnny was always doing something interesting. If he wasn't going someplace cool, he was meeting interesting people. He was going places. That was clear to Dixie. That was clear to everybody. But nothing at home seemed to change for her. She was still the shy, moderately attractive girl with big boobs. Growing up without siblings or any real friends from school, though, she'd grown used to a lonely existence. There was one constant in her life: Randal. But she was beginning to wonder if she should expect more.

On the surface, Johnny had changed. He no longer bullied Randal as he had during their youth. But on those occasions during college when Johnny returned to South Carolina during a break from classes, if he were to ask Randal how he was doing, he did so in the way a politician might ask about disadvantaged youth. He feigned interest but couldn't feign empathy, not towards his twin brother.

She noticed Johnny approaching in the distance. She stood and waved. He stopped, tipped his Ray Bans up on his forehead, waved back, and quickened his pace. He was wearing khaki pants, a white oxford shirt, and a tie.

As he was walking towards her, she began to realize that she was seeing Johnny differently than how she had growing up. She could see him as others did—handsome, confident, ambitious, and as someone whose orbit one was pulled toward, as though compelled by the force of gravity.

Over the recent years, as her feelings towards him thawed, her feelings for Randal seemed to do the opposite. The sympathy she'd had watching him grow up in Johnny's shadow had slowly turned to pity. She began to interpret Randal's feelings towards Johnny not as those of one who justifiably lived in fear of him, but as those of a smaller, jealous man.

* * *

Johnny took the stairs two at a time and gave Dixie a big hug. He then took a step back and held her hands in his. "Let me look at you. You're beautiful. How are you? How's my kid brother?"

Dixie smiled, knowing that though they were twins, since Johnny had been delivered first, he always referred to Randal as his kid brother. "Oh, he's fine, I guess. He's all caught up in some kind of weird communist thing. Frankly, it's embarrassing."

"Yea, Dad mentioned it." He chuckled. "He said he'd take care of it. But how about you? What brings you to my neck of the woods?"

"I'm here with Cindy. You remember Cindy, right?"

"Of course."

"Well, we're here with our sorority for a national convention of Greek organizations seeking to align themselves with President Kennedy's vision for the Peace Corps," she recited as she moved her head from side-to-side. "We all had to memorize that last part."

"That's wonderful. Good to see you're getting involved. But how did you pull yourselves away? You must be awfully busy."

"The conference ended earlier today, and the bus taking us back to Columbia won't leave until tomorrow morning. Basically, we have the whole afternoon and evening to ourselves, and we thought . . ." She paused at the sight of Johnny's face. "Johnny, what is it? Did you forget something at the office?"

"No, why do you say that?"

"It's just that it looked like you were off thinking about something other than what I was saying."

"Oh, sorry about that. Say, would you and Cindy like to go to a campus party tonight?"

* * *

Roscoe had just dropped off the keg and enough grain alcohol to kill a horse.

"So, what does this girl Cindy look like?" asked Luis as he poured another gallon bottle of grain alcohol into the trashcan.

Johnny was standing on the other side, dumping in powdered Kool-Aid and bags of ice and water from a hose running through the kitchen window to a spigot outside.

"Does it matter?" answered Johnny. "Just turn on your foreign accent, talk about your yacht and you'll spend the night in her pants. I assure you."

Johnny and Luis were still roommates, even after Nadia's unfortunate demise, but one wouldn't call them friends. The truth was that Caroline would likely never have given Johnny a second chance, if it had not been for Luis. All during that Christmas break, Luis begged her to take Johnny back—one phone call after another. "Caroline, please, you don't understand, she was blackmailing him! She had him doing drugs and not just pot. The bad stuff. He was messed up. But trust me, he loves you." When she continued to take his calls, Luis knew she'd been swayed—now, she just needed to have her ego stoked. "He's nothing without you."

"Then why did he encourage her when she showed up here? Why didn't he tell her to go back to her little island?"

"He didn't encourage her. Okay, so they fooled around a little on spring break, but once she showed up here—and trust me, he was shocked—she began stalking him. And then she lied about being pregnant."

"Really, Luis. Are you sure?"

"Yeah, I asked my dad to call in a favor. He got a look at the autopsy. She *wasn't* pregnant."

"Oh, that's such a relief. Thank you, Luis, for telling me. I really do want to give him a second chance. He does need me, doesn't he?"

"That's what everyone on campus is saying—Johnny Dunsmore is nothing without Caroline Thistle."

"You're a good friend, Luis. You know that?"

Luis had kept up the charade that they were good friends, so what choice did Johnny have? In front of Caroline, how could he not swear that he owed Luis everything? Over time, Johnny began to see Luis not as a friend, but as an accomplice, a co-conspirator, in everything.

Luis was simply one more person Johnny could use. That was how life worked. That was how Johnny saw it.

"And why am I trying to bed her tonight?" asked Luis.

"To occupy her. It's time for me to balance the scales and right a wrong."

* * *

When Dixie and Cindy hopped out of their taxi, they could hear a small party going on inside the home whose address Johnny had given her. The front door was partially open, so the girls walked in, looking for him. They saw him across the room filling a drink for a girl out of a trashcan.

Dixie recognized the girl as Caroline, whom she had met a couple of years earlier when she visited Johnny over Labor Day weekend. Dixie took Cindy by the hand, and they made their way through the small crowd. Johnny saw them advancing and broke into a big smile as he placed his arm around Caroline.

"Girls, so good of you to come. Caroline, you remember Dixie, don't you? Randal's girlfriend. And this is her friend, Cindy."

"Of course. Dixie, so good to see you again. And Cindy, welcome," remarked Caroline.

On cue, Luis walked up.

"Cindy," Johnny went on, "I'd like you to meet my good friend and roommate, Luis Sanchez."

Luis could turn his Panamanian accent up or down depending on the circumstances and the audience. In this case, he turned it up, and it worked. Cindy nearly melted on the spot, thinking she was in the presence of a very charming and sophisticated young man. Caroline rolled her eyes and walked off to talk to others.

The party at Johnny's place continued for another two hours before everyone headed out to other parties across campus and in the private homes rented by Georgetown students. Johnny, Caroline, Dixie, and Luis, hand-in-hand with Cindy, made their way to New South Hall, where Johnny knew there would be more than a party or two going on. After a while, Johnny suggested they head to the bars on M Street.

Luis and Cindy were getting on quite nicely. At around one o'clock in the morning, Cindy pulled Dixie to the side and told her she was leaving with Luis. Luis assured Dixie that he would make sure Cindy made the bus the next morning. Dixie reminded her that it was already "the next morning," and that the bus was leaving in eight hours.

"I'll be fine, Dixie." She then leaned in close and whispered, "And isn't he fine?"

And with that, Cindy was gone.

"Say, I should be getting you back to your hotel," Johnny said to Dixie.

"That's not necessary. Just help me get a taxi."

"Nonsense," said Caroline. "Johnny, don't you listen to her. You make sure she gets safely back to her hotel like a good Southern gentleman."

"Okay. I guess you're right," said Dixie. "Thanks, Johnny. And it was good to see you again, Caroline."

The girls hugged goodbye while Johnny hailed a taxi. As the taxi pulled up, Johnny told Caroline that he would head home after dropping Dixie off and that he'd see her tomorrow at the library. She agreed and gave him a squeeze on the arm and a quick kiss as he held the taxi door for Dixie. They got in, and he waved to Caroline as the taxi pulled away from the curb.

But they didn't go to her hotel.

"It's still early," he said. "How about one last drink at Old Ebbitt Grill?"

"Sure," she said.

* * *

"Johnny, good to see you," said the bar tender as he wiped down the bar top in front of Johnny and Dixie. "The usual?"

"You too, Alfred. And yes, the usual, but make it two and make it extra special for my extra special guest tonight," Johnny said as he winked at Dixie.

"You got it."

"Wow, the bar tender knows your name. You must come here a lot," Dixie said.

Johnny noticed the look of awe on her face as she took it all in.

"It's a popular watering hole for those of us who work on the Hill."

"The Hill?"

"Oh, excuse me. *Capitol* Hill," explained Johnny. "In fact, just since entering, I've already spotted two congressmen and a senator," he lied.

"You're kidding! Where?" she asked as her head spun around.

"No, no, no. Just because they're public servants doesn't mean they don't deserve a little privacy every now and then."

Dixie asked questions about life in Georgetown and where he wanted to go to law school. Johnny, in turn, wanted to know all about her life, her sorority, and who she had met at the conference. Dixie provided answers, and he feigned interest in those answers—but the truth was, all he could think about was the night when they were all fourteen years old and she'd embarrassed him in front of everyone. This afternoon, it had dawned on him—what better revenge than to make her boyfriend a cuckold?

One drink turned into two, which turned into three. By the time Johnny was done telling her about the famous people he'd met and about the important work he was doing, she was defenseless against his charms. He took her back to her hotel, walked her to her room, and when she opened the door, he placed one hand on her shoulder, gently turned her towards him, and kissed her. She offered no resistance and pulled him closer. He stepped into her room, and she shut the door. The scales had been rebalanced.

Chapter 25

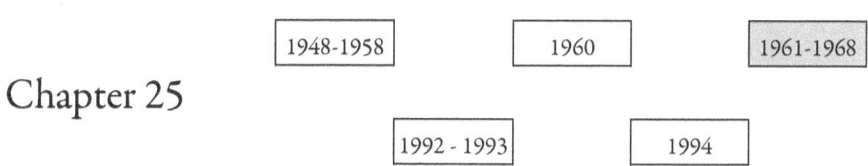

1965

Their night together in Washington, DC was the first of many for Johnny and Dixie. What had begun as revenge on Johnny's part had turned into pure lust. After college, Johnny attended law school at the University of Virginia. Colin had wanted Johnny to return to South Carolina for law school, where he would begin his political career, but Caroline's father, Terrance, argued that attending law school at the University of Virginia would open more doors and was more in keeping with the long game—the White House.

In the end, Terrance—or rather, Caroline—prevailed. Consequently, Johnny and Dixie only saw each other on those occasions when he returned to Columbia over a school break, which were rare since he spent his summers working in DC for law firms or judges—positions afforded to him by his excellent grades and his close relationship with the Thistle family.

Their separation in terms of both time and distance fueled their passion for each other. The cheapness of the hotels in which they met added to the intrigue and romance as far as Dixie was concerned. She believed the secrecy and intensity of their affair meant only one thing: Johnny loved her. She maintained this fiction throughout Johnny's courtship of Caroline. Not even their engagement and wedding ceremony could dispel her of the notion.

And oh, what a wedding it was.

* * *

Near the Nation's Capital
The week of June 7, 1965

The wedding was held at the Washington National Cathedral on Saturday, June 12th, with the reception to follow. But the wedding festivities began earlier that week when the Thistles opened their horse ranch to the wedding party and close family. The wedding party consisted of a dozen bridesmaids and a dozen groomsmen, so between this crowd and their significant others, plus close family, every room in the family compound was taken.

They spent their days riding, playing tennis, lawn bowling, or bird hunting, and the nights that followed were filled with gourmet meals and drinking into the early hours of the next day, only to be repeated. In a nod to tradition, Johnny and Caroline did not share a bed the week leading up to their nuptials, which only opened the door for Johnny and Dixie to sneak away for a quickie during the daylight hours, which they did—Dixie being Randal's plus one—often copulating in the barn.

Caroline's mother was in charge of the wedding, and she hired the best planners available. The only hiccup was the selection of the rooftop floor of the Hay-Adams Hotel as the wedding reception venue. Caroline was adamantly opposed to this location, due to it being where her fiancé had often met Island Girl. The memory still haunted her, though she knew she had no reason to doubt Johnny's loyalty again. The entire affair had shaken Johnny to the core. Johnny had been visibly upset, and it was only out of the goodness of her heart that Caroline had seen that Johnny was both repentant and in need of comfort. Luis made sure of that. She took him back and they were a couple again by the time they returned from Christmas break.

Caroline's mother was aware of the affair, but not the details, and Caroline intended to keep it that way, so she could hardly explain her opposition to the Hay Adams hotel. Instead, she argued hard for holding the reception at the Larz Anderson House owned by the Society of the Cincinnati.

"But Mother, don't you see? It's perfect. Father is a member of the Society. We'd be celebrating not just the birth of our life together, Johnny and I, but the birth of our country as well. What a wonderful backdrop, one we'll be able to trot out every election season. It's perfect."

"Dear, dear. You make a wonderful case. Maybe it's *you* who should run for office and not Johnny. But the space simply will not do. We're expecting a sit-down dinner for close to 400 people and the Larz Anderson House can only accommodate 130. So, you see, I have everything firmly under control. The Hay-Adams will do quite well."

And that was the end of that. They could have seated five hundred people if the venue could have handled it, for the wedding of Caroline Thistle was the highlight of the summer social calendar. The Thistles were nothing short of Southern blueblood aristocracy, a tier on the ladder of social hierarchy and political influence to which Colin Dunsmore aspired. They hailed from Richmond, Virginia, and their wealth was steeped in tobacco.

Over the previous 300 years, Thistles living in Virginia, who arrived from England as part of the great Puritan Migration, had grown, harvested, dried, aged, cured, rolled, packaged, transported, and sold tobacco in all forms, from leaves to cigarettes. Caroline's ancestors owned a company that became one of several assets of the American Tobacco Company when James Buchanon Duke bought it. The Thistles accepted stock in lieu of cash, a decision that made the family fabulously wealthy for generations to come, while still other Thistles were early investors in one of the first cigarette rolling machines.

There were so many fine people for the young couple to meet and greet at the reception, including senators, judges, congressmen, ambassadors, a few of Eleanor Thistle's theater friends from Broadway, and wealthy, highly sought-after donors to the worthiest of causes, political and charitable, that Caroline and Johnny hardly had time for their closest friends. So, when Caroline spied Johnny's old roommate, Luis Sanchez, across the room, gathered with their old college clique, she could hardly contain her excitement.

"Luis! Luis!" she called out. "It's so good of you to come."

"I was so very pleased to receive the invitation. How did you find me? You know, your beau here isn't the best when it comes to keeping up with some of his old friends," said Luis as he playfully punched Johnny in the shoulder.

"Don't I know it," said Caroline, who was standing on Johnny's other side, leaving him sandwiched between the two of them as they carried on their conversation. "I kept bugging and bugging Johnny here to find your address, your phone number, anything! Didn't I, sweetie?" she asked as she playfully rubbed the back of Johnny's neck. "Finally, I gave up, but then my father was able to track you down," Caroline explained. "He walked in one morning as we were going over the invitation list and heard me talk of you as one of Johnny's missing-in-action friends. It turns out he knows your father."

Luis smiled, placing an arm around Johnny's shoulders.

Johnny tried in vain to avoid his glare.

"Yes, he does," Luis said. "It seems your father, Caroline, has taken a keen interest in an area of the law in which my family has expertise."

"What area is that?" asked Caroline.

"International banking."

"Isn't that what you're studying?" she asked.

"Yes, he is," answered the handsome elderly man who had just joined their conversation.

Johnny still hadn't spoken a word and wasn't about to now.

"My dear, since your husband appears overwhelmed by the moment, allow me to introduce myself. I am Señor Sanchez, the Panamanian Ambassador to your lovely country and father of this young man," he explained, gesturing to Luis. "And yes, Luis is studying international banking and corporate law at the London School of Economics and he's doing quite well, I may add." Turning to Johnny, he continued, "And how are things with you, Johnny? It's been some time since we've seen each other, hasn't it? Now, when was the last time we were together?"

Johnny stood motionless, penned in by Luis on one side and Gilberto on the other.

His silence disturbed even Caroline.

"Johnny? What's wrong?" she asked.

"Graduation, I believe, Mr. Sanchez," answered Johnny, at last.

"Are you sure? I could have sworn it was over dinner one night in December when you and Luis were seniors. I was in town on business. We started the evening with drinks at my condo and then had a fine meal at Rive Gauche. Yes, I'm sure of it. You know, they know me there; it is my favorite restaurant in this city."

Gilberto never took his eyes off Johnny, letting the silence build.

"Well, maybe you are right," Gilberto responded. "Graduation week. Yes, of course, we would have seen each other that week. You and Luis were housemates and such good friends. Did Luis tell you the good news?"

"No, Father," said Luis. "I haven't had the chance yet."

"Oh, do tell, Luis," said Caroline.

"I am returning to America in the fall and will be taking a job with my father's firm. We're opening a branch in DC, and your father, Caroline, will be one of our DC office's first clients."

"Oh, how exciting. Then we'll all be able to see more of each other!" she said, glancing over at Johnny. Again, he was blank-faced and expressionless, though there appeared to be a gleam of sweat glistening on his upper lip.

"Of that, I can assure you," said Gilberto as he bowed, kissed Carline on the top of her hand, and slithered away.

* * *

Some might say that Johnny's drinking problem began the night he got married, but to anyone paying attention, it was clear that his issues began in college. Something snapped inside Johnny the night Nadia died. Caroline had taken him back, and as opposed to her being the object of pity on campus, as he had schemed with Luis, he was. She told him he could cry for his old flame since she had died horribly, but if he was going to do it then he needed to get it over with quickly and man up.

The curious thing was that Johnny didn't cry. Initially, his shock at seeing a dead body and of it being someone he'd known so well had ruled his emotions. But then, over dinner later that same night with Luis and Gilberto at Rive Gauche, as they carried on a conversation as if nothing had happened, the thing inside of him that snapped began to die.

What was it that snapped? What was it that had begun to die? Maybe it was that thread of humanity that Nadia had connected with—the thread of humanity inside Johnny that she had awakened. She was the first person he'd ever known for whom every human interaction wasn't a transaction. She'd feared there was a little Colonel Kurtz in him; she was right. For months, he was tormented by visions of her body draped across the bed, her head dangling over the edge and her bulging eyes staring blankly at him. But gradually, the visions faded. The drinking ensured that. So that was how the drinking started—first to forget, later to mask fear, then to fuel a false bravado, and ultimately, to hide from himself.

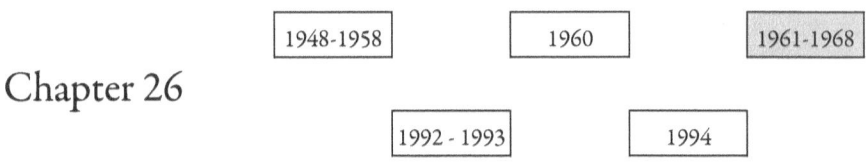

Chapter 26

FOUR YEARS LATER . . .
COLUMBIA, SOUTH CAROLINA
WEDNESDAY, MAY 22, 1966

"I am proud to introduce our president and fearless leader, Caroline Thistle Dunsmore."

Caroline rose from her table, leaving behind a picked-over fruit salad, and approached the front of the room as the audience politely clapped. Wearing an apricot-colored Cassini shift dress and matching pillbox hat, Caroline glided up the stairs with all the poise and grace of her perfectly coiffed bouffant hairstyle.

"She has some exciting news for us," said Dotty McQuillan, the long-standing historian and seemingly permanent secretary for the Columbia Neighborhood & Garden Beautification Society.

"Thank you, Dotty," said Caroline, positioning herself behind the podium and adjusting the microphone attached to it. "Ladies, thank you so much for being here today. I do have some exciting news. We've been hard at work planning next year's annual trip, and I am pleased to announce that we will be visiting the White House Rose Garden and East Garden. As many of you know, Bunny Mellon, at the behest of her dear friend, Jacqueline, recently redesigned these gardens. We will also be treated to a private tour of Bunny Mellon's gardens at her Oak Spring residence in Virginia."

The room broke into excited applause and general good cheer as the ladies turned towards each other, smiling and celebrating the thrilling news. A perk of Carloine's tenure as president was her ability to open doors of these sorts—for not everyone could. But she was a Thistle, which meant she could do things most people couldn't.

For the most part, Caroline loathed her time in Columbia. Her people were from Virginia, for goodness' sake. She missed the family ranch and taking quick jaunts to Martha's Vineyard or her family's beach house. But she was playing the role of the good wife, the dutiful wife, and all in the name of a good cause—putting Johnny in the White House. Once he got elected to Congress, they would buy a townhome in Georgetown, and she would be back amongst her people.

"Yes, isn't it wonderful?" she said, hands placed on each side of the podium, eyes roving from one side of the room to the other. Everyone continued clapping. Caroline's energy shifted, though, as she moved onto the next topic. "I'm afraid that I have some bad news, though. I was so hoping that my husband could address us today and share a few words. As you know he is a member of the Columbia City Council, and any day now is expected to *officially* announce that he will be running for the 74th district seat in the South Carolina House of Representatives."

Caroline, her hands still placed on each side of the podium, paused to give the ladies time to clap, which they did. She soaked in the grandeur of the moment. Now, with her right hand raised, signaling to them that the applause was both welcome and unexpected, she continued. "Yes, yes. We're very excited at the Dunsmore household, but I am afraid something unexpected has come up, and he can't join us today."

This time the clapping ceased, replaced by murmured disappointment.

"I know, I know. He works so hard. But he wanted me to let you know how much he appreciates each of you and the work we do."

Feelings of good cheer returned, along with polite clapping.

* * *

The tedious rhythm of the creaking bed frame and the rattle of the broken-down air-conditioner played as background music to the moaning of a sweaty Dixie LeMar rocking back and forth on all fours. She stared at the reflection in the mirror on the wall across the room of the man positioned behind her, as she met each of his lustful thrusts. She noticed he was staring at himself, too.

Afterward, while lying on the bed together and looking up at the ceiling of the seedy motel room off the state highway, where thankfully there was no mirror, Dixie started up again. "Look, Johnny, I'm tired of meeting like this. For one, it's hotter than six shades of hell in this room. Can't you at least get us a room with an AC that works? You told me you *own* this dump of a hotel."

"None of the AC units work well, sweetheart," Johnny answered casually as he rolled to his side and retrieved a cigarette from the bedside table.

"Why would you wanna own this dump, then?" she asked as she motioned for him to share the cigarette with her.

"Because it makes me money. Besides, I'm workin' on a solution to our little problem," he said as he passed the cigarette to her.

"And what *is* our little problem?" Dixie asked sarcastically.

"I've got my eyes on a little love nest for us. It'll be great. It's on Lake Murray. Very secluded. You can decorate it how you want. It'll be like home for us."

Dixie crossed her arms and rolled onto her side, facing away from Johnny.

Johnny rolled toward her and draped an arm over her waist. "Look. I know you want me to divorce Caroline, but I can't. We been over that. It'll kill any chances I have of getting elected. Our own private love nest is the best I can do right now. Besides, she's pregnant."

"Pregnant!" Dixie sat up and stared at Johnny. "Since when?"

"Now, calm down. I just found out myself."

"And when were you going to tell me?"

"I just did, for Pete's sake. Now lay off. What business is it of yours, anyway? You know I'm not leaving Caroline. Not *now*, anyway. Like I said, it will kill my chances of getting elected to the State House."

"But you don't love her. If you did, you wouldn't be porkin' me. And who cares about what goes on in the State House? It's not like y'all got any real power."

"Well, you'd be surprised—but this is just my first step. Governor of South Carolina is what I'm after, and then the White House."

"And you think the Thistle family can get you there?"

"Them and others."

Caroline slowly laid back down in bed next to Johnny, but turned so she was facing away from him again. "And where does that leave me?"

"You still gonna marry Randal, ain't ya?"

"Yeah. The date's set for next October. Not crazy about it, but everybody expects it. We've been friends for longer than I can remember."

"You love him?"

"Hell, I don't know. I know I used to . . . I guess I still do, but he makes it awful hard sometimes."

Johnny just laughed and reached for a new cigarette.

"What you laughin' at? You know it's true. What's with all this crazy political stuff he's gettin' into? In college, he was a communist. Remember that?" she asked as she rose up to her knees, leaned over Johnny, and grabbed the bottle of Old Grandad sitting on the bedside table next to the pack of Camels.

"Boy do I. But Dad put a stop to that, didn't he?" Johnny intercepted the bottle from Dixie, took a swig, and handed it back to her.

"He sure did," she said, laughing at the memory. "But now he's rambling on about some guy named Henry Marcuse. Says he's the father of the *New Left*, whatever that is. Randal has read all his books. I tell you what, from what he told me is in these books . . . that Marcuse fella has some crazy ideas."

They paused for a few moments, filling the silence with sighs of cigarette smoke and sips of bourbon. The air conditioner continued to wheeze.

Eventually, Dixie shrugged, shaking her head. "You gotta promise me your daddy won't fire him from his bank job."

"He could make it easier by showin' up and putting in an honest day's work," said Johnny.

"He thinks the work is beneath him. You should hear him go on about how he ain't appreciated."

"Don't worry. Daddy's workin' on something that'll benefit us all."

"Me too?" Dixie asked as she leaned over Johnny and swayed her chest seductively.

"You too," he answered with a wink and a smile.

* * *

Sweetwater Café in Columbia, South Carolina
Friday, June 10, 1966

Randal was seated in a booth reading a paperback when Dixie walked in. They had a standing lunch date at noon each Friday at the Sweetwater Café. Dixie loved the weekly Friday special: country fried steak, creamed corn, green beans, cornbread and cobbler for dessert—the fruit in the cobbler depending on the season. Randal didn't rise when she approached the table and instead kept on reading as she took a seat.

"Hi, honey. Have you been waiting long?" she asked.

"Yes, and you're late," he said as he tilted his book to the side and stared at her impatiently.

Dixie glanced at her watch. It was 12:03 p.m. She was *three minutes* late.

Randal put the book down and picked up the local free neighborhood paper. It was filled with news that he considered important, even if his daddy said it was a communist rag. "Did you see what they said about me?" he asked as he waved the paper at Dixie.

"No, dear. I didn't. Is it good?" she asked.

"You tell me," he answered smugly as he handed her the paper. "Start reading right here," he said and pointed to a paragraph halfway down the page. She took the paper and began to read. "Read it out loud, please."

Dixie looked up and saw Randal sitting erect with his hands folded neatly under his chin.

> "The march for feminism and free love held last week in the city park was a grand success, and its success is due to the tireless work of one man—Randal Dunsmore. Randal Dunsmore, like his father and brother, has a heart for the downtrodden and it shows. This reporter caught up with Randal and asked him what drove him. "It's simple really. I have a heart for the victims of this world, and I will be their champion."

"Do your parents know about this?" she asked. "Does your boss at the bank know about this?"

"Why do you have to bring them into it?" He slouched back into the booth and folded his arms across his chest. "I finally have something that is mine—*all* mine. The people who attend these rallies and sit-ins love me. Don't you see that?"

Dixie looked on sympathetically. She knew what it was like to crave love and attention, and she'd watched Randal grow up in his brother's shadow. But of all positions to take, all places to stake his claim, this wasn't it. "It's just that I worry that all your work on these rallies and the causes that are important to you will interfere with your job."

"You don't have to worry about my job. Dad told me he has something better lined up for me," Randal said as he picked up his fork and knife.

"That's great, sweetheart. What is it?" Dixie was trying her best to sound upbeat and supportive.

"I don't know. He just told me to meet him at his lawyer's office this afternoon."

* * *

*Law Offices of Ernest, Billings, and Treemont in Columbia, South Carolina
Later that afternoon*

"Bart, I'd like to introduce you to our son, Randal. And Randal, this man across the desk from us is someone you'll be seeing a lot more of—Mr. Bartholemew Tremont."

Bartholomew Tremont was a first-rate attorney specializing in tax planning, trusts, and estate work, and he spent a good deal of time representing charitable foundations.

"Randal, it's a pleasure to meet you," he said, extending a hand for a handshake. "I've heard a lot about you from your parents. We go way back, your father and I."

Bart had, indeed, heard a great deal about Randal, because Colin had come to him seeking advice on hands and knees. He and Barbara, frankly, didn't know what to do with Randal. He could barely hold onto a low-level managerial role at a bank in which they were the majority owners.

While Colin could handle criticism concerning nepotism, he couldn't handle Randal's bent towards activism. Anti-war protests and civil rights marches to end Jim Crow laws were in vogue in their Democratic Party circles, so he was fine with that—but advocating for communism or this New Left crap was a bridge too far. Something had to be done.

Besides, Colin couldn't forget about Terrance Thistle's warning at the JFK inauguration—he knew he couldn't let *anything* derail Johnny's chances for the White House.

"Son, we asked you to meet us here today because we have some exciting news for you," said Colin.

"That's right, darling," Barbara tacked on.

Randal's dull gaze moved from someplace over Bart's shoulder, out the window, then back to his mother and his father.

"Your mother and I have established a foundation to support causes we believe you will identify with."

Barbara and Colin looked at their son for a reaction of some sort. They received nothing.

Colin shifted in his seat and looked at Barbara for support.

"And the best part is—we are making you the chairman," she added.

That information evoked a response in Randal—a small one, but one that Colin noticed, and so, in relief and a bit of hope, Colin chimed in, "That's right, Randal. You are going to be the chairman of the Dunsmore Family Foundation. Your mother and I have seeded it with a generous donation of $8,000,000."

Randal was no longer slouching in his chair.

"Well, what do you think, son?" asked Colin.

This news came out of the blue, so a pause on Randal's part was not unexpected. Of course, he would have questions and thoughts. Who wouldn't?

"So, *I'll* decide how the money is spent?" he asked.

"Yes. Well, sort of. The Foundation will have a committee to vet all such decisions, but you'll be on that committee," his father answered.

"And who else?"

"Your mother and I—and Mr. Tremont, of course. And others."

"And I get to decide how the money in the foundation is invested, right?"

"Yes. Well, sort of. Again, we'll have a committee for that, too. But again, you'll be on that committee."

Randal's gaze passed from Bart to his parents and back. "So, this job you are giving me is very important, isn't it? I mean, an important job not just for me, but for the whole family."

"Oh, yes, indeed, son. Very important," said Colin as he looked to Barbara for affirmation and support.

"Yes, dear. Very important," added his mother.

"And, of course, the Dunsmore Foundation will certainly reflect well on Johnny, won't it?" asked Randal.

"Absolutely," answered his mother.

"You'll be performing a valuable service for the family," added his father.

"Well, an important job like this must certainly come with a substantial salary. It only makes sense."

Colin and Barbara did not answer the question but instead looked to Bart for help.

"Randal, your family's foundation must file records with government agencies, and your compensation will be public knowledge. So, it simply wouldn't look right in the public's eye for you to receive the kind of salary you might be hoping for. I'm sure you understand," said Bart.

"I'm sure I don't," said Randal as he sat straighter in his chair, with his hands folded neatly in his lap.

"Randal, not to worry," said Colin. "This brings us to the other reason for our meeting today. Your trust."

"I *have* a trust?" asked Randal.

"You most certainly do. Your mother and I set it up when you were born. The beneficiaries of this trust are you and your brother. Upon turning twenty-five, you can begin receiving distributions from the trust and do so for the rest of your life."

"Why can't I just have the money now?" he asked.

This really is infuriating, thought Colin. Here he was, setting up the dolt for life, and all he got in return was a sense of entitlement and bitterness.

"Well, your mother and I thought it best to do it this way. You see, we set aside money years ago, and we've been investing it ever since. The size of the portfolio is quite large now and will support a very generous lifestyle for you. Furthermore, your children and Johnny's will be the next generation of beneficiaries when you die. You see, we are creating generational wealth that will allow the Dunsmore clan to continue in its position of power and prominence in the community for generations to come."

"But I get to decide how the money is invested, right? And how much I can take out each year, right?"

"Not exactly. Again, there will be committees for this—trustees, they're called."

"So, you see, Randal," said Bart, "you won't need a large salary from the foundation. The trust will take care of you—for life."

Colin studied his son, wondering what in the world he was pondering.

"Okay. I'll do it. I'll be the chairman of the Dunsmore Family Foundation," Randal said.

Colin looked at Barbara. They shared a smile that was mixed with just a bit of exhaustion. Then, he glanced at Bart with a slight eyeroll, as if to say, "*I can't believe this is my son!*"

Chapter 27

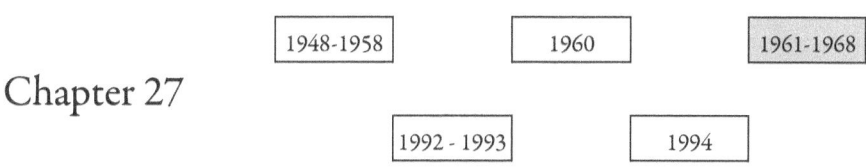

COLUMBIA, SOUTH CAROLINA
1966

Dixie and Randal were married in October. At first, the marriage gave Dixie hope—hope for a life with purpose. Randal, in his own estimation, was thriving as the chairman of the Dunsmore Family Foundation. Despite being initially impressed by the title, Dixie later was coming to understand that Randal did nothing. The perks Randal enjoyed, however, were seductive. They were fawned over by the press, wooed by the biggest charities around, and invited to every black-tie charity event in town, as well as those held in toney Charleston.

What became plainly evident to Dixie was that the charities that helped people in the ways they needed it most—homeless shelters, food banks, free medical care clinics—hosted the blandest parties. The national organizations that sought to cure diseases or save puppies or the environment for all of humanity, on the other hand, had the largest budgets for parties and entertainment. Randal was drawn to *those* sorts of charities. So, while he paid lip service to the poor, the Foundation's grants to the less glamorous charities were meager, at best. Gone were the heady days of his college youth, marching across campus, calling for an end to poverty and injustice.

It didn't take long for Dixie to grow weary of her new life, for it resembled, more and more, an updated version of how her life had been growing up. As an only child, Dixie lived a cloistered life, locked in a very small world. Often, an only child will mature more quickly than children with siblings because they spend such a large percentage of their formative years with their parents and in the world of adults. Not so for Dixie. She was raised by nannies who loved her, but who saw their job as caring for her as one would a small dog. The care she experienced as a child was steeped in condescension, and the weight of this upbringing seeped deep into her pores, rendering her emotionally handicapped, always seeing herself as being in the care of others.

As Dixie grew up, responsibility for her care did not travel far. Financially speaking, she was more than provided for. Her parents had set up a very generous trust for her benefit and heirs upon her death. The trust investments and disbursements were managed by her father, and the trust document spelled out that these trustee responsibilities would remain his until Dixie wedded and had a child, at which point her husband would take over.

As for children, Dixie wanted them, just not with Randal. It wasn't just the idea of Randal being the father figure in her children's lives that left her cold; it was also the idea of Randal siring the children to begin with. Their sex life was less than satisfactory and certainly not anything to brag about. And then there was Johnny. Now *that* was sex!

While arrogance may have been Johnny's first vice, followed closely by alcohol, coming in a close third was Dixie. His marriage to Caroline did not diminish his desire for Dixie. In contrast, when Dixie and Randal were married, Dixie tried to go straight and resist Johnny's invitations. But it was pointless. Had she married anyone else, there would be no way to explain why she was always around Johnny and the rest of the family. Johnny had hinted as much during her engagement to Randal when she was getting cold feet. In fact, their proximity to each other at family dinners and get-togethers heightened the sexual tension between the two of them.

Johnny's drinking convinced Dixie that he was miserable being married to Caroline, which only strengthened her resolve to wait out what she referred to privately with Johnny as his "sham marriage," at which point she'd often declare, "Johnny, you'll come running to me one day, I just know it."

The irony was that Dixie's marriage to Randal was also a sham. Growing up, Dixie and Randal were drawn to each other. They were fellow back-row kids in the classroom—a distinction they carried with them through much of life. Dixie felt sorry for Randal growing up, but their familiarity with each other bred contempt over time. Her empathy for Randal morphed into pity, and his compassion for her turned into loathing. Once married, when he complained about how Johnny was the Golden Child, she'd comment, "Then why don't you do something about it?" He always said he would; he never did. And not once did he ever encourage her to stand up to her parents and demand they notice her. Why would he? If she were to develop some level of self-respect, she might long for someone above his station in life. No, it was best for Randal if he kept Dixie down with him.

So, what had begun as revenge on Johnny's part—having sex in college with Dixie, his brother's girlfriend—turned into revenge on Dixie's part, when she had sex with Johnny, her husband's brother.

Chapter 28

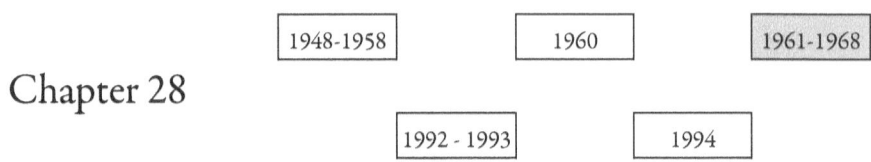

DUNSMORE ELECTION HEADQUARTERS IN COLUMBIA,
SOUTH CAROLINA
MONDAY, JULY 11, 1967

"Did everyone enjoy their Fourth of July break?" asked Caroline. Heads around the table nodded in unison. "Good. Then let's get to work. The election is going to be here before you know it. Stephen, what do you have for us?"

Stephen worked for a public relations firm out of Washington, DC. The Thistles had worked with them before and pushed hard for the Dunsmores to hire them. Seated around the table were Johnny and his father Colin, two of Stephen's associates, and Johnny's campaign manager. Johnny was the face of the campaign, the man of the people, that rare soul born with a magnetic personality, one that could both attract and repel. Johnny understood his role and that of everyone around the table—except for the campaign manager's, because it was Caroline who ran the show.

"The Dunsmore name is well known in South Carolina," said Stepehen. "That's not our problem. Our problem is your brand. Statewide polling—in the 74th District, specifically—indicates that folks know the Dunsmore name but think of you more as a business than a family. There's no humanity associated with the Dunsmore name."

"That's why we started that damn foundation," barked Colin.

"And that has helped," Stephen said, "but we need more. Voters need to see you as church-going people. They need to see you sitting in the pews, dropping off canned foods on the front porches of folks in need. That kind of stuff."

"Well, I don't want to, but I'll do it," said Colin.

"Colin, it's not necessary for you and Barbara to do anything. The voters want to see Johnny and Caroline attending church and performing acts of civil service."

Colin breathed a sigh of relief and Caroline nodded her head, taking notes. "And do you have a church picked out for us?"

"We do," Stephen answered. "And we need Randal and his wife Dixie sitting right next to you every Sunday. Those optics will mesh nicely with their role as the state's leading philanthropist."

* * *

On a state highway outside of Columbia . . .
Thursday, August 11, 1967,

The humidity weighed on Dixie like a water-soaked wool sweater. At church the previous Sunday, she had signed up to deliver some much-needed supplies to a family the congregation had adopted.

By the time Dixie had placed the diapers and canned goods in the backseat of her Pontiac Bonneville, she was in a full sweat. She went back inside to grab her purse and, on the way back to the car, noticed the heavy rain clouds in the distance.

"Oh, good Lord, we could use some rain."

She got in, started the car and pulled out of the driveway.

A half hour later, she was driving down a lonely state highway. As she drove, she reflected on her life in general, and on her life with Randal, specifically. She knew revenge sex was no basis for a relationship, and that was how matters had started off between her and Johnny.

But I want more from life, she thought. *I want more from Johnny. I want a life with Johnny.*

Dixie had complained to Randal that she was bored and didn't have any girlfriends to spend time with. "Sure, you do," he replied. "Last Saturday night, didn't we meet that couple raising money for the new museum in Charleston? Didn't it seem like I really hit it off with the husband, George? He was awfully impressed with the work I'm doing for the Family Foundation, don't you think? You could be friends with his wife, Charlotte." *Randal,* she thought, *you just don't get it. They aren't real friends; they just want your foundation's money.*

Dixie began to slow down, knowing she was getting close to the turnoff. That was when she saw Johnny's car parked towards the back of one of the many seedy motels she'd visited with him before. Only a few other cars were in the lot, and one was parked next to Johnny's.

No, it can't be . . . He wouldn't.

Dixie looked over her shoulder for any traffic behind her and then pulled off to the side of the two-lane state highway, made a U-turn, spraying gravel in her wake as she headed back towards the motel. She crept down the parking lot and parked a dozen spaces down from Johnny's car. She stepped out of her car taking care to shut the car door quietly and eased her way down the wall and peeked inside. The curtains were not closed completely, affording her a view of an all-too-common scene: Johnny positioned behind a woman on all fours. But this time, Dixie wasn't the woman, and neither was Caroline.

Dixie could have banged on the door and tried to barge in, but she didn't. She could have calmly waited outside and confronted Johnny, but she didn't. She was broken and didn't know what to do. How could she have fooled herself into thinking Johnny loved her? How could she have been so stupid?

Dixie made it back to her car and drove away. She continued down the state highway with a car full of diapers and missed the turnoff she'd been focused on finding just a few minutes earlier. The tears flowed and flowed. Sadness overcame her. But her mood turned into white-hot anger, and she banged her hands and her head on the steering wheel. If it weren't for the horn of the oncoming eighteen-wheeler, she likely wouldn't have swerved in time to avoid a head-on collision. Rattled by the near miss, she pulled into the parking lot of a small roadside diner. After collecting herself, she went inside.

The bell on the door jingled as she stepped inside. The waitress, taking care of the table closest to the door, turned her head over her shoulder to greet her. "Afternoon," she said. If she picked up on the fact that Dixie had been crying, it didn't show in her expression. "Have a seat. Someone will be right with ya."

Dixie made her way to the booth at the back of the diner—as far away from the others as possible. She sat with her back to the front door so no one could see her. The tears returned in full force, and she buried her face into the privacy of her hands.

The waitress placed a menu on the table, moved on to refill water glasses at another table, and did not notice Dixie crying.

A few minutes later, she returned. "What'll you have?"

Dixie's head was pitched forward, resting in her hands, obscuring her face. She said nothing. The waitress leaned down a bit to get a better look at Dixie. Then, she shrugged, grabbed the menu off the table, and headed up front to check on the others.

Dixie remained seated. She wanted to disappear, to be invisible. She tried to do just that. Then, a young man walked up and stood next to the booth where Dixie was sitting. She slowly lifted her head and saw a busboy wearing an apron and holding a glass of iced tea.

"For you, ma'am," he said, softly.

"Thank you."

"Stay as long as you like."

Dixie smiled at the young man, who looked down at his hands as he dried them on his apron and then returned to the kitchen.

* * *

Dixie never ordered anything that day and was not presented with a check for the iced tea, but she left two quarters on the tabletop anyway. She returned the next day, hoping to see the young man again. He was there. This time, she ordered the chicken salad plate and learned his name: Jeremiah Taylor.

She returned every day for the next week—each time ordering the same thing, each time trying to talk with Jeremiah. There was something about Jeremiah she was attracted to. He was kind to her. *Maybe it's as simple as that,* she thought.

Finally, after learning when he got off from work, she sat in the parking lot and waited for him to leave. He did and started walking down the road. She pulled out of the parking lot and slowed the car with her window lowered as she pulled up next to him.

"Jeremiah, where you goin'?"

"To the bus stop, ma'am."

"Jeremiah, we're the same age. You don't have to 'ma'am' me. Can I give you a ride somewhere?"

"No, ma'am."

"I said enough with the ma'ams. Now get in. It's 'bout to start rainin'."

Jeremiah looked at the clouds about to burst open and got in. Dixie pulled back onto the road, and before long, it did start raining. The rain came down in sheets, and Dixie pulled off onto the side of the road and put the car in park. "I don't like drivin' in storms like this. Can't hardly see where I'm goin'."

Jeremiah sat quietly in his seat, his eyes focused on the windshield. "It's for the best."

"What is?" Dixie asked. The car was still running, and she'd left the AC on but turned down the fan one notch so she could hear him more clearly. *He's so soft-spoken,* she thought.

"The rain."

"That's for sure. The heat's takin' a toll on me," she said.

"That's not what I'm talking about. With the rain, no one can see us together."

"And why would that be such a problem?" she asked.

Jeremiah turned and looked at her and held her gaze. "In case you haven't noticed, I'm a Black man and you're a White woman—a right pretty White woman—and we're in South Carolina."

"Fiddlesticks. I don't care."

"*You're* not the one they'd be coming for." Jeremiah reached down to pick up his backpack from the footwell. "It looks like the rain is slowing, so I'm gonna get out and walk from here. I appreciate your kindness."

"Jeremiah, you are the first man in a long time—and a stranger, to boot—who I can remember being genuinely kind to me." Dixie could see the confusion on his face. She reached over, placed her right hand on his left forearm and continued. "That day you brought me a glass of iced tea—it was nothin' to you, but to me, it was somethin'. You didn't have to. There was nothin' in it for you, and in the world I live in, no one does anything unless there's somethin' in it for them."

Jeremiah, with his backpack in his lap, cocked his head to one side and shot her an odd look. "What world you talking about? The White man's world?"

"Goodness, no. I've met some fine folks along the way, just none in my family, or my husband's family, or in the company they keep."

"You married?" he asked.

"Yes."

"Um, who to?"

"Randal Dunsmore," she answered.

With that, Jeremiah turned and opened the passenger side door. "Lordy, I'm getting out of this car, for sure. I gotta be goin', ma'am."

Dixie lunged and tried to grab hold of his arm again. "Jeremiah, please. Please, just sit with me a little longer and talk to me."

Jeremiah gave her a look that indicated he knew better than to play with fire, but she was beautiful, and it looked like the rain was starting up again.

Chapter 29

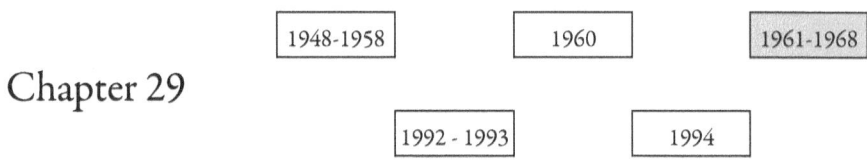

COLUMBIA, SOUTH CAROLINA
1968

As 1968 rolled in, the nation was a percolating cauldron of emotions, threatening to boil over at any moment. The situation in Vietnam appeared to be a war—or was it a police action and one without end? Domestically, racial tensions worsened by the day. Was Martin Luther King a unifier or a divider? Was he a communist, or were the reports just rumors spread by J. Edgar Hoover?

Johnny had distanced himself from his years working for Olin Johnston—an unrepentant segregationist. Johnny was now an ardent supporter of the civil rights movement. This position put him at the forefront of the growing influence of the more youthful members of the Democratic Party. The Party itself was in a state of flux: the older generation and established powerbrokers clung to segregation, while many politicians elsewhere cloaked themselves in the cause of the poor Blacks across the South and throughout the inner cities of the North.

For all of Johnny's blustering about voting rights, civil rights, and inequality, Dixie knew him to be of a different mind. It wasn't that he was a racist. He wasn't. He simply didn't care about them, or anybody other than himself, for that matter. The poor condition of Black neighborhoods and schools was simply a platform for him to campaign on and nothing more. Dixie was sure that the more dire their circumstances, the better it was for him, at least in his mind.

Dixie had grown to abhor politics, politicians, and the entire Dunsmore clan. Johnny's campaign for the South Carolina House of Representatives consumed the entire Dunsmore family. Randal was busy running the Dunsmore Foundation—at least he *thought* he was running it—and Johnny's side of the family was gearing up to run for the South Carolina House of Representatives. The election was less than a year away, and one would've thought Johnny was campaigning to be the next pope, given how seriously they took themselves.

"This is just the beginning, son, but one we have to get right," his father would say. "I can see the road to the White House laid right out in front of us. You're gonna win this year, then win reelection and hold that office while you run for the South Carolina Senate. Then, the US House of Representatives in '78 and the US Senate in '82. Win reelection in '88. In 1990, you'll come home and become governor of South Carolina. Then, after that—well, we'll have to see. Maybe serve two terms as governor and then run for president or go ahead and throw your hat in the ring in 1992 for the White House."

Dixie had heard it all before. They all had. For the first time ever, the brothers seemed to have carved out space for each other. They were both caught up in the excitement of the upcoming campaign. The Dunsmore Foundation fed Randal's feelings of entitlement and kept the Dunsmore name in the news.

The bottom line was that no one paid any attention to Dixie. Dixie never told Johnny she had caught him with another woman at the roadside motel. She broke it off with him, explaining that she wanted to build a life with Randal. "I owe him that much," she said. Johnny was miffed that anyone would turn him down, but he hardly had time to argue with her, between his marriage, his campaign, the family's business interests, and his other extracurricular liaisons.

Randal's arrogance and sense of entitlement had blossomed as soon as he was granted his lofty position at the top of the Dunsmore Family Foundation—which meant he'd also come to turn a blind eye to Dixie. Part of her wondered if Randal knew about her affair with Johnny and simply didn't care. Or was it that he was so detached from reality that he didn't even notice?

Deep down, she knew Randal had done nothing to earn the attention of others, and it was this reality he had to keep at bay. To do that, he'd taken to using one of his older brother's oldest tactics: belittling others in the name of uplifting himself. He'd developed a level of contempt for those around him. And for those closest? Cruelty. And who was the closest? *Dixie*.

Dixie was losing all patience with the Dunsmores. The last straw was presented to her one evening as she was getting ready for bed. She was watching television on the sofa and Randal was sitting in his recliner reading the paper.

"I'm heading up to bed. Do you want to keep the TV on?" she asked.

"No, bedtime sounds good. What do you say I join you?"

Dixie knew what he meant, but she just wasn't in the mood, partly because getting pregnant now seemed like her duty to the entire Dunsmore clan. Her in-laws were constantly reminding her that children and large families polled well.

She smiled demurely at Randal, and he followed her upstairs.

The next morning, Dixie was up first. She was in the kitchen and when she heard Randal in their bathroom, she ran to the bottom of the stairs. "Randal, honey, I have a bit of a headache. Could you bring me a few aspirin on the way down?"

"Sure thing."

The bottle in Randal's medicine cabinet was empty, so he rummaged through Dixie's trying to find some aspirin amongst all the bottles, lotions and jars.

A few minutes later, Randal entered the kitchen holding up a prescription bottle in his hand. "What the hell is this?" he demanded to know.

Dixie was cooking breakfast at the stove, and she looked over her shoulder and saw Randal holding her bottle of birth control pills. She turned back to the stove, flipped the pancakes, and said nothing.

Randal stormed out of the kitchen and flushed them down the toilet in the bathroom around the corner. He returned to the kitchen and stood silently until Dixie turned toward him, her apron securely around her waist and a spatula in her hand. "I'm calling your doctor and the pharmacy and telling them to never fill a prescription of birth control pills for you again *unless I tell them to*. Got that? You *will* have a child. Johnny and Caroline already have two. Do you understand me?"

"I understand. I'll have a child," she answered and turned her back on Randal and resumed her duties in the kitchen.

"Good." And with that, Randal stormed out of the house.

But it will be on my terms.

* * *

It was January, and Randal was in Charleston for the week. Dixie took a chance that Johnny would be working late. His office was in downtown Columbia in a building the Dunsmores owned. Johnny's campaign had rented one floor out to serve as his campaign headquarters. The chances of Johnny being there were strong.

Dixie drove by the building and saw that the light in his corner office was on, and his car parked in his reserved spot. She circled around to the back of the building, parked, and entered through a door she knew Johnny used on weekends and when working late. She had used it before. A few minutes later, she walked out of the elevator and into Johnny's office, where he was sitting on the sofa surrounded by folders and stacks of paper.

"I've missed you," she said.

Johnny smiled and stood up from the sofa as Dixie sauntered his way, and he reached for her hands and drew her to him.

* * *

Dixie got pregnant in February. She wanted to keep the news to herself until she began to show, but Randal was too excited and would not cooperate. When Martin Luther King was assassinated, he decided that the moment was too good to pass up and he leaked to the press that Randal Dunsmore, Chairman of the Dunsmore Foundation, and his wife Dixie were due in November and that if their child was a boy, they would name him Martin, and if a girl, Martina, in honor of Martin Luther King.

As for the child's paternity, Randal had every reason to believe the child was his. Why wouldn't he? But Johnny and Dixie had been hot and heavy as of late, and Johnny was having a big laugh, knowing it could be his—that was, until Dixie refused to abort the child.

* * *

The African Methodist Episcopal Church in Columbia, South Carolina
Sunday, April 7, 1968

The church was at capacity. Everyone arrived to mourn Martin Luther King's death earlier that week. The Dunsmores—Johnny and Caroline and Randal and Dixie—were in attendance so everyone could witness their deep sorrow. Even Colin and Barbara made it. The PR firm insisted.

When the service was over the church doors opened, Johnny and Caroline, arm-in-arm, were some of the first to exit. When Johnny saw the reporters and TV cameras amassed on the church lawn, he made a beeline for the wall of microphones. With Caroline holding a handkerchief and leaning on his left shoulder, he raised his right hand and very solemnly pronounced, "Please, please. This is a time for mourning." And then the two of them turned and walked away slowly, their heads bowed.

As they were doing so, Johnny spied Dixie talking to the pastor. He turned to Caroline. "Honey, I see the President of the local chapter of the NAACP standing over there by the coffee and donuts. Why don't you go chat him up while I have a word with the pastor?" Caroline smiled, gave him a quick peck on the cheek and made her way over to the coffee.

Johnny set off to say hello to the pastor. After having a quick word, he grabbed Dixie by the shoulder and maneuvered her away from the crowd and out of the way.

"What do you think you're doing?" he asked.

"What on earth do you mean?" Dixie was standing perfectly still with her hands folded in front of her.

"You know what I'm talking about," he said as he looked this way and that way to ensure they could not be overheard. "You're not going to have the baby, are you?"

"Of course, I am. Why wouldn't I? It's what everybody wants."

"Look, Dixie. Be reasonable. You and I both know the baby could be mine," said Johnny.

"Probably is," she answered.

"Then you gotta get rid of it. It could look like me."

"Wouldn't that be something?" said Dixie with a grin on her face.

"I'm serious. Now, I know a doctor who will take care of it and make it look like a miscarriage."

"I'm sure you do. But I'm having the baby." Dixie turned and started to walk away but Johnny grabbed her by the arm.

"Now, I mean it! I'm being very serious. Have you thought of what people will say if the baby looks like me?" asked Johnny.

"Yes. I have," she said as she pulled her arm free and walked away.

* * *

Dixie's defiance masked her sorrow. The joy that should have accompanied her pregnancy did not. On the contrary, for Dixie, the summer of 1968 was one of trepidation and a growing sense of loneliness. Throughout it all, Jeremiah was Dixie's life raft. Dixie would sit in the booth for hours, reading a book and waiting for Jeremiah to get off work. Carpentry was his true love; he only worked at the diner when he wasn't on a job site.

Sometimes they would take a drive down a lonely dirt road. Other times Dixie would bring a blanket, and they would find a place under a tree and talk. Were it not for him and the time they spent together, the harsh truth about Johnny, his selfishness, and who he was would have crushed her. She thought that getting pregnant under a cloud of suspicion and the anxiety it was causing Johnny would have brought her a sense of retribution. It did not.

Her marriage offered no relief, either. Randal and Dixie were moving quickly through stages. After the wedding, Randal and Dixie shared a certain bliss and she was hopeful for a fulfilling life filled with children, romance, affection, and purpose. But six months later, the romance was stilted, affection non-existent, and the desire for children strictly utilitarian.

Things might have turned out differently if only someone had noticed her perilous emotional state. No one did. Dixie went into labor early, and it was a difficult delivery, complicated by the fact that she was pregnant with twins—a girl who they named Rebeca and a boy who was named Joseph. Dixie died from complications and did not live to hold her children. The boy, Joseph, died two days later.

The Dunsmore family trumpeted their grief and rode it to victory that November when Johnny Dunsmore won the South Carolina 74th District seat in the House of Representatives. As for Randal, he told folks that everywhere he looked, he saw another painful reminder of his dear departed wife, so he took his baby daughter Rebeca and moved to Charleston.

PART FOUR

Ecclesiastes 12: 14 (14) For God will bring every deed into judgment, with every secret thing, whether good or evil.

Chapter 30

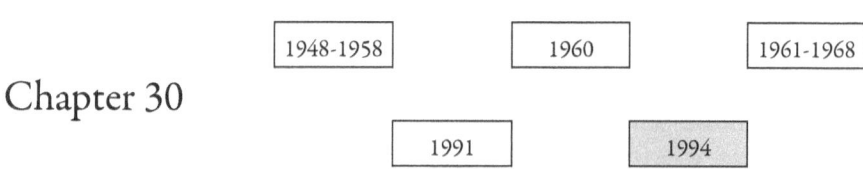

THE HIBERNIAN HALL IN CHARLESTON IN SOUTH CAROLINA
FRIDAY, JUNE 10, 1994

Walker's head snapped around, looking first at Eddie and then back at Governor Dunsmore and Luis Sanchez. *"What* did you just say?"

"I said, 'Mr. and Mrs. Luis Sanchez,'" answered Eddie. "That's the name of the couple y'all are gawking at."

Walker was jolted by the reality that Luis Sanchez is the name of the man he had been warned about just twenty-four hours ago while sitting in the living room of the Caribbean banker, Nigel Pinder. The last words of the mysterious gentlemen on the phone, Nash, still echoed in his mind: *"Be careful. One man you don't want to underestimate is Luis Sanchez."*

He looked back to Eddie. "You described them as a power couple. Say more."

"Well, Luis and his father, Gilberto, are the two names behind one of the world's fastest growing and most influential law firms. Their specialty is international corporate law and offshore banking. The firm is called Sanchez and Sanchez, and they work closely with lobbyists and the congressmen those lobbyists own, men with inordinate influence over banking and securities laws in this country."

"And the wife?" asked Isabelle.

"Yeah. She looks familiar," said Eddie's wife, Vanessa.

"I'm sure she does. Her name is Dominique Agdall. She was a *Sports Illustrated* swimsuit model about twenty years ago," said Eddie.

"I remember her now. She was on the covers of *Vogue*, *Glamour*, and other women's magazines," Vanessa said.

"That may be so," Eddie said. "But today she hosts parties where she raises thousands of dollars for political candidates and environmental and social causes."

"And Eddie, why do you know so much about them?" asked Walker. "Or is it the AG's office that has a special interest in them?"

"Both, and because of the company they keep."

"We need to talk," said Walker, but before they could, the crowd's attention was drawn to the front of the room, where the night's first speaker was taking the stage.

"Shush, you two," said Vanessa. "Randal Dunsmore is about to speak, and I want to hear what he has to say."

Randal Dunsmore stood with his hands clasped in front of him and his head bowed as the announcer—Natalie Hawthorne Cummings—both introduced him to the party and listed off a slew of his personal and professional achievements. Natalie was known about town as a matron of the arts and a champion of all things environmental. Tonight, the crowd had gathered to celebrate her for helping raise two million dollars to fight "irresponsible coastal development that poses an existential threat to our delicate ecosphere," as she put it.

"The opportunity tonight to stand before the fine people of Charleston—dare I say the *finest* for their unwavering support for the arts and the beautiful Lowcountry ecosphere—is one I shall forever cherish and take to my grave. And none of it would have been possible without the generous support of the Dunsmore Family Foundation," she said, concluding her introduction.

She expertly took two steps back from the podium and turned to applaud Randal Dunsmore as he approached the podium. He paused to air-kiss her once on each cheek before she turned and exited the stage. As Randal stood behind the podium, his hands confidently gripping each side, he began with remarks he had delivered countless times before.

"It gives me great pleasure to stand here today as the chairman of the Dunsmore Family Foundation. For the last thirty years, our family has humbly risen each morning, motivated by an unyielding desire to help those most vulnerable in our community. From my brother's office at the governor's mansion, to the grassroots across this fine state yearning for a better tomorrow—grassroots which we are proud to water and nurture from my offices—the Dunsmore name is one you have always been able to count on."

In anticipation of the inevitable applause, Randal paused, eyes roving over the crowd as if to thank each and every person clapping. "Tonight," he went on, "I am pleased to announce that on top of the two million dollars we helped Natalie raise, we are contributing an additional fifty thousand."

More applause followed. Everything was perfect, neatly scripted, that is until a disturbance arose from the back of the room.

Someone was yelling something, and not in an encouraging tone, but in an accusatory one; that much was clear before anyone could make out what the voice was saying. The voice grew louder, and the crowd parted as a young woman confidently approached the stage where all could hear what she had to say.

"Nonsense! The great biodiversity of the Lowcountry, the seashore, the salt marsh, the maritime forest, the tidal creeks and rivers, and the vast array of wildlife you pay lip service to are all threatened by the unhinged and unrestricted development fostered by the Dunsmores. Don't be fooled by this man's public stance on biodiversity!" she said, turning to face the crowd but pointing a finger like a dagger at Randal. "His position at the Dunsmore Family Foundation merely assures the *appearance* of activism, but the truth is that this is all for show! They merely pretend to put up a good fight but they knowingly wage a losing fight against the forces for unlimited expansion, forces fueled and profited from by companies this man and his brother, our governor, stand behind and protect."

The crowd in the front of the room had arranged itself in a semicircle behind the young woman, who stood alone at the foot of the stage. Murmurs spread across the great hall. Those in the crowd behind the first row strained to see who this woman was. She was standing with her feet shoulder-width apart and her hands clenched by her sides as she continued her verbal assault on Randal Dunsmore.

The police standing in front of the building strutted inside, and the buzz from the crowd grew louder as two uniformed officers quickly approached the woman, grabbing her by the arms, one on each side.

Randal Dunsmore held up his hand, and the officers stood down, released their grip on her, and then moved one step back. Though it appeared as if the woman had talked herself out, the defiant tone of her stance had not waned, and she stood her ground, her eyes locked in and staring up at Randal, who seemed incapable of looking at her, his eyes cast downward at his feet. Finally, he slowly raised his head and looked at the young woman before him.

After an uncomfortable moment of silence, he said, "Hello, Rebeca. It's been a long time."

Chapter 31

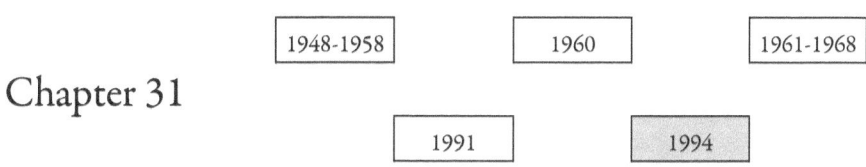

CHARLESTON
JUNE 13, 1994

Rebeca Dunsmore was pleased to be waking up in her own bed and not in a jail cell. She'd crashed the event at Hibernian Hall a couple of nights before knowing full well she could have been arrested and charged. Admittedly, she'd been counting on her father to tell the police to stand down, and luckily for her, he had. The flip side was that she knew he then expected an explanation. She would give him one, eventually. But first, she needed to gather more information.

Rebeca walked out of the home she was renting on Gadsden Street and headed west on Bull Street toward the Marina Variety Store to meet a man for breakfast. It had been his idea to meet there, and one she wholeheartedly supported. She was hoping their breakfast was as good as she remembered.

Rebeca hadn't lived in Charleston since graduating from high school in 1986, eight years ago. She'd ended up heading west to attend Arizona State University, intent on putting a couple of thousand miles between herself and Charleston. But as she walked down Bull Street enjoying the lemony scent of magnolia and crepe myrtle trees in bloom, she marveled at how little the city had changed over the years. She had to acknowledge that Charleston truly was a beautiful city. *It wasn't you, Charleston, that made me leave—it was him.*

* * *

It was a short walk to the Marina and Rebeca climbed the stairs and entered the restaurant right at eight o'clock that morning. She was meeting a man named Tad Torcher, a man she had met once before in Scottsdale, Arizona when he was there vacationing with his wife. Mr. Torcher was the attorney who helped manage a trust her mother's parents had set up for her. She had just turned twenty-one at the time of his visit and Mr. Torcher had explained that under the terms of the trust, she was entitled to begin receiving distributions and certain reporting as to the trust's performance.

He'd told her that if she ever had any questions about her trust and her rights as its sole beneficiary, to just give him a call. She'd done just that the previous week, which was why she was now standing next to the hostess and scanning the restaurant for any site of him. Her eyes met those of a man sitting in a booth by the window. He was casually reading the local paper while also keeping a lookout for her. Upon their mutual recognition, he raised his hand, and she made her way over to him.

"Rebeca Dunsmore," he said happily as he stood up from the booth to greet her. "So good to see you." He took a full appraisal of her standing in front of him, perhaps as a grandfather would.

"Thank you. And thank you for meeting with me."

"Of course, of course. I have a nine o'clock meeting here with a potential new client, so this works out perfectly. Oh, and before I forget, my wife sends her regards. She so enjoyed meeting you when we were together in Scottsdale. She hasn't stopped talking about that charming restaurant you recommended to us. Do you remember what it was called?"

"Durants."

"That's it. We just loved it. Well anyway, she sends her best."

"That's kind of her. Please tell her that I do the same."

They both took their seats, and the waitress filled her mug with coffee and topped off Tad's.

"Y'all know what you want, or do you need a few minutes?" the waitress asked.

Tad cast a look at Rebeca, who had not picked up the menu and then turned to the waitress. "Why don't you give us a few minutes? She just got here."

"No need to wait on my accord," Rebeca said. She turned to the waitress. "Do y'all still serve an omelet with crab meat?"

"We sure do."

"I'll have that and a glass of OJ," she said as she handed the menu back to the waitress. "Make that two," Tad said and then looked at Rebeca with a quizzical smile.

She shrugged and answered the question on his mind. "I used to come here a lot when I was a kid."

"It's my favorite breakfast spot in town, though the Misses wishes I didn't come here as often as I do," he said as he chuckled softly and patted his belly.

Their easy banter seemed to have stalled and was followed by a moment of silence as they each picked up their napkins and placed them in their laps.

"When my secretary told me you had called, I wasn't sure if I was surprised to hear from you or if it was a call I should have expected all along."

"Why do you say that?"

"Ms. Rebeca, you asked for this meeting, so why don't you tell me what's on your mind?"

"It's about my trust. I haven't received a report in some time. Mr. Torcher, is something wrong?"

"First of all, please call me Tad."

"I'll try." She gave him a weak smile. "You work for Dad, managing my trust. I used to get reports from you every quarter; I didn't understand them but I'm older now and I should be able to. I'm just surprised that I haven't received any communication from your office in close to a year."

Tad tended to his coffee while Rebeca was speaking, opening a packet of sugar and pouring it in. When she had finished, he picked up a spoon and stirred the contents. "Rebeca, I'm sorry to hear this," he said as he laid the spoon down on the table. "You see, I don't manage your account anymore. Your father fired me last October."

"Why?" she asked as she sat back in the booth and crossed her arms in front of her.

"I wish I knew," he said in a tone of exasperation. "I asked him that same question and all I got back was vague comments about him wanting to go in a different direction. I'm sorry. I wish I could tell you more."

"It doesn't make sense. You'd been working for him forever."

"Since you and your father arrived here in 1968," Tad clarified. "You were just an infant when I took on your account. I remember your father brought you to my office when he signed the papers. The babysitter had called in sick. You were just learning to crawl."

What a kind man, she thought.

Neither said a word and they both returned to eating their meals.

"I know it's none of my business, and I know you just said you haven't been receiving any reports on your trust, but what of distributions?" He dabbed his mouth with a napkin. "You should still be getting something."

"Dad's missed a couple and the ones I have received lately are puny." Rebeca put her knife and fork down and leaned slightly forward. "Mr. Torcher—*Tad*. I don't know what to do."

"Have you asked your father about it?"

Rebeca's gaze drifted out the window, to a sky that was a vibrant blue. The late-night thunderstorms had pushed the previous day's humidity aside and the marina was coming to life as boaters were unfurling the white sails of the ships that adorned the harbor like jewels. The peace and calm of the setting was lost on her, though, drowned out by the ugly business she had returned to Charleston to take care of.

As for his question, she responded with a question of her own. "Can you recommend an attorney for me?"

Tad Torcher didn't hesitate. "On a Trust & Estate matter like this, Walker Atkins is who you want to talk to."

Chapter 32

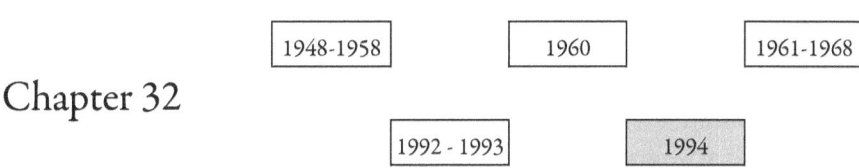

LATER THAT MORNING . . .
LAW OFFICES OF ATKINS & ATKINS

Walker was wrapping up a memo to the Gaston file and preparing for a meeting he had later in the day with Eddie Wentworth and the attorney general when Mrs. Beasley buzzed him in his office. "Mr. Atkins, a woman in the lobby is asking to see you."

He leaned forward far enough to depress the button and reply. "Mrs. Beasley, I need to stay focused on the day's agenda. Could you please schedule her for some time later in the week?"

"I've already suggested that, sir, but she insists on seeing you as soon as possible. She seems quite determined."

"Does she have a name?"

"Yes. Rebeca Dunsmore," replied Mrs. Beasley

Walker paused. This was an interesting development, indeed. After a moment of internal debate, he pressed the talk button again. "I'll meet her in the conference room."

Walker sat in his office for a few minutes to give Mrs. Beasley the time required to situate Rebeca Dunsmore in the conference room and deliver the obligatory coffee or water. When he entered, she was standing in front of the bookcase on the far wall, her back to him, looking at a book she had pulled from the shelf.

"Good afternoon, Miss Dunsmore. I'm Walker Atkins."

Rebeca turned and, holding the book in her left hand, extended her right to shake his. "Thank you for seeing me on such short notice and please, call me Rebeca."

Rebeca was about Isabelle's height, just shy of Walker at five foot ten. Her hair was thick, auburn, and very curly. It flowed naturally just beyond shoulder length and framed a face with an olive complexion. She had a small nose and brown eyes, and she wore a cream-colored sundress, a lightweight denim jacket accented by a wide saddle-colored belt, and a pair of Tecovas cowboy boots. Her hand was adorned with two turquoise rings, and she had multiple silver bangles around her wrists that jingled when they shook hands.

Nodding towards the book in her hand, Walker asked, "Something spark your interest?"

She turned the cover towards Walker so he could see the title.

"*The Dwelling Houses of Charleston* by Alice Huger Smith and her father," said Walker. "An excellent book, so I'm told."

"I'm admiring your book collection. Reading the titles reminds me of the extraordinary history of this town," she said.

"Yes. The good, the bad, and the ugly."

"True, but even so, what a beautiful city. It's only getting more beautiful, it would seem. Out of the ashes of Hurricane Hugo, Charleston appears to be experiencing a new renaissance. As I walked the streets earlier, I came across one renovation project after another. But I take it from your comment that this book does not interest you."

"No, that's not the case at all," Walker said. "If you live in this city, you can't help but become interested in its architecture, history, and beauty to some degree, but this book collection is my father's doing. He's the first Atkins in our firm's name and he is spending less time in the office and more time chasing his new passion—history, and specifically our city's history. He leads tours in the old historic part of town and collects first-edition books on the history of the Lowcountry. Hence, this collection. But I doubt you dropped in today to discuss my father's book collection. How can I help you, Rebeca?"

"You can help me sue Randal Dunsmore."

* * *

Walker excused himself, walked to the lobby, and asked Mrs. Beasley to call the AG's office and see if he could push his meeting with Eddie Wentworth back a half hour. He waited while she placed the call. After a long minute pacing his lobby, he saw Mrs. Beasley smile. "Thank you for your flexibility," she said and hung up. Upon returning to the conference room, he took a seat, leaving the chair at the end of the table open for Rebeca.

"Now, Rebeca, please tell me why you want to sue Randal Dunsmore," he said, energized by this turn of events.

"First of all, do you know who I am in relation to Randal Dunsmore?"

"Well, Rebeca, I believe I first laid eyes on you last Friday night at the fundraiser at Hibernian Hall. You made quite an impression and the rumor circulating after you were escorted from the building was that Randal Dunsmore is your father. How am I doing?"

"Spot on. Shall I pick up the story?"

"Please do."

* * *

Dixie LeMar Dunsmore, Randal's wife, and mother to Rebeca Dunsmore, died on October 10, 1968. Randal's brother, Johnny Dunsmore, was elected to his first statewide office in November of that year. Relations between Johnny and Randal, never good to begin with, deteriorated after Dixie's death. Randal abhorred living in Johnny's shadow, where he would reside if he remained in Columbia, South Carolina.

So, in early 1969, Randal and his daughter Rebeca moved to Charleston, where he bought a beautiful Georgian home on Murray Boulevard overlooking the area where Ashley River flowed into Charleston Harbor.

Randal threw himself into his duties as the chairman of the Dunsmore Family Foundation. By making noteworthy donations to the various charitable and cultural institutions around town, with the veiled promise of more to come, he quickly found himself invited to every educational event and soiree sponsored by the Charleston Historical Preservation Society, the Charleston Library Society, the Friends of the Gaillard, the Middleton Plantation Foundation, the Lowcountry Ecology Restoration Society, and numerous other historical and environmental societies.

Randal doled out donations at a controlled pace, fast enough to keep him on every important invitation list in town, but not too large for recipients to think they could take him for granted. Once the dance was over, the charity had more of the foundation's money and he had an honorary membership, a position on the board of directors, and a seat at the table. The transaction was complete: money in exchange for stature.

And what of Rebeca, his daughter? She was raised by nannies. Randal had neither the time nor the interest in being her father, except for when it benefited him. They were photographed visiting an orphanage, which the family foundation supported, and reading to underprivileged children in failing schools. They were photographed entering the South Carolina Society building on Meeting Street, ensuring that everyone saw Randal dropping Rebeca off for Cotillion dances.

Randal wasn't cruel. He didn't verbally or physically abuse his daughter. He was simply indifferent to her existence. Their relationship was cold, loveless. Rebeca saw other children run to their parents and jump into waiting arms. Her mother was dead, so only one pair of waiting arms was left. But when Rebeca ran to her father, he neither bent his knees nor opened his arms, so as she approached, she would slow down, knowing this time would be no different; she would come to a full stop a foot or so away, receive a pat on the head, and peer up into a sorrowful face—a face framed by an empty smile that felt more like a shut door than a love-filled welcoming.

And so, Randal and Rebeca grew up as housemates, and not as father and daughter. One benefit of the relationship was that as Randal dated, there was never a dynamic between the woman pursuing Randal and Rebeca. The women Randal dated all presumed they would have to win over Rebeca if they ever hoped to land Randal as a husband. Nothing could have been farther from the truth.

As Rebeca became a teenager, she hid her loneliness behind a sarcastic attitude and a tough, cynical veneer. She knew nothing about her mother, Dixie, other than she had died birthing Rebeca and her twin brother, Joseph. And as for Joseph, he died just a day or two after delivery. The tragedy of her mother's death, however, was not owned by Randal, but instead had been hijacked by his brother Johnny, for it seemed that during every election season when he was running for office, the Dunsmore campaign—and their willing accomplices in the press—would trot out stories of Dixie's death to remind the public of the family's great suffering.

Randal's loss was meant to make his brother more relatable—he too had suffered, and you could count on him to fight the good fight for you, a fight to end your suffering.

Like any girl in similar circumstances, Rebeca longed to know more about her mother. What was she like? What were her dreams? Was she pretty? What had she been like as a little girl?

One day, when she was thirteen and had been left at home alone on a Saturday night without a nanny, she snuck into the attic above her father's study. She had seen him pull a string to lower steps that led up into the attic and was curious. As a young girl, Randal never had to tell her not to climb the stairs because she was too small to reach the rope. When she asked him what was up there, he would respond vaguely and tell her it was just where daddy stored boring old business documents.

It was a little past 6:30 when Randal had left in a tuxedo to pick up his date for another charity event. It seemed as if that was all he did: attend fundraisers. She knew he wouldn't be home for hours. *Probably getting another dumb award*, she'd thought.

So, after he had left for the evening, she snuck into the attic. Her father was right—he stored a lot of business documents in the attic—but she was undeterred and kept opening boxes in the hope of turning up something from the days he was married to her mother. There was not a single picture of her mother anywhere in the house, not even a picture of their wedding. She knew they had to exist, though.

Rebeca's persistence paid off. She found a shoe box with a single Polaroid of her mother and a picture of her mother and father on their wedding day, framed and lying at the bottom of the box. She put the boxes in the attic back to how she had found them. She knew right where she was going to place the wedding picture—on the bookshelf in the drawing room.

Rebeca wondered how long it would take before her father discovered the wedding picture on the bookshelf and what his response would be. It didn't take long. A few nights later, she was sitting on the floor of the drawing room, her legs curled up beneath her, and reading a homework assignment. Her father walked in and picked up the framed wedding picture. Rebeca pretended not to notice and focused extra hard on her textbook, though she wasn't reading a word.

"Rebeca," her father said. Rebeca looked up. He was holding the picture carefully in his hands. "Your mother was a beautiful woman," he'd said. "And you are becoming one too. I know I'm not the best father, but you remind me so much of her that, at times, looking at you makes me awfully sad."

That was the closest he'd ever come to telling Rebeca that he loved her mother or her. Rebeca now knew that her father missed her mother and that her absence made him sad—but she also knew that her presence did, too.

Rebeca kept the Polaroid in the drawer of her bedside table. Hardly a day passed when she did not look at it. Her mother was beautiful, as her father had said. She had long blond hair that hung down past her shoulders. Her eyes were blue, and her complexion fair, features her mother had in common with Randal. While she loved the picture, looking at it made her feel even more alone in the world, for she looked nothing like her mother or her father.

Rebeca returned to the attic often on those evenings when her father left her at home alone. She combed through boxes, looking for anything that might educate her about her mother. One night, behind a wall of banker boxes, she found a trunk. Inside the trunk, she found a collection of high school annuals, a few old books, a letterman's jacket, and a shoebox covered with dust. It was filled with photos and newspaper clippings. As she thumbed through the box, she realized she was looking at family photos: Thanksgiving dinners, Christmas gatherings, pictures of her parents on what appeared to be dates. *Bingo.*

* * *

"Rebeca, thank you for sharing that with me," Walker said and stood up so he could refill her glass of water. "I can tell that your memories growing up still bring you pain."

She took a long sip of her water and cast her eyes towards a corner of the room. "Yes, a bit, but I've learned to cope. Talking about it helps." She turned her attention back to Walker. "But I also wanted to put to rest whatever rumors may be circulating about me since my unannounced appearance last Friday night at Randal's big gala."

"So, you didn't head west to join a commune?" Walker asked as a grin spread across his face.

"Now, *that's* a new one. No, not exactly. After I graduated high school, that would have been in 1986, I headed west, but not to join a commune. I attended Arizona State University."

"What took you to ASU?" Walker asked.

"Growing up here, I didn't have many friends. The other kids had moms; I didn't. The other kids played youth sports; my dad never signed me up. I withdrew. But I had books. Randal filled the shelves in our houses with books. I think he thought a home filled with books made him look cultured. Either way, because of that, books became my best friends. One book that I fell in love with was a collection of photographs by Ansel Adams. The hours I'd spent with that book also led me to a love for photography and the West. I particularly loved his photographs of a canyon east of Flagstaff, Arizona, called Canyon de Chelly. So, when I finished high school, I wanted to head west. I applied to ASU and was accepted."

"And photography? Did you pursue it?"

"Yes, but more as a hobby. I interned for a beautiful travel magazine called *Arizona Highways,* for which Ansel Adams was a contributor."

"Did you ever meet Ansel Adams?"

"No. He died in 1984, but I did meet other noteworthy characters from the Grand Canyon State while I was there—men and women who informed my worldview."

"Such as?"

"Let's leave that for another day. However, the sum effect of my experiences led me to attend law school at ASU. I graduated in the spring."

"Congratulations and welcome to the club," Walker said as he raised his cup of coffee in a toast. She returned the toast with her glass of water. "What will you do with your degree?"

"I have a few options, but right now I'm here taking care of some family business."

"Yes, that's right. You said you want to sue Randal Dunsmore, your father."

"That's right."

"Can you tell me why?" Walker asked.

"I am the sole beneficiary for a trust that he's doing a lousy job managing." She then filled him in on her breakfast meeting earlier that day with Tad Torcher, and Walker took a few notes throughout her spiel.

"I know Tad," he said, setting aside his pen. "They do good work at his office." He glanced at his watch and sighed. "Rebeca, I have to go now. I have another meeting out of the office, so we'll need to meet again to further investigate your concerns. Mrs. Beasley can set up a time."

"Okay. I'm ready to get started," Rebeca said enthusiastically.

Walker took his time collecting his pads and pens before responding. "Rebeca, when Tad asked you if you had asked your father about what was going on with your trust, he was putting you on the right path."

Rebeca looked away and Walker paused before continuing. "I don't practice family law, but because I work with families dealing with wills and trusts, I've seen how legal issues can tear a family apart. Suing your father . . . well, that's going to be emotional, regardless of how you may feel about him. So, I'll meet with you again, but I encourage you to talk with your father first and ask him what's going on."

"I'll think about it," she said.

Chapter 33

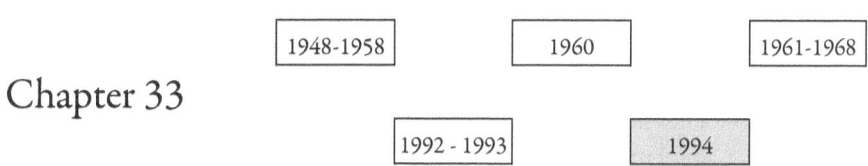

*THE ATTORNEY GENERAL'S OFFICE IN
DOWNTOWN CHARLESTON*

Walker was seated in the lobby of the Attorney General's Office in Charleston when Eddie Wentworth came streaming in through the front door. "Sorry, I'm late. Court went long. Follow me."

Walker set down the magazine he'd been reading and followed Eddie down the hall. The receptionist passed Eddie a stack of messages as he breezed by in what appeared to be a well-choreographed dance. Eddie was thumbing through them, head down, as he maneuvered the hallway, dodging other busy attorneys and talking to Walker at the same time.

"You guys stay late last Friday night?" Eddie asked.

Eddie opened the door ahead of Walker and let him enter. Eddie stepped in, closed the door, placed his briefcase on a credenza, hung his jacket on the back of the door, and plopped himself in the chair behind his desk.

"No, we left soon after all the commotion at the end," Walker answered.

Eddie was opening drawers and pulling out a fresh legal pad and pen while he was talking. "Yeah, how about that? So, that girl who barged in is Randal Dunsmore's daughter?"

"Apparently so." Walker hadn't yet told Eddie about the meeting he'd just had with Rebeca and decided not to bring it up until they'd formally decided to work together. "How about you and Vanessa? Did y'all stick around?"

"Nah, we made a quick exit. The kids stayed with Vanessa's parents for the night, so ... we had the house to ourselves ..."

"Say no more." Walker shared a good-natured smile with his old friend.

"But enough about all that. I've been looking forward to this meeting. You seemed pretty worked up when I told you that the man standing next to Governor Dunsmore was named Luis Sanchez. You want to tell me more about that?"

"You're not going to *believe* what I learned on my trip to the Bahamas."

"Go on," said Eddie.

Walker took the next fifteen minutes briefing Eddie about his meetings with Nigel Pinder, Eli's connection in Nassau, and his meeting with Anthony Fergusson—the lawyer acting as the registered agent for the host of companies in South Carolina that had defrauded Walker's clients, the Gastons—and about the mysterious man on the phone named Nash.

"So, let me get this straight. This guy named Nash was able to determine that Anthony Ferguson was calling the law firm of Sanchez & Sanchez. Is that right?"

"Not just the firm and not the firm's main line, but Luis Sanchez's *direct* line." Walker paused for dramatic effect. "Honestly, between you and me, I think Nash is CIA. And he knows Eli. I tell you, the more I learn about Eli's time away, the more I'm convinced he was a spy or something."

"You're not the only one. Of all the rumors surrounding that whole affair, that is my favorite. But anyway, back to the Sanchez law firm. What do you make of it all?" asked Eddie.

"The law firm of Sanchez & Sanchez includes one *Luis Sanchez*—the guy standing next to our governor at the event last night. What are the odds of that? The inference is clear: Anthony Ferguson has Luis Sanchez's direct phone line, Luis Sanchez is buddies with our governor, and our governor is somehow tied in with what is going on at Palmetto Lending Tree and the other companies."

Eddie nodded in agreement. "Well, if all that is true, then this changes things. This is Big-League stuff."

"Yep." Walker and Eddie shared the second smile of the meeting.

"Walker, what do you say we get the AG on the phone?"

* * *

The phone was answered and the call transferred.

"Langston here," said South Carolina Attorney General Joshua Langston.

"Hey, boss. Eddie here, and I've got Walker Atkins sitting across from me, ready to report on what he learned during his trip to the Bahamas."

"Excellent. What do you have for me?"

Walker spent the next fifteen minutes giving Joshua the same update he'd given Eddie. Joshua asked a few questions but, for the most part, let Walker talk.

"Okay. I agree that seeing Johnny Dunsmore standing with Luis Sanchez last Friday night was a hell of a coincidence, but it's not proof of a crime. I don't know what you expect the AG's office to do with this information," said Joshua.

"Well, boss," said Eddie. "There's more. This matter came to our attention because Walker represents the Gastons. We figured that what happened to them wasn't likely to be a one-off event and that there would be other victims out there."

"Agreed."

"Last week, while Walker was in the Bahamas, our staff combed through tips left on our hotline and looked for activity similar to what the Gastons have experienced. We had a few hits. Now, Walker is not comfortable contacting the people lodging these complaints and soliciting work, but someone from our office certainly can call them. We could refer the civil matters to Walker while we investigate the criminal matters," Eddie suggested.

"Sure. Works for me. But again, what do you expect to accomplish concerning Johnny Dunsmore?" the AG asked.

"If a grand jury investigation into Palmetto Lending Tree leaks, we might just rattle Governor Dunsmore's cage."

"Yeah. But the identity of a grand jury investigation isn't supposed to leak—is it?"

"Um, of course not, boss. I'm aware of that. I wasn't suggesting . . . um, anything nefarious. It's just that sometimes, word of a grand jury *does* leak."

"I'm aware of that. And I'm also aware of who the primary target of these investigations is—it's Palmetto Lending Tree and its sister companies. We're not looking at the governor. If other stuff falls out, so be it.

We'll follow the evidence. Have I made myself clear?" the AG wanted to know.

"Yes sir," Eddie responded.

"Now, Walker, are you comfortable with this?" the AG asked.

"Absolutely. I'm meeting with my clients this afternoon, the Gastons. I won't mention my work with your office, but I'll have enough of my work to show them that they have a fighting chance of keeping their home. And if your office sends more clients my way, I'll provide them with the same aggressive representation."

"I'm sure you will. Anything else?"

"No, sir," said Eddie.

"Okay. Keep me posted."

* * *

On his walk back to his office, Walker mentally rehashed the previous several weeks, beginning with the chance encounter with Governor Johnny Dunsmore in the Men's Grill at the club.

Here I am, barely three weeks later, looking at being on the other side of the table from that ass and the most powerful family in the state on several matters: helping the Gastons; working with the Attorney General's Office as they investigate what I'm sure are front companies for your predatory loans and other criminal activity and, very likely, representing your niece, Rebeca, as she sues your brother.

This was too good.

* * *

When Walker got back to his office, Hugh and Loraine Gaston were waiting for him in the conference room. He entered the room and saw the Gastons sitting side by side, Hugh with a cup of coffee and Loraine with a glass of water.

"I see that Mrs. Beasley took care of you," Walker said as he pulled a chair out and took a seat across the table. "Hugh and Loraine, this meeting won't take long, and it probably could have been handled by phone. But, as I'll explain, not much is going to happen for the next several months and I wanted the three of us to get together one more time so I can answer any questions you may have."

"Thank you. We so appreciate your help," said Loraine. "I guess we're still just really in the dark. We haven't received any other notices from the bank since we first met with you."

"Okay. So, let me tell you what will happen, in broad strokes. The one letter you received from the bank informing you that you were in default started a clock running. The law in South Carolina states that a lender must commence a Foreclosure Action 120 days from the Default Date. The bank will file a complaint with the court to initiate a Foreclosure Action. We will have thirty days from the date they file this complaint to file an answer to their Complaint. So, our answer will be due no later than October 13th."

Walker perceived some confusion on Loraine's face.

"And don't worry about the calendar. Our office will keep track of everything," he added.

"Oh, it's not that," said Loraine. "We're sure you will. Hugh and I are just amazed that you never look at any notes. Aren't we, Hugh?"

Hugh nodded that he was. "And what will our Answer be?" he asked.

Walker nodded, as if to humbly say, *Thank you*. "Since we first met, I've done some digging and learned more about Palmetto Lending Tree, Coastal Savings & Loan, and the others. Simply stated, you were the victim of a predatory loan and bank fraud," explained Walker. "The bank lied to you when they told you your deposits were insured. I have more work to do, and I may develop other arguments, but *we will have an Answer*."

"And you think this will work?" asked Loraine.

"I can't make any promises, but I have a high degree of confidence that when we are done, Coastal Savings and Loan and the other entities will not be able to kick you out of your house. I don't know what remedy the court will finally arrive at, but we'll get a better idea after we go through the discovery stage."

"What's the discovery stage?" asked Loraine.

"Don't worry about that. I'll let you know when the time comes but know this: I'm working on your behalf. Go about your lives. They can't do anything to you right now."

Walker saw Loraine turn towards her husband, squeeze his hand, and smile.

"You see, honey? I told you everything would be okay."

Who said being a lawyer didn't have its rewards?

Chapter 34

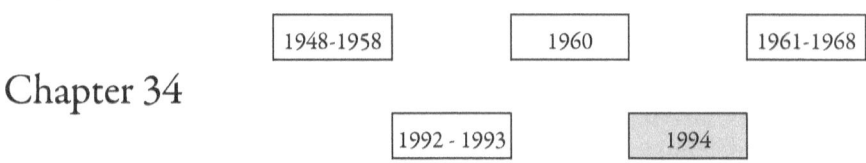

LAW OFFICES OF ATKINS & ATKINS
THURSDAY, JUNE 16, 1994

Walker was back in the conference room sitting across from Rebeca Dunsmore. She was wearing a yellow sundress and sandals, and Walker could see a large manila folder jutting out of her purse, which she had placed on the table. Once Mrs. Beasley had finished delivering the cups of coffee and the pitcher of water, Rebeca was on her feet in a flash, pulling the folder from her purse.

"This is a copy of the document creating my trust," she said.

Walker was sitting back in his chair, his two hands flat on the table in front of him. "Rebeca, I appreciate your determination. Mrs. Beasley told me you called our office first thing yesterday morning to arrange this meeting. But I need to know—have you met with your father yet?"

Still standing, Rebeca placed both hands on her hips. "Yes."

Walker waited for more. Nothing was forthcoming. "Well? What did he have to say?"

Rebeca took a seat and sighed in exasperation. "I asked him why he fired Mr. Torcher and why I hadn't received any quarterly reports lately. You'll never guess what he told me."

"What?"

"He said that I had to talk to his wife—that *she* was helping with the trust now."

"Huh? You're right, I would have never guessed that. Did you discuss anything else with your father?"

"No. It was really awkward. We sort of agreed to get together for dinner soon, but that was all."

"Okay. Well, before we come back to his answer to your question and the role his wife is playing, what can you tell me about your trust?"

Rebeca opened the folder and slid two documents across the table. "I'm what you call a *trust fund baby*. I'm sure you're familiar with that term in your line of work."

Walker nodded that he was.

"Well, I wasn't familiar with that term until I took a Trusts & Estates class in law school at Arizona State. You see, I'm the beneficiary of these two trusts, one set up by my father's parents—*the Dunsmore Trust*—and one by my mother's parents—*the LeMar Trust*." She tapped the papers in front of her. "These copies are for you. I figured you might as well look at both of them."

Rebeca sat anxiously at the end of her chair while Walker scanned the first trust document, looking for the telltale signs of whether the trust was filled with standard boilerplate provisions or whether he was dealing with something unusual. Upon first glance, the document and the trust it created appeared rather typical.

"Of course, I'll need to read these documents carefully, but from the looks of the trust you call the *Dunsmore Trust,* I suspect you aren't receiving any money from it right now," said Walker.

"That's right. Randal does, but I'm next in line once he dies. But take a closer look at the other document—the LeMar Trust." Walker picked it up and began to thumb through it as well while Rebeca told him what she thought she knew. "I've read the trust document, and mind you, I had one class in law school on Trusts & Estates, so I need your help. But as I read it, the trust document states that when Dixie LeMar—my mom— got married, her husband would take over trustee responsibilities once she had a child. Until my mom married Randal, her father, my grandfather, was the trustee. Well, when she married Randal, they had me and he became the trustee, and he still is today, but he's doing a lousy job."

Walker put the document down and leaned back in his chair. "When you say he's doing a lousy job, what do you mean?" He didn't wait for an answer. "You see, it's not as easy to remove a trustee as one might think. If the trust isn't making much money, that's not grounds for removal.

Our courts, and the common law tradition that many of our trust and estates laws rest upon, don't want trustees looking over their shoulders and feeling like they could get sued if a trust they are managing doesn't grow at a suitably fast rate, because that type of pressure might encourage trustees to take unnecessary risks and end up losing money. The law will never fault a conservative approach to fiduciary responsibilities."

"That much I know," said Rebeca. "My problem is that I know nothing about what is happening with the trust. I don't know what is in the trust. I don't know how much it's worth anymore. Remember, I haven't received a single report since Mr. Torcher's report in August of last year. My father prepares the trust's tax returns, and the trust pays any taxes that are due. If the trust has other expenses, I wouldn't know because I see nothing."

"You mentioned when we met Monday that the distributions you receive from the trust are small..."

"They certainly are. Randal did pay my college and law school tuition out of the trust. Heaven forbid dear old Dad ever pay for anything himself! I bartended a bit to make ends meet. If you're ever in Tempe, check out Lonnegan's. Their house band is fantastic—the Dave Dodt Band."

"I'll do that," Walker said, grinning. "I attended Georgetown University. We had our fair share of great bars."

Walker pushed his chair back and stood up to stretch his legs. "Well, Rebeca, what you are describing constitutes a breach of his fiduciary responsibility. As a trustee, your father must provide you with regular reports and an accounting of the trust's performance. But before we file a lawsuit, let's see if we can get him to do exactly that."

"Okay, but let's say he does. Let's say he provides reports, but I still think he's doing a bad job. How long do I have to put up with him as the trustee? I mean, do I *ever* get control of the LeMar Trust?" Rebeca asked.

"Good question." Walker sat back down and pulled his chair up close to the table. "A trust must end, and all the assets must vest in one or more beneficiaries within twenty-one years of the death of a life-in-being when the trust was created." Walker picked up the trust document. "Let me see if I can find the controlling provision. Okay, here it is. The lives-in-being provision in this trust is standard. It's called a 'savings clause' or a 'Kennedy clause.' Instead of identifying a life-in-being that might be hard to track down, the attorney who wrote this document used a life-in-being known to the public. This trust must end within twenty-one years of the death of a then-living descendant of John F. Kennedy. I believe JFK has two kids alive today who were alive when this trust was created, so assuming they enjoy an average life expectancy, this trust isn't ending anytime soon, as long as there is a beneficiary in waiting."

"Is this what is called the rule against perpetuities?" she asked.

"Yep."

"I missed that question on my Trust & Estate exam."

"Most people do."

"And who is the beneficiary in waiting?" Rebeca asked.

"Do you have any siblings or children?"

"No."

"Then *you* are. The trust will end, and all the assets will be distributed when you die or when your children die, assuming you go on to have any—but no later than twenty-one years after the last of the two Kennedy kids dies."

"So, what you're saying is that I'm stuck with Randal as the trustee?"

"Yes, but not if he has breached his fiduciary responsibilities and we can convince a court that he needs replacing. So, let's return to that discussion you had with your dad."

"Yeah, all he said was that I had to talk to his new wife. Do you know her?"

"No. But everybody knows *who* she is—the head-turning socialite, Blythe Cavendish Dunsmore."

Chapter 35

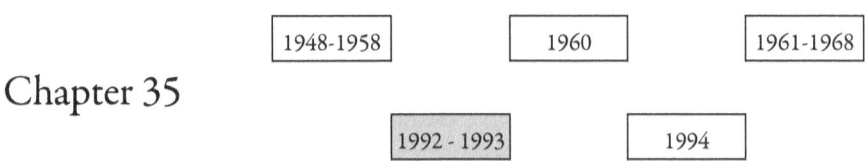

WEST HOLLYWOOD, CALIFORNIA
JANUARY 6, 1992

Danielle Brown—also known as "Danny Brown," with the stage name of "Amber Peaches"—parked her brand-new Jeep Grand Cherokee in the parking lot behind Tattle Tails and waved at Hank as she stepped out of the car. She was wearing impossibly tight blue jeans, a plaid halter-top, and sneakers. Hank, who was guarding the back door, was six foot seven and weighed just over three hundred pounds. He'd lost a little weight since his playing days in the NFL, a career cut short by one too many knee surgeries and the resulting addiction to pain killers.

"Danny, I gotta say, I'm surprised to see you here. I figured you would have blown town by now."

"Had to say goodbye to the girls first."

"We're gonna miss ya. You ain't like the other girls. You got tits *and* brains."

"That's sweet of you to say. And don't forget my fine ass," she said as she entered the nightclub.

Although it was sunny and seventy-five degrees outside, you wouldn't know from inside Tattle Tails or any other strip club in the area. There were no windows or clocks to hint at the time of day, just bone-rattling music heavy on the bass, fog from the machine rolling across the stage, and cigarette smoke illuminated by red and blue flood lights. *Sweet Child of Mine* by Guns & Roses was blaring, and that meant Chastity was on the main stage; she was twenty-two, or so she said, but barely looked a day over eighteen. The guys loved her.

Danny wasn't sure what was more depressing—the inside of a strip club midafternoon, with only one or two girls on stage and maybe a dozen men scattered about, no two sitting together, or the same club at midnight with over a hundred men leering at and cheering on a dozen dancers taking up every stage in the club.

Danny was just glad to be leaving this life. She saw who she was looking for sitting at the bar, reading the race sheet. Owing to her reputation, she felt the eyes of half the room follow her as she walked towards the bar.

"Well, if it ain't the widow maker," said Dexter Childress.

"Drop it, Dexter."

"Buy you a drink?"

"Cup of coffee."

"Coffee? What gives?"

"I'm hitting the road just as soon as I collect from Sammy. He owes me two weeks' pay and then I'm out of here."

"Still got your heart set on Charleston?"

"Yeah. You could use a fresh start, too. Why don't you come with me?"

Dexter was a lawyer who represented people who wanted to break the law and get away with it—or at least skirt the law and use it to their advantage, typically at the expense of some other poor, unsuspecting soul who thought the law would protect them.

Dexter had recently represented Danny in a matter involving one Matthew Corrigan, a very wealthy man with whom she was having an affair. The only thing more embarrassing to the man's family than the fact that he had left the lion's share of his estate to her was how he died. It seems she boinked him to death, hence the moniker, "the widow maker." The last thing the old man saw was her body impaled on his, riding him like a bull. She had been the one to call 911, and she'd answered the door wearing nothing more than a house coat.

Despite protests from his wife and children, it seemed likely the man's entire estate would be left to her—his will expressed as much. Matters turned against her, though, when it surfaced that she was aware of his weak heart and that he was under a doctor's strict orders to refrain from vigorous physical activity—including sexual intercourse. The toxicology report explained the empty bottle of Viagra found in her purse and turned a contest over a last will and testament into a police murder investigation.

The family's desire for privacy carried the day, though, and they prevailed on the police to drop the investigation and asked Danny to accept a cash settlement.

"Maybe I will, but not just yet. Gotta a few things cookin' here," said Dexter.

"But we're good, right? The wire for your fees came through, right?"

"Yeah. We're good."

"And that envelope on the bar in front of you—it's got what I came here for?"

"You're all set," he said as he reached back over his shoulder to retrieve the envelope and handed it to her. "I'm gonna miss your style."

About then, a group of dancers came up to hug Danny.

"You're our hero, you know that, right?" said one of the girls, the other five nodding in unison. "We hate to see you go. We're gonna miss you."

A few of the girls were crying.

"I'm gonna miss you girls, too. Now don't forget what I was always tellin' ya."

"Yeah, we know," said one of the girls.

All five of them, in unison, chimed in, "'Keep your tits high and your prices higher.'"

"That's right. *We* own *them*, not the other way around."

Hugs were exchanged, and tears were shed. Danny collected her last pay from Sammy, an envelope full of cash, and said her goodbyes. She was about to start for the door but paused to take both of Dexter's hands in hers.

"I meant what I said, Dexter. Come with me to Charleston."

"Nah. You're still determined to land you a rich husband. I'd just get in the way, sugar."

"Yeah, maybe so. The money I got will set me up, but it won't last forever, at least not for how I plan on living. So, falling in love with a rich guy ain't just a good idea, it's a necessity."

"Or at least fallin' in love with his *money*, right?" said Dexter with a sly grin.

"Hell, it's easier to fall in love with a rich guy than a poor one—the parties are better! Besides, I'm getting too old for this game," she said as she cast her eyes around the club one last time. "The talent's getting younger and younger, and I ain't."

"Does that mean we've seen the last of Amber Peaches?"

Danny leaned in, kissed Dexter on the lips, and then whispered in his ear, "The world has, but I'll always perform for you."

And with that, Danny Brown walked out of Tattle Tails for good, slid into her car and tossed the envelope Dexter had handed her onto the passenger side seat. As she pulled out of the parking lot, destination Charlston, she caught a glimpse of her old life in the rearview mirror: Amber Peaches, stripped bare, on a stage or on her back, selling her dignity to the highest bidder.

Then, her eyes drifted to her new life, contained inside the envelope to her right: a driver's license, birth certificate, social security card, credit cards, and information for a bank account holding her newfound wealth.

It was everything she would need to become Blythe Cavendish.

Chapter 36

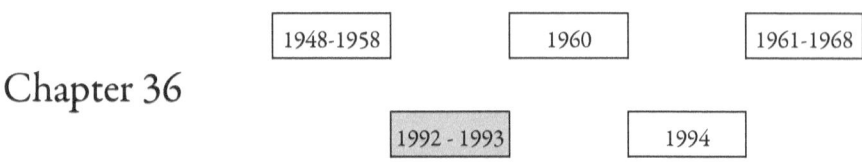

CHARLESTON, SOUTH CAROLINA
EARLY 1992

Danny—now *Blythe*—had fallen in love with Charleston, or at least the idea of Charleston, after watching *Gone with the Wind* at the Wiltern Theater on Wilshire Boulevard. While Charleston was never featured in the movie, it was where Rhett Butler, a character she loved, was from. She'd also read an article in a travel magazine extolling the virtues of the city and talking about how it had recovered from Hurricane Hugo.

Prior to leaving LA, she spent time in a public library researching the city, its history, and what life was like today. When she arrived in Charleston, she knew where she wanted to live, which organizations and clubs to join, and the families that mattered. And she had a plan.

It was a simple plan: the right neighborhood, the right church, the right club, the right people. She started by meeting with a private banker at a local bank, where she opened a checking account into which she deposited the proceeds of the Carrigan Family shakedown. She asked for a referral to a wealth manager, which he gladly provided. Then he went one further and introduced her to the development directors at several of the city's more well-established cultural institutions. By the end of January, she had joined several prominent organizations and clubs around town, including the Charleston Historical Preservation Society, the Charleston Library Society, and the Friends of the Gaillard.

The cherry on top was the home she purchased on South Battery Street overlooking White Point Garden and Charleston Harbor. Anytime homes in that part of town changed hands, it was news, even more so when the buyer was a newcomer to town—and even more so when the buyer was a beautiful, single woman nobody had ever heard of or knew anything about.

Rumors quickly sprouted and spread about who she was and where she'd come from. As for where her wealth came from, she was astute enough to know that new money bragged, and old money did not. She played it cool and allowed rumors to grow and take hold—rumors, some of which, she started herself. It was said she was an heir to a large family fortune in California with roots in the almond business. She had learned a lot about the almond business from one of her regular clients when she was high-priced call girl; the client owned several thousand acres of almond trees. If pressed for details about her family's business, she could carry it off.

Blythe had enough from her settlement with the Carrigans to live out her days happily, if modestly, but she had developed a taste for extraordinary wealth while living in LA and would not be content until she had the same for herself. She wanted more, and how much more could only be measured against what others had. Envy and greed were driving the bus now.

* * *

It was a Sunday afternoon in March, and the weather was picture perfect. The azaleas were in full bloom, peppermint peach trees could be spotted here and there, and the musky scent of the wisteria lay gently across the city. Blythe waved at a friend of hers named Cathy, whom she'd met at one of her High Impact Aerobics classes. She paused at the top of the stairs of the Charleston Library Society until Cathy caught up with her and then they entered together. They were attending a book signing before heading to dinner.

Single and attractive, they turned heads wherever they went. Blythe was wearing a simple, white dress by Anne Klein. The shoulder pads delivered a regal heir, and the bold blue belt accented her thin waist and ample bust. They each took a glass of rosé from the table and stepped to the side to survey the crowd and pick out where they wanted to sit.

"Who's the man talking to Pat Conroy?" asked Blythe in a whisper.

"That's Randal Dunsmore," said Cathy.

"And the woman he's with?"

"A Middleton. Her first name escapes me."

"I see him around quite a bit, but not always with the same woman. Who is Randal Dunsmore?" Blythe asked.

"I forget you're still new to town. Randal is Johnny Dunsmore's little brother."

"*The* Johnny Dunsmore who is our governor?" asked Blythe, although she knew exactly who he was.

"One and the same. Randal is the chairman of the Dunsmore Family Foundation. They support every charity and good cause in town. Randal is invited to every party, and he has a wonderful home not too far from yours. Would you like to meet him? I could introduce you. His daughter and my youngest sister went to school together."

"Daughter?"

"He's a widower. Tragic, really. His wife died giving birth to twins, and only one of the children survived. Her name is Rebeca." Something else Blythe also knew. "But she's away at college or something."

"Sure. Why not?"

* * *

Randal didn't know what hit him. Blythe's years as Danielle Brown, the high-class hooker rubbing elbows with LA corporate titans and Hollywood moguls, and as Amber Peaches, the strip club star, prepared her to go forth with the utmost grace and decorum at a posh Charleston event, but to also work Randal over in the bedroom in ways he had only imagined.

They quickly became an item. She was his plus one at every social event in the Lowcountry. She was a fixture in the galleries along State Street and Broad Street and became a friend and patron to more than one up-and-coming artist. When the date was set, an invitation to their wedding became the most sought-after on the social calendar, at least by women. The date was April 10, 1993. Masters weekend.

The large number of Dunsmore family and friends attending the wedding masked the fact that Blythe Cavendish had precisely zero friends or family from the West Coast in attendance. She allowed the rumors of a contentious battle over the family estate in California to explain their absence—rumors she'd authored. The wedding was a grand affair and was talked about for weeks. The happy couple honeymooned in Europe for a month and returned to set up housekeeping.

For Randal, life was good. He had finally found a woman who respected him and looked up to him, a woman who shared his same lofty opinion of himself, a woman who put his needs above her own, a woman who didn't want children, and a woman who would make Randal a man other men envied. And for Blythe, she too had found what she was looking for.

Chapter 37

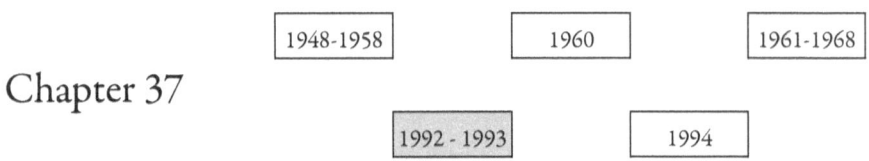

CHARLESTON, SOUTH CAROLINA
OCTOBER 8, 1993

Not long after Blythe and Randal returned from their Honeymoon, cogs within the Dunsmore family machinery noticed a disturbing pattern: Blythe's spending. She went to lunch every day, treating friends, old and new, and she was an easy mark for the proprietors of the King Street jewelry and clothing stores, her reputation amongst the art galleries having already been firmly established.

Blythe had methodically sought out someone like Randal when she hit town in early 1992: someone wealthy, well-connected, and, most importantly, someone who needed her more than he perceived she needed him. With Randal, she'd scored a bullseye on all but one of her desired attributes. While Randal lived a life of wealth, he wasn't wealthy himself.

Randal was a trust fund baby. The trust his parents had established and generously seeded for him and his brothers' benefit was not theirs to control. Colin and Barbara controlled it. They were the trustees and employed experts to run and administer the trust. Colin used the trust distributions as handcuffs, ensuring that his two boys did as they were told. If they performed as expected, the distributions were generous; if they did not, distributions were not. Furthermore, neither Johnny nor Randal could touch the body or corpus of the trust, for it had to be preserved for future generations; upon their deaths, their children would become the next generation of beneficiaries.

On the surface, none of this was apparent. Randal lived in a lavish home south of Broad Street with an envied view of the harbor. Furthermore, his credentials as wealthy and well-connected were burnished by his presence at every high-society event in town. As the chairman of the Dunsmore Family Foundation, he was held up and praised as a generous benefactor to all the right causes. Who could blame Blythe for misreading the situation? Randal had lived his entire adult life allowing people to conclude he was something he wasn't.

There were a few in town who suspected the emperor had no clothes and they were the store owners and foundations who cashed the checks that paid the balances due on his tabs and honored the charitable pledges. The checks these stores and foundations deposited were signed by authorized signatories on checking accounts in the name of the Dunsmore Family Trust or the Dunsmore Family Foundation; rare was the day Randal wrote a check out of a personal checking account.

Blythe got her first look behind the curtain when, much to her embarrassment, her credit was denied at a small gallery along State Street. Blythe and several girlfriends had enjoyed lunch at 82 Queen and were strolling down State Street when they came upon one of her favorite galleries. They stepped in, and the proprietor rushed out of his back office to greet and fawn over Blythe. She took her time selecting a painting with a price tag she was sure her friends would gab about to others. When the proprietor asked her to follow him to the back office, he explained that the bank had been instructed not to honor the check. To save face, she purchased the painting with a personal check of her own, a detail she kept from her girlfriends waiting out front.

Blythe had no intention of keeping the painting; if she had to spend her own money, then it wasn't worth it. No, she would call the gallery the next morning, explain that it didn't fit the space she'd had in mind, and have them pick it up.

In the meantime, Blythe had to get to the bottom of whatever was going on. How could she walk into any restaurant, shop, or gallery in town not knowing whether her credit would be denied? What if Randal was broke? For as much time as she'd spent on her back beneath Randal, she could make more money as a hooker to the Hollywood and corporate elite than she could carrying on as Mrs. Randal Dunsmore. But no, she wasn't going back.

Randal, sweetheart, there must be money somewhere. That's clear from how you live. It's just a matter of getting my hands on it. But first, I need to get my hands on you, she thought. *And by the time I'm done with you, you'll tell me everything I need to know.*

Chapter 38

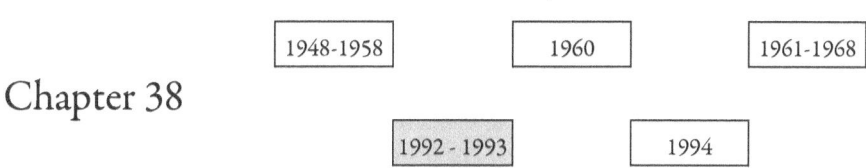

The Drawing Room in Randal Dunsmore's Home

"I'm in here, darling!" Blythe called out from the drawing room—a room adorned with pictures of men on horses surrounded by hunting dogs and the other equine accouterments designed to convince a visitor that Randal hunted and rode horses.

She had selected a long silk nightgown with a slit running from the floor to her hip for the evening. When Randal entered the room, he found his bride lying across the sofa by a crackling fire, holding a champagne flute seductively in her hands. She rose from the sofa and waltzed over to the bar and stood with her back to him so that her left leg emerged through the slit in her gown. She proceeded to make him an Old Fashioned, taking her time while she knew he had to be admiring the view. She turned, walked towards him, and stopped just inches away. He took the glass from her hand and took a sip, and she demurely began removing his tie, casting her eyes up at him with her head cocked to the side as a wickedly delicious smile spread across her beautiful face. She removed his shirt, dropped to her knees, and unzipped his pants. Randal moaned audibly.

This is too easy, she thought. Within a few minutes, Randal was sitting in a straight-backed chair, entirely nude, with his hands bound behind his back and his feet tied securely to the legs of the chair.

"Where did you get those?" he panted, referring to the ties around his wrists and ankles.

"Don't you worry about that," she said, thinking of how she'd hid them behind the pillows on the sofa earlier that day. She then stood before him and allowed her gown to fall to the floor. And she began.

Taking her time, she asked him about his day. He tried to answer coherently, but she knew the blood was fleeing his brain. She returned to the task at hand. Then, stopping again, she announced, "I need to check on dinner. I had the help prepare something and place it in the refrigerator. I just need to put it in the oven to warm things up. Don't go anywhere," she said mischievously, knowing full well he couldn't even if he tried.

She sauntered back into the room a few minutes later.

"Miss me?" She stood immediately in front of him and looked down at his predicament. "Looks like I've still got your attention," she said seductively. "I think it's time to take things up a notch."

Randal grinned and moaned his affirmation. She placed a pillow behind his back, moving his rear closer to the front edge of the chair. "That's better," she said. She checked the ties binding him to the chair, retying them tighter than before. She then walked over to the writing desk in the corner of the room, returned with a sleep mask she had stashed there earlier in the day, placed it over his eyes, and tied a Hermes scarf around his head so the mask would not slip off. She stepped back and admired her handiwork, wondering if Randal was growing a little concerned. *He should be*, she thought as she waited for his attention to flag a bit, and then she began all over again.

After a while, she stopped to make herself a drink and then again, a bit later, to freshen up her drink. And she would start over again. This pattern continued for another two hours, her finding a reason to stop and delay matters only to start up again once his interest waned. From her experience, she knew that the swelling would become painful before long. Finally, when he couldn't take much more, she asked, "Don't you want to know about my day?"

"What?" he managed to ask. Randal was no longer merely breathing heavily—he was gasping for air.

"*My day*," she said. "Don't you want to know about my day?"

"Sure, but can we talk about it later?" And then, out of nowhere, he felt the searing bite of the end of a riding crop slashing through the air and striking the inside of one thigh and then the other. He screamed in a mixture of fear and pain.

"No, we can't," she barked. Then she paused and leaned over him, her mouth just inches from his left ear, and whispered in a calm, seductive voice that demonstrated her total control of the situation, "Now, let me tell you about my day." And she did, beginning with her embarrassment at the art gallery and the purchase she had made. "I was going to return the painting, but I've decided to keep it. You'll reimburse me. I know you've got the money."

Blythe did not forget the leverage she held in her hands, and she slowed things down, prolonging Randal's predicament. "I have questions, though, Darling—questions you're going to answer for me."

"O-okay," he stammered. "Anything you want to know. Just ask me. *Please*, ask me."

And she did. He was treated to the sting of the riding crop when he was slow to answer or when Blythe felt he wasn't forthcoming. The combination of the stick she held in one hand and the carrot she had in the other left Randal confused and on the precipice of a chasm of delirium and agony. It wasn't long before Randal was broken; from that point forward, he answered her questions obediently. By the end of the evening, Blythe had a clearer picture of Randal's financial situation. She patted Randal on the head and left him tied to the chair, his cooperation unrequited.

Chapter 39

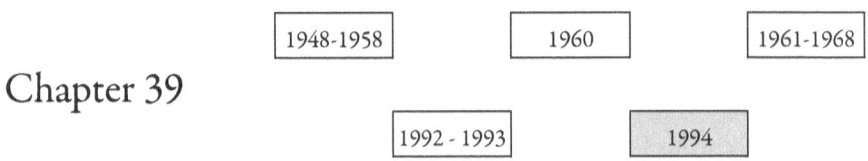

LAW OFFICES OF ATKINS & ATKINS
MONDAY, JULY 11, 1994

Walker was fighting a three-front war against the Dunsmores. He was fighting to have Randal Dunsmore removed as the trustee for Rebeca's trust. He was assisting the Attorney General's Office in their investigation of numerous companies which Walker was convinced were owned by the Dunsmores hiding behind banking secrecy laws, and he was fighting on behalf of the Gastons and others who had been injured by the actions of these companies.

The Gastons were no longer his only clients. As promised, Eddie's efforts at the AG's office turned up numerous other victims of the predatory loans and fraudulent real estate and investment schemes proffered by the companies the AG was investigating. Since litigation was not Walker's forte, he knew he needed help, and he knew where to find it—right across the hall.

Abigail Baker had been Monty Atkins's secretary when he opened his law office in Charleston in the early 1970s. Abigail was smart and a hard worker. She became Monty's paralegal and most trusted confidant at the office. When Monty found himself in deep water—nearly bankrupt and seemingly at the mercy of a vindictive banker in town—Abigail had been one of the few people to stand by him. She went back to school and earned her law degree and cut her teeth working for a litigation specialist in Atlanta before returning to Charleston where she stepped away from practicing law while her children were young. A year ago, with her youngest in the first grade, she called Monty looking for part-time work; he hired her over the phone.

Abigail was thrilled with the opportunity to assist Walker, and she took responsibility for the initial client interviews with the others—discovered by the Attorney General's Office—who had stories like that of the Gastons. Doing so freed up Walker to focus on Rebeca's battle with her father.

* * *

Walker entered his office's conference room holding a pen, legal pad, and manila folder in his left hand. He saw Rebeca standing in front of the bookshelf, his back to him, reading a selection from his father's extensive collection.

"Good morning, Rebeca."

"And good morning to you." She returned the book to the shelf and then met Walker at the end of the table where they shook hands. They each returned to their side of the table and took their seats. Rebeca picked up the coffee mug in front of her and took a sip.

"I see Mrs. Beasley already took care of you," remarked Walker as he nodded to the pot of coffee on the table along with a tray of cream, sugar and a single remaining mug. "Thanks for agreeing to meet with me this morning. I hope I didn't cut short any travel plans. A lot of folks around here use the Fourth of July to launch a two-week vacation."

"No, not at all; I stayed in town," she said, making herself comfortable. "I made it out to Folly Beach for a few days last week. I've reconnected with a few old high school friends since I've been back."

"And how has that been?"

"It was nice—even if it was overshadowed by the fact that I've been elevated to minor celebrity status since I barged into the fundraiser at the Hibernian Hall a month ago." She smirked at Walker from above her mug before taking a sip.

He laughed. "I'm sure. I also saw an article in the *Post & Courier* last week, in which you were quoted extensively. Something about a lawsuit to stop further real estate development along the coast."

"Yeah, that was me. I'm working with a national environmental advocacy group called Meaningful Stewardship. They're opening a local chapter in Charleston. We're focused on slowing reckless development along the fragile coastline—developments that threaten ecosystems that future generations and habitats will depend upon. Our other major focus in this part of the world is overfishing."

"Well, you've been busy, it would seem."

"I have. And you? Do we have a case against my father?"

"I believe we do. I contacted Tad Torcher, and he confirmed what you shared with me from your meeting with him."

"Why did you have to do that? Did you doubt me?" she asked.

"No, but I need him to testify to what he told you in the form of an affidavit, which I have right here," Walker said as he patted his hand on the manila folder he'd brought with him to this meeting.

"Of course. Sorry to have questioned you."

"No, that's quite all right. I'm going to need you to sign one as well. Here's a draft of one that I prepared," Walker said as he removed it from the folder and slid it across the table. She picked it up and scanned the first page. "I'll need you to review it as soon as possible," Walker added. "If you need to make changes, my associate, Abigail Baker, can make the changes and then you'll need to sign it. Mrs. Beasley is a notary, and she'll oversee that."

"This is great. Thank you! Wow, we're really going to do this."

Walker paused to gather his thoughts and then looked right into her eyes. "Rebeca, I want to remind you that what we're doing is bound to stir up emotions, for you and your father. This isn't going to be easy." He waited for a response from her. She sat with her hands crossed in front of her, fingers interlaced and resting on the table. It did not appear a response was going to happen, and so he cleared his throat and added, "I contacted your father and told him I was representing you. I asked him to send me a recent statement."

"Well, what did he say?" asked Rebeca.

"He hemmed and hawed about going through proper channels and that he'd have to get back to me, but he couldn't get off the phone fast enough. I followed up by sending him a certified letter demanding an accounting of trust activity. He refused delivery. That was over a week ago, and now he won't return my calls."

"Walker, don't think I haven't thought about this. I know it will be emotional. It is already, but I've made up my mind," she said, her eyes never breaking away from his.

"Okay."

"So, is it time to sue Randal?" she asked.

"No. Our first step is to petition the court to remove him on the grounds that he refuses to comply with the most basic duties to keep beneficiaries informed. Once we get our hands on the records detailing the trust's activity over the last few years, you'll have a clearer picture of what transpired, and then you can decide whether to sue him. But first things first. Let's get you a new trustee."

"I couldn't agree more."

* * *

After Rebeca signed her affidavit, Walker turned his attention to the stack of affidavits Abigail had assembled following her interviews with the Gastons and the other clients they had signed up. While there were differences in the fact patterns of these new client cases, they all had one thing in common: they were facing a foreclosure action filed by either Palmetto Lending Tree or Coastal Savings & Loan. The defenses Abigail and Walker would formulate against the foreclosure actions would also form the basis for the complaint each client would file against Palmetto Lending Tree and Coastal Savings & Loan in search of damages for their predatory and deceitful business practices.

Walker stood up from behind his desk and walked slowly about his office. It was time to call Eddie at the AG's office and see how things were proceeding on his front. He made the call and pushed the speaker button. The call was answered, and he was transferred to Eddie's office.

"What's up?" Eddie said.

"Just called to see how the grand jury proceedings were going," Walker answered.

"They're going," said Eddie. "The first batch of subpoenas went out a couple of weeks ago to purported victims of the target companies. We'll be taking their testimony before the grand jury for the next couple of days. We're taking a break now. The folks who testified this morning all had similar stories. These companies are dirty."

"Awesome!" Walker had stopped pacing and was leaning over his desk, a huge smile across his face. Their testimony would only help in his defense of the foreclosure actions his clients were facing.

"Yes, it is, but the real fun begins when we start taking the testimony of the officers of these companies. We blanketed the city with process servers so that every subpoena we're issuing was served on these guys within a half hour of each other."

"That's excellent. I'd love to be a fly on those walls," Walker said. "Thanks and keep me posted."

"Happily."

* * *

The subpoenaed companies' employees ran for cover.

It was as if a small bomb had gone off. They stormed into the office of the president of each company with questions the president couldn't answer: *Am I going to jail? Do I need an attorney? Do I have to go? Will the company pay for my attorney? What's going on?*

When it became obvious he didn't have answers, they ceased asking questions and commenced with declaratory statements: *I'm not going to jail for some rich guy. I didn't do anything wrong. I only did what I was told to do. Somebody better fix this.*

Their reaction was consistent with human nature and exactly what the AG's office anticipated and hoped for. Attorney General Joshua Langston was adamant that the target of the investigation was the people who decided to foist fraudulent business practices on the public. He was not interested in going after low-level employees who were following orders. Instead, he hoped to flip them so they would testify against the higher-ups and, most of all, the owners of these businesses who profited most from this criminal behavior.

Word spread through these offices like wildfire, and by the end of the day, the other officers in these companies were huddled in the president's office behind closed doors while the subpoenaed employees were gathered in the parking lot about to head home, scared and angry. The presidents of these companies all called the person to whom they reported to find out what the hell was going on and what they were supposed to do. None of them knew at the time that they were all calling the same person.

* * *

Law Offices of Anthony Ferguson
Nassau, Bahamas
Tuesday, July 12, 1994

It takes three data points to form a pattern, but Anthony Ferguson had a pretty good idea of what was happening after the second phone call. After the tenth, there was no doubt. The South Carolina Attorney General's Office was sniffing around the operations of the various Palmetto companies. What did the AG's office know? How did this get started? How would it play out?

He couldn't help but recall that strange visitor back in June—the man who had arrived and disappeared all in a day, never heard from again, who represented clients who had been injured by questionable practices carried out by a host of companies in South Carolina that were all domiciled in the Caribbean and for which he was the registered agent.

"Hadn't he left behind his business card?" Ferguson rummaged through his desk and found what he was looking for. He pulled the card from the back of the top center drawer, held it up, and said out loud to the room: "Walker Atkins. What are you up to?"

Anthony Ferguson called the Miami offices of the law firm of Sanchez & Sanchez. Luis Sanchez was not available. Anthony left a message. By the end of the day, when Luis had not returned his call, he dialed his direct line and explained the situation. As Anthony suspected, the first question out of his mouth was simple: *How did this get started?*

He shared with him his suspicions, and by the close of business in Charleston the next day, Luis had passed along these suspicions to others, and the presidents of each of the target companies had a local lawyer on their side.

Chapter 40

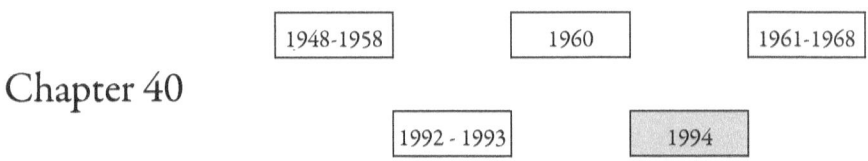

RANDAL DUNSMORE'S HOME
MURRAY BOULEVARD, CHARLESTON
FRIDAY, JULY 15, 1994

Colin Dunsmore and his two sons gathered in Randal's home office on the third floor of his palatial home overlooking the Ashley River, where it flowed into Charleston Harbor. Though it was his son's home, Colin sat behind the antique writer's desk in the office while Johnny paced the room and Randal slumped in a chair in the corner.

"Boys, we're four months out from the election. We don't need this kind of attention," said Colin, vocalizing the obvious.

"It's not my fault," said Randal. "I have nothing to do with how those businesses are run."

"Shut up, *Grundel*," said Johnny.

"Both of you, shut up!" snapped Colin. "Now, Johnny," he went on, "you told me that Luis Sanchez gave you a call and that he has some idea as to why Palmetto Lending Tree and the rest of those companies have all been subpoenaed. So, what's going on?"

"It seems that when the subpoenas were delivered Monday, everyone that received one—and make no mistake about it, *every* officer at Palmetto Lending Tree, Palmetto Quick Cash, the whole lot of them, received one—called Anthony Fergusson in the Bahamas. Well, it turns out that Walker Atkins, an attorney here in town—"

"Yeah, I know who Walker Atkins is. Get to the point," his father barked.

"Walker Atkins visited Anthony Ferguson's office in June. Said he was representing clients who'd been injured by Palmetto Lending Tree's predatory business practices and that Walker knew that the true owners of Palmetto Lending Tree were hiding behind the Bahamas banking laws. He threatened Anthony with legal action and then offered him a way out if he'd roll over on the true owners."

"Anthony didn't squeal, did he?"

"No, of course not," Johnny said. "Monday, when he began receiving the calls, Anthony remembered Walker's visit in back in June. He called Luis Sanchez back in June when Atkins visited and then he called him again Monday when he started receiving panicky phone calls from the company presidents who were subpoenaed."

Colin rocked back and forth in his chair. "I still don't get it. What does Walker's visit to Ferguson's office on a private, civil matter in June have to do with a grand jury criminal investigation now? Maybe it's just a coincidence."

"It's not. After Luis called me yesterday, I had the records at Palmetto Lending Tree and Coastal S&L searched and we found that Walker Atkins is representing several borrowers who we are foreclosing on."

Colin nodded. Some dots were taking shape and aligning.

"And then I called our source in the AG's office. According to him, Eddie Wentworth, the attorney in the AG's office heading up the investigation, is a close friend of Walker's," explained Johnny. "The AG's office hired Walker Atkins under some sort of co-investigative collaboration agreement. Eddie Wentworth and Walker Atkins are working together."

Colin nodded as if it all made sense now. "A couple of Boy Scouts." Colin scoffed. "Anything else?"

"After just a few days of testimony from people claiming they were victims of these companies, the AG's office is confident they can put together a case against Palmetto Lending Tree and the rest of the front companies."

"The bastards at the AG's office can investigate all they want. They'll never get to us," insisted Colin.

"I'm not so sure." Johnny paused in front of the window, raking his hands nervously through his hair as he looked outside. "It's on public record that we're part owners of Coastal Savings & Loan, and they're wrapped up in all this. That's incriminating."

"Not at a level that ties them to the actions of the other companies. The aggressive practices of those other companies are what's drawing the attention of the AG," continued Colin. "Not anything that Coastal S&L is doing. Besides, we're minority owners."

"Aggressive? Don't you mean *criminal?*" asked Randal sarcastically.

"Shut up, Grundel."

"Shut up, *both of you*," said Colin.

Everyone in the room was silent for a few moments.

Then, Johnny spoke up. "According to our mole, the attorney general won't be happy if all they do is convict a few low-level employees or simply fine the companies; their real target are the *owners* of these companies—and that's us."

"They'll never make the connection," Colin said dismissively. "Their efforts will run into a wall, a dead end—courtesy of your pal, Luis Sanchez. As you know, every single one of those companies is owned by a faceless partnership or corporate entity in the Caribbean, and the money we receive from those companies is wired to our offshore bank accounts also in the Caribbean. We're bulletproof."

Colin cleared his throat and went on. "However, these investigations by the AG's office aren't the only problem our business interests are facing, are they? No, they're not. We're now facing a rash of lawsuits by environmental wackos who are slowing down our oceanside real estate developments and adding to the costs."

"Yeah, and whose fault is that, *Grundel?*" asked Johnny. "It ain't mine."

Randal returned to looking out the window.

"So, Randal, what are we doing about your daughter, Rebeca? She's the face of these groups suing the developers, after all. Please tell me that she does not know about our involvement with them," said Colin, "because she continually intimates that we are involved."

"She can't prove anything. She thinks that because we are part-owners of Coastal S&L, there's no difference between the developers, the bank, and our family since Coastal S&L makes loans to the developers she hates. She lumps us all together—can't help herself."

"That may be the case, but it's bad press for me," said Johnny, who had stopped pacing long enough to stand over Randal and prod him in the chest with his finger. "You're becoming an embarrassment to this family. You can't control your own daughter."

"That's *enough*, Johnny. And stop that pacing. I'm getting seasick just watching you," said Colin. "Yes, there's a chance that either a leak from the AG's office or fallout from the lawsuits could make it into the news and wash up on Johnny. You've got a comfortable lead in the polls, but we'll take nothing for granted. We're playing the long game here. Our goal is the White House, and we all have our role to play. That means you too, Randal."

Randal nodded his head dutifully as he returned to looking out the window.

"So, this is how we'll play it," said Colin. "Johnny, if the grand jury investigation makes it to the press and if word gets out that the beneficial owners are hiding behind bank secrecy laws, then you take a hard stance against corrupt businesses that hide behind these laws and offshore bank accounts. This position will draw national attention, which is good for our image. You'll push for help at the federal level. Commissions will convene, and Congress will call for harsher banking laws."

Johnny nodded.

Collin gave him a pointed look. "Then, pull in Luis and his old man," he said, noticing Johnny's face deflate slightly, wilting along with his posture. "I know you've gained a strange aversion to utilizing their connections, but they are a powerful family and a valuable asset."

"I'm aware of that," Johnny said. In a whisper, he added, "More than you know."

Colin shrugged it off. "Their connections on Capitol Hill will ensure that these pointless laws are passed—and that, to the public, will make it look like DC is tackling the problem. And business will continue as usual."

Johnny sighed, nodding, and Randal continued looking out the window.

"Randal, have the Dunsmore Foundation donate to the environmental group your daughter Rebeca is involved with—the one suing the developers. That will set us on the right side of things. Make sure our donation is big enough to make the paper, but not too big. Got it?"

Randal nodded silently.

"Johnny," Colin went on, barking orders like a general, "talk up the importance of environmental stewardship at your campaign stops. We'll turn this crap to our advantage."

Johnny, who was sitting now, leaned back in his chair and smiled.

"Is there anything else, boys?" asked Colin.

Randal sheepishly raised his hand.

"Well, what is it?" asked Colin.

"The suits aren't the only thing Rebeca is up to," Randal confessed, voice soft.

Johnny and Colin looked at each other, and then Randal, waiting for him to continue.

"She hired an attorney and has petitioned the court to have me removed as the trustee of the LeMar trust—the one Dixie's parents set up for her," explained Randal.

"When did this happen?" asked Colin, clearly perturbed by this latest revelation.

"The petition was filed yesterday."

"And who's the attorney?"

"Walker Atkins."

"You're kidding," remarked Johnny.

"I wish I was."

"Well, that's curious. But look, while it's not good news, it ain't the worst news, either. Just handle it, Randal. Give her what she wants and make this go away. And if that doesn't shut her up, we'll go back to the press and paint her as greedy—as the black sheep of the family. Again, use it to our advantage."

"Greedy?" asked Randal. "How so?"

"Oh, you know. The usual. The ungrateful child who was raised by a loving father but fell in with some leftist commies. Have a few stories run with pictures of you and that broad you married—maybe walking out of church or something wholesome like that. That'll play well when your daughter is trying to portray herself as a morally superior environmental warrior. Like I said, it ain't good news, Randal, but if that's the worst news you have for us, then it ain't so bad."

Colin held is son's gaze for a moment before Randal broke it off and turned back to the window and the view outside. "What is it, son?" But Randal didn't have to say a word, fear was etched into every wrinkle of his brow.

Chapter 41

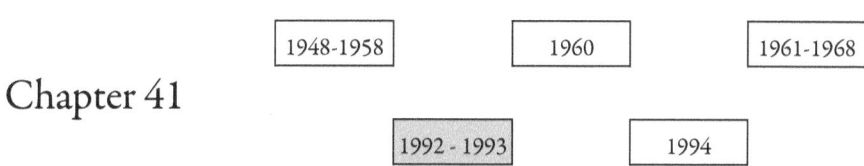

RANDAL DUNSMORE'S HOME OFFICE
CHARLESTON, SOUTH CAROLINA
OCTOBER 9, 1993

The day after Blythe had tied Randal to the chair, armed with copies of both the Dunsmore Trust and the LeMar Trust—documents that Randal turned over without a whimper—Blythe faxed them to Dexter Childress in Los Angeles. She wanted him to explain the documents to her. He was a trained attorney, after all.

Blythe telephoned Dexter from Randal's desk. Randal was asleep in one of the guest rooms downstairs, exhausted from the previous evening's festivities. "Hey, honey. Have you had a chance to review the docs I faxed you?" she asked.

"I sure did, but why don't you tell me what is going on?"

She told him everything, including how she came into possession of the trust documents she had faxed him and everything Randal had divulged to her.

"So, Amber Peaches is alive and well," he said.

"For the moment. Now tell me what you've learned from reading what I faxed you."

"From the Dunsmore Trust, you get nothing," said Dexter. "The beneficiaries are Randal and his brother, Johnny, and their descendants. Randal gets regular distributions but from what he told you last night, the folks that manage that trust watch it like a hawk. You *could* have kids with him and then when Randal dies, your kids would get money from the trust," Dexter said with a chuckle, "but that's the closest you'll get to that payout."

"Procreate with that guy? Not on your life!" Blythe said. "What about the LeMar Trust, the one his daughter Rebeca gets money from? Anything there?"

"Nope. Even if you had kids with him, they wouldn't receive anything under it. Only the descendants of Rebeca's mother receive anything, and Rebeca is the only heir. Even if Randal had other children, they wouldn't receive anything, because the trust only benefits the heirs of Dixie Dunsmore."

"What the hell am I supposed to do?" she asked. "I didn't marry limp-dick for his charm and good looks. I married him for his money!"

"Don't worry. I gotta plan."

"Let's hear it."

"You see, Randal is the trustee for the LeMar Trust. He controls the investments and the distributions to any current heirs as long as he is alive. The only living beneficiary is his daughter, Rebeca. Correct?"

"Yeah. They're not close."

"Does the trust send her money?"

"Yes. Randal told me he paid her college tuition with the trust and that he sends her money quarterly."

"Does he manage it all?" asked Dexter.

"No. There's an accountant and stockbroker that do all the work."

"Well, that's about to change, baby cakes."

"What do you mean?" asked Blythe.

"The firm of Dexter Childress is about to take over as manager of the LeMar Trust. You and me, babe. We're going to move the LeMar Trust investments into ventures that *we're* behind. We're going to pay ourselves fat fees. We're going to get rich."

"What about his daughter, Rebeca?"

"We'll keep a checking account active in Charleston, and we'll keep sending her money, so she doesn't get suspicious. Not too much, though. And you keep Randal in line. Sounds like last night was quite a night..."

"Oh, it was, honey. Putty in my hands."

"I'm sure, but how long will he stay down? I doubt you'll be able to coax him back into the chair. What are you gonna do if he protests?" asked Dexter.

"You still know that guy who develops film regardless of what's on it?"
"Of course."
"Then we've got nothing to worry about."

* * *

By the end of the next week, Dexter was up and running with fake letterhead, business cards, and an operational plan. At Blythe's direction, Randal called the CPA firm of Torcher and Banks and fired them. Blythe was sitting across the desk from him when he made the call. The next call was to Dexter Childress. She dialed the number and put the phone on speaker while they waited for Dexter to answer. He did, and after a few pleasantries, he began faxing very official-looking paperwork to Randal for his signature while describing his extensive experience in the field of investments and trust management. Blythe placed each signature page in front of Randal, and by the time the phone call was over, he had signed every document. Blythe faxed the signed pages to Dexter and promised to mail him the originals later that day.

"You've made a wise decision, Randal," said Dexter. "I look forward to working with you."

Randal didn't seem to know what to say, so he said nothing.

"And we look forward to working with you too, Mr. Childress," replied Blythe and the call ended.

* * *

Randal knew that the next steps were crucial. He would have to wire the money in the trust from the local bank in Charleston to a bank in California that Dexter selected and also transfer the custodial responsibilities for the stocks and bonds the trust owned from Paine Weber, where they were currently held, to Biltmore Strickland Brokerage, a small shop in Los Angelas. Dexter had a contact inside Biltmore Strickland and once Dexter's guy at Biltmore Strickland became the custodian of the stocks and bonds, Dexter could direct their sale as he wished without drawing the attention of a compliance department in a larger institution.

If he was going to man up and put a stop to what Blythe was doing, it would have to be now. The game was over once she and Dexter had control of the trust assets.

"Randal, sweetheart, we're almost done," said Blythe. That morning, the bank and the brokerage houses faxed the necessary paperwork, which she had completed; all that was needed was his signature. But faxed authorizations of this sort would not suffice. Randal knew he would have to go to the bank and execute the wire transfer. A notary would have to certify that Randal had signed the custodial transfer authorization documents before Blythe could fax them to Paine Weber. Even after receiving the notarized authorizations, Randal knew from previous dealings with Paine Weber that they may telephone and ask him to confirm the authorization verbally. Randal knew this was crunch time.

He suspected that Blythe did too. Something broke inside him the night Blythe tied him to the chair, and he'd been searching for a modicum of self-respect ever since that evening. He knew this was his chance. If he was ever going to recover, he had to take a stand now.

"Now all you need to do is take care of this last bit of paperwork, and you'll never have to worry about any of this again." The words dripped from her mouth, as soft as honey-butter. She slid the paperwork over the desk's smooth, mahogany surface, and handed him a pen. She was sitting in his chair, behind his antique writing desk in his home office.

Randal merely stared at it.

She cleared her throat. "Just a signature away from enjoying our breakfast, dear," she said, referring to the scent of pancakes floating up the stairwell from the kitchen. She tapped the place for him to sign.

"No," he finally blurted out, shoving the paperwork back across the desk.

Blythe gave him a look of incredulity and outrage. "*What* did you say?"

"You heard me. I said *no*. I'm not doing it." Randal looked her hard in the eyes. "That money is Rebeca's, and I'm the trustee. I won't allow it. You and Dexter, or whoever he is, can go to hell. I'm putting a stop to this now."

Blythe didn't move and didn't say a word. Rather, she stood up and left the room.

* * *

Randal breathed a sigh of relief. He had done it. He hated confrontation, but by the looks of things, Blythe having left the room, he had won. He had stood up to her. Soon, he would file for divorce, he thought. He'd get his life back. His finances back.

But then, she strolled back into the room and tossed an envelope on the desk before him.

"Open it," she demanded.

He did, and whatever vestige of manhood that he had been clinging to just a moment ago died permanently. Inside the envelope were pictures of that night—of him tied to the chair, stark naked and sweating like a pig. One might argue that positive identification was not possible in that an eye mask was tied securely around his head with a Hermes scarf, but the Dunsmore family portrait hanging prominently on the wall behind him in every picture removed any such doubt.

"I want these documents signed, notarized, and faxed by the end of the day. And if you get any crazy ideas about trying to wrestle these pictures away from me, understand this: Dexter has copies, and he's holding the negatives. If the money is not wired to the new bank account by the end of today, he will mail copies of the pictures to the Charleston newspapers. And if the paperwork transferring custodial care of the stocks and bonds is not processed by the end of tomorrow, he will mail copies of these pictures to the Charleston newspapers."

Randal sat there in complete horror and shock. This woman was blackmailing him!

"Oh, and one more thing, sweetheart. Don't even *think* about divorcing me. I look forward to being Mrs. Randal Dunsmore until I'm done with you."

Chapter 42

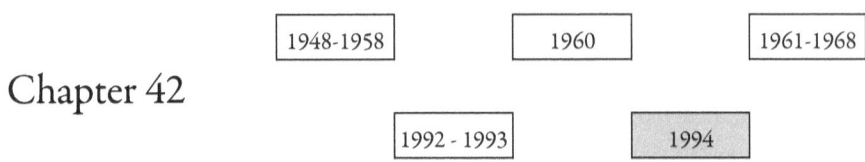

THE ATTORNEY GENERAL'S CHARLESTON SATELLITE OFFICE
WEDNESDAY, AUGUST 3, 1994

Attorney General Joshua Langston was slumped in a chair twirling a rubber band in his hands and sitting across the desk from Eddie Wentworth. Joshua had loosened his tie when he entered Eddie's office and draped his jacket over the back of the chair. His shirt was crumpled; the humidity of the late summer had won. Walker was sitting in the chair next to him. Eddie wasn't making eye-contact with anyone.

"So, what you're telling me is that after over a week of testimony from the presidents, vice-presidents, and CFOs of every company under our radar—Palmetto Lending Tree, Palmetto Quick Cash, Coastal Savings & Loan, the whole lot of them—you've got *nothing*. Am I hearing that correctly?" asked Joshua. Eddie and Walker remained silent. "Well, Eddie, this is your show. Tell me something."

"They were tipped off as to what the victims testified to earlier in the investigation," Eddie insisted. "They had to be," he said, slamming his fist on the desk. "It's the only explanation."

"Walker, what do you think? Is Eddie right?"

"Yes, sir, I believe he is. The testimony of every subpoenaed witness was remarkably similar. Seemed rehearsed."

"Did they all hire the same attorney to help them prepare for their appearance before a grand jury? That would explain it," Joshua remarked.

"It would, but no," Eddie said. "We had folks scouring the parking lot and the lobby of our building. Every witness had their own attorney."

Joshua, still slumped over in his chair, stared up at the ceiling and kept twirling the rubber band. "So, what did they say? What was the 'remarkably similar' testimony of the witnesses?"

"Well, first of all, not a single officer in these companies knows who the real owners are. When asked, they all answered that they were owned by an LLC or a partnership of some sort," explained Eddie.

"And do we know anything about these companies?" Joshua asked.

Eddie looked to Walker.

"Each company they named was one of the companies I discovered, and each one is located in the Caribbean," explained Walker.

Joshua nodded as if this was exactly what he'd expected them to find. "But no one could give you the name of a single *person*. Is that right?"

"That's right," said Eddie. "There's more. Every witness admitted that the business practices the victims testified to did, in fact, take place, but they denied *knowing* the practices were against the law. They were adamant about that, insisting they thought everything they were doing was above board."

"And who developed the business practices they so effectively implemented?" asked Joshua.

"We don't know. We asked them, of course. Each one said they didn't know, either," said Eddie.

"So, we're to believe that manuals just *magically* appeared on their desks instructing them to sell fraudulent financial services and how to do so?" Joshua asked sarcastically.

"One name *did* pop up," Eddie said.

Joshua sat up in his chair and shrugged, as if to say, *What are you waiting for? What name?*

"A few guys took the fifth when we started homing in on who was in charge, but those that talked all fingered the same guy—a lawyer named Anthony Ferguson," Eddie said.

"He's the man I visited in the Bahamas in June," Walker said.

Joshua sat up quickly in his chair with a note of hope in his voice. "Then let's get him in here."

"Not that simple," explained Eddie. "The extradition treaty we signed a few years ago with the Bahamas doesn't go into effect until September 22nd of this year. We figure he'll be into the wind by then."

Joshua slumped back down in his chair and returned to twirling the rubber band. He saw Walker and Eddie exchange a glance. "What?" he asked. "Please tell me one of you has an idea. So far, this whole investigation has been a bust. You do realize I'm up for reelection, right?"

Eddie spoke up. "We want to subpoena the Dunsmores."

"Which one?" Joshua asked, doing nothing to mask an incredulous stare.

"Johnny. His old man, Colin. Whoever makes the decisions for their family business," answered Eddie. "The Dunsmores are minority owners of Coastal S&L, and we have testimony from several clients of the S&L that they were sold high-yield bonds by account managers at Coastal, who told them that the FDIC guaranteed the investment. This is a slam dunk—fraud, and a clear violation of securities law. We can nail the Dunsmores with this."

"Walker, what are your thoughts?" asked Joshua.

"Eddie and I have gone back and forth on this strategy and I'm sure the Dunsmores are dirty, but I'm not as confident as Eddie that we can get to the Dunsmores. As minority owners, they can easily claim ignorance about the practices employed by the bank and who authored them. The law does not automatically assign liability to minority shareholders, even in closely held corporations. In fact, the Dunsmores are just as likely to claim victim status and sue Coastal S&L for breach of duties owed by the majority shareholders to minority shareholders. They'd do it just for show and then drop the suit when it was convenient."

"But this could help us," argued Eddie. "If they file a suit, we may learn the identity of the true owners behind the faceless corporations and partnerships that are the majority shareholders of Coastal S&L, along with the Dunsmores. I'd wager my kids that it's the same group of people who own Palmetto Lending Tree and all the other companies."

Joshua was shaking his head. "I gotta agree with Walker. The Dunsmores will *threaten* a suit and make noise, but they may never *actually* file a suit. They'll just use their bully pulpit to help Johnny get reelected," Joshua said. "No, I'm afraid that calling Colin or Johnny Dunsmore to the stand is a dangerous game. It's an election year, and he's on the other side of the aisle. If we call him before the grand jury, it's bound to leak. Hell, they'd leak the story *themselves*—and that bastard Johnny will use it against me in my reelection bid for the Attorney General's Office."

"Okay, that may all be true, but we're running out of options. Where's the satisfaction if we send a few lackeys to jail and fine the companies but don't get at the *real* perpetrators? Where's the deterrence? They'll just do it again," Eddie said, openly frustrated.

"I hear you, Eddie. I do," said Joshua. "But I need to sleep on this one. Let's finish up the week and see if we learn anything useful from the remaining witnesses. Offer immunity to some of the officers if they help find out who the owners are. And then the three of us should get on a call next week."

"Okay, boss," said Eddie. "Will do."

* * *

Randal's Home Office
August 5, 1994

The three men were in the usual positions for their weekly Friday strategy session: Johnny pacing the room, a drink in his hand; Colin situated behind Randal's desk, taking charge; and Randal in the chair by the window, his mind elsewhere.

"Johnny, what's the latest from our man inside the AG's office?" Colin demanded.

"It's all good. They got nothing. Our guy gave Anthony Ferguson the lowdown on what all the poor schmucks testified to, so we knew what we were dealing with. Ferguson found each of them their own attorney so their testimony wouldn't look coordinated." And his father joined him in laughter as they said, in unison, *"But it was."*

"That's great. Love it. So, they got nothing, huh?" said Colin.

"The AG's office has no idea that we're the largest shareholders in those companies and he'll never find out. There are a couple of things, though," Johnny said. "They may try to extradite Ferguson, so in mid-September, he needs to take a vacation."

"Sure, why not? He's earned it. Anything else?" Colin asked.

"Yeah, Eddie Wentworth wants to subpoena us and try to indict Coastal S&L."

"You're kidding!"

"Nope. I'm not. The AG ain't too keen on it, though. Said he wants to think about it. They're going to finish up taking the testimony of a few other witnesses they haven't gotten to and then decide."

Colin groaned in dissatisfaction. "How's Joshua Langston doing in his bid for reelection?" Colin asked.

"He's cruising. Skip Jackson isn't proving to be much of a challenge," Johnny answered.

"Well, that's about to change. We're going to get out ahead of Langston and leak a story that the AG's office is looking for an excuse to subpoena *you*, Johnny," Colin said.

"Me?"

"Yep. You see, they're bungling an important investigation and weaponizing the AG's office at the same time in an attempt to bring down an important public servant." Colin could hide neither his smile nor his contempt for the AG's office as he laid out the hitjob he envisioned one of their lackeys in the press writing.

"I love it," Johnny said.

* * *

By the end of the following week, news broke of a poll, a poll conducted by an agency the Dunsmores kept in their back pocket, that showed Joshua Langston's opponent in the race for Attorney General, Skip Jackson, closing in on him. The story was bolstered by the Dunsmores' announcement that they were endorsing Skip Jackson in his race and would put the full weight of their resources behind getting him elected. The landscape for Joshua Langston and for Eddie and Walker worsened when they each read the lead editorial in the Sunday morning edition of the local paper.

"Does the State of South Carolina Need to Clean House at the Attorney General's Office?"
August 14, 1994

Evidence has surfaced that local attorney Walker Atkins has colluded with his old high school friend Eddie Wentworth at the Attorney General's Office to smear several prominent local companies and the reputations of the men and women who work there. Walker Atkins represents several clients who have failed to pay their mortgages on beachfront homes and who now want to blame the companies that built the houses, developed the properties, loaned them the money, and anyone else they can think of rather than repay their loans.

The word is that Walker Atkins promised his clients that if they signed with him, they would never have to repay the money they owed—a bold assurance that flies in the face of the Rules of Professional Conduct written by the well-respected American Bar Association. Mr. Walker Atkins apparently conspired with Eddie Wentworth, a senior prosecutor in the Attorney General's Office, to use the full force of the State's prosecutorial powers to gather evidence and to bully and threaten the companies that Walker Atkins is suing with fines and jail time if they don't drop the foreclosure proceedings and settle with his clients out of court.

But the conspiracy does not stop with Eddie Wentworth. The Post & Courier has proof that at Langston's suggestion, the Attorney General's Office hired Walker Atkins as a "consultant" in order to hide his involvement and better collude. With Walker Atkins supplying the names of people he wanted prosecuted, the Attorney General's Office subpoenaed people who, through no fault of their own, found themselves in Walker Atkin's crosshairs as they sat through hours of humiliating questioning at the hands of career-obsessed prosecutors.

The grand jury testimony has yet to turn up what the Attorney General's Office was looking for: a single guilty party. Desperate to justify the grand jury proceedings and the subpoenas issued to these companies, the Attorney General's Office is now contemplating issuing a subpoena to our sitting governor, Johnny Dunsmore. What's in it for Walker Atkins? Money. What's in it for Eddie Wentworth? Money, very likely. It's easy to imagine Walker Atkins cutting his friend in on a piece of the action. But as for Eddie Wentworth, it's no secret he has an eye on his boss's job, and his boss, Joshua Langston, has his eye on the governor's—perhaps not this election cycle, but one day. Of that, no one should doubt.

Voters have a chance to stop Attorney General Langston's climb to that office this November as he seeks reelection against the reinvigorated campaign of a promising up-and-comer, Skip Jackson.

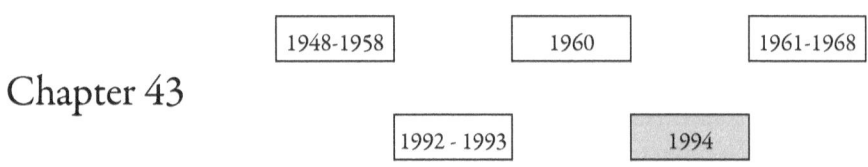

Chapter 43

SALTY MIKE'S
CHARLESTON, SOUTH CAROLINA
WEDNESDAY, AUGUST 24, 1994

Whenever Eddie and Walker got together to catch up over a couple of beers, they would meet at Carolina's on Exchange Street. But that was not the case tonight. Carolina's was too high-profile, populated as it was by the young professional crowd in Charleston. They knew they were taking a big risk meeting in public in the first place, so they chose to meet at a table at the back of Salty Mike's instead.

"We should come here more often," Walker said as he looked around the bar.

The clientele consisted of fisherman, dock workers, a couple of white-collar guys, truck drivers, and a few college kids. It was a true dive-bar. The smell of pluff mud from the salt marshes floated in on the breeze coming across the harbor.

"Can you smell it?" asked Walker. "The smell of pluff mud brings me home like no other."

Eddie was too preoccupied to notice. "Do you know why pluff mud smells the way it does?" he asked.

"Oh, no, I have no idea . . . please, tell me," Walker said sarcastically, trying to lighten the mood a little bit. Everyone who'd grown up in the Lowcountry knew precisely why pluff mud had such a distinct odor.

"Because it's comprised of decaying plant and animal matter," Eddie said without looking up from his bottle. "That's you and me—decaying plant and animal matter feeding the ecosystem of crooks, thieves, and liars that run this town."

"Look, Eddie, I'm sure that once the investigation is completed, you'll be cleared."

"Maybe, maybe not, but it doesn't matter. I know how this works. Last week they put me on administrative leave. That was step one," Eddie said as he looked at Walker.

"Eddie, I'm so sorry."

"It's okay. Joshua had to do it. He had to distance himself from me. Skip Jackson is gaining on him in the polls. What a tool that guy is! I don't know why Joshua ever hired him. Tomorrow, the AG will announce that they've opened an investigation into whether you and I conspired to bring down the governor and the companies we were investigating. Joshua gave me a heads-up this afternoon. I'm telling you this because you may need to hire your own attorney."

Walker nodded his appreciation for the news. He wasn't surprised. It'd already occurred to him that he'd probably need to find his own lawyer.

"My fate now hangs in the balance of the election. If Joshua is reelected, the investigation will be quietly wrapped up. I'll be sanctioned and nothing more. And a few months later, you'll see a one-paragraph article in the paper stating that I have resigned from the Attorney General's Office and returned to private practice. If Skip Jackson wins, there's no telling what he might do. Either way, my future with the AG's office is over."

Walker didn't know what to say, so he kept silent.

"Heh . . ." Eddie shook his head. "I guess the silver lining is Vanessa and I won't have to worry about whether we'll have to move back to Columbia. Maybe I can get a job here working at Salty Mike's," he said, smiling for the first time since they'd sat down. "I'm sorry to go on like this . . . I know the last week or so hasn't been a picnic for you, either."

Walker shook his head, indicating he agreed, but that he didn't want to dwell on it.

"I read that the local Bar Association has opened an ethics investigation into your conduct," Eddie went on.

"Yeah. Dad is encouraging me to hire an attorney. He agrees with you that I may need one if I am swept up with you in the AG's investigation."

"He's right, you know. Having your own attorney will help you keep your mind on your clients."

"Well, that's become a whole lot easier," Walker said. "In the wake of the Ed Op and the other stories the paper ran, I've lost about half of the clients I was representing in foreclosure actions brought by Palmetto Lending Tree and Coastal S&L."

"What about the Gastons? Are they still with you?"

"Yeah, they are," Walker said as he smiled and stared at his beer bottle. "They came by the office and asked a few questions but said they had the utmost faith in me."

"That's great. Good for you."

The two of them slipped into a moment of silence and drank their beers.

"Eddie, do you want to shoot a game of pool?"

"Nah. How about a bucket of shrimp and another beer? Then we head home and see our wives."

"Sounds perfect. Oh, and Eddie, remember, 'For those who love God . . .'"

"'. . . all things work together for good.' Thanks for the reminder, buddy. Appreciate it."

They clinked their beer bottles and ordered that bucket of shrimp.

* * *

Two days later . . .
Randal's Home Office
Friday, August 26, 1994

Randal was sitting in his home office—three flights above the sidewalk outside—when he heard his father and brother enter the house. He couldn't make out what they were saying, but he heard laughter from the bottom of the stairwell, and it certainly sounded like they were in a good mood. *Sound really travels in these old houses.* He knew Johnny would stop at his bar and pour himself a drink before mounting the stairs, and that delay would buy him some time, but even so, Randal needed to end the call fast.

"So, you'll send the requested docs in time?" Randal confirmed with a sigh of relief.

"You can count on it," said the voice on the other end of the line.

Randal hung up, ending the call as he heard his father and brother summit the steps. The door to his office was closed but that didn't stop Johnny from walking in without knocking.

Colin was huffing and puffing and sweating profusely. "When are you going to put an elevator in this godforsaken house? I hate these old homes that everyone here is so in love with."

"An acquired taste, I guess," Randal said as he rose from behind his desk and took a seat in the chair next to the window.

Colin plopped himself down in the chair that Randal had been sitting in, took a long swig of his drink and inventory of his two sons.

"We certainly showed that a-hole, Joshua, and his two Boy Scouts, didn't we?" boasted Johnny.

"We sure as hell did," Colin said as he banged his right hand down on Randal's desk.

"A thing of beauty, Pops. We couldn't have scripted it any better. The latest polls have me in front by eighteen points," said Johnny.

"And what about Skip Jackson? Is he going to pull this off?"

"He's got a real chance," said Johnny. "But he needs something else to talk about on his campaign stops. He's not the best on the stump; unless he's super prepared or fed talking points, he comes across as flat. He doesn't ad-lib well on the trail."

"Not like *you*, Johnny," remarked Randal as he picked at his fingernails.

"Shut up, *Grundle*."

Colin just shook his head in disgust. "We'll get to you in a minute, Randal."

"Initially, when the stories broke, he climbed quickly in the polls, but he's since plateaued," Johnny said.

"What do you suggest?" asked Colin.

"The story of collusion between Walker Atkins and the AG's office was a stroke of genius, but it's run its course. At the end of the day, most folks in these parts have a high opinion of the Atkins family—especially Walker's aloof brother, Eli. The man's a folk hero, and Walker has been carried along on his coattails. We need to freshen the story up. Let's have the attorneys for the subpoenaed companies push the negotiations with the State to a conclusion, and then we use our friends in the press to run a line of stories along a different angle."

"And what would this different angle be?" asked Colin.

"Let's take the side of Walker's clients," Johnny said, brows raised. "We'll excoriate the companies the AG's office was investigating—accuse them of predatory practices. Once the attorneys have negotiated weak settlements and small fines, we criticize the AG's office for not doing a better job. We hang them out to dry because the corporate bad guys got away with it again, and on the campaign trail, I'll call for tougher laws against offshore banking and the wall of secrecy corporate crooks hide behind. After everything cools down, we'll see that the officers running those companies get nice little bonuses."

Colin leaned back in his chair, his elbows perched on the armrests and his fingertips pressed together in a steeple-like formation. After a moment, a smile broke across his face.

"Perfect. Love it. Get it done," Colin said to Johnny.

"Will do," said Johnny, returning the smile.

"Now, Randal," Colin said, rotating his chair in Randal's direction. "How are things between you and Rebeca and her environmental groups? What's the latest on the lawsuits they've filed?"

"Rebeca has been silenced, at least for a while," said Randal. "The financial gift we made to her environmental foundation shut her up. I heard that she wanted to reject the gift and do so publicly, but the group's chairman overruled her. One of the stories you had planted mentioned that his annual compensation is a percentage of donations to the foundation, so he had a financial incentive to accept the gift."

"Of course he did," said Johnny. "Just another lazy commie."

Colin nodded in agreement; Randal said nothing.

"And the lawsuits against the developers?" probed Colin.

"Going nowhere. The group's ability to pay their lawyers depends upon their ability to raise money. You were right, Dad," Randal said with a sigh. "Rebeca looked like a spoiled little brat criticizing the family that made a gift to her foundation. When word of our sizeable donation hit the street, donations from other sources dried up; everyone figured they had enough cash and some of the real zealots thought the group had sold out by taking our money."

"You mean sizeable *pledge*, don't you?" asked Colin.

"Yes, I meant to say sizeable pledge. We made a small donation and a sizeable pledge."

"A pledge we have no intention of keeping, I may add," said Colin as he chuckled and cast a glance Johnny's way. Johnny smiled and raised his glass.

Randal ignored the celebration taking place in front of him. "Our attorneys think they'll be out of funds by year-end. We'll be able to settle by making small contributions to their cause and planting a few more trees."

"Well done, Randal," said Colin in a rare show of approval. "Well done."

Randal smiled weekly and nodded his appreciation towards his father. He stole a glance at Johnny to see his reaction. Nothing. Johnny was staring at his shoes.

"And that matter over the trust," Colin added, and Randal felt himself go into a cold sweat. "Does your daughter still want you removed as the trustee?"

"She's asked for some documents, and my advisors are gathering them," Randal answered, vaguely.

"Excellent. That should end that. Well, then, I think we're done here," said Colin.

Johnny returned his empty glass to the bar behind him and reached for his jacket. Colin rose from the chair and did the same.

It was late August, and the heat and humidity were each pushing ninety. The Lowcountry was the last place anyone wanted to be at this time of year. Colin had a plane on the runway fired up, with a flight plan for Aspen, Colorado. Johnny and his wife would be making a few campaign stops in Greenville and other parts of the Upcountry. At least it would be a little cooler there.

As for Randal, he was resigned to spending the weekend alone in Charleston.

"Where's that wife of yours?" asked Colin.

"California," he said truthfully.

"California! Again?"

"Visiting family again," he lied.

"I thought she didn't get along with them."

"She's trying to make amends."

"Well, get her back here soon, will ya? It's important the voters see us all as one big happy family," said Colin as he struggled to pass his trailing arm through his jacket sleeve. Despite his mental fortitude, his body was aging. Too much alcohol and restaurant food and no exercise were taking its toll. It was impossible to ignore.

"Don't worry," said Randal. "I have a feeling she'll be returning to Charleston sooner rather than later."

* * *

Until a week ago, "that wife" of Randal's knew nothing of Rebeca's efforts to remove her father as the trustee for the LeMar Trust. When he received the notice that she was seeking his removal, he told no one, not even Blythe. He was scared to death of what she might do—of what she and that snake, Dexter Childress, might do.

On the seventeenth of August, at the hearing to replace him, Randal appeared in court and pled innocence and a slight bit of incompetence. He explained that he changed CPA firms and brokerage houses and that some things had fallen through the cracks in the process.

"That's on me, Your Honor, and I will see to it that Rebeca receives everything she has asked for," he said.

"Well, she's asking that the court remove *you* as trustee. Are you saying you're giving that up?"

"No, Your Honor. I meant that I'll produce all the documents she requested."

"Yes, you will. I'll give you two weeks to produce tax returns, bank statements, monthly statements on the trust's performance, and records of every transaction and expense going back to the effective date of the last report Rebeca Dunsmore received," ordered the judge.

"Your Honor, I'm afraid that with everyone's summer travel plans, that two weeks is just not enough time," said Randal.

The judge paused to think about what Randal had said. It was hard to deny that there was a bit of truth to it.

"All right," the judge relented, as he leaned over his desk and stared down his nose at the calendar. "I'll give you until 5:00 p.m. on Friday, September 9th to get it done. Everyone should be back from Labor Day travels by then and ready to return to work."

The parties agreed, the gavel was struck, and everyone filed out of the courtroom.

The extra time for document preparation was the least of Randal's concerns. His big concern—his *only* concern, in fact—was what to tell

Blythe and Dexter. What would they do when they found out? Would they release the pictures Blythe took of him in the most compromising of situations?

A few days after the judge had ordered that he produce the documents, he finally summoned the courage to call Blythe at the Waldorf Astoria in Beverly Hills, where she was staying, and told her the bad news. She didn't take it well, and neither did Dexter, who happened to be in the room when he called. They calmed down after a few moments, and Dexter told Randal not to do anything stupid, and to give him time to come up with a plan.

They called back and said they would be returning to Charleston, and Dexter said that they had a plan. That was who Randal had been talking to on the phone when Colin and Johnny were barging up the stairs.

Colin and Johnny had shown themselves out, leaving Randal alone in his study, when a question crossed his mind, and not for the first time: *I wonder what they did with the trust assets?*

Chapter 44

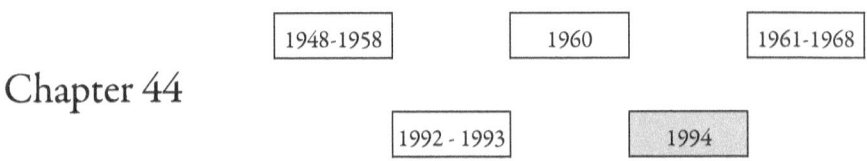

LOS ANGELAS, CALIFORNIA
1994

When Dexter told Randal that he had a plan, he didn't tell him what it was. Dexter's plan was simple and straightforward. Lie. Lie about *everything*. Lie about what they had done with the assets. One of the documents Randal had been blackmailed into signing transferred custodial control from Paine Weber to Biltmore Strickland Brokerage in LA. Dexter had a friend who worked there named Zed Renfro. With Zed managing the account, Dexter could buy and sell the stocks and bonds in the portfolio without fear of oversight—and that was exactly what he did.

"Sweet Cheeks, what this trust fund needs is some diversification. We need to invest in ventures that generate some *real* cash and not the kind we'll pay taxes on," Dexter told Blythe.

Dexter began selling stocks and bonds, not all of them, but as needed to free up cash to invest in businesses they knew a thing or two about—*flesh*.

Within a few months, Blythe and Dexter had bought Tattle Tails—the strip club where Blythe used to work—and they were running a call-girl operation that catered to the whims of the high-rollers in LA, the wealthiest of the wealthiest who saw everything and everyone as something they could buy. On the other end of the spectrum, Dexter ran a loan shark operation praying on people on the bottom rung of society's ladder with predatory loans that carried interest rates borrowers couldn't afford.

As for the world of narcotics, he refused to touch the stuff—as a user or distributor—but he was more than willing to provide the operating cash to local dealers who needed to buy in bulk and pay for product coming across the border before taking possession themselves. As a lender, he collected his ten percent fee off the top for facilitating these types of transactions—transactions in which his money was out for only a few days.

Business was good, and Dexter and Blythe were looking to expand, so the news from Randal that a judge in Charleston was demanding that Randal produce financial reports and bank statements for the benefit of a poor little rich girl named Rebeca was not welcome.

Nevertheless, Dexter knew what to do. He would simply *forge* the requested documents.

He took the bank statements and the monthly statements that the Charleston-based firm of Torcher & Banks produced for Rebeca—copies of which Randal had willingly handed over—and gave them to an associate. This associate was told to forge similar-looking monthly statements, to make it look as if his office had produced them. Dexter told his buddy that the reports had to show some activity because it would look suspicious if they reported that no stocks or bonds had been bought or sold.

Dexter, working with his pal Zed Renfro, crafted quite a fictitious tale that included months and months of statements detailing the strategic sale and purchase of stocks and bonds inside the LeMar Trust.

When Blythe flew back to Charleston the day before the court-ordered deadline to produce the documents, she did so with several banker-boxes filled with very official-looking statements and reports—all confirming that Rebeca's trust was in good hands.

* * *

Law Offices of Atkins & Atkins
Friday, September 9, 1994

Abigail stuck her head into Walker's office. "Well, Randal Dunsmore made the deadline with an hour to spare," she said. "A courier just dropped off four banker boxes. Do you want to start going through them with me?"

"I'm expecting a call from Eddie Wentworth. Could you take a quick look at the docs and let me know what you think? I won't have time to take a deep dive until this weekend."

"You got it. You want the door shut or open?" she asked.

"Shut please," he said, and the phone rang right on cue.

"Eddie, it's been a long week. Do you have any good news for me?" Walker asked.

Eddie was still on administrative leave, but his old secretary was providing him with regular updates as to what was happening in the office. "I'm afraid not. Joshua's going to shut down the grand jury next week. They negotiated a few feeble fines against the companies but nothing of consequence. Nothing's going to change. Joshua had to end things and get the stories off the front pages. He's taken a beating."

"Yeah. I was afraid this was what you'd be telling me. I saw a poll in the paper recently saying the race was fifty-fifty. Skip Jackson's run a solid campaign."

"Well, he certainly had enough money to do so. I think the Dunsmores have spent more money getting him elected than they've spent on Johnny Dunsmore's campaign."

"And what about you, Eddie? Are you still on leave?" asked Walker.

"Afraid so. I'm thinking about calling it quits. To hell with them. I wonder if Salty Mike's is hiring?" Eddie laughed as he said this, bringing a smile to Walker's face. "Hey, I've got to end this call. Vannesa and I are heading to The Abaco for dinner tonight. Want to join us?"

"Can't. We have plans, but I'll be in touch."

* * *

Walker found Abigail in the conference room. All four banker boxes were on the table. She was standing over one of them and placing a stack of folders back in the box.

"What's your initial impression?" Walker asked.

"I only had time to take a quick look, but it appears as if everything you asked for is here," she said as she waved her hand over the table. "Bank statements, copies of tax returns, brokerage statements, etc. And it's well organized."

Walker cocked his head to one side and rubbed his chin.

"You look disappointed," Abigail said.

"I know I shouldn't be. For Rebeca's sake I hope all is in order, but I was really hoping to get Rebeca what she wants, which is a new trustee."

"Even if he's doing a good job for her?"

"Yes. Even if he's doing a good job for her. Family can be tough, and she doesn't have a good relationship with him."

"I understand. Are you going to stay and go over these docs now?"

"No, not now. I'll come by this weekend and take a look. Right now, I need to get going. Isabelle and I are having Rebeca over for dinner. I've been meaning to get the two of them together. Rebeca is an amateur photographer, and she is interested in learning about the photo exhibit Izzy is putting together. I need to pick up a couple of bottles of wine on the way home and clean the BBQ before Rebeca arrives."

"Are you going to tell her what I just told you? That everything appears to be in order?"

"No. I'll tell her that they met the deadline and produced the requested docs, but just barely, and so I didn't have time to review them. No reason to put a damper on the evening. Right?"

"Right. You deserve a relaxing evening. See you Monday, boss."

"See you Monday."

* * *

Walker stopped by a wine and cheese shop on his way home and almost got run over as he was lost in his thoughts and not paying attention. What a summer it had been. Over the Memorial Day weekend, he was excited about the chance to help the Gastons. Then the case developed such that he got the opportunity to work with his good friend Eddie and maybe bring down some bad guys. Early on, it looked like the Dunsmore family were the bad guys. And then Rebeca Dunsmore walks into his office, and he felt like he'd hit the trifecta! Now, with Labor Day in our rearview mirror, summer is over, and nothing was going right. Eddie was about to lose his job. It looked like Rebeca was going to be stuck with Randal as the trustee for her trust. Johnny Dunsmore would be reelected in a landslide and Joshua Langston may lose his bid for reelection as the State's attorney general to a Dunsmore lackey. The Dunsmores were winning on every front. How did everything go so wrong? Maybe Eddie was right—maybe people like the two of them were nothing more than decaying plant and animal matter feeding the ecosystem of crooks, thieves, and liars who ran this town.

Chapter 45

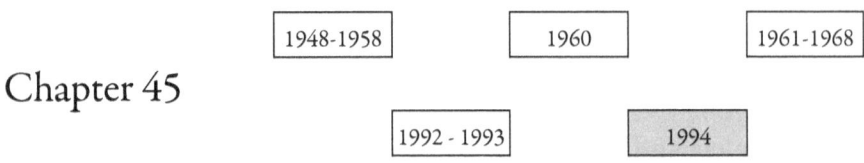

WALKER AND ISABELLE'S HOME ON TRADD STREET
SEPTEMBER 9, 1994

Rebeca and Isabelle hit it off wonderfully. They sat on their screened-in porch and enjoyed a glass of wine while Peter and Anna ran around in the backyard.

"They're adorable," Rebeca said to Izzy, giving her a warm smile.

"Thank you. They bring us more joy than we could ever have imagined. They are a handful, though. What about you, Rebeca—anyone in your life?"

Rebeca smiled before answering. "Yes, I believe there is. A boy I met at ASU. His name is James. He's from Wyoming—a real cowboy. We've been dating for a little over a year. I miss him."

"I know a little about what is going on," said Izzy, "but Walker keeps most of his work confidential. Are you planning on staying in Charleston for long? Sounds like you have a reason to return to Phoenix."

"I'll be returning to Phoenix—and probably fairly soon. I signed a lease on a place through the end of the month. A lot depends on whether the court will allow me to replace my dad as trustee of my trust. When I returned to Charleston back in May, I wasn't looking forward to it. My childhood wasn't abusive or anything—it was just bland. The house I grew up in was loveless. But I've been pleasantly surprised by how much I've enjoyed my time here. Growing up here, I took for granted what a beautiful city Charleston is."

"Well, if you must return after your lease has run out, you are always welcome to stay with us. We have a small guest room upstairs."

"Thank you. That's kind of you," said Rebeca.

About then, Walker entered the room with an opened bottle of white wine and proceeded to refill everyone's glasses. "The grill is almost ready," he said, topping off Rebeca's. "I'll put the steaks on in a few minutes."

"Sounds good." Izzy stood up with her refilled glass of wine, making her way toward the kitchen. "I need just a few minutes to finish making the salad and to prepare the kids' meal."

"Can I help?" asked Rebeca.

"Sure."

Fifteen minutes later, Peter and Anna were eating their dinner at a small table in the corner of the kitchen reserved for them while Walker, Izzy, and Rebeca sat at the table Izzy had prepared on the porch. They held hands, and Walker said grace, thanking the Lord for the food and the company. It was a wonderful evening, the kind that made Rebeca admit to longing for a family of her own—not like the one she'd grown up in, but like the one she was surrounded by at that moment.

* * *

After dinner, Izzy and Rebeca cleaned the kitchen while Walker read Peter and Anna a quick story, said prayers with them, and tucked them in. When he rejoined Rebeca and Isabelle on the porch, they were looking at photographs Rebeca had taken of the Grand Canyon.

"Honey, you have to see these," said Izzy. "They are wonderful!"

"Thank you," said Rebeca.

"Walker and I are planning a big vacation next summer with the kids, and we've been thinking about driving west and seeing the Grand Canyon, San Francisco, and then, of course, Disneyland."

"If you do, please plan a day in Phoenix so I can show you around."

Walker looked through the photo album, commented on the beautiful pictures, and passed the album back to Izzy before pulling out another album from a box Rebeca had retrieved from her car.

"Oh, those aren't photos I took," Rebeca said, quickly. "Those are just some old family photo albums I found when rummaging around in Randal's attic."

Walker started to put the album back in the box, but Rebeca said, "It's okay. You can look at them. I'd like to look at them, too, actually."

"Okay," said Walker. Izzy was already sitting on the couch to his right, and Rebeca left her chair across from them to sit to his left. Between them, he turned the pages of the photo album—the three of them taking it all in. Throughout it all, Rebeca narrated her life growing up in Charleston as Randal Dunsmore's only child.

Walker was turning a page and then stopped and flipped back to the previous page. He lowered his head and took a hard look at one photo, in particular.

"Where was this taken?" he asked.

Rebeca pushed a few stray strands of hair behind her ear and leaned in to get a closer look.

"That was taken on Uncle Luis's boat, the *Peristeria*," she said, pointing a finger to a younger version of Johnny Dunsmore. "And that's Uncle Johnny—our fearless governor—and his wife, Caroline. And that's me standing between my dad and some girl. I don't remember her name. She was just his flavor of the month. His girlfriends—they came and went."

"Who's Uncle Luis?" asked Walker.

"He wasn't *really* my uncle. That's just what we called him. Our families went on vacations together—often to the Caribbean. He was a friend of Uncle Johnny's from college."

"And this guy, on the end. Do you know who he is?" asked Walker.

"You mean the guy with the huge ears?" asked Rebeca, laughing.

"Yeah, that guy," answered Walker.

"Don't know his name, but he was always around. I called him Dumbo—not to his face, of course. That was my nickname for him. I think he worked for Uncle Luis and his dad."

"What is it?" asked Izzy, noticing Walker's face.

"I met him in the Bahamas back in June. I'd swear to it. The guy at the end of the row in this picture—his name is Anthony Ferguson. Rebeca, do you know when this was taken?"

"Well, I think I was about fifteen in this picture. That was during spring break, so that would make it 1981."

"Who is Anthony Ferguson?" asked Izzy.

"He's the dead-beat attorney behind all the companies Eddie and I have been pursuing," Walker revealed, hardly able to keep his voice down. "This is it! This is the irrefutable link we've been looking for."

"I don't understand. What link?" asked Rebeca.

"The grand jury that Eddie headed up was investigating a host of companies, all possibly in cahoots with one another, that we believed were defrauding innocent folks in town, like the Gastons."

"Yes, honey, I'm aware of all that."

"Well, we kept running into a stone wall. Every company under investigation was owned by a partnership or other company domiciled in the Caribbean, and each of those companies or partnerships was, in turn, owned by another faceless company. We could never determine who the real owners were—the so-called *beneficial* owners."

"And this picture answers that question for you?" asked Rebeca, skeptically.

"Kind of. It confirms our suspicions. We suspect that your extended family, Rebeca, are the beneficial owners," Walker explained, choosing his words carefully. "We suspect they are the people behind these companies." Turning to Izzy, he added, "Sweetheart, do you remember the fundraiser at the Hibernian Hall back in June?"

"The one where I stormed in and called my father a hypocrite in front of the whole town?" asked Rebeca, as if doing so was the most normal thing in the world.

"That's the one," said Walker, and the three of them laughed.

"That was where we saw Johnny and his wife standing next to the strikingly handsome couple," Izzy noted.

"That was Luis Sanchez with his supermodel wife by his side," Walker went on. "They are still connected, to this day. That proves it. Luis Sanchez is *Uncle Luis*. This picture is of an unholy alliance: Johnny Dunsmore, our governor; Luis Sanchez, the co-founder of a law firm specializing in setting up offshore companies and hiding assets; and Anthony Ferguson, the registered agent for *every* company the Attorney General's Office has been investigating."

"But I thought the AG was going to shut the investigation down," said Izzy. "You said that Joshua was in a hurry to bury it and move on."

"Well, if the public could see this picture, they may insist he reopen it," Walker speculated. He turned to Rebeca and added, "Can I have this picture?"

"Be my guest," she answered as a smile of satisfaction tinged with hope spread across her face.

Chapter 46

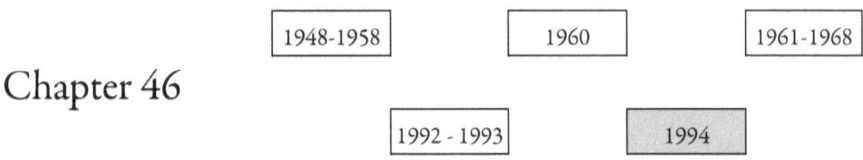

LAW OFFICES OF ATKINS & ATKINS
SATURDAY, SEPTEMBER 10, 1994

Walker began his day with a run through the neighborhood. It was a beautiful Saturday morning, accented by a chill in the air—an unexpected gift for this time of year. His thoughts were focused on the significance of the picture he had come across the night before. As he ran along the Battery, he strategized his next steps, and by the time he jogged up to the front of his house, he had a game plan in place. But first, breakfast with the family. The four of them enjoyed pancakes on the screened-in porch and made plans for a picnic later that afternoon.

At nine o'clock that morning, Walker entered the solitude of his office dressed in blue jeans, a faded golf shirt, and an old pair of running shoes. While he enjoyed the energy of his firm when it was humming and alive with activity during the week, there was something about the peace and quiet of empty hallways and offices that he really loved. Maybe it was the sense of being free of disturbances that allowed him to focus. There'd be no unexpected phone calls from clients, judges, or opposing counsel. The agenda for the day was his to control, and for now, there were only two action items on his list.

The first thing he did was call Joshua Langston at his home. Joshua had given him his private number earlier that summer—"For emergencies only," he'd said, "and don't you dare share it with anyone."

On the fifth ring, he picked up. "Joshua Langston here."

"Joshua, its Walker Atkins."

A short pause followed. "This better be an emergency."

"It's not—but you're gonna want to hear what I have to say." Walker then told him about dinner with Rebeca the night before and the picture he had in his possession. After which, he asked the question he needed an answer to the most: "Eddie told me late yesterday that you're planning to wrap up the grand jury investigation sometime this week. Does this latest development change that?"

"Walker, if that photograph in your possession were to turn up in the newspaper for all the public to see, what choice would I have?"

If it was possible to hear someone smile over the phone, then this would have been one of those moments—for both Walker and Joshua. They then discussed which reporters in town would be most receptive to running a story.

"Joshua, I'll contact the newspaper tomorrow morning first thing. Now, I hope you enjoy the rest of your weekend, and thanks for taking my call."

"Are you kidding? Best news I've had in a while! Thanks, Walker."

* * *

Walker moved on to agenda item number two: reviewing the four boxes of documents Randal Dunsmore had dropped off the day before.

Walker expected that upon investigating the contents of the four boxes, he would have to report to Rebeca that although the trust's performance might not be as strong as she would like, there was little he could do for her. After all, Randal had satisfied his duty to provide these reports without any evidence of malfeasance.

After an hour of going through the boxes, he had to admit that all looked in order. The portfolio was doing reasonably well—certainly in line with the overall market's performance. Nothing jumped out at him. He'd never heard of the brokerage firm in California that Randal was using, however, which was a bit bothersome. *Why not stick with one of the big boys on Wall Street?*

He suspected that since Randal's wife was from California, she was having some sway over Randal's decisions, and this presented a potential problem. So, for that reason, he kept plowing away, looking for anything that might raise a flag.

After a few hours, he took a break and walked around the office. He kept thinking there had to be some reason to fire Tad Torcher and the Wall Street brokerage firm, but he couldn't find it. The new team Randal had assembled hadn't made any significant changes to the portfolio. Walker kept thinking that if you're going to go to the trouble of changing financial advisors, aren't you going to pick someone with a different investment philosophy? It just didn't make sense.

Something was eating at Walker. He decided to give Tad Torcher a call. Maybe he'd know something. Owing to it being the weekend, he didn't expect to reach him at his office. The answering machine picked up when he called. "Tad, it's Walker Atkins. I'm working with Rebeca Dunsmore on some estate planning and I'm wondering if you could give me a call Monday. That's all. Hope you enjoy your weekend."

Walker closed the office and walked down to White Point Garden, where he met Izzy and the kids for an afternoon picnic.

Chapter 47

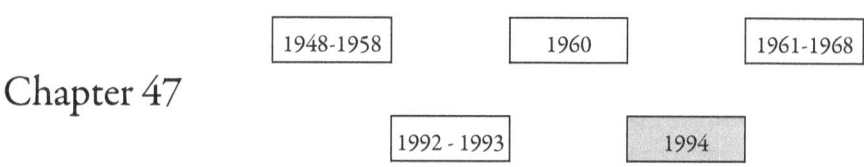

THE LAW OFFICES OF ATKINS & ATKINS
MONDAY, SEPTEMBER 12, 1994

Walker's first action item of the day was to reach out to a trusted political reporter at the *Post & Courier* who was thrilled to receive the call. He said he would drop by personally to pick up the photo. "I'll leave it in an envelope at the front desk," Walker had said.

After handing Mrs. Beasley the envelope with the photograph, Walker stopped in the breakroom to refill his coffee cup. On his way back to his office, he observed the other attorneys in their offices busy at work. Phones ringing. Clients waiting in the lobby. It was a good day. He saw Abigail enter her office and he followed her, stopping at the threshold and quietly knocking on the door frame.

"Good morning, boss," Abigal said. "Good weekend? Oh, how was your dinner with Rebeca?"

Leaning against the door frame with one foot crossed over the other and a huge smile on his face, he answered, "Wonderful."

Abigail looked at him curiously. "I guess so," she said as she put her purse down on the credenza behind her desk.

Walker then brought her up to speed on the latest developments in their representation of the Gastons and their other clients.

"I can't believe she had a photograph of the three of them!" Abigail exclaimed. "Walker, this is wonderful news. We have new life." She paced—more like bounced up and down—back and forth behind her desk.

"I thought you'd like it. When is the lender's deadline for filing the foreclosure action against the Gastons?"

"This Wednesday, and we're coming up on the same deadline for our other similarly situated clients over the next couple of weeks. We could use some help formulating a strong defense. Hopefully, a reinvigorated grand jury investigation will do that for us."

"I gave the reporter your name. If he needs any background for his story, I instructed him to call you."

"My pleasure," she said as she came out from her desk. They high-fived and Walker tuned to leave her office.

As he walked down the hallway towards his office, he could hear her shout, "YES, YES, YES!"

It was going to be a good day.

* * *

Walker had hardly settled himself behind his desk when Mrs. Beasley buzzed him. "I have Tad Torcher on the line. He said you left him a message over the weekend."

"Yes, I did. Please patch through."

"Walker, Tad Torcher here."

"Thanks for getting back to me so quickly," Walker replied.

"Not a problem. I can't tell you what a coincidence it was when I walked in this morning and listened to your voicemail."

"Why is that?" asked Walker.

"Because I received something in the mail last week, and I made a mental note to call you."

"Well, here I am. What's on your mind?"

"As you know, when Randal fired me, it came out of the blue. I asked him why, but he couldn't come up with a good reason. Anyway, I had forgotten all about it until back in June when his daughter Rebeca invited me to breakfast. What a delightful young woman. Anyway, when Randal fired me, I prepared the necessary paperwork to close out matters and sent the files to Randal's house, as he'd directed, and that was that. Like I said, I'd forgotten all about it. But then, last week, I got a notice from the IRS concerning the most recent tax return that had been filed for the trust..."

"Tad, why would you receive notices from the IRS about the trust's tax returns if you're not working for the trust anymore?" Walker asked.

"Well, there was some paperwork that didn't get handled properly. I was listed as an authorized representative with the IRS for all tax matters pertaining to the LeMar Trust—this is typical in our industry, standard operating procedure. As an authorized representative, whenever the IRS sends notices to Randal, the trustee, I'm copied. Well, neither Randal nor anyone in my office filed the proper form with the IRS to cancel my Power of Attorney."

"So, that's why you received the notice last week."

"That's right," he answered.

"Well, what did the notice from the IRS say?" Walker asked.

* * *

Thirty minutes later, the phone call ended. Walker could hardly contain his excitement. He ran across the hall to Abigail's office and told her what he'd learned. They strategized for a moment, then went to work. By the end of the day, they had drafted a motion for a Temporary Restraining Order, supported by an affidavit Tad Torcher was happy to sign. If granted, this would prevent Randal Dunsmore, Dexter Childress, or anyone from their camp from buying or selling any securities or other assets on behalf of the LeMar Trust. In this motion, Walker also sought an emergency hearing to have Randal Dunsmore immediately removed as trustee.

Walker was at the courthouse five minutes before it opened the next morning with the motion in hand. Immediately upon filing it, Walker was granted a private audience with the judge in the judge's quarters to argue his case. Walker showed the judge an affidavit that Tad Torcher had signed earlier that day. Having convinced the judge that his client could suffer immediate and irreparable harm if this order was not granted, the judge issued the TRO and set an emergency hearing for the following Monday.

At Walker's suggestion, the judge's clerk faxed the order to a superior court in Los Angeles County, and an officer of the LA court delivered the order to the local California bank listed in Randal's document production and to Biltmore Strickland Brokerage before informing Randal Dunsmore. By the end of the day, the judge had received confirmation that the orders had been delivered to those two institutions. It was too late to serve the order on Randal; that would have to wait until the next day.

* * * *

Offices of the Dunsmore Family Foundation
Charleston, South Carolina
Wednesday, September 14, 1994

Everything was spiraling out of control for Randal.

He stared out the window of the office he leased at the corner of East Bay and Stoll's Alley overlooking Charleston Harbor, trying to think if there was anything he could do to head off the coming storm. There wasn't—and he decided it was best to tell Blythe sooner rather than later.

Randal took a chance that Blythe would be having lunch at 82 Queen with friends. He knew he shouldn't show up unannounced, but a part of him was simply beyond caring. In a daze, he made the short walk over to the restaurant. He walked inside, right past the hostess, and before he knew it, he was standing in front of Blythe and her friends, all gathered around a large circular table.

"I need to speak with you," he told her bluntly. "Now, and in private."

Before she could argue, he'd grabbed her arm and escorted her outside.

"What is it? My God!" Blythe asked, eyes wide. "Did somebody *die?*"

"I don't know what you and that guy Dexter have been up to, but it must be pretty bad for the judge to issue an order like this," said Randal as he shook the order that he'd been served just a half hour ago.

"What are you talking about, Randal? What's in this paper you're holding up that's worth embarrassing me in front of my friends over?" she demanded to know.

"It's an order from the judge compelling me to appear in court and explain to him what's been going on with Rebeca's trust. It seems the judge is suspicious. Do you know *why* he might be suspicious, *Blythe?*"

Blythe looked away, avoiding eye contact.

"Dexter needs to get back here in a hurry and you two better fix this— whatever *this* is."

"It's going to be worse for you if *you* don't fix it," she insisted.

"No can do. I don't have that kind of juice."

"True. But your daddy does. Call him. *Now*."

Randal had expected this reaction from her, and on the walk over, he'd thought about what he would say. He'd come prepared. "No. I'm done. I don't care anymore. Do what you want with the pictures. I know I'm a joke in this town, anyway," he said, relishing the look on Blythe's face as he'd thoroughly disarmed her.

He turned and walked away, leaving Blythe alone on the street, her cup of she-crab soup getting cold at the table with her friends—and for the first time in a long time, Randal felt like a man.

* * *

Later that day . . .
Los Angeles, California

"Hello, Sweet Cheeks. I wasn't expecting to hear from you today," Dexter said when he heard Blythe's voice on the other end of the phone.

"Oh, Dexter, we got trouble."

The first thing Dexter did after Blythe told him about the court order was call Zed Renfro, his buddy at the local brokerage, and tell him to sell the remaining stocks in the portfolio. The receptionist told him that Zed was unavailable and that his account had been handed over to a new manager. This new manager explained that he was holding a court order that prohibited all trading in the account. Dexter hung up, hopped in his car, and sped off to the bank.

"I'm sorry, sir, but a freeze has been placed on your account. I'm afraid I can't help you," said the teller behind the plexiglass.

At this point, Dexter knew that talking to a manager would do no good. He also knew that he was screwed if he couldn't convince the judge that no funny business was going on. When Blythe called, he wasn't worried. They'd liquidate the stocks and leave town for a while. Business would slow down, except at Tattle Tails; he had a good manager who could run things, and the chances of anyone tracing ownership of that joint to him and Blythe were nearly zero. But now, with his cash frozen and much of it on the street, he was in a jam.

Complicating matters was that he'd made commitments to some bad people who would expect him to live up to his end of the bargain. No, it was critical that he kept the engine running—and that meant showing up for the emergency hearing next Monday wearing his best suit and conning the judge into lifting the court order long enough for him to liquidate and leave the country. He'd bring Blythe with him if he could—but first things first, he'd take care of himself.

* * *

Walker Atkin's living room, at the end of the day . . .

"Honey, come in here! You need to see this!" Walker shouted from the living room. He was sitting on the sofa with a beer in hand, watching the local news.

Isabelle was in the kitchen preparing the kids' dinner. She stepped into the living room. "What is it?"

"Did you read the story in the paper this morning that included the picture we found in Rebeca's photo album last Friday?" Walker asked.

"Sure did. Loved it."

"Well, the AG held a press conference today and Channel Five covered it."

Isabelle dried her hands on her apron and took a seat next to Walker on the sofa as they both looked on.

"Earlier today, Joshua Langston, the State's embattled attorney general, held a press conference. We have a recording of the event that we're going to show you."

> "It's wonderful to see so many members of the press here today. Earlier this week, it was reported by some of you that my office was ending the grand jury investigation into the conduct of several local businesses. A few amongst you even commented that this likely marked the end of my career as the State's attorney general. Well, I'm happy to report that that news has been greatly exaggerated. Considering recent developments that were reported in this morning's edition of the *Post & Courier*, we will not be dismissing the grand jury. In fact, very soon, we will be issuing new subpoenas.

Isabelle turned to her husband on the sofa and took both his hands in hers. "Good for you, Walker. Good for you."

It had been a good week.

Chapter 48

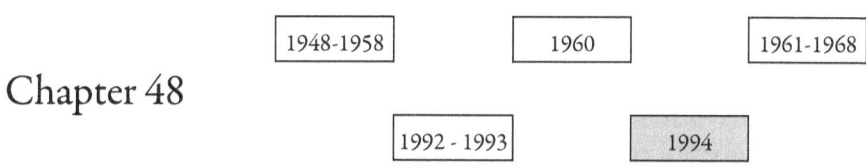

JUDGE RAWLING'S COURTROOM
CHARLESTON, SOUTH CAROLINA
SEPTEMBER 19, 1994

"All rise."

Walker and Rebeca, at one table, and Randal Dunsmore and his attorney, Homer Radcliffe, at another, all remained standing until the judge took his seat. Normally, bench trials didn't draw a crowd, but due to Rebeca's newfound notoriety as the point of the spear in a host of lawsuits brought to protect the local ecology, and as the "rich little girl" suing her father for control of her trust, the court room was about half full of journalists, news reporters, and curious onlookers.

"The matter before us is simple," announced the judge. "Counsel for the plaintiff in this matter, Ms. Rebeca Dunsmore, has brought a motion to have Randal Dunsmore removed as the trustee of a trust established by the plaintiff's parents. The plaintiff further seeks to have her attorney, Mr. Walker Atkins, appointed as the temporary trustee until a permanent trustee can be named. Mr. Atkins, are you ready to call your first witness?"

"I am, Your Honor."

"Please proceed."

"Thank you, Your Honor. We call Mr. Dexter Childress to the stand."

As Dexter walked from the back of the courtroom to the witness stand, Walker almost felt sorry for him. He had not deposed the man but knew exactly what the man was going to say. He also thought Dexter

Childress looked ridiculous in the three-piece suit he was wearing. It was close to ninety degrees and threatening to rain. Even from his table, Walker could see the man was struggling with the heat. *You think you're sweating now, just wait till I'm done with you.*

"Mr. Childress, you're the financial advisor Randal Dunsmore hired to help him with his custodial duties. Is that correct?" Walker asked.

"That's right. I come highly recommended."

"I'm sure you do."

Walker then went through the statements meticulously, establishing that Dexter had sold only a few stocks that were in the portfolio when he took over, and that he'd directed the brokerage to wire the proceeds from the sale to a bank account opened at a local California bank in the name of the LeMar Trust. When Walker asked Dexter to explain his rationale for making the trades, his attorney objected, arguing that the trust fund's performance had tracked that of the overall market and that poor performance was not ground for removing a trustee.

The judge sustained the objection.

"No further questions, Your Honor," Walker said, concluding his examination of this witness. "But I reserve the right to recall Dexter Childress to the stand."

The judge nodded. "Very well. Mr. Childress, you are excused from the stand but must remain in this courtroom. I hope to wrap this up today, and I don't want to have to track you down."

"No problem, Your Honor," said Mr. Childress. He stood from the witness stand and slowly swaggered through the gate separating the attorneys and their clients from the gallery, taking a seat next to Blythe behind Randal Dunsmore.

Walker saw him pat Blythe on the leg and thought he looked far too confident in himself and in his performance. *Downright cocky. If he only knew.*

"Your Honor, I'd now like to call Mr. Tad Torcher to the stand." Walker stole a glimpse at Dexter. No reaction.

After establishing who Tad was and what his previous role had been in relation to the trust, Walker homed in on recent events. "Mr. Torcher, in your capacity as the CPA who prepared the tax returns for the trust, were you regularly notified by the IRS of any matters pertaining to the returns?" Walker asked.

"Yes, I was," Ted replied with confidence. "When Randal Dunsmore hired me over twenty years ago, we completed the paperwork with the IRS so that I was listed as an authorized representative for all tax matters pertaining to the LeMar Trust. This is typical in our industry. As an authorized representative, whenever the IRS sent notices to Randal Dunsmore, the trustee, I also received a copy."

"And when you were fired by Randal Dunsmore, did you file any paperwork removing you as an authorized representative?"

"No, I didn't. Neither did Randal. It was an oversight on his part and mine, but I accept responsibility," Tad explained.

"And have you continued to receive notices from the IRS concerning the trust?" Walker asked.

"Yes. I received one two weeks ago."

Walker was getting into a nice flow and rhythm with Tad. He stole a glimpse of Randal's camp and noticed that his attorney was leaning back over the railing, having a heated conversation with Dexter. That brought a discreet smile to Walker's face.

"Mr. Torcher, would you please tell this court what the notice from the IRS pertained to?"

"The IRS notice reported that the last tax return was incompatible with the information they had gathered from the various 1099 forms the IRS had received concerning the trust."

"I'm sorry, Mr. Torcher, but I'm just a lowly attorney. Could you explain to me and the court what you're talking about?"

"Sure. When you sell a stock, the brokerage that sells it on your behalf issues a Form-1099 to you and the IRS. This form identifies the name of the stock that was sold, the date it was sold, and the price per share at which it was sold."

"So, you're saying that the IRS received copies of these 1099 forms from the brokerage firm indicating that the trust had sold some stocks, but that when the tax return for the trust was filed, it did not list the revenue from the sales of these stocks."

"That's right."

"Mr. Torcher, I'm looking at the most recent statement prepared by the brokerage firm that Randal switched to, and according to this statement, of the twenty-five stocks in the portfolio when they took over, they only sold four of those stocks in the last year. So, how much revenue did they fail to report?"

Homer Radcliffe, Randal's attorney, leaped to his feet. "Objection! Calls for speculation."

Homer Radcliff looked desperate to slow down Walker's momentum in any way possible. He wasn't going to. "I withdraw the question."

"Your Honor, I would like to draw this court's attention to Exhibit A," Walker continued as he handed copies to the judge, opposing counsel, and Tad Torcher on the stand. "Mr. Torcher, could you please tell the court what Exhibit A is?"

"Certainly. This is an affidavit prepared by a registered agent of the DTC listing every stock the LeMar Trust has bought or sold over the last twelve months."

"Could you please tell us what the DTC is?" Walker asked.

"The DTC is the Depository Trust Corporation," Tad explained. "They maintain records of every stock transaction in the country and a list of who owns what stocks and what stocks in each company are owned by whom. As a CPA who also has a few licenses with the SEC, and because I've been at this game a while, I'm owed a few favors. I placed a call to a friend of mine at the DTC to find out what stocks the LeMar Trust has bought or sold since Randal took the account away from me. This is it," he said as he waved the report over his head.

"And of the twenty-five stocks that were in the LeMar Trust when you were involved, how many have been sold?" Walker asked.

"Over half of them. They've sold over half of them."

"Did they buy new stocks?"

"Not according to this report."

"What do you think they did with all the money?" asked Walker. He fully expected an objection to his question from opposing counsel, but from the look on the man's face, he was clearly too stunned to say anything.

"I don't know," said Tad. "But I do know one thing..."

"And what's that?" asked Walker.

"They're going to owe a boatload in taxes."

Randal's lawyer had no questions at this time for Mr. Tad Torcher but reserved the right to recall him to the stand.

The thrashing only continued.

"Call your next witness," said the judge.

"The plaintiff calls Mr. Boatwright," said Walker.

For the first time, Dexter appeared to be nervous. Sweat was clearly visible on his face.

"Mr. Boatwright," Walker began, "could you state your full name and occupation?"

"My name is Cantor Boatwright, and I am President of Biltmore Strickland Brokerage."

"Now, you heard Mr. Childress testify about the accuracy of monthly statements from your firm pertaining to an account held in the name of the LeMar Trust. Does your brokerage have an account in the name of the LeMar Trust?"

"We do."

"Now, I'm going to show you the statements Mr. Childress went over with me this morning. They have been marked as Exhibit A. Would you take a look at them for me?"

Walker passed a stack of statements to Mr. Boatwright, who thumbed through them.

"Could you tell the court what you are looking at?"

"Forgeries," he answered.

"Excuse me," Walker said, brows raised. "Did you say forgeries?"

"I did," Mr. Boatwright confirmed. "These are forged statements made to look like a statement that my firm would produce."

"How can you be so sure?" asked Walker.

"Because after I received a court order last week putting a freeze on the account, I printed out the last twelve month-ending statements for the account. I became suspicious when I learned that Mr. Childress had called our office that same day and directed his account manager to sell the remaining stocks in the account and to wire him the money, pronto."

"Would you look at the statements that Mr. Childress produced and then look at the statements you brought with you and tell me if you see any differences?"

"The statements you just handed me, the statements Mr. Childress walked us through, were printed at our office using our software, but they were printed for a fake account. You see, the trades that these statements show as having happened do not show up on the statements for the account that I printed out and that's because they never happened. I had my IT guy look into it, and he confirmed that that was the case. A fake account was created and a fake record of buying and selling stocks was created for the account."

"So, someone in your office created a fake account and printed fake reports on activity for the LeMar Trust that—to the untrained eye—would look legitimate," said Walker.

"Correct," Mr. Boatwright confirmed with a sigh.

"Do you have any idea who set all this up?"

"I know *exactly* who did it. Zed Renfro. I fired him last week and informed the police and the Securities and Exchange Commission of what I discovered. He denied any wrongdoing, but when we showed him the security camera footage of him entering the offices after hours with Mr. Dexter Childress, he crumbled and admitted to everything."

About that time, Dexter bolted from his chair and fled for the exit in the back of the courtroom, only to be tackled to the ground by a security guard who hadn't lost a step from his days on the field.

Judge Rawlins was on his feet, hammering his gavel and screaming for order. "Officer, arrest that man and make sure you read him his rights! He's going to need them."

The courtroom was stunned. Walker, like everyone else, was watching the events unfold in the back with an expression of shock. He glanced at the opposing counsel and the two of them shared a look of utter dismay. He couldn't find Blythe anywhere in the courtroom and figured she must have scurried away in the midst of all the chaos. Walker fell back into his chair and took it all in as the judge, who was seated now, made his pronouncement.

"Randal Dunsmore, you are officially removed as the trustee for the LeMar Trust," he said, eyeing Randal's camp critically, "and Mr. Walker Atkins is hereby named the temporary trustee. As for you, Mr. Childress—you are under arrest."

Walker turned towards Rebeca and smiled. He saw tears beginning to form in her eyes.

"Thank you," she said.

Walker just smiled.

Randal began making his way to the exit only to pause for a moment in silent deliberation. Then, he turned on his heel and approached his daughter. "Rebeca," he called out quietly, and she turned to look at him but remained silent.

"I'm sorry."

"What are you sorry for?" she asked, unconvinced.

He leaned over the railing, reaching out for her hand and holding it in his, as if clinging to a relationship they never had. "I'm sorry . . . for *everything*."

Rebeca looked at him in a way that suggested she had accepted his apology. He shook her hand gently in a show of agreement, not knowing whether it was the beginning or the end. They stared at each other for a moment, and then Randal turned to leave, but before making it to the door, he turned back with one last comment.

"Rebeca?"

She was waiting alongside Walker as he gathered his papers, and she again gave Randal her attention.

"The Dunsmore family is poison. Leave town. Leave us all behind. Don't let the venom oozing from our family's pores affect you. You're from better stock."

Chapter 49

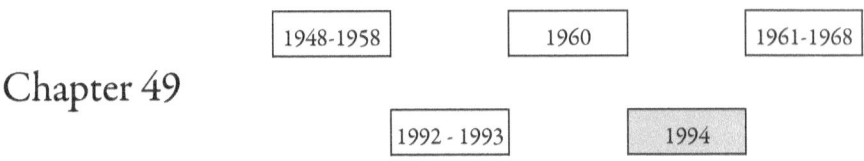

CHARLESTON COUNTY SUPERIOR COURT JAIL
WEDNESDAY, SEPTEMBER 21, 1994

"Dexter, you got a visitor," said the guard.
It's about time, Dexter thought.

It had been over a week since the hearing, and Dexter was still sitting in jail, having been denied bail, and waiting to see if Blythe would pay him a visit. He walked into the room reserved for such visits, his ankles chained together, slowing his pace, and his hands handcuffed in front of him. Blythe was sitting in the chair across from the table where a prison guard told her to sit. The guard refused to remove the handcuffs but did step outside, giving the two of them some privacy.

"What took you so long, Sweet Cakes? I'm dyin' in here. You gotta get me out."

"I'm not even supposed to be here. My attorney told me to stay away."

"You got *yourself* an attorney? What for?"

"What do you mean, *what for?* You said we'd skate! You said you could pull this off. That lawyer, Walker Atkins—he made you look like a fool." She paused, and in that moment, Dexter saw something in her that he often saw only in himself: the ability to betray an ally in the name of saving your own skin. "You're going down, Dexter," she said, as though to confirm his fear, "and you ain't taking me with you."

The laugh that erupted from his throat was half-bark and half-crow. "Oh, yes, I am! But only if you don't cooperate with me," he noted, raising his brows at her. "Have you lost faith in me, already? Don't give up on me now, Sweet Cakes."

She looked away. No reaction.

"What? Have you reconciled with—what was it you called him? *Limp dick?*"

Blythe didn't even flinch.

He kept pushing. "You think Randal's gonna save you? Don't bet on it. He's probably lawyered up too."

Blythe sat taller in her chair and looked off into the corner. Dexter knew that even if he was right about this, she'd never admit it.

"Look, we can still beat this," he pressed. "Just hear me out."

Blythe looked back, meeting Dexter's eyes, but showed no signs of softening. "It all starts and ends with that bitch, *Rebeca*," she said, spitting out the name. "She started all this."

"You're right. The way I see it, it's simple. She's the only beneficiary of the trust. If she goes away, the trust is wrapped up, and the trust assets go to Randal," Dexter said, speaking softly so they would not be overheard.

Blythe's ears seemed to perk up. "Goes away?" she echoed.

He nodded. "The trust assets will pour into her estate, and since she doesn't have a husband or any children, unless she's got a will, everything flows upstream to her daddy. To your husband, limp-dick himself."

Blythe looked away, but this time it was to contemplate what Dexter had just said.

"I see I've got your attention," he said. "There's more. If Rebeca *goes away*, there's no one to claim they've been damaged by how we managed the trust. No one damaged means there's no one to press charges against me. Randal will keep his mouth shut. They'll have to release me."

Dexter now had Blythe's full attention.

"Finally, that brings us to Randal. I'm sure *he* has a will."

Blythe nodded her head.

"And does dear ol' Randal leave you anything in his will?"

"Don't know," she said.

"Well, he should. I'll bet if you hand him the negatives, he'll leave you everything, and that will include the assets of the LeMar Trust that will flow into his estate if anything . . ." He paused, raising his eyebrows. ". . . unfortunate happens to Rebeca."

Blythe hesitated before speaking, but the wheels were clearly turning.

"So, if Rebeca were to go away," repeated Blythe. "And if Randal were too..."

"*Now* you're getting it. I'm gonna give you a phone number, Sweet Cakes, and I want you to memorize it. When you get to your car, write it down so you don't forget. When you get home, call it and ask for Tommy. Tell him about our Rebeca problem. He'll know what to do. Then, tear up that number and go about your business. Before you know it, everything will be taken care of."

* * *

Randal Dunsmore's Home
Friday, September 23, 1994

At just over 12,000 square feet, one would assume that the size of Randal's home was more than adequate for two people—but from Blythe's perspective, it wasn't nearly large enough. Not with the way things now stood between them.

Since the courtroom fiasco a week and a half ago, Blythe had been relegated to a guest room on the backside of the ground floor complete with its own side entrance. It had been the nanny's quarters when Rebeca was a child. She was pacing her room, wearing her bra and panties, remembering her conversation with Dexter in jail just two days ago. He'd made it clear what needed to happen for the two of them to walk away with their freedom and Randal's money.

But what if Dexter's plan didn't work? In that case, Dexter was looking at prison, that was clear. But what about her? With her in bed with him in more ways than one, she rightfully feared for her freedom. Could she avoid the same fate?

She figured that Randal was the key to her freedom, or at least her best shot at it, but she feared that Randal was a little wiser now and knew that too. One way or another, she had to get Randal to use his family's influence to keep her out of jail. They each had something the other wanted. But who would broach the subject first? Randal, wanting the pictures back, or Blythe, wanting to stay out of prison? Oh, and one other thing she couldn't forget: she had to persuade him to put her in his will.

"*What to wear?*" she asked herself as she stood in front of her closet. Most of her clothes were still in the master bedroom closet upstairs. She decided less was more and removed her bra and panties and put on a simple white skirt and a thin, satin blue top. No slip. Barefoot.

* * *

Randal was sitting on the veranda, reflecting on the past couple of weeks. A copy of Michael Crichton's latest novel, Disclosure, sat on the table next to him. In the book, the protagonist, a man, must prove that he was sexually harassed by a fellow employee, a woman, instead of the other way around. Two weeks ago, Randal wouldn't have touched the book; it hit too close to home. But recent developments had dealt him a new hand. The deck had been reshuffled.

He was content to let Blythe remain in the house; it fed his sense of empowerment. He knew she was home; he'd seen her enter the side entrance about an hour ago. But how long should he let her live there? Divorce was inevitable. He was tired and ready to move on. They each had a great deal to lose: for him, what remained of his reputation, and for her, freedom. Who would make the first move? *I can afford to be patient*, he thought.

* * *

Randal's attention was broken by the sound of his wife's voice.

"I've brought you a drink, darling," she said.

Randal looked up as she was approaching him, the sun over her back, shedding light, so to speak, on what she had decided not to wear.

He smiled at the vision, hoping she would interpret it as warm and welcoming, and as a sign of his piqued curiosity. *Looks like she did,* he thought as she stopped short of Randal and bent over slowly, the top two buttons of her blouse undone, and placed his drink on the table. "Darling, can we talk?"

He was going to enjoy this.

"You talk, I'll listen," said Randal.

"I owe you a huge apology," she said as she down next to him demurely, her head bowed.

"You're kidding, right? You owe me an *apology?*" He laughed. "You owe me *more* than that—and from where I sit, there's no way you can repay me or undo what you've done."

"Won't you at least let me try?" she begged.

Over the next forty minutes, his wife said everything she could think of to persuade him to use his family's influence to keep a local prosecutor from bringing charges against her.

Randal wouldn't budge. He knew what he wanted, and he would get there eventually. But he was going to make her sweat for what she had done. "Blythe, cut the crap. You don't love me. You never did. I was an easy mark. I get it. But no more. So, this is how it's going to go down. I'll put you in my will and take care of you now, but you're not getting more than Rebeca. She'll get the lion's share of my estate when I die. In exchange, you'll help Walker Atkins track down the money you and Dexter stole from the trust, and you'll turn over the title to every asset you purchased with the money. I'll talk to Dad, and we'll use our influence to keep you out of jail. And when it's all over, I'll divorce you."

"But what's to keep you from changing the will after everything has blown over and after I've helped you recover the money in the trust?" she asked.

"Well, that brings us to the pictures you've been blackmailing me with."

"Honey, like I said, if you take care of me, you can have the pictures."

"Oh, I know. You've promised me you'll turn over every copy and all the negatives—but what keeps *you* from holding back a set of copies to use against me later?"

"I wouldn't do that, Randal. I'll turn them all over. You have my word."

"I'll have more than that," he said as he leaned forward and looked down her blouse.

"What are you talking about?" she asked, wearily. She began to button her blouse.

"I'll have my own pictures. Call it mutually assured destruction. Now get inside and strip. I think you know which chair to sit in."

Chapter 50

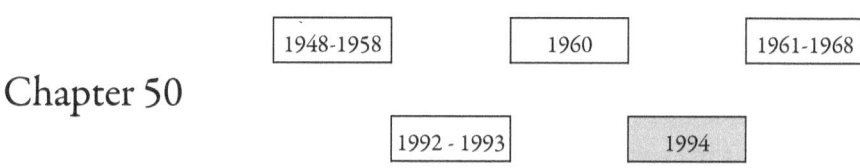

CHARLESTON
SEPTEMBER 1994

Johnny Dunsmore's march to the White House ran into a brick wall on Wednesday, September 14th when his bid for reelection was jeopardized by the story the *Post & Courier* ran on the front page linking Johnny and Luis Sanchez with Anthony Ferguson—the dirty banker from the Bahamas who was knee-deep in the fraudulent activities the grand jury was investigating.

The reporter who ran the story included two photographs. One was a photo that featured Johnny, Luis Sanchez, and Anthony Ferguson on the Sanchezes' yacht, and the other was a recent one of Johnny and Luis Sanchez standing side-by-side at the fundraiser at Hibernian Hall in June of that year. These photos made it easy to tie the governor and Luis Sanchez together in a shared conspiracy with Anthony Ferguson. After reading the story, there was one thing everybody could agree on: Johnny Dunsmore had some explaining to do.

The story was picked up by the *Wall Street Journal*, and an investigative reporter who had been on the trail of the Sanchez family ran with it. The story took on a life of its own. Johnny's in-laws, the Thistles, were dragged into the mess as well. It seemed that Luis Sanchez and his father, Gilberto Sanchez, and Johnny's father-in-law, Terrance Thistle, were entangled in the savings and loan crisis that unfolded in the 1980s. They had repeatedly gathered politicians, lobbyists, and owners of savings and loan banks on junkets where they discussed banking legislation. These same politicians went on to pass legislation that opened the lines of business and types of loans that an S&L could engage in.

Privy to advanced knowledge of these backroom deals, the Dunsmores bought Coastal Savings & Loan from the family that owned it and did so despite the bank's precarious financial position, confident in the knowledge that forthcoming legislation would open the floodgates to new, more lucrative business. Deregulation was the name of the game, and laws passed by both the Carter and Reagan administrations contributed to a Wild West mentality that spurred reckless loans that, when combined with illegal behavior by owners of savings and loan institutions, lead to asset bubbles. These assets inflated in value to unsustainable heights, real estate in the case of the S&Ls, only to later collapse.

More pictures surfaced in stories uncovered by the *Wall Street Journal* of politicians and judges cavorting with beautiful young women aboard the *Peristeria*—the Sanchezes' 187-foot-long, triple-masted sailing yacht. By the end of the week, the media was calling for congressional investigations into the undue influence in the nation's banking system. Influential members of the House of Representatives who were up for reelection heard the cries for justice, and subpoenas were being prepared and attorneys hired. The Thistles were outraged, Johnny Dunsmore was on the defensive, and the Sanchezes were seething.

And at the center of all of it stood Rebeca Dunsmore.

Amidst all the denials and dissembling, her testimony would tie all the parties together.

* * *

Wadmalaw River, Johns Island
Wednesday, September 28, 1994

Johnny had the place to himself, at least for the next half hour or so. The house was owned by his wife—or, more accurately, it was owned by a multigenerational trust domiciled in the Caribbean and established for his wife's benefit. It was his oasis, a forty-minute drive from downtown Charleston, and a place to which he could retreat and be left alone. His wife was in Nantucket but would be home sometime next week.

He was sitting in an Adirondack chair at the end of the dock with a cigar in one hand and a tumbler of whiskey in the other. The setting sun cast an orangish-red haze from across the Wadmalaw River, and bolts of lightning far in the distance foreshadowed a coming storm.

Johnny heard a car door shut, but instead of greeting his guest, he stayed put. A few minutes later, knowing he couldn't avoid the inevitable, he stood and walked back towards the house. As he did, he saw Luis Sanchez and his father, Gilberto, waiting for him.

* * *

Johnny stood barefoot with his back to the dock and his right hand gripping the sliding screen door, his empty drink glass in his left hand. He was still dressed in the khaki pants and white oxford shirt he'd put on that morning, but he had removed his tie on the drive over. Sitting on his sofa was Gilberto Sanchez, his left ankle crossed over his right knee. His son, Luis, poured himself a drink at Johnny's bar.

"So nice of you to invite us over, Johnny," said Gilberto, mildly. "Can my son pour you another drink? Bourbon is your preference, I believe."

"You invited yourself," Johnny clarified. "And no. I can pour my own drinks."

"Yes, you've become quite adept at that over the years, haven't you?" Gilberto asked.

Johnny's gaze drifted from Gilberto to Luis and back to Gilberto as he struggled to grasp how far he'd fallen since first meeting these two monsters.

"Johnny, I want to tell you something." Gilberto paused to sip from his drink—keeping his eyes locked eerily on Johnny the whole time. "I want to tell you what I told Luis before he headed off for his freshman year at Georgetown all those years ago. Would you like to hear what I told him?"

"Do I have a choice?"

"No, you don't." His face hardened. "And *sit down*," he said, pointing at a chair on the other side of the coffee table. He did so with the sort of authority that Johnny was used to hearing only from his own father. "Your pacing has always been an annoyance."

Johnny didn't want to sit anywhere near them, so he leaned against a table positioned along the wall, by the exit to the dock placing Gilberto between him and Luis, who was still standing by the bar. He wondered for a moment if he could make it to the end of the dock, dive off and swim away.

"I said to him, son, we help people hide their sins. Darkness abhors the light. We help keep the light at bay. Graft, bribery, tax evasion, theft, and deceit are all as old as time. We need not encourage such behavior in men, for it is their nature. We simply ease their fears of being caught and ease their conscience along the way by shielding them from the shame of others knowing what kind of men they truly are.

"We remove the guardrails. You might even say we lead them into temptation by eliminating the consequences of their actions. When we do, they do the rest. They'll willingly place their head in the lion's mouth for a few moments of fame and glory. And *we're* the lion's mouth. That control over others, the power to shut the lion's mouth, is what *we* possess.

"So, I told my son that while he was at Georgetown—walking the halls with the sons and daughters of parents who are in Congress and courthouses—he needed to befriend them, get to know them, and most of all, get to know their weaknesses." He paused, giving Johnny a sadistic sort of grin. "And then *remove the guardrails.*"

Johnny's breathing was labored. His eyes abandoned Gilberto and drifted to somebody he had once considered his best friend. Luis was leaning against the bar top, almost mirroring Johnny's stance across from him.

"Imagine my excitement," Luis's father went on, "when my son told me that he had met just such a man in his first week of college. Do you know who that man was, Johnny?"

Johnny remained silent. He knew damn well *who that man was.*

"That man was *you.*"

Luis cleared his throat. Johnny realized he was even holding his whiskey in the same hand—that they were, in every way, mirrored. "Before you start thinking you're special, *El Jefe*," Luis said with a conspiratorial grin, "please know that you're not. You aren't the only man we own. There are plenty of others just like you. It's just that right now, you're the only one whose failures threaten to expose much of what we have built."

Johnny set his whiskey aside, finally summoning the power to speak. "I don't know what you're talking about, Luis."

"I'm talking about your niece, Rebeca Dunsmore. She knows too much, and the public loves her. They believe whatever she says. Now, we all know that a grand jury here in South Carolina has called her to testify, but it gets worse. Our sources tell us that she will be called to testify before a special committee that Congress will convene shortly. They're planning on her being the first witness, and the hearings will be televised for all to see. Other witnesses they may call will know far more than she does, but she presents the human element—the little girl dragged along on scandalous vacations with her father and uncle, on yachts populated with hookers and politicians, and of course, me and my father. She's the pretty face. She's the witness the public will remember. And worst of all, she's the only witness we can't persuade to lie or to remain quiet."

"So, Johnny, you see our problem, don't you?" asked Gilberto.

Suddenly, rage replaced Johnny's fear. How *dare* they come in here, into his home, and threaten him like this! They thought they *owned* him? He'd show them who really owned this town.

"I do see *your* problem, Gilberto," Johnny said boldly. "You stand to lose a lot."

"So do you," Luis countered, but Johnny only laughed.

"Not as much as either of you," he said. "The public loves me too—more than Rebeca, by far, I'd wager, but it isn't a competition about who the public loves more. It's a competition of who the public *hates* more. In this case, who do you think they would *hate* more?"

Neither Gilberto nor Luis said anything.

"I think we all know the answer to that," he continued. "They would hate you—foreigners corrupting our system of government. I'll be granted immunity so fast your head will spin. And I know everything there is to know about Sanchez & Sanchez, and the rest of your clientele. You're not the only ones with power here!" He picked up his drink and hurled it over Luis's head towards the front door, at which he was now pointing. "SO, KINDLY GO FUCK YOURSELF AND LEAVE MY HOUSE NOW!"

The veins were bulging in Johnny's neck as he screamed at Luis and Gilberto, who both remained eerily calm. Luis then reached into his inside coat pocket, pulled out an envelope, and tossed it onto the coffee table, separating the sofa from where Johnny was standing.

"Open it," demanded Luis.

Johnny took a step forward and bent over to pick up the envelope. As he opened it, memories he thought the bottle had killed came rushing back. He was holding photos of Nadia's dead body stretched out on the bed—photos of the last night Johnny ever saw her.

Johnny attempted to regain his composure.

"This means nothing. This was years ago. You can't tie her death to me. These pictures clearly show the logo of the building on the pillows. That condo was leased in *your* name, Gilberto. These pictures indict *you*," he said as he tossed the pictures at the old man.

Luis then reached into the inside coat pocket on the other side, pulled out another envelope, and tossed it at Johnny. It hit Johnny in the chest and fell to the floor. Johnny didn't have to be told what to do. He opened it and began to thumb through a legal document.

"What is this?"

"That, my dear friend, is the lease on the condo where her body was found. If you flip to the last page, you'll see *you* were the tenant. That's your signature at the bottom."

Johnny was reeling. "This is a fraud! I didn't sign this, and you know it. This will never work. Her body was found in an alley. The police said she died from a drug overdose."

"Johnny, do you remember Lucius from your days at Georgetown?" asked Gilberto. "He was the doorman at the condo building as you may remember. We recently tracked him down and gave him a job at one of our properties in the Caribbean. He's doing great. Yes, we overpay him for what he does, but rewarding loyalty is important in our family. Well, you'll be delighted to know that he still remembers you. When we brought up your name, he asked how you were doing and whether you were still peddling drugs or whether you had left that life behind."

Johnny couldn't take any more of this and launched himself over the coffee table at Gilberto. Luis pulled Johnny off his father, but Johnny was not easily subdued—that was, until Luis pointed a pistol at him.

"Sit down," Luis demanded.

Johnny couldn't catch his breath. He was hyperventilating—trying to figure out what the hell was going on. He reluctantly took a seat. Everything was reaching a peak. The memories of Nadia's bloated, puce face and his tie around her throat, the way he'd vomited his DNA all over the scene of the crime, only to be carried away and cared for by Luis . . .

Gilberto recomposed himself, walked over to the bar to pour himself a drink, and then returned and stood next to his son, who was still holding the pistol on Johnny.

"Johnny, you and your father have proven to be very resourceful over the years, and believe me when I tell you that Luis and I want nothing more than to see you in the White House—but, to us, you are nothing more than an investment, and like all investments, they carry potential risks and rewards. What we must decide is whether sticking with you is worth the risk. You see, you have become a loose end, as has your niece, Rebeca. The question is, which of these loose ends do we tie up? The decision is yours, Johnny."

Johnny sat on the sofa, fighting the urge to throw up. "Tie up that loose end named Rebeca, or else we'll be forced to tie up *two* loose ends."

Chapter 51

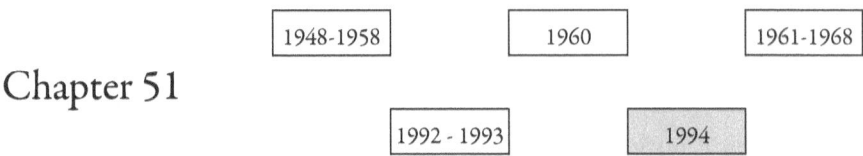

CHARLESTON

Blythe wanted Rebeca dead, but she didn't want to phone the number Dexter had given her when they met in jail. She knew the man named Tommy, who would answer the call. She remembered meeting him a few times at Tattle Tales when she was dancing and she did not want him in her life. Rebeca needed to die, but hiring Tommy to kill Rebeca felt like a bad move. It created a *loose end*.

Blythe realized that there was only way to go about this—she would have to do it herself. *She* would kill Rebeca, but that didn't mean she couldn't *implicate* Tommy.

Blythe would often visit Homer Bosco's office under the guise of wanting an update on how Dexter was doing; Homer was Dexter's attorney. On several of her trips to Homer's office, Blythe would secretly place calls to the number Dexter had given her. She'd wait until the call was answered and then hang up. A couple of times, Tommy called back. Once, while Bosco's receptionist stepped into the bathroom and when Homer wasn't in the office, she wrote Tommy's number down on the pink pad used to record phone calls with the simple message: "Tommy says to call him. You'll know what it's about." She placed the slip towards the back of the top drawer of Bosco's desk and returned to her seat in the conference room before the receptionist returned to her desk.

* * *

Sunday, October 2, 1994

Dexter was in jail pending his trial, and not likely to be released anytime soon, which meant it was time to move on to the next step.

Blythe had followed Rebeca earlier in the evening and learned she was out with friends. It was a perfect night to kill someone. It was a new moon, so the visibility was low. The October weather was unseasonably cold and blustery, making it difficult to hear anything over the wind, and it was sometime after midnight, rendering it unlikely anyone was out for a stroll.

Blythe parked a couple of blocks from the house Rebeca had rented and walked the rest of the way, taking care to avoid streetlights. Rebeca had rented a small, two-story Charleston single house off Gadsden Street just north of Bull Street. Blythe had scouted the neighborhood earlier and knew that the house immediately south of Rebeca's was vacant, awaiting a major remodel, so she made her way to the backside of Rebeca's house from Bull Street. As she approached, she saw someone else walk up the stairs and down the piazza and knock on the front door. He was wearing a hoodie, and judging from his gait, Blythe assumed the person was a man.

And not just a man, but a *familiar* man, somehow.

She took cover behind a tree, watching as Rebeca opened the door, but wisely did not let the man in a hoodie inside. From where Blythe was standing, it looked like the man was doing all the talking. Eventually, Rebeca opened the door and let the man in. *Why? Interesting.* Did she know this guy, after all?

Blythe closed the distance between herself and the house, pulled herself up over the railing on the south side of the piazza, and discreetly peered through the window.

* * *

If Johnny had had a plan as to how to kill Rebeca, he abandoned it early on. Rebeca was sitting on the sofa while Johnny was pacing to and fro, holding the pistol in his right hand and running his left hand through his hair.

"Why couldn't you leave well enough alone?" he mumbled. "Why did you have to show someone that photograph?"

Johnny was visibly drunk and struggling to keep a grip on things.

"What are you talking about?" asked Rebeca.

"The photo taken on the boat!"

"So that's it, Uncle Johnny. You're afraid of the Sanchezes. Are you going to kill me now? Did they send you or was this your idea?"

"Don't call me *Uncle Johnny*."

"Why not? Is it because you're not my uncle? Is it because you're actually my father?"

Johnny stopped pacing and looked at her, then started pacing again.

"Don't give me that look," Rebeca argued. "I've seen the old family photos and how you and my mom looked at each other."

That got his attention.

"That's right, Uncle Johnny. Anyone with eyes could tell you two had a thing for each other. Should I dispense with the uncle nonsense and just call you father? We look alike, you know. We both have dark, curly hair. Dark complexions. I look nothing like Randal."

"I'm not your father," Johnny insisted.

"Sure you are. Randal certainly isn't. You know he's sterile, don't you?"

Johnny stopped pacing again and looked at Rebeca, who was sitting calmly on the sofa.

"Yep. When I was about thirteen, I came home from school and saw the light blinking on the answering machine. I knew there was a message waiting, and I listened to it. Thought it might be for me. It was from a fertility clinic, and they were asking that Randal give them a call. Now *why* would he be going to a fertility clinic? Well, he knew someone had played the message, but didn't know who. He fired the maid in case she heard it. I never told him I was the one who listened to the message, but I think he might have known all along. He looked at me differently from that point on. So, yeah, Randal's not my dad—so, that leaves you. And you know what? I'm tired of the lies, Johnny. It's time the world knew the truth."

Whether Johnny was predestined for the path he followed or whether his downward spiral was triggered in college after Nadia's death is anyone's guess. But one thing was objectively true: something died inside Johnny the night he saw Nadia lying dead in a pool of blood. At first, the alcohol numbed his conscience, but at some point, it took over and fueled his dissent into the abyss. Any chance to recover his soul on his own was long gone, but that didn't relieve him of the responsibility for his actions—even now, when he could only engage with the world around him from the reptilian portion of his brain.

Johnny steadied himself, lifted the gun, and pointed it at Rebeca.

Rebeca lunged at Johnny from the sofa and knocked the pistol out of his hand. She tackled him to the ground, but even in his drunken stupor, he was just too strong and pushed her away. He got to his feet and saw that she was reaching for the gun. He grabbed the fireplace poker and buried it into the base of her skull, leaving her face down, blood seeping across the floor.

As Johnny stood over her, the front door opened, drawing his attention to Blythe.

"Hello, Johnny."

Chapter 52

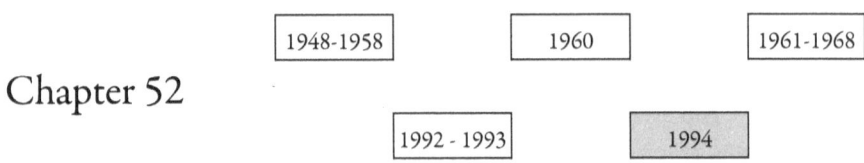

Randal's Veranda
Sunday, October 2, 1994

Randal was sitting in a rocking chair, holding a cup of freshly brewed coffee and enjoying a peaceful morning on his veranda. He was dressed in sweatpants and a thin cotton sweater owing to the early-morning chill in the air. Over the seawall, sailboats powered by the ocean breeze slipped by as the sound of church bells rang across the Holy City.

His peace was interrupted by the footsteps of two uniformed police officers walking towards him.

"Mr. Dunsmore? Are you Mr. Randal Dunsmore?"

"Yes, officers. What can I do for you?"

* * *

The officers were looking at it as a robbery gone bad. They believed that Rebeca Dunsmore had walked downstairs and surprised the burglar, and that she may have tried to interfere because there was evidence of a struggle. Items were stolen, including her purse and her car. Police found the vehicle abandoned twenty miles away, off the side of the Savannah Highway. Rebeca was found lying on the floor by the hearth, bludgeoned by the fireplace poker and barely hanging on to life.

"Are you sure it's *my* Rebeca?" Randal asked, clinging to some vestige of hope, to anything.

"Yes, sir. We are," responded one of the officers. "Her purse was taken, so we couldn't find a driver's license or any ID, but we know it's your daughter. The mail on the kitchen counter was addressed to her. She's been taken to the emergency room. Mr. Dunsmore, we're very sorry."

Randal, who stood when the officers arrived, slumped back into the rocking chair. Numb. Not sure what to feel beyond loss. *This can't be happening!* he thought.

"Mr. Dunsmore, is your wife here? Can she give you a ride to the hospital?"

Randal hadn't seen Blythe since she slithered out sometime late in the afternoon the day before. "She's not feeling well. I can drive myself."

* * *

As the shock wore off, Randal began to question the cops' findings. He was sitting in the emergency room lobby, waiting to see his daughter and wondering who could have done this. Burglary as an explanation made no sense, but attempted murder did.

It struck him how Rebeca's death would take the heat off several people, his wife included. All matters concerning the trust would go away, and no doubt she'd never expect him to go after her and Dexter over trust mismanagement, given that he was not a beneficiary and that they were holding the incriminating photographs.

About then, a nurse told him he could see her. Nothing could've prepared him for the sight he was faced with moments later. As Randal stood over her, he realized he had loved Rebeca, despite it all.

When he left the hospital, he returned to the question: Who else besides Blythe and Dexter would benefit from Rebeca's death?

The answer to that question was easy: Gilberto Sanchez. Luis Sanchez. His father. *And Johnny.*

* * *

Thirty minutes after leaving the hospital, Randal was outside his father's suite at the Charleston Place Hotel, banging on the door, demanding to be let in.

Colin opened the door, and Randal burst into the room and saw Johnny standing by the window, clearly drunk. For some reason, the sight of his drunk brother pissed him off even more, and before he could stop himself, Randal was flying across the room, barreling towards Johnny.

He had him on the ground in seconds.

"What the hell is going on?" Colin demanded to know.

Randal was sitting on Johnny's chest, slamming his fists into Johnny's face. "You bastard! You tried to kill her! I know you did! *You fucking bastard!*"

"Get off him—right now!" Colin demanded, attempting to swat Randal away, but he was an old man now and didn't have the strength he used to.

Randal shook him off, hit Johnny a few more times, and then stood up on his own accord, mostly because he wanted his brother to explain himself. Once he'd gotten answers, maybe then Randal would return to beating Johnny to within an inch of his life.

"Randal, what the hell are you talking about? Who tried to kill who?" Colin asked.

"It was both of you! You were both in on it!"

"In on what?" asked Colin.

"Rebeca was attacked early this morning in her home. She's in a coma. I just came from the hospital. Her chances don't look good."

"Attacked?" repeated Colin. The shock on his face was remarkable. Either he was a great actor, or genuinely concerned and uninvolved in the attack.

"You heard me," Randal went on. "The cops came by my house today. She was found in her home this morning. She had been attending church at St. Michael's with a friend who gave her a ride to church each Sunday. Her friend honked her horn, and when Rebeca didn't come out, she investigated. The front door was open, and when she walked in, she saw Rebeca on the floor by the fireplace—blood everywhere."

"Oh, good Lord. Son, I'm so sorry. I truly am," Colin said, and for the first time in Randal's life, it looked like he actually meant it. "You say she's alive, though. In a coma?"

"Yes, but it doesn't look good."

"We'll send someone to her at once," Colin offered, springing into action. "We'll demand a copy of the police report. We'll get details on this assault and track down the perpetrators at once. Rebeca may hate us, but she's a Dunsmore. We'll protect her."

This took Randal aback thoroughly. "You didn't do it," he realized. "You're not behind this attack on her?"

"What are you talking about? Of course not!" Colin barked.

Randal turned his gaze to Johnny.

"Johnny, you look drunker than usual," said Randal. "Guilty conscience?"

Johnny remained silent.

"You think your brother attacked Rebeca?" asked Colin.

"Who has the most to lose if it all comes out about what our family and the Sanchez family have been up to all these years? Who has the most to gain if it can all be swept away? It's *you*, Johnny. It's you!"

"Nonsense," said Colin. "Now that's enough."

"Johnny, there's nothing you won't do to get to the White House, is there?" asked Randal.

Johnny still had not said a word. He took a swig of his drink and stumbled to the bar to prepare himself another.

"Don't you think you've had enough, son?" asked Colin.

Johnny said nothing. He then poured his drink and drank it in one gulp, the reflection of his father and brother staring back at him in the mirror over the bar.

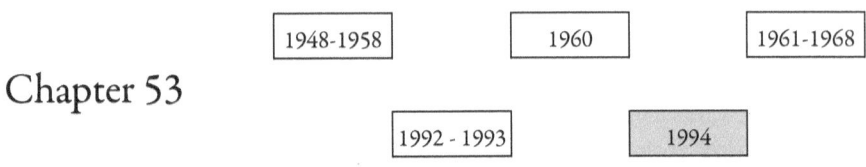

Chapter 53

LAW OFFICES OF ATKINS & ATKINS
MONDAY, OCTOBER 3, 1994

Walker was at his desk drafting a will for a new client when Mrs. Beasley buzzed him. "Mr. Atkins, I have your wife on the line."

"Thank you. Please patch her through."

"Oh, Walker. It's terrible, just terrible—"

"Honey, what is it? Are you okay?" Walker could tell Izzy was upset and crying. He could hear what sounded like traffic in the background.

"Rebeca was attacked in her home early Sunday morning. She's in a coma."

"*What?* Where are you getting this?" he asked, hoping that her information was wrong. "And where are you? I hear a lot of noise in the background."

"I heard it on the radio. I'm calling you from a payphone. I pulled over at the first gas station I came to. Oh, Walker, who could have done this?"

* * *

Walker ran to the conference room and turned the TV to a local station that was running with the story and learned that she had been taken to MUSC Hospital. Twenty minutes later, he was talking to the doctor outside her room.

* * *

"Dr. Fedor, I'm Walker Atkins—a close friend and her attorney. What can you tell me about her condition?"

"She's in a coma."

"Yes, I know. It's all over the news. But what more can you tell me? What are her chances of recovery?"

"First of all, it's way too early to know for sure, but I don't think the prognosis is good. She lost a lot of blood, and the brain trauma looks severe," he explained.

"What's the best-case scenario?" Walker asked.

"That she recovers consciousness, of course," the doctor replied. "But even so, she would likely suffer significant long-term consequences such as impaired vision, slurred speech, cognitive impairment—"

"And the worst case?"

"That she doesn't die and lives out her days in a persistent vegetative state."

* * *

It was all Walker could do to keep his emotions in check as he walked back into his office. He'd grown quite fond of Rebeca. His wife Isabelle had too. At his office, everyone joined him in the lobby and brought them up to speed. Prayers were said and a few tears were shed. Not knowing what to do, everyone returned to their office and began going through the motions of caring about what they had scheduled to do that day.

When Walker sat down at his desk, he saw a message: "Urgent: Call Eddie Wentworth."

Eddie picked up quickly. "I guess you've heard," said Eddie. Eddie had quietly been reinstated at work as a result of the news reports that substantiated the attorney general's reasons for calling the grand jury to investigate the Dunsmores.

Walker shared with him what the doctor had told him.

"Well, that aligns with what our office learned from the police department," Eddie said, sighing in resignation. "You know what this means, don't ya?"

"I hadn't really had the time to think about it. Still trying to process it all. Why don't you tell me."

"Without Rebeca's testimony, we don't have much," Eddie said. "And we can't find Anthony Ferguson anywhere. The guy has vanished. Oh, and the boys in DC have apparently lost interest. Senator Cochrane, who was chairing the congressional hearings to investigate offshore banking activities said—get this—'Her demise really lets the steam out of our investigation.' What a loser."

Walker felt fifty pounds heavier as he slumped at his desk. "Does any of this surprise you, Eddie?" Walker had grown as cynical as Eddie had in recent months about the work they were doing to bring down the corporate bad guys.

"No, it doesn't. And on that note, I'll leave you with one more bit of *good* news," he said sarcastically. "Last Friday afternoon, Palmetto Lending Tree, Palmetto Realty, Palmetto Quick Cash, and the cast of Grand Ocean Pavilions LLCs all filed for bankruptcy protection. We just learned this morning."

Walker groaned audibly.

"It may be time for another trip to Salty Mike's," Eddie said.

* * *

Fifteen minutes later...

As Walker was digesting the news Eddie shared with him, Abigail knocked on his door.

"Come in, Abigail." Her mascara was smeared, and she made no effort to hide her emotions. She walked in and stood on the other side of his desk and flailed her arms in exasperation. "What now?" she asked.

"Have a seat. I have more to tell you," he said, and then he told her that the companies they'd been pursuing on behalf of the Gastons and their other clients had all filed bankruptcy.

"So that means that even if we win in court, we lose because the companies are bankrupt and won't have money to pay any judgments." Walker nodded that she was right. "But what about the foreclosure actions against the Gastons and the others? What happens to those?" she asked.

"I don't know yet. It will depend on whether the lenders sold their loan portfolios before filing bankruptcy. So, we've got some work to do."

Abigail and Walker were quiet. The specter of Rebeca's condition hovered over them.

"And what about the matter of Rebeca's trust?" Abigail asked.

Walker was too numb to think constructively. He was fighting back tears. "Abigail, let's talk about it tomorrow. I gotta get out of here."

* * *

Walker left the office early that afternoon and went for a run, hoping to clear his mind. When he entered the house, covered in sweat, the television in the living room was turned to a station airing live news, and he found Isabelle on the screened-in porch reading to Anna and Peter.

He filled a glass with water and joined her. She looked up and smiled weakly at him.

"Hey, kids, Daddy and I need to talk," she said. "We'll finish this story later. Why don't you run outside and play?"

The kids took off and Walker and Izzy walked back inside and sat next to each other on the sofa. The emotions Walker had been holding back all day came pouring forth. He put his head on his wife's shoulder and just cried. He was exhausted, physically from the run, and mentally and emotionally from everything else. No words were exchanged. Izzy was there for him, and this was all he needed at the moment.

Their attention was drawn to the news reporter on the TV: "And now, we're going live to a press conference that has been called by our governor, Johnny Dunsmore. We've been told that he'll be making remarks about the recent assault on his niece, Rebeca Dunsmore, who we understand remains in a coma:

> "As I stand here today, our family is gathered, expressing our great sorrow and shock over what has befallen my beautiful niece, Rebeca Dunsmore. You will notice, however, that her father, Randal Dunsmore, my beloved brother, and his wife, Blythe, are not with us. They have asked to be given their privacy as they process everything. I'm sure you understand."

Walker's tears stopped as his sorrow dissipated. The governor continued:

> "As your governor, if I am reelected, fighting crime will be at the top of my agenda. But in order to do my job, I need your help. I need you to not only return me to the governor's mansion, but I need you to put Skip Jackson in the Attorney General's Office."

Walker's sorrow had now fully morphed into disgust and Isabelle was on her feet staring at the television in disbelief. She turned to her husband, and with tears of anger streaming down her face, her right hand balled up with her index finger extended and pounding the air, she spoke to him clearly, concisely, forcefully. "Rebeca Dunsmore needs an attorney now more than ever. Walker, you be that man!"

Chapter 54

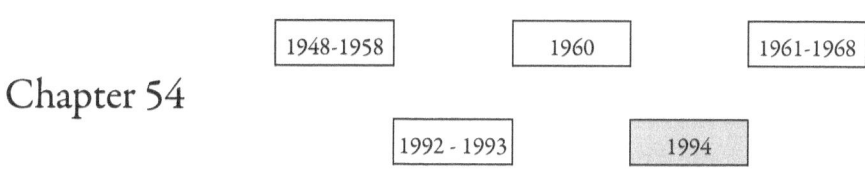

LAW OFFICES OF ATKINS & ATKINS
TUESDAY, OCTOBER 4, 1994

Walker arrived at the office early. It was amazing what a good night's sleep was capable of. That, plus Isabelle's love and support, was *invaluable*. He was at his desk scribbling notes on a legal pad when Abigail stuck her head in his office.

"Morning, boss," she said and then kept on towards her office.

"Abigail," Walker shouted. "Do you have a minute?"

She returned and stepped into his office. "Of course." She moved to have a seat in the chair across from the desk where Walker was seated.

"I want to apologize for my behavior yesterday afternoon," Walker said. "It was unprofessional."

"Apology not necessary. That wasn't unprofessional—that was *human*."

Walker smiled. "You ready to get back to work?"

"Absolutely," she said.

Walker stood from his desk and handed her a legal pad and pen.

"Will we be filing a motion to have you appointed as Rebeca Dunsmore's legal guardian while she's in a coma?" asked Abigail.

"Yes," answered Walker. "But I expect that her father, Randal, will too. Rebeca's condition changes everything. If Randal becomes her guardian, he can shut down the suit to have himself removed as trustee of her trust."

"Doesn't that mean he has a conflict of interest?" asked Abigail.

"Yes, which is what we'll argue before Judge Rawlings. But it gets worse. As the only beneficiary under the terms of the LeMar Trust, if Rebeca were to die, the assets of the trust become her property and flow into her estate, and in South Carolina, if you die without a will, the assets in your estate pass to your children first and then to her siblings."

"And she doesn't have a will, does she?" said Abigail.

"That's right. I drafted one for her, but she hadn't signed it yet."

"She doesn't have any children or siblings, either," added Abigail.

"Correct."

"Which means the assets pass to her parents," she said.

"Which means her father, Randal."

"Which is why he can't become her legal guardian," Abigail concluded.

"Exactly."

* * *

Meanwhile, a few blocks away in the Charleston County Jail...

"Well done, Sweet Cheeks," Dexter said. "I heard the news."

"I don't know what you're talking about," Blythe said in a sing-song voice, conveying just enough insincerity to earn her a conspiratorial smile from across the table.

"Of course, you don't. Now, it's time to get me outta here. I need you to call my lawyer and get the wheels in motion. He'll know what to do. Without Rebeca around, there's no one to press charges."

Blythe's face fell slightly. "Oh, she's still around, honey."

"True, but the news coming across the TV ain't good. She could be in a coma for years, they say. She's as good as dead. Besides, they can't keep me locked up without an injured party or witness," explained Dexter.

"Won't her attorney, Walker Atkins, keep the fight going?"

"He can try, but you can stop him."

"*How*, honey? How can I stop him? Tell me what to do, and I'll do it."

"Atkins may ask the court to make him Rebeca's guardian," Dexter said. "We can't let that happen. *Randal* should be her guardian, and the court will support him—he's her father, after all. You gotta keep Randal on a short leash a little longer. Make sure he becomes Rebeca's guardian. Then he can shut down her investigation into what we were doing with her trust. Got it?"

"Got it," she answered with a devilish smile.

"Once it's shut down and I'm out of here, we'll sell the rest of the stocks in dear ol' Rebeca's trust, disappear for a while, and then come back when the pressure is off. I'm thinkin' Fiji. You and me, babe. Let's go to Fiji."

"Let's."

* * *

Charleston County Superior Court
Judge Daggett's Courtroom
Wednesday, October 5, 1994

"All rise, the Honorable Judge Daggett presiding," the bailiff announced.

The judge took his seat and told everyone else in the courtroom that they could as well.

"I have a busy docket today, so let's get right to it," he said. He tilted his head forward so that he could look over his readers and see the court room more clearly. "Mr. Bosco, it's always good to see you in my courtroom."

"Thank you, Your Honor, and it's always a pleasure to be here. Today, I'm representing Mr. Dexter Childress, and we are—"

"I know why you're here. I read your brief," the judge said. "Just get to the point."

"Judge Daggett, while my client is distraught over young Rebeca Dunsmore's situation, it leaves this court without its key witness or an injured party. We are asking that all charges be dropped and that my client, Mr. Childress, be immediately released."

"But Mr. Bosco, we still *have* an injured party—Rebeca Dunsmore. Now, I understand your client's situation and the injustice he would suffer were he held in jail indefinitely while we wait and see if Ms. Dunsmore recovers. But there are other matters to consider."

* * *

Meanwhile, down the hall in Judge Rawlings's quarters . . .

Blythe was sitting in a small waiting room outside the judge's chambers hoping for an audience. She was dressed tastefully but still in a manner she knew even happily married men wouldn't fail to notice. The matronly secretary guarding the entrance to the judge's chambers was not impressed.

Blythe knew that Dexter was down the hall with his attorney waiting to argue for his release, but Dexter getting out of jail no longer aligned with her plans. He didn't need to know that, though, of course.

Blythe wanted him to go on thinking that they were in cahoots together. She'd seen how the other half lived, and Dexter didn't fit in that world. She had sold her body to men who lived amongst the other half, and to Randal in exchange for his wedding vows—and she was *sick* of prostituting herself. Dexter had proven useful, but she had grown weary of him. No, she had to stop the judge down the hall from releasing Dexter.

The phone buzzed, and the judge's secretary answered. Blythe looked on and it was clear to her that the secretary was not pleased. "I'll send her right in," she said.

"The judge will see you now," she said, refusing to look directly at Blythe.

* * *

The judge rose from behind his desk when she entered. Blythe thought he looked older and less formidable without his black robe on.

"Thank you for seeing me," she said.

"Of course. Now, what can I do for you?" he asked as he led her over to the sofa. He took a seat in a chair at one end and poured each of them a glass of water from the pitcher on the coffee table.

"Your Honor, this is all so embarrassing, but I can't stay silent any longer. You see, Dexter Childress has been blackmailing me and my husband, Randal," she confessed quietly.

"And how has he been blackmailing you?" he asked.

"It's all my fault. I knew Dexter when I lived in Los Angelas, before I moved to Charleston. We used to be lovers. This was before I met Randal and fell in love with him. I left LA to leave behind the life I was living—a life I'm not proud of. Well, Dexter followed me out here. He knew things about me, and he knew he could ruin my new life here—the life Randal and I were building. Your Honor, it pains me to say this, but Dexter Childress has sway over me; he's like a bad drug. Anyway, shortly after he arrived, I had an affair with him. It didn't last long, and I came to my senses and broke it off with him."

"And he used this against you to get control over Rebeca Dunsmore's trust?"

"Yes, Your Honor. You see, Randal found out about it. Dexter told him, and then he threatened to go public with it. Randal knew it would reflect poorly on his work for the Dunsmore Family Foundation, and then there's his brother Johnny's bid for reelection next month. Randal was so forgiving of me. Dexter wanted control of his daughter's trust, and Randal gave it to him."

"Mrs. Dunsmore, I find this all rather difficult to believe. This is the twentieth century; infidelity is rather common. I don't see how your affair with Dexter Childress would negatively affect your brother-in-law's reelection bid. Unsavory allegations didn't keep Bill Clinton out of the White House. Besides, if you were serious about keeping Dexter Childress behind bars, you'd be telling this story to the judge across the hall; I understand he's hearing a motion right now to have Mr. Childress released."

"Well, with all due respect, Your Honor, Bill Clinton might not be president today had there been *pictures* of his indiscretions, and you'll hopefully understand why I'm not in the courtroom across the hall publicly arguing my case once you see these."

Blythe then demurely reached into her purse and withdrew a stack of pictures and placed them in front of Judge Rawlings—photos of her naked, tied to a chair, and blindfolded. They were, of course, a copy of the photos Randal had taken. He'd given her a set as a reminder of the deal they had reached.

"Dexter took these of me," she said, doing her best to act mortified. "I know what you're thinking—it was stupid of me to pose this way. When I did, I didn't know he would use them against me."

The judge looked through them quickly and handed them back.

"In the pictures, you can clearly see the Dunsmore family portrait on the wall," she went on to add. "Dexter figured that folks would think that either Randal took the pictures and that we were into all sorts of kinky stuff or that someone I was fooling around with had. You see, Your Honor, I was afraid that my history in California, which I alluded to, would have come out and that everything I had run from would catch up with me. It would have devastated Randal and his family. Randal has been so good to me."

* * *

Meanwhile, back in Judge Daggett's courtroom . . .

"So, Mr. Bosco, I'm inclined to allow your client's release, but also to keep Walker Atkins on as the temporary trustee until the courts sort matters out," Judge Rawlings explained. "And furthermore, Mr. Bosco, before I would allow Dexter Childress to resume his responsibilities for Ms. Dunsmore's trust, I would need to hear from Randal Dunsmore. He may have something to say about all this."

Homer Bosco was not deterred. "Your Honor, I have the transcript from the court proceedings that led to my client's arrest. If I may approach the bench, Your Honor, then I could show you the testimony from Randal Dunsmore, where he testified that he had willingly hired my client and approved of the job he was doing."

The judge flicked his wrist, indicating he could approach, took the transcript from the attorney, and began reviewing the referenced testimony.

"Mr. Bosco, I'm going to—"

Before he could finish his sentence, the bailiff from across the hall came barging in the courtroom. "Your Honor, please, may I have a moment of your time? It's important."

"What's so important that you would interrupt my courtroom like this?"

"Your Honor, may I approach the bench? I have a note from Judge Rawlings. He says it's urgent that you read it."

The judge waved him forward, and the bailiff approached quickly and handed him the note. The judge put his glasses on, unfolded the note, and read it. He looked up and across the courtroom at Dexter Childress, read the note again, and then with the crack of the gavel, the judge pronounced, "Motion denied."

Chapter 55

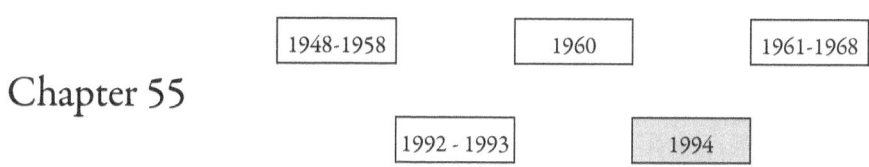

Blythe had learned a lot from Dexter. She'd learned that under the LeMar Trust, if Rebeca died now, without children, siblings, or a will, the trust would dissolve and all the assets in the trust—which she knew to be worth over $30 million—would flow up to her father's estate. The final piece of the puzzle had also recently fallen into place. As part of their Faustian bargain, Randal had rewritten his will, leaving the lion's share to Rebeca, but he had also left a remainder interest to Blythe. Of course, if Rebeca died, it *all* would go to Blythe.

But only if Randal died too.

* * *

Lockwood Marina
Friday, October 7, 1994

Blythe was wearing dark blue jeans, a black blouse, black sweater and brown deck shoes. The cloud cover obscured what moonlight there was. Visible stars were few and far between. She hadn't seen a single soul on the walk from her car, which she parked far away from any streetlights. At the end of the pier, she saw the embers of a cigarette glowing, and as she got closer, she could see the man holding it. When she arrived at the boat, she didn't wait to be asked aboard.

"Well, I got your message. I'm here," he said with an attitude. He was sitting in the captain's chair with a beer in one hand and his cigarette in the other. "What do you want?" asked Johnny.

"You can do something for me."

"And why should I?"

"Because I saw you try to kill Rebeca," she answered.

"Okay, I thought that would be your play. And that's why I'm here. To put an end to this." He stood from his chair and jabbed his right index finger in Blythe's direction. "To put to rest any notions you may have that *you have* anything on me. Because you don't," he insisted. He sat back in his chair and took a long drag on his cigarette.

Blythe remained silent.

Johnny continued, "You can't blackmail me without implicating yourself, because they're going to ask what *you* were doing there."

"Your DNA is all over that living room. The results will be back from the lab soon, so I'm told." She had no idea if that was true.

"So, what? They'll never think of asking for a DNA sample from me. Why would they?" he asked, looking quite pleased with himself.

"Your right—*on their own*, they'll never think of asking you for a sample. That's where I come in. I'm the little birdie that could whisper in their ear," she said, hoping Johnny picked up how pleased she was with herself.

Johnny remained silent and took a nervous drag on his cigarette.

"Oh, Johnny dear, you really should be nicer to me. If it comes to that, you might need an alibi. I'd be happy to tell everyone you and I were shacked up in a hotel room somewhere."

"And how's that going to help me? The election is just a month away. Last I checked, infidelity doesn't poll well."

"Neither does attempted murder."

They both remained silent.

"Like I said, Blythe—what do you want?"

"I need you to kill your brother for me."

"Why? What's he done to you?" he asked, as if having a good reason was reason enough.

"For money. It's like this. If Rebeca dies, the assets in her trust flow into her estate. We have it on good word that Rebeca doesn't have a will and since she has no siblings or children her estate flows to her father, dear old Randal. And your brother loves me so much that he recently amended his will. When he dies, I get everything."

Johnny was chuckling.

"What's so funny?"

"Oh, nothing. So, how much is Rebeca's trust worth?"

"Over thirty million dollars."

Johnny walked over to the cooler and pulled out two beers, opening one for her. He passed it over, likely buying himself time to think. "And if I do this, we're even. Right?" Johnny asked as he pulled the tab on his can.

"You'll never hear from me again."

Chapter 56

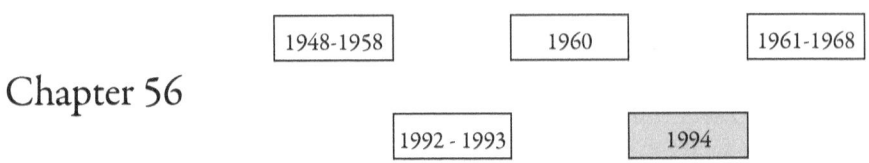

CHARLESTON COUNTY COURTHOUSE
JUDGE RAWLING'S COURTROOM
FRIDAY, OCTOBER 14, 1994

The session was scheduled to start in fifteen minutes and already the courtroom was filled to capacity, as every seat was taken and people were standing across the back wall: Journalists, TV reporters, members of the public, and other attorneys who wouldn't miss this show for the world.

The matter before the court today was the motion Walker had filed the previous week to be named Rebeca's legal guardian. She was in a coma, and medical decisions would have to be made. Word of the motion leaked, and Walker was excoriated by the press and the public alike. Walker's actions were met with derision, seeing as her father, Randal, was the obvious legal guardian. In his motion, Walker argued that Randal had a conflict of interest, because he stood to profit from Rebeca's death.

The public was aghast. Walker knew, though, that as her attorney, he was obligated to advocate for her best interests, regardless of the popularity of the position he might take. The judge granted Walker his motion for a hearing. Of course, Randal would have something to say about it all.

Which was another reason why the courtroom was full.

Randal was dead.

* * *

Randal's body was discovered by the maid in the bathtub off the bedroom he had shared with his brother Johnny growing up in the family home outside Columbia, South Carolina. The cause of death was either the slit wrists or the excessive quantity of pills and alcohol he had consumed.

"Frankly, from a review of the toxicology report, given all that he ingested and when I believe he took the pills, I don't know how he managed to hold the razor blade," remarked the pathologist assigned to the case.

The police did not find a note, but it wasn't hard to deduce what drove Randal to take his own life. Sitting on the edge of the bathtub was a picture of Randal and Rebeca's mother, Dixie—the photo Rebeca had placed in the drawing room of his home in Charleston when Rebeca was a teenager.

What the pathologists did not know was that Randal consumed the pills unknowingly, as Blythe had crushed them up and mixed them into his drinks. She had paid him an unannounced visit under the ruse of wanting to give their marriage one more chance. Randal had retreated to his childhood home—a place he hadn't visited in years—to find some privacy, knowing his parents were in Washington, DC. She followed him there.

Despite Blythe's petitioning, he wasn't having it; he was content, however, to watch her beg and prostitute herself, at least emotionally, as she tried in vain to persuade him that she had changed. Randal was enjoying his newfound respect. However, once the pills took effect, it was simply a matter of getting him upstairs and into the bathroom. She couldn't handle this on her own; Johnny would have to help. What choice did he have? They were in this together.

* * *

The next day, Johnny was back on stage, behind a wall of microphones, again pleading for privacy as the family digested yet another tragedy. Blythe was present, standing just behind Johnny, with a handkerchief dabbing her nonexistent tears.

* * *

"All rise, the Honorable Judge Rawlings presiding."

Judge Rawlings brought the gavel down several times, gathering the room's attention. Walker was seated at his table along with Abigail. He looked around the room and saw Johnny Dunsmore sitting with opposing counsel at the table where Randal would have sat. Folks approached him to shake his hand and express their deep sorrow for his loss. In the back of the room, Walker spotted Blythe wearing a hat and a pair of large sunglasses, hoping to remain inconspicuous.

The courtroom eventually settled down.

"Looks like we have a full house today," he said as he eased into his chair. "In all my years on the bench, I have never seen a case quite like this one. I have read the briefs from counsel and am ready to state my findings. It's late, and I'm tired, so I'm asking that prevailing counsel draft the official orders no later than Monday morning, which is when I will sign them.

"The first motion before the court is to remove Randal Dunsmore as the trustee for the LeMar Trust. Because of an earlier ruling from this bench, Mr. Walker Atkins currently serves as the temporary trustee. However, considering Randal Dunsmore's unfortunate death, matters have taken a turn. The motion before the court now is who to name as the permanent successor trustee. The document that created the LeMar trust is vague in this respect—a common fault of family trusts of that generation—so I will look elsewhere for guidance.

"The law begs the question: What is in the best interests of the trust beneficiaries? Since Rebeca Dunsmore is the only current beneficiary of the trust, the matter is further complicated by the fact that she is currently in a coma, from which she may never recover. So, this court must also decide who Rebeca Dunsmore's guardian will be. Were her father alive, the answer to that question would be easy: Randal would be Rebeca's guardian, and this court would also restore him as the trustee for her trust.

"However, as we are all painfully aware, Randal Dunsmore recently took his own life. So, we must now take his last will and testament into consideration. Randal Dunsmore's will states that his brother, Johnny Dunsmore, shall be the executor of his estate. I see that we have Governor Dunsmore in the courtroom with us this afternoon."

Johnny nodded his head towards the judge.

"First, let me say how sorry we all are for your loss," the judge said.

"Thank you, Your Honor. That means a lot."

"Governor Dunsmore, you are a busy man. Are you prepared to serve as executor of your brother's estate?"

"Yes, Your Honor."

"Further, are you prepared to serve as the legal guardian for his daughter, Rebeca Dunsmore, your niece?"

"Yes, Your Honor."

"Your Honor, if I may?" Walker interjected.

"Yes, Mr. Atkins. Do you have a problem with the governor serving as legal guardian for Rebeca Dunsmore?"

"Yes, Your Honor, I do," Walker said, and there was at once murmuring the crowd of those in attendance. "Ms. Dunsmore does not have a will. She doesn't have any siblings or children either. Under South Carolina law, if Rebeca Dunsmore were to die, her estate would pass to her father. But he is no longer with us, which means that it then passes to her aunts and uncles. Johnny Dunsmore is her only uncle, and she has no aunts. Johnny Dunsmore will have a conflict of interest. He will be asked to make medical decisions concerning Rebeca Dunsmore, including whether to remove life-sustaining support, knowing that he stands to inherit more than thirty million dollars from Rebeca upon her death."

The buzz from the courtroom was overwhelming. Judge Rawlings brought down his gavel repeatedly to restore order. Blythe, sitting in the back row, saw the carpet being ripped from under her—and throughout it all, Johnny Dunsmore was resolute, stoic, a picture of calm.

"Mr. Atkins, are you suggesting that our governor would *kill* his niece for financial gain?" asked an incredulous Judge Rawlings.

"Your Honor, may I speak?" asked Johnny Dunsmore, who was now standing as flashbulbs popped across the courtroom.

"Of course. By all means."

"Mr. Atkins has a reputation in town as being an excellent attorney, and that reputation is well-deserved. He's simply doing his job, advocating for his client. I don't fault him and ask that this court not do so, either."

"Thank you, Governor, for your mature approach to such a sensitive subject," said Judge Rawlings. "Mr. Atkins, your objection is noted for the record, but my order stands. Governor Dunsmore is hereby appointed the guardian for Rebeca Dunsmore and the trustee for her trust."

And with that, the gavel came down.

* * *

Reporters fled from the room; each determined that their story would hit the wires first. Vans decorated with logos from local news stations were on the street outside, and their intrepid investigative reporters, all sporting fresh haircuts and new suits, were speaking into their microphones in their most serious, hard-hitting voices.

In the courtroom, Walker Atkins sat at the table and tried to make sense of what had just happened. He watched as the attorney for Johnny Dunsmore—a high-priced suit from Atlanta—quietly yet smugly celebrate with Johnny and Colin Dunsmore.

Walker Atkins *hated* Johnny Dunsmore. He hated them all. But what could he do? The judge had just allowed an insincere "man of the people," a heartless political animal who would do anything to remain in power, gut his client's position with the utterance of empty platitudes.

Walker finished packing his briefcase and was going to shake the hand of opposing counsel when he noticed that someone from the back of the courtroom had caught Johnny's attention. Walker looked to the back of the courtroom where Johnny's gaze was cast at Blythe Cavendish, sitting alone, and then back at Johnny.

The look on Johnny's face was one of victory. The look on Blythe's face? Pure rage.

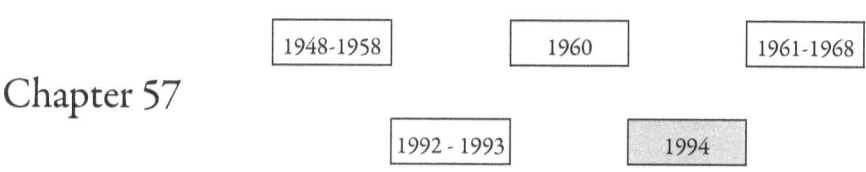

Chapter 57

It was a short walk from the courthouse to the jail where Dexter was being held. Blythe knew that for appearance's sake, she should wait a day or two before confronting him, but anger blinded her. It seemed that after everything, Dexter was to blame. *She* was supposed to inherit everything if Rebeca and Randal died. That was what Dexter had said would happen. That was why she'd had gone to Rebeca's house that night to kill her. That was why she had helped Johnny kill Randal. Good god! She was both an accessory to attempted murder, and a murderer as well.

Twenty minutes after leaving the courthouse, still seething, she was sitting across from Dexter in the same room in which, just over three weeks ago, they had talked about killing Rebeca.

"What are you laughing about?" she demanded when Dexter didn't even bother to say hello and instead, burst into laughter.

"Oh, Sweet Cakes. This is *rich*. You don't get it, do you?"

"You told me that if Randal put me in his will, I would inherit everything once he and Rebeca *both* died!" she said, furiously.

"I did. I did, indeed," Dexter said, grinning widely. He finally stopped laughing.

"Then tell me what's going on!"

"And why should I?" asked Dexter, clearly bitter. This took Blythe aback. Something had changed, but she wasn't sure what. "You were going to leave me here, weren't you?"

Despite her best effort, her face fell. "What do you mean?" she said, but even to her own ears, she didn't sound sincere.

"I *know*," said Dexter, eyes hardening. "I know you were behind whatever has kept me locked up these last few weeks. I heard that you paid a visit to the judge across the hall while my hearing was going on. I don't know what was in that note the bailiff handed my judge, but I got a pretty good idea that whatever it was explains why I'm still sitting here."

Blythe said nothing, looking off into the corner of the room.

"Nothin' to say, Sweet Cakes? Not as smart as you think you are, are you? You want to know what went wrong with your plan? You want to know *why* the governor stands to inherit everything and why you're getting nothing? You got the order wrong, honey."

"What do you mean?" she asked.

"You got the order of *deaths* wrong. If Rebeca had died before Randal, then all the assets of her trust would have become *her* assets as of the day she died—they would have been part of her estate and would have passed to Randal. But Randal died first; Rebeca is still clinging to life. When she dies, her dad will not be around to inherit anything; he's dead. You made sure of that, didn't you?" he added, and Blythe flinched at the surety of his words. "So, without siblings, children, or parents, like the judge said, the next family members in line to inherit when someone dies are the aunts and uncles—and in this case, that means Uncle Johnny, the governor. So, you see, you got the order wrong. You should've made sure Rebeca died before Randal died. I'm also betting that Johnny Dunsmore understood *all* this when you two were killing his brother."

Blythe had to swallow a gasp.

"I'm right, aren't I?" asked Dexter, but he didn't have to ask. He knew her well, and even if she was good at hiding things from the world, she'd never been good at hiding things from *him*.

Dexter sat back in his chair, clearly pleased with himself.

"Shouldn't have double-crossed me," he said.

"Will I get anything?" was all she could bring herself to ask.

"Sure, with Rebeca out of the way, you'll get everything Randal owned—but from what I remember you saying, he didn't own jack-shit, not even the house he lived in. Didn't *you* tell me it's owned by the family foundation along with his fancy cars?"

Blythe sighed, exasperated. "Yes."

Dexter started laughing again, but this time, it was more of a chuckle. "That Johnny Dunsmore is one smart cookie."

Blythe began to cry, no longer angry.

"You look scared, Blythe, and I think I know why. You never called Tommy, did you? You decided to do the dirty work yourself."

She said nothing.

For a breath, Dexter's eyes softened. It looked like he might even feel sorry for her. "Well, since you didn't call Tommy, they got nothin' on me. But you? That's another matter."

Blythe's anger had passed and had been replaced with blinding fear. Her heart lodged itself in her throat. How would she get out of this? *Could* she? Now that Johnny was done with her, would he try to eradicate her as a loose thread?

She got up, moving to leave, only for Dexter to say one more thing: "Hey, Sweet Cakes, did you know that South Carolina has the death penalty?"

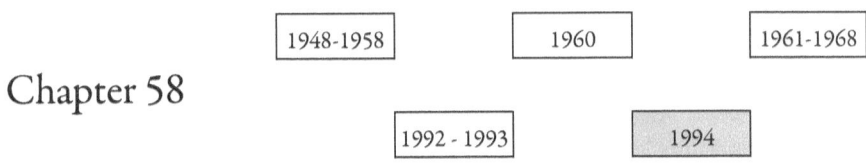

Chapter 58

WALKER AND ISABELLE'S SCREENED-IN PORCH
FRIDAY, OCTOBER 14, 1994

After the mayhem at the courthouse earlier that afternoon, Walker hadn't gone back to the office. Instead, he had come straight home, changed, and put on his running shoes. He needed to unwind, and a run was just what the doctor ordered. Six miles later, he walked back through the front door and greeted his wife with a tired and somewhat resigned smile. She kissed him tenderly and led him to the backyard, where he played with the kids while she prepared dinner.

Once dinner was over, Walker and Isabelle put the kids to bed. After everything that had happened, they were overdue for some quality time together with a glass of wine on the back porch.

"Tell me what's on your mind. It'll do you good," Izzy suggested. "I'll just listen."

"They're going to get away with it," Walker said with miserable certainty. He'd thought about it from every angle during his run. "They're going to get away with *everything*."

"Go on."

"The money that Rebeca's grandparents left her will end up in Johnny Dunsmore's hands. If she dies, her estate will pass upstream to Johnny. That's a lost cause, and ultimately, I don't have any control over any of that anymore."

He paused, sighed, and took a long sip of wine.

Izzy cleared her throat. "And what about the Gastons?" she asked.

"There's still a huge mess surrounding the grand jury investigations. The investigation into Palmetto Tree Lending and the other fraudulent companies didn't lead to justice for Loraine and Hugh and the others, because we could never find out who owns those companies. The true owners aren't faceless partnerships and companies, but the people behind those faceless partnerships and companies who use bank secrecy laws to hide their identity."

"Though you're pretty sure the Dunsmores *are* the beneficial owners of those companies," said Izzy.

"Absolutely," said Walker. "I'm sure of it, but we can't prove it. When they flushed those companies through bankruptcy, they guaranteed that the real victims would still be victims, because there was no money in those companies to compensate anybody. The Dunsmores hid all the money they made in offshore accounts set up for them by that snake, Luis Sanchez. To top it off, it looks like Johnny Dunsmore is cruising to reelection, and that stooge he's supporting for AG, Skip Jackson, is leading Joshua Langston in the polls. If that guy becomes the next AG, he'll shut down any investigations that might lead back to the Dunsmores or the Sanchez family."

"Honey, I'm so sorry."

"When all this started, I was hoping I could help Rebeca Dunsmore, and I wanted to help the Gastons keep their home. I pulled Eddie into this mess, too, because I saw us playing the role of the hero together. We were going to put away the bad guys. And now it looks like the bad guys will get away with everything."

He shook his head, staring miserably into the dark night. It was chilly on the porch, but Walker wasn't ready to go indoors. He was still so unsettled with more on his mind to share with Izzy, and the cold kept him awake, sharp, and attuned to what their time together might bring.

"And here I sit," he went on. "Helpless to do anything. Same old, same old. The little kid still tied to the chair," said Walker who was ready to keep going when Isabelle placed her hand on his shoulder. She knew where this was going.

"Walker, do you see yourself as helpless, or is it that you believe *everyone else* sees you that way?" she asked.

"Izzy, do you know what it's like to be known as *Eli's little brother?* He's a hero in this town—meanwhile, I'm immortalized as the kid tied to the chair, helpless, defenseless. Eli saved the day, and my life has never been the same. I saw myself as finally getting a chance to be the hero. I would make a *new* name for myself. People would start thinking of Eli as *my* big brother, and not me as *his* little brother. I was going to be the hero. Instead, I'm a joke. I'm the guy who accused our governor of wanting to kill his niece so he could get even richer. Man, did I screw up."

Walker was sitting at the end of the sofa, slumped over with his head in his hands, tears rolling down his face.

"Walker Atkins, you know I love you, but you need to listen to me now. You did your best, and you did what you thought was right. That day in your past when you were tied to the chair by that monster who beat your father to within an inch of his life—that day you can't even *remember*, even as someone who has nearly perfect recall—well, guess what? You were defenseless that day. Utterly defenseless. If your brother Eli and the police hadn't arrived when they did, you'd be dead. So, your brother Eli *is* a hero. You know who else is a hero?"

Walker shook his head.

"Your father. He walked into an unknown situation controlled by a savage killer, and he did it without any concern for his life, but to protect you and your mother. They didn't plan to be heroes—they did what they thought was right. And that's what you've done. You did what you thought was right. You came across people on the side of the road who needed help, and you helped them. Rebeca and the Gastons. I'm proud of you. But I'm sick and tired of you placing yourself in Eli's shadow and playing the victim. It ain't sexy. Worse, it's killing you—it's holding you back. If others still see you as the helpless little kid, then they don't know you. That's their problem; don't make it yours."

Walker pulled his face out of his hands and then sat back on the sofa.

Izzy moved to the front of the sofa and turned to face him. "The only person whose opinion of you matters is the Lord's, and you know what He thinks of you."

The room was quiet—wonderfully quiet.

Walker smiled, nodded, and started crying again, but this time happily.

"You know what you need?" asked Izzy. "A day off. Tomorrow is Saturday."

"And it's the opening of your photography exhibit. Let's make a day of it."

"I was hoping you'd say that."

"Absolutely. Sounds perfect. Let's grab a quick bite and spend the afternoon at the exhibit. Izzy, let's celebrate you." He paused, looking at his wife with love. "Oh, and honey—there's one more thing. What you said to me just a minute ago..."

Izzy raised her brows in open question.

"Thanks," he said. "I needed to hear it."

"Yeah, you did. Ya big goof." Then she kissed him and wiped away his tears.

* * *

After an early lunch at Poogan's Porch on Queen Street, Walker and Isabelle walked a few blocks east to the location of what was once a slave auction house on Chalmers Street, known as Ryan's Auction Mart.

"I can't wait to see what y'all have done inside that old building," said Walker.

"We've had to do more than we expected, that's for sure," Isabelle said. "The poor lighting was the biggest challenge. The building was abandoned in 1987, when the art museum was closed. The City of Charleston bought the building in 1988, and Mayor Joe assures us that the City is going to open a new museum inside, but until then, it just sits empty. And the price was right. The City set the rent at $1.00 as long as we purchased liability insurance."

"Excellent."

The exhibit Isabelle put together was entitled, "Reckonings and Reconstructions: Forgotten Photographic Artists of the American South." She'd finally landed an underwriter in late June, a family in town that wished to remain anonymous. The goal was to hold the event at the same time as the annual Home and Garden tours throughout Charleston in the fall, leaving Isabelle without much time to pull it together—but she had.

"As we all know, the poverty in the South after the Civil War was devastating," she went on to tell Walker. "The challenges of reconstruction, the impact of slavery's legacy, and the ensuing poverty were felt deep into the twentieth century by Black and White people alike. We've collected an exhibit of photographs that capture what life was like. Many of the photographs are on loan from other collections. As for the photographers—the artists—while many of them have passed away, I'm thrilled that we will have as many of the living artists here as we do. Some of them will be here for the duration, and we'll also be hosting classes for folks who want to learn the art of photography, as well as listen to daily lectures at the Dock Street Theater by some artists and other art historians interested in the subject matter."

"Baby Doll, as usual, you've outdone yourself."

"Thank you, sweetie."

When they entered the exhibit, a few people pulled Isabelle aside to congratulate her on the job she'd done. Walker kept going, knowing she would catch up when she could. He owned an Olympus digital camera that Isabelle had given him a couple of birthdays ago, but he only used it to take pictures of the kids. Walking the exhibit confirmed in his mind that photography done right was, indeed, an art form. He knew this because he knew he could never produce the beautiful, poignant photographs that graced the walls of the exhibit.

As he approached the end of one wall of exhibits, he saw an elderly Black woman sitting in a rocking chair, needlepointing. Across from her was a wall covered with black-and-white photographs of various scenes in front of a rundown ramshackle house. In one scene, two children who appeared to be about four years old, one black and one white, were playing. The little girl, the white child, wore what appeared to be newer clothes, while the little Black boy was barefoot, shirtless, and wearing jean shorts. In the photograph, sitting on the porch, sat a young man smiling as the children played in the dirt lot in front of the house.

"You like that photograph?" asked the elderly Black woman.

"Yes, I do. Are you the artist?"

"I am."

"And did you take it with that camera on the table next to you?"

"I did. That camera is a Leica M2. It's simple. A mechanical camera. No batteries. It has a shutter speed dial and a range finder. That means the rest is up to me. Just the way I like it. When I was a younger woman, I developed my own film, too. Don't have the eyes fo' it today."

"You obviously know what you're talking about. For me, I just love looking at these black-and-white photos."

"And you like *that* one, especially. The one of the two children—the little White girl and little Black boy, playing together without a care in the world."

"I do. There's something about it that is familiar, but I can't put my finger on it," said Walker.

"Maybe that's because that little girl is yo' client, Mr. Atkins." The woman paused, looking at him in eyes. "The girl sittin' in a coma over in the hospital."

Walker's head spun around, and he looked at the old woman. Then, he turned back to the photograph and focused on the little girl, and it hit him. The night they had Rebeca over for dinner, they had gone through old photo albums, and he had seen pictures of her as a little girl.

He turned back to look at the woman, this time more slowly. "You say that the little girl in this photograph is my client?"

"Mmhmm. That be Miss Rebeca as a little girl."

"And the boy in the picture?" asked Walker.

"Her brother, Joseph. My great-grandson."

"And the young man on the porch?"

"That's my grandson, Jeremiah—the father to those two children. They be twins."

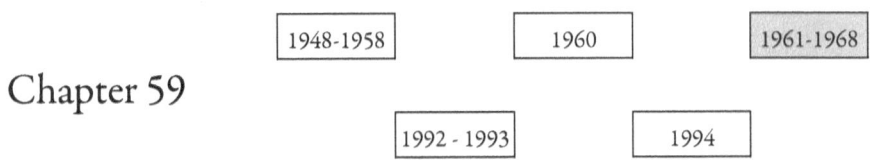

Chapter 59

Columbia, South Carolina
Summer 1968

Throughout the summer of 1968, Dixie and Jeremiah had continued to see each other. For Dixie, Jeremiah was a life raft. Were it not for him and the time they spent together, the harsh truth about Johnny and his heartless infidelity would have crushed her. Her marriage offered no relief.

What Jeremiah and Dixie had together was different than anything either of them had experienced before. They got to hear what the other's lives were like—something neither of them had ever had a chance to do. Though their lives up till then bore little in common, there were one or two things that they did share: hormones and a physical attraction to each other. But it was more than that. They were falling in love.

So, it was only a matter of time before these two healthy young folks shared more than a picnic blanket. And when they did, the excruciating joy Dixie took from Jeremiah's affection cast her into deep despair. What was she to do? She was trapped in a loveless marriage with a cowardly man and in love with a tender, caring man, but a love their respective cultures told them was forbidden.

"If you're so miserable, why do you stick around?" Jeremiah asked one afternoon as the two of them were lazily sprawled across a picnic blanket under the shade of a live oak tree.

"Don't know, Jeremiah."

She was lying on her stomach, her chin resting on her clasped hands. She turned towards Jeremiah and looked at him.

"I'm guessin' it's cause a you."

Jeremiah, lying next to her and with obvious concern for Dixie written across his furrowed brow, asked her a simple question that moved her closer to a deeper awakening.

"But what do you do all day while I'm at work?"

"That's part of the problem. I got nothin' to do. I should be crankin' out babies and makin' a home for my husband and volunteering at the church like so many others, but the thought of it all is just too depressin'. Life with Randal is boring. I can't pretend we're in love anymore, and that's what I've been doin' for the longest time—*pretending*."

"Then, I'll ask you again: If you're so miserable, why do you stick around?"

Dixie looked away and then slowly sat up with her back turned towards Jeremiah, her arms wrapped tightly around her knees, and in a moment of apparent shame answered his question.

"It's the money, Jeremiah."

"The Dunsmores got *that* kind of money? Enough to sell your life for it?"

"Oh, they got money, all right, but I ain't talkin' about theirs. I'm talkin' about mine. You see, my daddy, he's got me tied up pretty good with a trust he left me. He put money into the trust, and he doles out the money to me every so often—not too much, but enough to keep me around. You know what I mean?"

"No."

"Well, I can't get my hands on the money, and he can cut me off quick as lightning if I don't behave. Worse than that, once Randal and I have a baby, Randal becomes the trustee, and he'll make all the decisions. They *own* me."

"Don't *you* ever get the money, like when your pappy dies?"

"No. My kids get it, then their kids do. Like I said, they own me."

Jeremiah, now sitting up on his knees, placed a comforting hand on her shoulder. "Only if you let 'em. Only if you're willing to sell."

"What are you talking about?" she asked as she turned towards him.

"Forget the money. Forget your trust. Run away with me. Save up that trust money you get every so often. I got a little money set aside. We'll head to New York. I got family in Buffalo, and then from there, we'll head to Canada. I'm thinkin' Toronto. Folks in Canada, they'd have no problem with us bein' White and Black. I can get work anywhere. Good carpenters are always in demand."

"Oh, Jeremiah," she said, patting her pregnant belly. "If only it was that easy."

* * *

For Dixie, the hypocrisy of the Dunsmore clan had grown too much to bear. The Dunsmore Family Foundation made donations to local food banks, churches, and homeless shelters, but these donations were small when compared to the donations made to the arts in Charleston. The Dunsmores made sure their donations in Columbia received sufficient press, along with pictures of Johnny, Caroline, Randal, and Dixie. The donations in Charleston, while never mentioned in the press, were whispered about in the drawing rooms of Charleston south of Broad Street, which brought Randal the acclaim and social panache he so craved.

Yes, the hypocrisy was proving too much for Dixie. But again, what was she to do about all this angst? An interesting and unintended consequence of the Dunsmore's politically driven decision to become church-going people was that for the first time, Dixie heard the Gospel. One Sunday morning while sitting in the pews of the church the Dunsmore handlers recommended that they attend, she heard a message from the pastor that resonated with her. He preached on the Book of Ecclesiastes.

"I'll say it again, it's all vanity we strive for," said the pastor. "Our toil, our folly, our deeds, our striving for wealth, power, and status. To what end? For the same end comes to us all. And then what? What will you say on that fateful day, when you stand before the Creator? What is it you have done that will impress Him, the Creator of all?

And then he closed with the last scripture from this curious book in the Bible, a book she had never heard of before: *"For God will bring every deed into judgment, with every secret thing, whether good or evil."*

It was all vanity. Everything.

Never were truer words shouted from a pulpit about the Dunsmores than those she heard that day. And as for *her* life, could she boast of anything different? No. Her acts would be revealed. There was nothing she could do. It would all come out. She did not love Randal. She did not love Johnny. She loved Jeremiah. She was having someone's child. She felt certain it was Jeremiah's, but only the Lord knew for sure. But she knew this much—she would raise the child with Jeremiah.

After the pastor finished his sermon, she sat in the pew as the others drifted out to share lukewarm coffee and bland donuts, and she felt a comfort come over her she had never experienced. The truth. She could handle the truth. So, she made a decision for herself—and it was a big one.

* * *

October 10, 1968

Dixie waited till Randal left for the office. She pulled a tan suitcase decorated with images of airplanes out from under her bed and packed a few items. She collected what money she had and then took cash from a strongbox she knew Randal kept in his study, along with her passport. All told, she had a little over five hundred dollars. She sat at the kitchen table and wrote a letter, sealed it in an envelope and placed that envelope at the bottom of the suitcase. She placed her suitcase in the trunk of her car and then went back inside.

Dixie didn't know how to pray, but she figured the good Lord would know what was troubling her, so she dropped to her knees and began. "Lord, I guess this is it. I may be making the second or third biggest mistake of my life, but since I'm tryin' to undo the first couple of mistakes, it feels like the right thing. I'm worried about this baby, though," she added, holding the swell of her eight-month pregnant belly. "It ain't done nothin' wrong. Whatever happens to me, just please take care of this child."

And with that, Dixie walked out of the door of her spacious, split-level home and into a future which she could only hope and pray was better than what she was leaving behind. She pulled out of her driveway, drove down her quiet street, and headed for the state highway that would take her into Jeremiah's world.

Dixie had been driving to the general part of town where Jeremiah lived for nearly a year but still did not know where he lived. On one occasion, before she was showing, she met his parents for a meal at the diner where she'd first met Jeremiah. Jeremiah had told her that his parents were not thrilled that their son was enamored with a White woman—a *married* one, at that—and one connected to the most politically powerful family in South Carolina.

The last time they were together, Dixie told Jeremiah she had decided to leave Randal and head to Canada with him. Jeremiah was overjoyed.

"Are you going to tell your parents?" she asked.

Jeremiah, moving food around his plate with his fork and avoiding eye contact with Dixie, raised his head and stared out the window. "I got family here, and I love them, but I'm ready to move on," he'd surprised her by saying. "I see so much confusion amongst my people. Some are angry, and I mean burn-down-the-city angry at the killing of Martin Luther, and I get it. And others seem resigned to second-class citizenship. Maybe I'm just a coward, but I don't want to fight the fight. I love what I do—building things. Could be a house or just a bookshelf. But I'm not cut out for living like this, always steering clear of White folks the way my parents and grandparents do. I get why they're that way, but it just ain't for me."

"And what about me, Jeremiah? Where do I fit in?"

Still staring out the window, he turned slowly and looked at Dixie. "Dixie, I love you. What else you wanna hear?"

With that, they paid the check and walked out of the diner, hand in hand—folks in the other booths shaking their heads.

* * *

Dixie met Jeremiah at the diner, and ten minutes later they were heading north in his car. They ditched her car in case Randal came looking for them or alerted the police. In answer to her earlier question about whether he had told his parents, Jeremiah explained that he'd left them a letter. In that letter, he didn't tell them where he was going but promised to get in touch with them once it was safe to do so. The contractions started soon after.

"I thought you had another month to go," Jeremiah said, frantically.

"Me too, honey. Me too. Just keep drivin', Jeremiah. Keep drivin'," she said.

"Are you crazy? And what—have that baby *here in the car?*"

"Well, we can't go to a hospital," she said. "Agh! Jeez, it hurts."

The contractions were coming faster. Dixie was having this baby, and she was going to have it soon. The only question was *where*.

"That's it. We're headed to my grandma's house. She's a doula. She's delivered hundreds of babies," Jeremiah said. He made a U-turn and headed back. "Twenty minutes, honey. You can make it."

Dixie answered with a long, miserable moan.

Jeremiah hit the gas pedal.

* * *

Fifteen minutes later, Jeremiah came flying down the gravel road off the state highway toward his grandmother's house. Doretha Middleton was a doula and had been delivering babies and helping newborns and their mothers since she was a girl. The only training she'd received came from helping her mother and grandmother do the same.

Jeremiah pulled up to the front of the house, kicking dirt up in his wake.

"Grandma, come quick!" he yelled.

Doretha was in the kitchen when she heard someone calling out her name. She was washing tomatoes she had picked from her garden that morning, cursing under her breath as she said, "Who is out there makin' such a ruckus? With twenty-five kids and grandkids, it's a miracle I ever get a moment of silence 'round here."

"Grandma!" Jeremiah shouted again.

"I'm comin', I'm comin'," she said as she walked out the front screen door, drying her hands on her apron. Standing on the front step, she saw Jeremiah helping a very pregnant woman in obvious distress out of the car.

Doretha took immediate control of the situation.

Jeremiah carried Dixie into the house and placed her on his grandma's bed.

Dixie was suffering. The pain was overwhelming, and there was no slowing down nature at this point.

"What can I do?" asked Jeremiah, panicking.

"Just talk to her, child," she said, wisely. "I've brought hundreds of babies into the world, and by and large, babies deliver themselves. There ain't no stopping it."

"Don't thing go wrong sometimes?" Jeremiah asked, glancing nervously at Dixie, who was delirious with pain.

"From time to time," Doretha admitted. "In those cases, I do what I can, and I pray. More often than people would believe, mother and child come through just fine—momma a little worse for wear, but fine just the same."

However, Doretha feared this delivery was not shaping up to be one of those times.

Jeremiah was sitting in a chair beside the bed, his head leaning over Dixie's face, holding her left hand in his two hands.

"Is everything gonna be okay, Grandma?"

Doretha was silent.

"Grandma! Is everything gonna be okay?"

"Jeremiah, go get your momma."

"Why? What's wrong? Shouldn't we take her to the hospital?" he asked.

"Ain't no time for that. Now go. Fetch your momma. I'm gonna need help."

* * *

The hospital where Esther worked was a twenty-minute drive without traffic. Jeremiah prayed the cops wouldn't stop him. His mother was reading a magazine in the cafeteria on her lunch break when she heard someone call out her name. Looking up, she saw her son frantically approaching the table.

"Momma, Grandma needs you. Come quick."

Her son was scared, that was clear, and that was all she needed to know. She grabbed her purse and quickly left with Jeremiah. He sped back towards Grandma's house and told her what was happening. Fifteen minutes later, Jeremiah came to a screeching halt in his grandma's front yard and bounded through the front door, his mother behind him.

Doretha was a large woman—strong, too. But there was only so much one person could do. Esther and Jeremiah found her sitting in a rocking chair Jeremiah had built especially for her and holding not one, but two babies in her arms. The pain and exhaustion on her face were eased only by the inexplicable joy that accompanies the miracle of birth; God's power of creation played out, again and again, every day, everywhere—a miracle that never ceases to amaze.

Doretha looked at her grandson, who was standing just a few feet away, his arms straight by his side, and spoke to him as if she owed him an explanation, an apology. "I did what I could. But she lost too much blood. You see, the first baby was breach, and the second one didn't wanna wait, and then the cords got wrapped—" Doretha looked up at her daughter standing before her, as if pleading for mercy, and then at her grandson. "There was just too much bleedin' and no way to stop it."

Jeremiah was numb. The look on his grandmother's face at that moment was so full of sorrow. Jeremiah slowly walked into the bedroom. At the sight of Dixie's pale form, he burst into tears. Behind him, he heard his mom talking to his grandmother.

"You did good, Momma. You did mighty good. Because of you, there are two more of God's miracles in this world."

Doretha leaned her head towards the shoulder where Esther's hand was resting so she could feel it pressed against her tear-stained face.

While it wasn't known to the folks in the house that day, the Lord had answered the prayer Dixie had prayed earlier that morning while on her knees. He had taken care of not one, but *two* babies.

Chapter 60

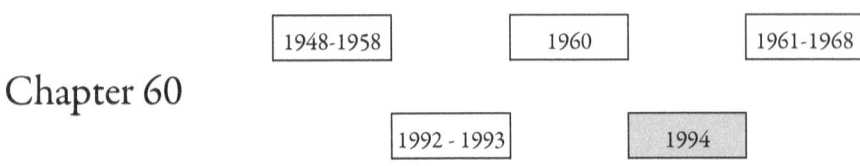

THE DRAWING ROOM IN JUDGE RAWLINGS'S HOUSE
SATURDAY EVENING, OCTOBER 15, 1994

"Your Honor, I know what I am asking for is out of the ordinary, but you said yourself, yesterday in court, that you had never seen a case quite like this one," said Walker.

Judge Rawlings had been sitting in his reading chair in the corner of the drawing room enjoying a book on revolutionary war history when Walker Atkins knocked on the front door and asked for a private audience. Standing beside him was his wife, Isabelle, and an elderly woman dressed in the fashion of a bygone era. Walker introduced this woman to Judge Rawling as Mrs. Doretha Middleton—Rebeca Dunsmore's great-grandmother.

Curiosity getting the better of him, the judge welcomed the party into his house and gave Walker the audience he requested. Twenty minutes later, after Doretha had told him her story, the judge wondered out loud what he had gotten himself into.

"So, what you're telling me, Mrs. Middleton, is that your grandson, Jeremiah Taylor, was having an affair with Dixie Dunsmore while she was married to Randal Dunsmore."

"Yes, sir," she said with a nod.

"And the two of them were about to run away together when Dixie went into labor."

She nodded once again.

"And that *you* delivered Rebeca Dunsmore and her twin brother," he said.

"Yes, sir. I did. I did my best."

"I'm sure you did," said the judge. He then stood and began to pace slowly. "I'm sure you know what this means, Mr. Atkins."

"I most certainly do. That's why we're here," answered Walker.

"But why did you have to bring it to me tonight? Why couldn't it wait till Monday morning? What's the big rush?"

"Your Honor, you might want to freshen up your drink before hearing the rest of the story," said Walker.

The judge did precisely that and then resumed his position in his chair. Walker then looked at Doretha and said, "Go on. It's time."

Chapter 61

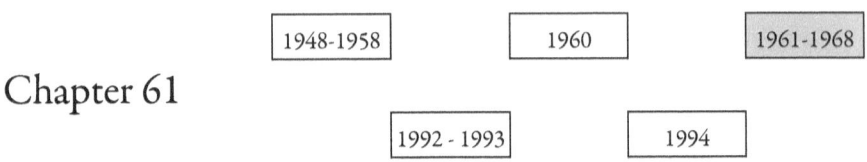

LEXINGTON COUNTY, SOUTH CAROLINA
OUTSIDE COLUMBIA
OCTOBER 10, 1968

This time, it was Esther who took charge. She pulled the cover over Dixie's head, took her son by the hand, and led him into the front room where Doretha was rocking the two newborns.

"They gonna be hungry soon," Doretha said.

"I know, Momma, but we got bigger problems on our hands right now."

In the bedroom behind her lay the body of the former Mrs. Randal Dunsmore, of the powerful Dunsmore family—the Dunsmore family whose son, Johnny, was running for the State House of Representatives; the Dunsmore family who controlled the Democratic Party in South Carolina; the Dunsmore family who owned the press, the sheriff's office, and the bank that held the mortgage on the home in which Esther and her husband Earl had raised their son Jeremiah and his three siblings.

"Jeremiah."

"Yes, Ma?"

"Get a hold of yourself," Esther said. "I need you to fetch your daddy."

Earl Taylor worked at the textile mill as his dad had before him.

"Yes, Ma."

Jeremiah started towards the door, but before leaving, he turned and walked back towards his grandmother. He knelt before her and looked at the two beautiful children resting in her lap.

"Grandma D?"

Doretha was rocking the children slowly. She looked at her grandson kneeling before her.

"Yes, child?"

"Thank you."

She smiled, and a tear crept down her face from the corner of her eye. "Now, go, like your momma asked. Get your daddy. He'll know what to do."

* * *

Earl didn't know what to do. He sat in the passenger's seat as his son drove them back to Grandma D's house and told him what had happened. His mood went from shock to anger at his son, to fear for his son's life. The Dunsmores held all the cards. What he needed to do was reshuffle the deck. By the time they pulled into Grandma D's front yard, Earl was ready to deal.

Standing in the front room, with Dixie Dunsmore still lying under a blanket in the bedroom, Earl paced, asked questions, and confirmed the best course of action.

"You want to bring Randal Dunsmore *here*?" asked his wife Esther, flabbergasted.

"That's right. Get him on our turf."

"And how do you propose to do that?" asked Doretha.

"Well, you just told me that Dixie's housekeeper is Wanda, your niece," said Earl.

"That's right. But what does Wanda have to do with anything?"

"I'm getting to that. Now, Jeremiah," said Earl as he turned his attention back to his son.

"Yes, Daddy?"

"How many folks were in the diner when you met Dixie earlier today?"

"Maybe six or so."

"And they was our people, you say?"

"Yes, sir."

Earl stopped pacing and looked out the window. "Okay, then. Esther, you go to Randal Dunsmore's house and wait for him to come home. Anybody asks what you doin' there, you tell them you're there about Wanda. Jeremiah, you sho Wanda is workin' today?"

"That's what Dixie told me this mornin'."

Nodding his head, Earl continued, "So, Esther, you're there to give Wanda a ride home so she don't have to take the bus, case any busybodies ask."

"And what am I supposed to tell Mr. Dunsmore when he comes home to get him to come to our house?" his wife asked, her hands on her hips.

Earl shrugged. "I figure the truth will work jus' fine."

* * *

Esther Taylor was parked in front of Randal Dunsmore's house when Randal pulled into his driveway. She waited until he was out of his car before getting out of hers and then, very cautiously, she approached Randal Dunsmore.

"Mr. Dunsmore, my name is Esther Taylor. I'm your housekeeper Wanda's aunt."

"Is there a problem? Is Wanda okay?"

"Oh, Wanda's fine."

"Then I must ask—what are you doing here?"

Remembering her husband's comment earlier that the truth should work, she launched into what she had practiced on the drive over: "Mr. Dunsmore, your wife was set to run away with my son, Jeremiah, but then she went into labor and my son drove her to my mother's house, her being a doula. The good news is that she gave birth to twins. The bad news is that your wife died during delivery."

Esther waited for his reaction but from where she stood, he was too stunned to make any sense of what she had just told him.

"Dead? My wife, Dixie?"

"That's right, sir. I'm so sorry."

"What did you say your name was?"

"Esther Taylor," she answered somewhat reluctantly because she didn't like the look on his face.

"I'm calling the police," he said as he fished his keys out of his pocket and started towards the front door to his house.

"Mr. Dunsmore, you might want to think this through a bit before you do that. Come with me. See the babies. Let's make sure it's your wife we're talking about."

Esther thought that last comment might have done the trick because he stopped short of entering his house and cast a look back at her.

"Talk with my husband," Esther said, trying to coerce Randal away from the house. "There will always be a chance to call the police if you still think that's what's best."

* * *

Thirty minutes later, Randal was standing in the front room of Grandma Doretha's house, having confirmed that the body under the cover in the backroom was his late wife.

Randal was a mixture of panic, rage, and, above all, confusion. What had his wife been doing with this negro? Randal was pacing back and forth as Esther, Earl, Doretha, and Jeremiah looked on. And then suddenly, Randal lunged at Jeremiah and tackled him to the floor, screaming that he was going to kill him.

Randal was brought to his senses when he felt the barrel of a shotgun placed against the back of his head.

"Get off my boy."

Randal stood up, brushed the dirt off his pants in vain effort to reestablish his dignity, and stepped back several feet. He took a deep breath and addressed Earl from across the room. "Mr. Taylor, I don't know what you think is going to happen here, but I do. I'm going to call the police and see to it that your boy hangs for what he's done to my wife."

"No, you ain't. What happened here is what happens sometimes. Havin' a baby can be messy, and we got two babies here, and the first one, the girl, she was breech—a serious complication under the best of conditions. And with her baby brother right behind her, it's a miracle anybody lived. Ain't that right, Doretha?"

Doretha nodded her head that it was so.

Randal's anger dissipated, and sadness seeped in.

"The way I see it, you lost a wife, but the world gained two beautiful children," said Earl. "Grandma D has delivered more babies in this county than anybody can count. Nobody could have done a better job of it."

"But if you'd taken her to a hospital, she might have lived," said a tearful Randal.

"That may be so, but we'll never know," answered Earl. "The question you might want to be askin' was what was your wife doin' with my boy,

Jeremiah? I got a pretty good idea, and you ain't gonna like it, but I'm bettin' you ain't the father."

"Ain't the father! Look, boy—now you better—"

"Now, don't be goin' there," interrupted Earl as he lowered the shotgun slowly from his shoulder and rested the barrel in his left hand, pointing at Randal.

Randal glared at Earl and the shotgun he was holding. "The babies are White. Anyone can see that I'm the father!"

"Well, they's White *now*. Let's give it a few days. Betwixt now and then, we still have your wife's dead body in this house. Now, what are we to do about that?"

"I'm calling the sheriff."

"You sure you want to do that? How's that gonna look to folks headin' to the polls in a couple of weeks, what with your brother runnin' for office? My folks like to talk, and your folks ain't too forgivin' when their women stray. From where I'm standing, my son's life will be in danger if it becomes known that he was messin' with your wife, and I will not stand for that. And your family's good name and political hopes and dreams will fade into the mist, for sure."

"So, what are you suggesting?" asked Randal.

"We gots to move the babies and your wife to your place and then agree on what happened."

"What makes you think I don't want the police brought in? Why should I go along with these lies?"

"Because I'm bettin' your pappy will cut you off if he finds out you couldn't keep your woman from strayin'—with a Black boy, no less—and I figure you're more attached to his money than you are to the memory of your dead wife."

* * *

Randal agreed with the general plan, but complexities abounded.

First, he would have to tell Dixie's parents. But when and what would he tell them?

Esther found Dixie's suitcase in Jeremiah's car, and after some pressure from his father, Jeremiah confessed that they were running away together. Armed with this information, even Randal began to doubt he was the father.

All parties understood that time was of the essence if they were going to act. They couldn't wait too long to move Dixie's body if the county coroner were called in. He might grow suspicious if he was called a few days after Dixie had died.

And then there were the babies to worry about. Jeremiah's mother and grandmother said it was too early to move them. Being twins and having come early, they were undersized and could be expected to lose weight over the next twenty-four hours. The twins could not be moved. They were adamant.

What to do? Sure, people could be paid off, but each payoff was a potential loose end; someone might talk. No, they needed a story in which everyone was invested.

Eventually, they agreed on a story: Dixie died giving birth at home. Dixie's housekeeper, Wanda, walked into Dixie's bathroom and found her passed out on the floor. She panicked and did the only thing she knew to do—she took Dixie's car and drove to her Great Aunt Doretha's house. Doretha returned with Wanda and concluded that Dixie must have slipped and hit her head getting out of the bathtub. In the meantime, she had gone into labor, and it was too late to move her to a hospital. While Doretha tended to Dixie, Wanda drove to Randal's office and spotted him leaving the building for a meeting. By the time he made it to his house, it was too late to move her to the hospital. Doretha did all she could do and managed to deliver the babies, but Dixie died.

Had they thought of everything? Why didn't Wanda use the phone to call for help? Doretha didn't have a phone. Okay, but she could have called someone else. True, but Wanda was only sixteen and not very bright. What about the bloody sheets on Doretha's bed? Esther said they should replace Dixie's sheet with the bloody sheets from Doretha's bed. Everyone agreed. So again—had they thought of everything? Probably not, but they were all counting on the Dunsmores being so afraid of the truth coming out that they'd suppress any prying eyes.

* * *

So, the decision was made. Dixie's body was moved back to her house. Doretha went with them. Randal broke the news to his parents. Dixie's parents were in Hawaii on vacation. It took Randal a little time to track them down, but he did and placed the call. They were heartbroken but took solace in knowing they would soon hold their grandchildren—twins, a boy and a girl.

Randal didn't bring his parents into the loop until after Dixie's body had been moved, and while he didn't like the plan, it was too late to object. He called Johnny and they all met up at Randal's house. Colin then called the family doctor, Dr. Curtis Wagner.

Dr. Wagner was an administrator and the director of the best hospital in town. He hadn't practiced much medicine lately—his time taken up with fundraising, hiring, firing, and the like—but he knew of Esther and Doretha's reputation. He had argued before the state legislature that doulas with a lifetime of experience should be allowed to become certified midwives without having to take a full curriculum of the state-required classes. He marched with Martin Luther and was a friend to the Black community in South Carolina. He said he would vouch for the work Doretha did. Though Randal had committed to the plan, he still wondered whether Dixie's life could have been saved.

"Randal, between you and me, it's a miracle she saved the babies," said Dr. Wagner on the day he'd been summoned to the house. "Twins, coming before term, one of them breach . . . it's truly a miracle."

"But could *you* have saved Dixie?" Randal wanted to know.

"Am I going to have to testify? Will there be an inquiry of sorts?" the good doctor asked.

"No," said Randal.

Dr. Wagner considered his answer and then placed a hand on Randal's shoulder. "I can't say for sure, son."

The doctor stayed until the ambulance took Dixie's body to the funeral home. Now came the moment of truth. Would they be able to keep Dr. Wagner from wanting to see the babies? They weren't present, as they were at Doretha's house with Earl and Jeremiah's sister, Bernice.

"Now, let's look at the babies," said Dr. Wagner. "Twins, you say. My, my . . ."

The strategy for keeping Dr. Wagner from insisting on seeing the babies was something Esther had come up with, and they had all rehearsed their parts. Colin Dunsmore did not like what he was being asked to say but had to admit it could work.

"Dr. Wagner, they're resting now, and we need to let that happen while we prepare to feed them. My daughter Bernice will be by later with the formula from the druggist. We'll wake them when it's feeding time."

"That's fine, Esther, but as a doctor, I think I should take look and see if they appear healthy. That's all."

"Dr. Wagner, do you remember when I publicly expressed my hesitation in letting doulas become midwives?" asked Colin Dunsmore. "You were testifying before the state senate, and I let my feelings on the subject be known."

"I do. We were sharing a drink together."

"And do you remember what I said?" asked Colin.

Dr. Wagner did, but he wasn't going to repeat it in the present company, so he just nodded.

"I said that they were nothing but uneducated negroes. Well, I was wrong," continued Colin. "Mrs. Middleton—Grandma D, as everyone calls her—brought those two babies into this world. It's a miracle. I don't think someone with a fancy degree could have done any better. Yes, we've lost our precious Dixie, but she's gone on to meet Jesus."

Jeremiah was standing in the corner, a witness to everything, and he knew that if Dixie were alive, hearing this claptrap would have killed her.

"I've spoken briefly with Randal about this, but we're thinking that our family foundation might want to build a prenatal wing for your hospital in honor of Dixie Dunsmore and Doretha Middleton."

Dr. Wagner turned to Doretha. "Grandma D, how do the twins look to you?"

"Them babies is right as rain, Dr. Wagner. They gonna be just fine," Doretha insisted.

Dr. Wagner smiled weakly at everyone present. "This goes against my better judgment," he said, more to himself than anyone else. "I really should insist on seeing those babies, but it does seem as though they are in competent hands." He looked to Barbara. "Will you be staying here at the house for a while, Mrs. Dunsmore?"

"Yes, I'll stay for a few days," she reassured him. "It's no bother. I'll stay in the guest room. Once Dixie's parents return, we'll see what help will be needed."

"You can count on us to make the necessary arrangements," added Colin.

"And what about you, Doretha?" asked Dr. Wagner.

"Yes, sir. I'll be right here with babies. They gotta rockin' chair in the nursery upstairs. If I need any shuteye, this sofa here will do fine."

All seemed to be under control. The LeMars would arrive in a couple of days. They were vacationing in Hawaii, and it would take a few days for them to get home. Their daughter's funeral would, of course, wait until their return.

At last, Dr. Wagner left, and everyone relaxed.

"Well, we got through the hardest part," said Colin as he faced his son, Randal.

"Not a bad performance for a couple of *uneducated negroes*," said Esther. "Did you really say that?"

"Maybe I was wrong," said Colin.

"Maybe?"

"Look. We're in this together. Let's not forget that."

Doretha placed a hand on her daughter's shoulder and slowly shook her head. Esther relented.

* * *

After Dr. Wagner left, it was decided that for appearance's sake, Doretha and Barbara would sleep at Randal's house for a night or two. They couldn't risk word getting out that they hadn't stayed to watch the babies.

Randal was emotionally exhausted and was ready for his father to leave. But no, his father, perpetually in control, couldn't let the day end without putting his stamp on matters.

"Randal, Johnny, let's step outside for a moment," Colin said.

The three of them went into the backyard and stood silently while they each lit a cigarette.

"This is a fine mess, son. Dixie runnin' off with a colored boy. For God's sake." He shook his head, knocking the ash off his cigarette butt. "What's been going on?"

"I don't know, Daddy. But it's not what it seems. Besides, we have it all under control."

Johnny, who reeked of alcohol, seemed to decide it was his job to address the elephant in the room. "Are you sure you're the father of those two babies?"

"Go to hell, Johnny. Of course, I am!" Randal retorted.

"Johnny ain't wrong to ask, because if you ain't and that boy Jeremiah is . . ." Colin shook his head again, at a loss. "Well, we can't afford to have word of this getting out."

"What are you saying?" asked Randal.

"If them babies turn up Black in a day or two, well . . . other arrangements will have to be made."

"Other arrangements? You mean find someone else to raise them?"

"That's not what I'm sayin'," said Colin.

Randal shuddered at the thought as his father's true intentions became clear. He looked to Johnny for help, but of course he wasn't any. He just turned away and occupied himself by blowing smoke rings.

"Hell, the donations from our family practically built the hospital Dr. Wagner runs. While the good doctor is fillin' out the death certificate for your dead wife, what's another two?"

Yes, all was under control.

* * *

Doretha waited until she was sure the unholy trinity below had disbanded and then quietly closed the nursery window overlooking the backyard. She took a seat in the rocking chair next to an empty crib and whispered, "Dear Lord, show me the way."

* * *

Doretha was out of the house early the next day. She walked to the nearest bus stop, caught a ride, then hoofed it home as fast as her legs could carry her. The babies were asleep, and her daughter Esther was in the kitchen preparing some more formula. Doretha hurried into the room without so much as a hello. She gently un-swaddled the babies and started her inspection. It was as she feared.

"Um . . ." She paused. "That woman be havin' some splainin' to do. Guess that ain't happenin', though, she bein' dead and all."

Esther entered the room. "Momma, what's going on?"

"Come here, child, and take a look at this," replied Doretha.

"Oh my. This changes things."

"In more ways than you know," Doretha said.

* * *

This time, when Randal entered the house, Earl searched him for a weapon.

"Just what do you think you're doing?" asked Randal.

"Takin' prophylactic measures," Earl said, giving Randal a hard look. "Somethin' my son should a done."

"What do you mean?" Randal asked. Earl finished patting him down, after which Randal charged deeper into the house, searching for the twins. "Where are they?"

He found them sharing a bassinet with Doretha next to them in a rocking chair. He peered inside and then stood up slowly and mumbled to himself, "Oh, dear Lord." He then turned and saw Esther and Earl Taylor standing behind him.

"So, the baby boy is Black," said Randal as he ran his hand across his scalp.

"Yes, he is," said Earl in a voice tinged with pride and trepidation.

"And the girl is White?"

"For the time bein'..."

"She's White, and I believe she will stay White," said Esther. "It's not unheard of, Mr. Dunsmore, for parents of mixed race who have twins to have one child of their mother's skin color and the other with their father's."

Randal's mind was racing. How could this have happened? Only days ago, his wife was pregnant with *his* child.

And now, Dixie was dead. *Dead.* After having packed her bags on her final day alive, ready to leave him for a Black man named Jeremiah she'd met at some restaurant. And now, Randal was being told he *wasn't* the father.

It was too much.

It was all too much, and yet it was still getting worse. Randal reflected on the night before, when he and his father and brother had stood outside smoking cigarettes. He thought of his father's insinuation about what would need to happen if the babies turned out Black instead of White.

His father's words suddenly seemed pregnant with wisdom.

"I'll raise them," Randal said. "You have my word. And Jeremiah can come see them whenever he wants to. You have my word."

"*You'll* raise them? We have *your* word? One White child and one Black child, and you gonna raise them both? You must take us for fools," said Earl. "You expect us to believe you? No, sir. You lyin' as sho as the sun is shinin'. You won't be takin' these two babies back home with you so you can oversee their unfortunate deaths. No, sir."

"I'm going to leave with the babies—now, *today*." Randal glared at the man standing in front of him. "Bring them to me. And Jeremiah. Where's Jeremiah? I need to see him right now."

Earl stood before him like a bulwark, refusing to step aside. "That ain't happnin' and he ain't here."

"No, I mean it. Now, bring me the babies. Now!" he shouted.

"The boy is staying with us," said Esther.

Randal looked about the room at one determined face after another. They had discussed all of this already. This had been their plan. They'd keep the Black baby, and they'd hand over the girl, and that would be the end of it.

"But the word is out that Dixie had twins," he argued. "Dr. Wagner knows. Dixie's parents know. They are on their way back from Hawaii and are expecting to see their grandchildren. What's going to happen when there's just one baby?" Randal felt himself tearing at the seams. "For God's sake, I see no way out of all this!"

"Well, we do." Tipping the shotgun towards Randal, Earl explained the situation clearly. "You take the girl. We take the boy. You'll be givin' us a little money to help with expenses. Jeremiah will take the boy and leave the state. We have family elsewhere, and they'll be fine."

"But that won't work," explained Randal. "Like I said, too many people—including Dr. Wagner—know that Dixie gave birth to twins."

"Well, there's one baby now," replied Earl. "Doretha, tell us, what did this boy's daddy say late yesterday?"

"That his family done built the town hospital and that the good doctor owed them."

"Anything else, Doretha? Did he say anything else?"

"Yes, he did. He said, 'While the good doctor is fillin' out the death certificate for your dead wife, what's another two?' He was talkin' about the babies," she added pointedly. "I heard him loud an' clear."

Earl stared at the little man in front of him. "So, you see, Randal, we done you a favor. The good doctor's only gonna have to fill out one extra death certificate. Now take your baby girl with you and get the hell out of here."

Dr. Wagner's Office
Lexington County Regional Hospital

The following week, Colin Dunsmore visited Dr. Wagner and explained how one of the two babies failed to thrive.

"I don't understand. Mrs. Middleton said the babies looked fine last week when I was in Randal's living room. Failed to thrive, you say?" asked Dr. Wagner.

"That's right," Colin said. "The little boy didn't make it. We buried him in our backyard. We wanted to avoid any fuss, so we held a small, private ceremony. You see, we have a small plot where our ancestors are all buried. We buried the boy—Randal named him Joseph—right next to his great grandfather, Ian Dunsmore."

Dr. Wagner wrinkled his brow and shuffled a few papers on his desk. He was trying to think of what questions he should be asking.

Colin interrupted his thinking. "You know, Dr. Wagner, in addition to doing something in honor of Doretha Middleton and their daughter-in-law, Dixie, we want to build something to honor young Joseph Dunsmore—a pediatric center, perhaps."

Dr. Wagner was leaning back in his chair now, only half listening to Colin. "When did you say the boy died?"

"Sunday."

Silence held court as the two men stared at each other.

Colin said, "We held the sweetest little ceremony the following day."

"I assume Dixie's parents attended," Dr. Wagner said.

"Why, no, they didn't. They were making their way back from Hawaii, but we decided not to wait. We figured their minds would be set on their daughter, Dixie, bless her heart, and we didn't want little Joseph's ceremony to add to their grief while traveling."

Dr. Wagner couldn't shake his suspicions. This whole thing had been strange from the get-go, but to now say one of the babies died and was hastily buried, without an autopsy or any legal recognition, such as a birth or death certificate—

It wasn't adding up. But he knew he wasn't in a position to challenge the Dunsmores. Few were.

"Well, it sounds like everything has been taken care of," he said, though the words didn't feel at home in his mouth. He figured the sooner he could wash his hands of all this, the better.

"Pert near. We do, however, have a small matter of paperwork," said Colin as he slid two birth certificates and one death certificate across the table for Dr. Wagner to sign. "What you've got there is a birth certificate for our beautiful granddaughter, Rebeca, and both a birth certificate and a death certificate for little Joseph. Would you sign off on this for us, Doctor?"

Dr. Wagner picked up the documents. He'd seen this coming. "I see you have them all filled out already," he said, smile wooden. "How . . . efficient."

"Least I can do. I know how busy you are, so I had one of your staff complete them. I hope you don't mind."

As Dr. Wagner was staring at the forms and wrestling with the gnawing feeling inside that something wasn't right, Colin spoke up. "You know, as I said, my wife and I want to build that pediatrics center for your hospital. After we buried little Joseph, we got to talking and decided to build it in his honor and name it after him. But as I sit here today, it strikes me that folks around here never knew him. How could they? He passed after only a few days, gone home to be with his maker, God rest his soul. Don't make sense to name the facility after someone folks around here couldn't feel passionate about. No, I'm rethinking that part of our venture, and I'm thinking the name needs to be one that resonates with the fine people of Richland County. Do you know whose name I'm thinking of?"

Dr. Wagner, who was twirling a pen and trying to make sense of what was eating at him, looked up at Colin with an expression that conveyed that he did not know.

"Why, *your name*, of course. The Wagner Center for Pediatric Medicine." Colin gave him a knowing smile. "How does that sound?"

Dr. Wagner paused and repeated the name to himself in a quiet voice, as if he were the only one in the room. "The Wagner Center for Pediatric Medicine." He then smiled, pleased that his contributions would finally be recognized, and picked up the certificates in front of him, signing off on all three. Colin placed them in an envelope that was already stamped and addressed to the Office of Vital Statistics in Columbia, South Carolina.

Colin Dunsmore and Dr. Wagner met each other's eyes.

"Why, Colin," Dr. Wager said, "I'd be honored. Humbled and honored."

* * *

Johnny Dunsmore cruised to victory in his run for the 74th district seat in the South Carolina House of Representatives. Jeremiah and little baby Joseph left town with a suitcase full of cash, courtesy of Colin Dunsmore. As for Randal, he told folks that everywhere he looked, he saw another painful reminder of his dear departed wife, so he took his baby daughter Rebeca and moved to Charleston.

Chapter 62

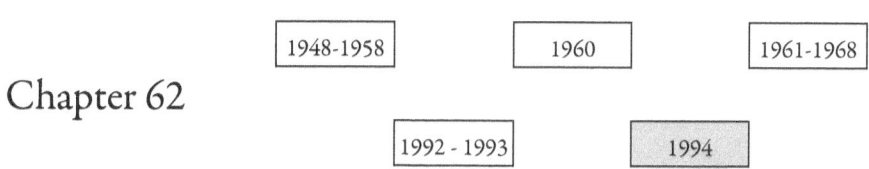

THE DRAWING ROOM IN JUDGE RAWLINGS'S HOUSE
SATURDAY EVENING, OCTOBER 15, 1994

Walker was sitting on the edge of his seat, leaning forward, his elbows resting on his knees, and his hands pressed together as if he were saying grace.

"So, you see, Your Honor, we're here tonight because of what the Dunsmores might do if they find out what Mrs. Middleton knows. You heard her say that Colin Dunsmore was prepared to kill the babies to protect his son's political future. Do you think there's anything they won't do now to keep this story from surfacing?"

"I hear you," said Judge Rawlings, "but I'm not ready to believe that our governor—or his father, for that matter—is capable of murder."

The judge turned to Mrs. Middleton. "Mrs. Middleton, you say your great-grandson, Joseph Taylor, is alive."

"He is." Mrs. Middleton was sitting on the sofa, with her hands folded neatly in her lap.

"Then, we're going to have to meet him. He's going to need to show up in my courtroom."

"I hear you, but I'm not ready to believe that you can protect him from our governor—or his father, for that matter," she said emphatically, echoing the judge's words verbatim.

Walker suppressed a laugh with a fake cough.

The judge took a seat and looked at the distinguished woman sitting on the couch across from him. "Okay," he said with a sigh. "This is what I'm prepared to do."

* * *

Early the next morning...
Sunday, October 16, 1994

It was late by the time they left Judge Rawlings's house and Doretha Middleton was tired. They took her back to the hotel where she was staying and told her they would pick her up early the next morning.

A van from the nursing home where she lived had driven her down to Charleston for the photo exhibit, and the hotel manager had arranged for a nurse to be on call, were one necessary. Doretha was now sitting in the front passenger seat of Abigail Baker's car, and Isabelle was seated in the back. They were on their way to the nursing home to meet Esther Taylor, Doretha Middleton's daughter and the director of the nursing home where she lived. Two and a half hours later, they pulled into the driveway of the Grace & Mercy Senior Living facility, and Esther Taylor walked out the front door along with an orderly pushing a wheelchair.

As Abigail turned the engine off and stepped out of the car, Esther was waiting to greet her.

"My name is Esther Taylor. You must be Isabelle Atkins."

"No. My name is Abigail Baker. Isabelle is in the back seat helping your mother."

"That won't be necessary," she said before turning to the orderly. "Charles, please see that Mother gets to her room." Turning back to Abigail, Esther added, "Thank you for making the drive, but as I said on the phone last night, I have nothing further to say. Now, if you will excuse me, I have a busy day ahead of me."

Esther walked back to the other side of the car and held the door open while Charles helped Doretha into the wheelchair.

"Mother, where's your bag?"

Doretha was silent.

"Mother!"

"In the trunk," she answered.

Isabelle had exited the car and was now standing alongside Abigail, both staring at Esther until she spoke up.

"Could you please open the trunk?"

"Esther, we know your son Jeremiah was Rebeca's father and that Rebeca has a twin."

Esther went rigid. Turning to Charles, she said, "Take Mother to her room." Once they were safe inside the building, she turned back to Abigail and Isabelle. "Let me guess. My mother showed you a picture of a young Black man and two small children, one White and one Black, and she told you they were her great-grandchildren. Is that right?"

"That's right," answered Abigail.

"My mother is ninety-two years old and is still angry that we have placed her here. She gets her revenge by concocting stories that place her in the middle of some big conspiracy or fantastic narrative. She does this to demonstrate to anyone who will listen that she belongs on the outside and not in this 'jail,' as she refers to it. A few weeks ago, she was telling folks that she was supposed to be sitting on the bus with Rosa Parks that day but that she came down with walking pneumonia and couldn't make it."

"Mrs. Taylor, I don't believe you," said Abigail. "Your mother's story contained too many details to be the product of her imagination. Frankly, it rang of the truth. I believe you're scared."

Esther did not reply and instead started walking back towards the nursing home's front door.

"Mrs. Taylor, I don't know if it will make a difference, but your son stands to become the beneficiary of a substantial trust that his mother's parents established," Abigail said.

Mrs. Taylor stopped and turned towards Isabelle and Abigail. "Do you two ladies have any children of your own?"

"Yes, we both do," Isabelle answered.

"What's your price?" Esther asked.

"Excuse me?" Isabelle said.

"You heard me. How much money would it take for you two to put your child's life at risk?"

"Mrs. Taylor, that's not what I was implying," Abigail said. But it was too late. Esther was on her way back inside the nursing home.

"We can protect you!" Abigail shouted. "We can protect Joseph!"

Esther stopped, turning back towards them. "Since you seem to know who you must protect us from, then you should know that you can't. Now please, just leave us alone." And she walked back inside.

* * *

Abigail and Isabelle drove away in silence, back towards Charleston. Beyond agreeing they were hungry and would stop for lunch, neither said a word. Twenty minutes later, they were standing in front of a meat-and-three diner, waiting for it to open for lunch. It being Sunday, the owners could expect a good crowd once church let out. The sign on the window announced that the special was country-fried steak with mashed potatoes and green beans. They didn't have to wait long; the owner opened the front door, and they were seated in a booth in the back corner.

Isabelle broke the silence. "She's scared. I just know it."

"She is. But how do we get her to help us locate Joseph? Without him, all we have is a fantastic story made up by a lonely old woman."

"Saturday, when Mrs. Middleton told us the story, she mentioned that her daughter Esther was working as a midwife at the county hospital. She was very proud of her daughter and of how she was well respected at the hospital."

"Okay. But what's your point?" asked Abigail.

"A young Black woman working in a hospital in this state in the 1960s had to be better than most just to be recognized as adequate. For a hospital to give Esther any real responsibility, she must have been *exceptional* and probably gained some confidence in her dealings with White people. Esther and her mother are from different generations. Mrs. Middleton would have been leery of White people and had learned to avoid conflict with them. But not so for Esther. I'll bet she marched and stood with MLK. I'll bet she hated having to hide the truth all those years ago."

"I believe you're right. Esther would have done whatever she could to preserve the truth and make a straight path for her grandson," said Abigail.

"So, what would she have done?" asked Isabelle.

"What any responsible medical professional would have done. She would have recorded two *live* births," answered Abigail, eyes wide. "Rebeca and Joseph."

"But only one death," Isabelle added with a smile.

And they both said in unison: "Dixie's."

Chapter 63

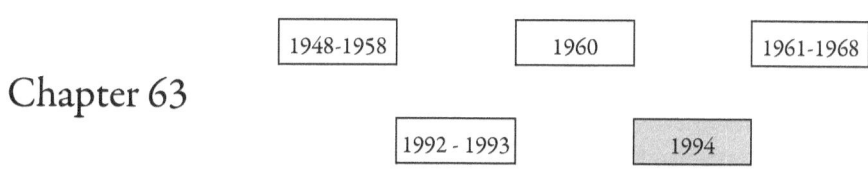

JUDGE RAWLINGS'S HOUSE
MONDAY, OCTOBER 17, 1994

Walker Atkins and Judge Rawlings were sitting in the judge's quarters at a table listening to the frustrated voice of Bob Gideon, the Dunsmore's high-priced attorney from Atlanta, playing through the speaker phone.

"Your Honor, did our local counsel deliver a draft of the order you requested Friday?"

"Yes, he did," answered the Judge.

"Then why are you postponing its effective date for a week?" he asked in exasperation.

"Because Rebeca Dunsmore may have a twin brother, which changes . . . everything."

"Your Honor, this is unprecedented," he said.

"Mr. Gideon, I agree, it is," said Judge Rawlings. "But it doesn't change my decision. Understand that nothing has really changed. The order your office drafted is acceptable, so long as another heir to Rebeca Dunsmore's estate does not turn up. Mr. Atkins believes he has located just such an heir, so I will not sign or enter the order with an effective date of last Friday, as originally intended. Instead, I am giving Mr. Atkins one week to locate this person and deliver them to my courtroom. If he doesn't do so by 9:00 a.m. next Monday, then I'll sign the order."

Mr. Gideon didn't miss a beat, and he quickly pulled his wildcard. "And what if medical decisions concerning Rebeca Dunsmore need to be made *this* week, Your Honor? Who will make them?"

"We will cross that bridge if and when we get there, Mr. Gideon," said the judge.

The call ended, and the judge stood to put his robe on, as he was due in the courtroom. But before leaving, he turned to Walker. "I don't know at this point if I want there to be a twin brother out there or not. But I do know this: this mess ends next Monday. You will get no further reprieves."

"Understood," Walker replied.

* * *

As Walker left the judge's quarters and walked back to his office, his head was spinning. It's all coming together, he thought. Walker hoped and prayed that Joseph did exist and that they could find him. Because if he did and they could, then Walker would win—beating back the Dunsmores and serving his client, Rebeca, in the process. He'd be known as the man who'd exposed the Dunsmores, not just as crooked but quite possibly as murderers. And finally, most of all, he'd no longer be seen as the defenseless little boy, tied to the chair waiting to be rescued by his older brother, Eli. He'd be free. He'd be free of all of it.

Everything depended on finding Joseph. Walker had told the judge that his wife and Abigail Baker had driven Mrs. Doretha Middleton back to the nursing home in Columbia—that they had located Rebeca's grandmother, Esther Taylor, and were hot on Joseph's trail. Walker had not told the judge, however, that Esther had been entirely uncooperative and that they had no idea where the trail began or might end.

Walker glanced at his watch; it was 9:30. Isabelle and Abigail were due to be knee-deep in government records by now. Yesterday, after their lunch outside Columbia, they'd called Walker and told him they were going to stay and look for birth certificates and death certificates that might back up Mrs. Middleton's story.

At the time, Walker had thought it was a great idea, but after leaving the judge's quarters, he knew that unless Joseph showed up in the courtroom, those certificates added up to nothing more than smoke. They needed a fire.

South Carolina Vital Records Office
Columbia, South Carolina
Monday, October 17, 1994

While Walker had been on the call with Judge Rawlings and the Dunsmores' lawyer, Abigail and Isabelle had been waiting outside of the South Carolina Vital Records Office in Columbia, waiting for it to open. As soon as it did, they found their way down the hall and began interrogating the clerk behind a plexiglass window. The clerk wasn't very helpful, but she eventually acquiesced to Abigail's request to let them sit in front of the microfiche machine and research the records themselves.

They started by searching for Rebeca's birth. Rebeca was born on October 10, 1968. Records were not stored by date of birth; they were recorded in chronological order according to the assigned Birth Certificate Number. A ledger at the front listed in what months and years one could find a particular range of birth certificate numbers. Armed with this information, they found the birth certificates for both Rebeca Dunsmore and Joseph Dunsmore. The mother listed on each birth certificate was Dixie LeMar Dunsmore, and the father was listed as Randal Dunsmore. The birth certificates were registered in Richland County on October 22, 1968, and the attending physician was listed as Dr. Wagner.

Next up was finding the corresponding death certificates for Dixie and Joseph.

These records were stored differently, but it didn't take too long for Abigail and Isabelle to find them. Sure enough, all was in order. The death certificate for Dixie showed that she'd died on the tenth of October, the same day the twins were born, and the death certificate for Joseph listed the twelfth as the day he died.

So far, the public records supported the story the Dunsmores had been peddling for the last twenty-six years. However, now the *real* work began—the hunt for the birth certificates that they theorized Esther would have recorded herself.

According to Doretha Middleton, Jeremiah left town with baby Joseph to hide the baby from the Dunsmores. Were this the case, Abigail and Isabelle surmised that Esther would have wanted to give the child every chance to succeed in life—and that would've required a legitimate birth certificate.

They began the hunt. After forty minutes—*bingo!* They found Joseph's birth certificate.

Esther Taylor had mailed in Joseph's birth certificate from the neighboring county—Lexington County—and she had done so on an earlier date than the date that Dr. Wagner's office had mailed Rebeca's birth certificate. As a result, the records were recorded four days apart by different clerks. Esther listed herself as the attending midwife, and the date of birth was October 10, 1968. The child's name was different, however. Rather than Joseph Dunsmore, the child's name was listed as Joseph Jeremiah Taylor. The child's father was accurately listed as Jeremiah Taylor.

Esther's commitment to accuracy didn't waver when she'd written in Joseph's mother as Dixie LeMar Dunsmore. However, now the question was: How could Dixie LeMar Dunsmore give birth to twins in Richmond County and another child in Lexington County on the same day?

The answer: She couldn't.

Abigail and Isabelle high-fived each other, made multiple copies of what they had found, and headed back to the nursing home to confront Esther. But first, a phone call to Walker with the good news.

* * *

Abigail and Isabelle walked through the front door of the Grace and Mercy Nursing Home and asked to see Esther Taylor. After a short wait, Esther met them in the lobby.

"Is there someplace we can speak quietly?" asked Abigail.

Reluctantly, Esther led them back to her office. Esther remained standing, so Isabelle and Abigail did too.

After an awkward moment, Esther spoke up. "Now, what can I do for you?"

"Mrs. Taylor, all three of us *are* mothers," Isabelle began. "And as you so clearly pointed out yesterday, there's *nothing* we wouldn't do to protect our children. And there's no amount of money that would change that." Isabelle looked at Abigail, who nodded for her to continue. "Mrs. Taylor, we have proof that the Dunsmores have been lying all these years about what *really* happened with Dixie, Rebeca, and Joseph. We know that your grandson, Joseph, didn't die when he was two days old."

As Isabelle was talking, Abigail reached into her briefcase and pulled out the microfiche copy of Joseph's birth certificate, which Esther had recorded all those years ago.

Esther picked it up, looked at it as if she were seeing a long lost loved one, held it close to her chest, and wept. Izzy and Abigail looked at each other with a shared expression of hope. Was this Esther's confession? They waited patiently for her to say something, and were shocked when she whispered, "They killed my baby . . . Jeremiah, they killed him . . ."

Esther reached for the corner of the desk to keep from falling. Isabelle and Abigail caught her and helped her to the sofa.

"*Who* killed him?" asked Isabelle as she took a seat next to Esther.

"The Dunsmores! Who do you think?" she said in anger. She collected herself and smiled at Isabelle, whispering, "I'm sorry."

"No need to apologize," Isabelle said, squeezing Mrs. Taylor's hand.

Abigail took a seat on Mrs. Taylor's other side.

Esther turned and looked at her kindly and continued, "I know they did. After the twins were born, Jeremiah took off with little Joseph and headed for Buffalo, New York, where we had family. He'd planned on moving to Toronto with Miss Dixie, where he believed they'd be more accepting of a biracial couple."

"Did he ever return to South Carolina?" asked Isabelle.

"Yes, once. That photograph Mother showed you was taken when he visited. He wanted to return permanently, but it wasn't safe, so he went back to New York. He ended up staying put in Buffalo until he got drafted. He tried to get out of it and argued that he was a single parent, but they said he had to go, anyway. So, he went to Canada instead. A lot of men did. After Jimmy Carter pardoned all the draft dodgers, he felt it was safe to come back to America. Well, he did and moved to California. He was struggling financially, though, and wanted to move back to South Carolina, where he had family and a support system."

"But it wasn't safe to return, was it?" Isabelle muttered, and Esther's eyes met hers.

She nodded, grimly. "No, it wasn't safe, but my Jeremiah was sick of runnin' and he had a child to take care of—and even though we were family, we didn't have money to help him in the way he needed."

"What did he do?"

"He did the one thing he never should've done," Esther said, tearing up again. "He came back to South Carolina to confront Colin Dunsmore.

He said if Mr. Dunsmore didn't give him money, he'd go public with the whole story."

Izzy and Abigail looked at one another in shock.

"My baby was found dead in a back alley from a heroin overdose." She scoffed, brushing away a tear. There was anger in her eyes, but it was eclipsed by grief. "But I know they killed him. My son was *not* a druggie," she said firmly. "I sought out the coroner, who pronounced his death an overdose, and I asked for his autopsy. The toxicology report indicated an overdose, but the mortician who buried him told me there were no signs of drug use—no track marks on his arms or legs, *nothing*."

Esther staired at Izzy and Abigail, still clutching Joseph's birth certificate to her chest, and whispered, "So, you see. I have a right to fear the Dunsmores. Joseph is safe, and that's the way he's going to stay."

"But Mrs. Taylor—"

"*But* nothing. I understand why you are here today, and I hold no grudge against you, but I'm asking you to leave us alone. If news of this ever becomes public, I am prepared to deny it and blame it all on the rantings of an old woman."

"No, you will not."

All three heads turned and saw Doretha Middleton stepping into her daughter's office from around the corner.

"The problem with these big offices is that someone can crack the door and listen to everything bein' said before anyone is the wiser. Now, Esther, I love you dearly, but you gonna listen to me," she said, raising her brows at her daughter. "I spent my life bein' afraid, livin' in the shadows, tryin' to stay outta trouble. No more. Do you know what the Lord tells us more than anything else?"

This was not a rhetorical question. Doretha was waiting for an answer.

"Yes, Momma, I do."

"He tells us not to be afraid. That's right. Now, I've spent time with these two fine women and Isabelle's husband. They good people. It's time we put these Dunsmores down."

* * *

MUSC Hospital
Charleston, South Carolina
Later that same day

Walker was sitting at Rebeca's bedside in the hospital going through a stack of documents Mrs. Beasley had dropped off for him to review when he heard a knock on the door and saw his brother Eli poke his head in.

"Hey, Walkie-Talkie, you want some company?"

Walker let the document he was holding fall into his lap. "Love some. Come on in."

Eli stood at the end of Rebeca's bed. "Any change?"

"No. Nothing."

"Little brother, you look tired. What are you doing here?"

"If what Mrs. Middleton is telling us is true, then the Dunsmores were capable of murdering two babies twenty-five years ago when Johnny was just starting his political career. Do you think they would stop short of murdering Rebeca *now* to protect it?" he asked.

"So you're keeping guard?"

"Yeah. At least until this whole thing plays out."

"But what if there's no truth to it? What if she doesn't have a twin brother?" Eli asked.

"Good news. I got off the phone with Izzy a while ago. He's real. Joseph is alive and he's ready to testify—here, in Charleston."

"Wow. That's huge. Way to go."

"Don't credit me. That belongs to Izzy and Abigail."

"What happens next?" Eli asked.

"We've got to transport Joseph here without the Dunsmores finding out. No doubt they're looking for him too. We have the benefit of a head-start, but they have the advantage of being ruthless."

Eli nodded in agreement.

Walker was looking into his hands resting in his lap, searching for the right words.

"Big brother, I need to brainstorm. I need a good plan. You wanna do that with me? You wanna help?"

A smile from ear-to-ear spread across Eli's face. "So, little brother is ready to admit he can't take on the world alone."

"Yeah, yeah, yeah," he said. "Do you want to help or not?"

"Love to."

Chapter 64

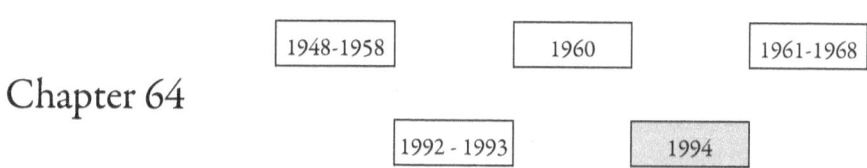

RANDAL DUNSMORE'S HOME
TUESDAY, OCTOBER 18, 1994

Johnny and Colin Dunsmore were meeting in Randal's home office. Randal couldn't join them, of course, because he was dead. Johnny had been in Columbia the day before carrying out duties as governor and then had a few campaign stops late in the day, so while he had spoken with his father the day before, he had only done so briefly.

"I can't believe this is happening," Johnny said. "How did Walker Atkins find out Rebeca's brother was alive?"

"Hell if I know. I just know we have to find him before he does."

"But we searched for him for years and couldn't find him. How do you expect us to now?"

"We need help. Get Luis Sanchez on the phone," said Colin.

The last person Johnny wanted to call was Luis Sanchez. "Dad, we don't need him. We can take care of this ourselves," he said as he resumed pacing.

Colin was sitting behind Randal's desk. "You think I don't know?"

Johnny paused, staring at his father. "What?" His hands shook as he took a long swig of his drink to cushion the blow of what he feared was coming next.

"Of course, I know," Colin added. "I've known for some time."

Johnny stared at his father in disbelief. What *exactly* did he know? Could he somehow know about Nadia? For the last thirty years, Johnny had done all he could to bury the memory of her. He was sure that no one knew outside of Luis and Gilberto Sanchez. Lord knew he'd tried to forget.

"I don't know what you're talkin' about, Dad. We don't need them." He chugged his drink and reached for the bottle to refill it.

"Son, I know all about *Island Girl*." Colin's tone was cavalier, but it still struck Johnny like a physical blow. His dad waved a hand dismissively. "I've seen the photographs. Why do you think I've been doing business with Luis and Gilberto all these years? I know what they're capable of."

"I-I didn't kill her, I swear." Johnny hoped his father didn't notice how bad he was shaking.

Colin rose from his seat, walked around the desk, and stood face to face with his son.

Johnny searched his father's eyes for a flicker of empathy but found only smoldering fire and brimstone.

"I know what the Sanchezes are capable of," Colin said simply, "and I know what *you're* capable of. Randal committed *suicide?* Right. You think I believe that? And Rebeca was the victim of a burglary gone bad? Are you kidding me? You fucked up. That ungrateful bitch, Rebeca, is still alive, and you better pray she doesn't come out of the coma."

Colin swatted his son's drink out of his hands; it shattered on the floor. "We're so close to the White House, I can taste it," he said, gripping his son's collar. "You win reelection here in South Carolina, wait out Billy Boy until his time is up, and then, it's our turn. Now, pull it together and get your old college roommate on the phone."

* * *

Thirty minutes later . . .

"Luis, thanks for coming to the phone," Colin Dunsmore said, having finally convinced Johnny that their only option was to contact the Sanchezes. "I have Johnny here with me. We have a situation we believe you can help with."

Colin spent the next ten minutes bringing Luis up to speed about the lawsuit involving his granddaughter's trust. He ended with the latest news that the judge had delayed signing the order that would make Johnny the trustee for Rebeca's trust as well as her legal guardian.

"So, you see, if this Joseph shows up and a paternity test proves that he is Rebeca's brother, then we're going to have to explain a lie we've been telling for the last twenty-five years," Colin explained.

"You mean the story you've been telling every election season—that your grandson had died at the age of two days old—was a lie, and he's out there somewhere right now?" Luis laughed softly.

Colin didn't answer, and sat rigidly in place, awaiting Luis's counsel.

"I'm going to guess that Randal wasn't the father, either," Luis said.

His comment was met with silence.

"What do you expect *us* to do?" asked Luis.

"To do what we can't do," said Colin, firmly. "Our hands are tied with the election coming up. We can't push to have that girl Rebeca unplugged. She's in a coma, and if she's taken off life support, she'll be dead in a day or so. How would that look to voters?"

Luis repeated himself, more slowly this time, as if to a child, *"What do you expect us to do?"*

"Take care of the *situation*!" Johnny interjected. "Take care of Rebeca. Can't you sneak someone into the hospital and give her an injection or something?"

"You watch too many movies. It's not that easy. Besides, my father and I have been talking. We're not so sure the Dunsmores are worth investing in anymore. Why should we help you out of this mess?"

"Look, you piece of shit," Johnny said, just drunk enough to not be afraid, "if Joseph turns up and a paternity test proves they're brother and sister, then I'm done, and I'll take you down with me. And before you threaten to hang Island Girl's murder on me, don't waste your breath. I'll lead with it. I'll put *you* on the defensive. By the time I'm through, in the public's eyes, I'll be a *victim* of your blackmail. We still have enough juice to get the hearings into offshore banking kick-started again."

After a moment of silence, Luis spoke up. "Wouldn't it make more sense to find Joseph before they do?"

Colin smiled at Johnny and picked up the conversation. "Yes, which is where you come in. You have more resources than we do."

"Well, first things first, shouldn't we track the steps of this attorney, Walker Atkins? He'll probably lead us right to him, don't you think?" asked Luis.

"We thought of that, and before we called you, we did some recon ourselves. Walker Atkins is sitting in the hospital room with Rebeca."

"Yeah, I guess he suspects someone might try to harm her," said Johnny in an effort to get a laugh. No one laughed.

"We've got a man watching him. If he goes anywhere, we'll know," Colin said.

Johnny held up his hand to get his dad's attention. "Hold on, Luis." Then, turning to his dad, he said, "He's paging me."

"Hang on, Luis. Our guy is paging us," said Colin. "Let us call him on the other line and see what's up. Don't hang up. We'll be right back."

Johnny called his guy, learned what he needed to know, and switched back to the line Luis was holding on.

"Okay. This is interesting. Walker's brother, Eli, and his father-in-law, Quaid Dawson, just paid Walker a visit at the hospital. They were all in Rebeca's hospital room for about ten minutes and then left. Eli got into Quaid's truck, and they drove off together. We told our man to let us know where they're going."

"And you're saying this is good information?" asked Luis, skeptically.

"Absolutely. The three of them go way back. Quaid's wealthy—he can get stuff done—and he has helped the brothers out of a jam or two before."

"Okay. When you know more, call us back," said Luis.

"Will do," said Colin.

"Oh, and one more thing," Luis said. "If either of you ever threaten me again, I'll kill you."

* * *

Later that Tuesday in Randal's home office . . .

"Luis, it's Colin and Johnny here again. We have more information."

"Go on," said Luis.

"Eli Atkins and Quaid Dawson just pulled up to the Johns Island Airport, where Quaid Dawson hangs his plane. We made a call and learned that he filed a flight plan for McClellan-Palomar Airport, in Carlsbad, California. That must be where Joseph lives."

"What kind of plane does this Mr. Quaid Dawson fly?" asked Luis.

"A King Air 260," answered Johnny.

"A real slug. They'll have to refuel twice and spend the night somewhere. We'll take our Gulfstream and beat them there. Fax me pictures of what these men look like, and I'll have my men waiting for them at the airport when they land. We'll trail them to where Joseph lives. If the man they lead us to is the Joseph you fear, then you have nothing to fear."

* * *

MUSC Hospital, Rebeca's Room
Tuesday evening . . .

The hospital staff earlier in the day had wheeled in a small cot for Walker to sleep on. The previous two nights, he'd slept, in vain, in a chair.

Walker was going over in his mind, for the umpteenth time, the plan he and Eli had come up with the night before to deliver Joseph Taylor, Rebeca's twin brother, safely to the Superior Court in downtown Charleston. All the wheels were in motion. While he was watching Rebeca in her hospital room, Isabelle and Abigail were on their way back to Charleston with Mrs. Doretha Middleton. Eli and Quaid were somewhere over Tennessee. But what was Joseph up to right now?

More importantly, what were the Dunsmores up to?

* * *

McClellan-Palomar Airport in Carlsbad, California
Wednesday, October 19, 1994

Two dangerous-looking men were sitting in their car in the Carlsbad parking lot airport, waiting for the arrival of a King Air 260 and looking at a faxed photo of men supposedly on the flight whom they were to follow. The man in the passenger seat was looking through his binoculars and reciting the tail number of a plane that had just touched down to his partner.

"That's it."

"So, we're not supposed to take these guys out. Is that right?"

"That's right, unless, of course, they give us no choice. We're supposed to follow them and see where they go. The boss says they're gonna lead us to some Black guy, twenty-six years old, and *that's* the guy we take out."

They watched as the two men exited the plane and approached a man leaning on a four-door Mercedes Benz S 600 Sedan parked on the tarmac. The men shook hands, got in the car, and drove off. The hitmen that Gilberto Sanchez hired followed them.

* * *

"Travis, it's good to see you," said Eli. "You remember Quaid Dawson, don't you?"

"I do, indeed. And good to see you, my friend. It's been too long," Travis said as he pulled out of the airport.

Travis McCoy was the scion of a wealthy Texas oil family. Travis lived to gamble on the golf course, and he had developed a reputation far and wide doing so—which, by his own admission, made his job as a hustler more difficult but more satisfying when he won.

Travis and Eli had met over fifteen years ago in the Bahamas and were paired against each other in a match folks still talked about.

"So, what keeps you busy these days, Travis? You still scouring the world, looking for the rarest of the rare?" asked Eli.

"I am, indeed. I've heard rumors that a first edition copy of *The Wealth of Nations* signed by Adam Smith himself, and a few other eighteenth century luminaries, has surfaced; I'm keen to own it. But I doubt you flew out here to discuss my latest hobby," he said, eyeing Eli, "and I see you didn't bring your clubs with you. So, let's have it."

"Why don't we rent some?" Eli suggested, clapping McCoy on the shoulder. "Let's drive down to Torrey Pines. We'll take the long way. And let me know if the grey Ford Mustang that followed us out of the airport is still on our tail. I'll fill you in as we go."

* * *

"So, we're a diversion," Travis remarked.

"That's right," said Eli. "Joseph Taylor, the guy my brother needs in court tomorrow morning, lives in Portland, Oregon. In fact, he should be landing in Atlanta soon."

"If the Dunsmores are as powerful and well connected as you say, aren't you taking a big risk putting Joseph Taylor on a commercial flight? Couldn't they search airline manifests and be waiting for him?" Travis asked.

"They could but they wouldn't find him. Joseph is travelling under the name of Royce Jones. You remember Nash, of course, from our time together in the Bahamas."

"Yeah, we still keep in touch."

"I spoke to Nash late Monday night. He arranged for a commercial flight from Portland, Oregon to Atlanta, Georgia for a man named Royce Jones, Then, yesterday, he had a travel agency he's worked with before deliver Joseph his airline ticket and an Oregon driver's license for a Royce Jones, complete with his picture."

"Incredible," Quaid said.

"Yes, he is," Travis said. "So, how much longer do you want me to pretend to drive around like I know where I'm going?"

"Shouldn't be much longer if Joseph's flight into Atlanta was on time. We're waiting to hear that he is safely in our hands. We have a trusted driver meeting him at the airport. He's going to drive him to Charleston tonight and provide safe housing until he's due in court. Our guy in Atlanta will call Walker from a gas station once they are safely on their way back to Charleston. So, if that phone you have in your car actually works, it shouldn't be much longer until we get the call."

"It works," said Travis. And as if on demand, the phone rang, and Travis punched a button on the handset. "Travis McCoy here."

"Travis? Walker Atkins here. Good to hear from you, and thanks for your help."

"What's the good word?" asked Travis.

"The eagle has landed."

"That's great news. We'll talk soon," said Travis as he disconnected the call.

Eli and Quaid had heard Walker over the speakerphone and were laughing and high fiving in the back seat.

"And our timing is perfect," said Travis. "Here's the exit for Torrey Pines."

They pulled in and parked, and Eli exited the car and walked over to the grey Ford Mustang that had parked a few rows over. He wrapped his knuckles against the driver's side window until the driver lowered it and stared at Eli.

"You guys bring your clubs?" asked Eli.

Chapter 65

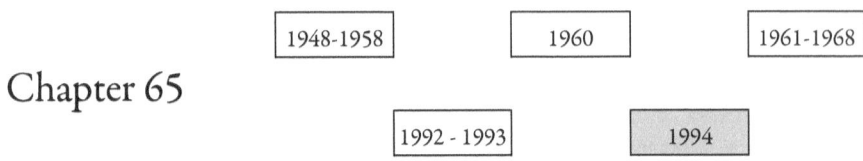

CHARLESTON COUNTY COURTHOUSE
JUDGE RAWLINGS'S COURTROOM
THURSDAY, OCTOBER 20, 1994

Walker was waiting next to the elevator in the underground parking lot beneath the courthouse for his star witness to arrive. Eddie Wentworth had picked up Joseph Taylor the day before at the Atlanta airport and had driven him to Charleston, where he spent the night at Eddie's house. Joshua Langston had arranged for a state trooper to stand outside of Rebeca's hospital room. They were leaving nothing to chance.

Walker saw a police car pull into the parking lot, and he waited, though not patiently, for Eddie and the officers to escort Joseph Taylor into the building. Walker couldn't remember the last time he was this excited to enter a courtroom. The car doors opened, and Walker saw Eddie and a young Black man get out of the back seat and walk towards him.

"Walker Atkins, I'd like to introduce you to Joseph Taylor," Eddie said. "And Joseph, this is Walker Atkins, your sister's attorney."

"Joseph, I can't tell you how happy I am to meet you. I have so many questions," he said as he chuckled lightly. "But that's going to have to wait. We're wanted in court. Are you ready for this?"

"I am," Jospeh said. "And I have a lot of questions for you too. But before we go in there, I want to say one thing . . . Thank you for what you have done for my sister and for my family."

Walker shook his head in recognition of the genuine sentiment, and then shook it again as he turned and pressed the elevator button in an attempt to ward off the tears.

* * *

Judge Rawlings's Courtroom

Judge Rawlings gaveled the courtroom to order.

"I issued my order last Friday naming Governor Dunsmore as Rebeca Dunsmore's legal guardian as well as the trustee for a trust established by Rebeca's grandmother on the grounds that the law, the facts, and considerations for practicality called for it. It was brought to my attention after I rendered this decision that Rebeca may have a twin brother who is alive. Now, we all know the story the Dunsmores have told us for years about how Randal's son—who was Rebeca's twin brother—died at birth along with their mother, Randal's first wife. If this twin brother is actually alive, then it is relevant for at least two reasons.

"First, I made Johnny Dunsmore the trustee under the assumption that Rebeca was the only beneficiary of the trust. If she has a twin brother who is alive, then I must reconsider.

"The second reason—and the more burning question before this court, as well as the distinguished members of the press who have descended on our fair city like a band of jackals—is why the Dunsmore family, from top to bottom, including our governor, has told us that this twin brother died at birth if the brother is in fact alive? Therefore, the purpose of this hearing is to determine whether Rebeca Dunsmore has a twin brother.

"Mr. Atkins, you may call your first witness."

Walker's first witness was Esther Taylor, who testified to the events of October 10, 1968, and the role she'd played. She testified that she had in fact recorded a separate birth certificate in the neighboring county for Joseph and that she was aware that Colin had seen to it that both a birth certificate and a fraudulent death certificate were recorded for Joseph in Richland County.

Walker's next witness was the Medical University of South Carolina lab technician who conducted the paternity test and testified that Rebeca and Joseph were, indeed, brother and sister.

Walker then put Joseph on the stand so the folks in the courtroom could meet him. His presence—his flesh and blood—was all the testimony he needed to provide.

The final testimony, and the testimony that sealed the fate of Johnny Dunsmore, was that of Doretha Midleton, who tearfully recounted the story of how she'd overheard Colin, Johnny, and Randal Dunsmore plot the murder of her two great-grandchildren and what she did to save their lives.

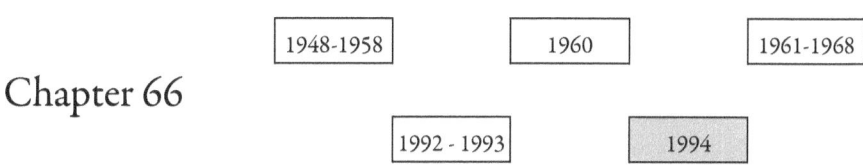

Chapter 66

NINE MONTHS LATER AT ELI'S RESTAURANT, THE ABACO
JUNE 1995

Walker and Isabelle, Eli and Rachel, Eddie and Vannesa, Abigail and her husband Tim, and Monty and Emmylou were gathered around the bar on the outside deck awaiting the guests of honor. The wine was flowing, and the croaking frogs and chirping cicadas provided background music for the evening.

When Joseph and Rebeca Taylor summited the top step and joined the crowd at the bar, the cheers were not limited to their group. Their story was widely known and celebrated. They were minor celebrities and every patron sitting on the deck clapped and cheered when they appeared.

Rebeca walked with a cane and was assisted by her brother, Joseph. Walker pulled up a stool and Isabelle helped her get settled. She had come out of her coma in February, to the surprise of every doctor that had examined her condition. The men and women in prayer groups across the Lowcountry were not surprised.

Rebeca was not comfortable with the attention but took it in stride. While their group enjoyed a wonderful meal Eli's kitchen had prepared, well-wishers from other tables came by to speak with Joseph and Rebeca. Walker and Eli were sitting side by side at the other end of the table, taking it all in and sharing a laugh between them about something Eli had said. Izzy walked over, sat down between them, and with each of her hands, grasped one of theirs.

"What's going on, you two?" she asked.

Walker cocked his head and looked at his beautiful, loving wife. "Oh, we're just thinking about how blessed we are."

"Yeah, we are, ya big goof," she said and then planted a kiss on him.

* * *

Throughout the evening, everyone in the group swapped stories of days past and looked forward to more times together. Little needed to be said about the "Dunsmore Affair," as it had come to be referred to in the press. The coverage following the final hearing had been unrelenting and every detail of the fallout was delivered in vivid color.

In a nutshell, Johnny was not reelected as governor, but Joshua *was* reelected as the attorney general. His opponent, Skip Jackson, was revealed to be the office mole who had been leaking news to the Dunsmore family and was now serving a two-year term in a federal prison.

The Dunsmores hired a slick PR firm out of New York to deal with the fallout, but nothing could be done once Rebeca recovered consciousness and identified Johnny Dunsmore as her assailant. Once that happened, the rest of the clan turned into a circular firing squad: Johnny implicating Blythe, Blythe implicating Johnny and Dexter, and Dexter implicating Blythe and Johnny. The phone calls Blythe made from the law offices of Homer Boscoe to the phone number for Tommy, the hitman recommended to her by Dexter, at first bolstered Blythe's claim that Dexter had ordered the hit on Rebeca—the thinking being that the attorney phoned Tommy on Dexter's behalf. However, the story fell apart when office records showed that Blythe was at the attorney's office every time the calls were made, but the same could not be said for the attorney. Tommy's ironclad alibi didn't help Blythe's story either.

Dexter pled guilty to everything he was charged with, but his sentence was reduced to time served because he helped Walker recover the assets he had stolen from Rebeca's trust. Dexter collected the money on the street and arranged for someone to purchase Tattle Tails from the trust.

As for Blythe and Johnny, they were sitting in jail, without parole, waiting to be tried for murder. Johnny could afford the best defense possible; Blythe could not. However, the fanfare that would follow her case attracted the attention of a media-obsessed attorney who typically only represented Hollywood stars. He took the case at no charge. The television exposure and the book rights would pay handsomely.

Rebeca was also able to help the AG's office establish a connection between the Dunsmores and the host of companies that had preyed on Loraine and Hugh Gaston. The law firm of Sanchez and Sanchez closed their Miami office and decided to lay low for a while. The bankruptcy court took a dim view of people using the bankruptcy code to shield themselves from criminal behavior and, using its broad powers, seized and sold the assets of the Dunsmore clan so that damages the Gastons and other victims had been awarded in civil suits Walker and other attorneys in town won for their clients could be paid.

It was all too much for Colin Dunsmore and he took the cowardly way out by putting his World War Two service revolver to his head and splattering his brains across the wall of his suite at the Charleston Place Hotel.

Colin's wife, Barbara, checked herself into the Betty Ford Center with no plans of leaving, ever.

Johnny's wife, Caroline, divorced him quicker than you can say Marlborough Lights. She retreated to the family ranch in Virginia where she remained hidden for several months. The latest rumors swirling about the tobacco heir had her traipsing about Austria and Switzerland on the arm of a minor prince from Liechtenstein.

Doretha had made one more trip back to Charleston to visit Rebeca in the hospital, but she was slipping and wouldn't be traveling anymore; she was almost ninety-three years old, so this was to be expected. Esther was looking forward to retiring from her position at the nursing home—everyone assumed she was waiting for her mother to pass—and spending time with her grandchildren.

Joseph had enjoyed his time in the South but would be returning to his home in Oregon. He was engaged to a girl from Portland and looked forward to building a family there.

Finally, there was Rebeca. She was the reason they were gathered around the table and the reason for the upbeat mood. Since coming out of the coma, her condition had continually improved. Her speech was slurred and probably always would be, but she was walking, and cognitively, she was returning to normal and on her way back to being Rebeca. Her brother asked her to move to Oregon with him until she fully recovered. They had become close, and she was tempted, but she declined and said she wanted to stay in the Lowcountry. With the money from the trust which she now shared with her brother, for which Walker was happily serving as trustee, she could afford the care and treatment she needed right where she was. Rebeca and Joseph planned to visit each other regularly, and she was thrilled when her future sister-in-law asked her to be one of her bridesmaids.

When the bankruptcy court ordered the sale of the home she grew up in with Randal, she was given time to remove any personal effects. Joseph retrieved boxes and other items she knew were in the attic and they went through them together.

They came across a small, tan suitcase decorated with images of airplanes that she had never seen. At the bottom of the suitcase, they found a letter in an unaddressed envelope dated October 10, 1968.

> *"My dearest child,*
>
> *I don't know if you are a boy or a girl as I write this, because you haven't been born yet. I'm leaving my husband today so I can live my life with your father, Jeremiah, a man I love very much. We don't know what lies ahead of us, and to be honest, I'm scared. But I know what lies behind me—a lifetime of mistakes. But the preacher at church tells me that makes no difference because He came to save us, not because of what we've done right but because of all that we've done wrong. Well, that's me, for sure. I've done a lot wrong. But there's one thing I'm gonna get right, and that's having you, being your momma, and setting you on your way.*
>
> *I look forward to meeting you. It shouldn't be long now.*
>
> *Love,*
>
> *Your Momma*

The End

Afterword

This book is a work of fiction. When I reach into the past, however, I try to portray it accurately. The Dunsmore family, the bad guys in this story, are powerful within the Democratic Party in South Carolina. This book takes place between 1954 and 1994, during which time the Democratic Party won most elections in South Carolina. That had been the case since the end of the Civil War. Once I decided that my bad guy would be a politician, given the timeframe in which this story occurs, this person had to be a member of the Democratic Party. The story would not have made sense if the Dunsmores had been members of the Republican Party. If you're a Democrat, don't take this story personally. I have tremendous disdain for politics and most politicians. Furthermore, no politician needs any author's help being made to look bad. They are quite capable of doing so themselves, as they prove most every day.

In chapter nineteen, Nadia finds Johnny sitting in the carols of the ground floor of the Riggs Library. This scene occurs in 1960. However, the scene I described could not have happened as I described it, because in 1960, the Riggs Library was housed inside Healy Hall and students sitting inside the library would not have been visible to people on the front lawn outside. The scene I described could have taken place in the Lauinger Memorial Library, which does have a ground floor visible to all outside, and which is often referred to by Georgetown students as the 'fishbowl.' Lauinger was not opened until 1970 when it became the main library on campus.

In chapter eighteen, Johnny Dunsmore has dinner with his girlfriend, Caroline Thistle, and her parents at a restaurant called 1789. This scene occurs in 1960. However, the restaurant named 1789, which is one block from the Georgetown campus, did not open until 1962.

Acknowledgements

I enjoy writing books. I enjoy crafting the story and figuring out both what the story is and how to tell it. Along the way, I will reach out to someone who has expertise in an area and seek help. While I went to law school, it was a long time ago and I only practiced for a couple of years. As a result, while I may know what questions to ask, I have long since forgotten the answers. I want to thank Jeff and Carter for their help with the trust and estate matters that came up as I was writing this book. You know who you are. Thank you. I took certain liberties with procedural matters, for instance, when it comes to probating a will or seeking court ordered custody over an incapacitated individual, but I did so to move the story along. As for the courtroom proceedings, I didn't seek the input of a litigator and it no doubt shows. I take full responsibility for all mistakes in this book.

When it came to turning the manuscript into a readable book, I couldn't have done it without the excellent editing services of Bublish. com. They also designed the cover. Thank you.

This is my third book, but I still feel new to the game. I drew energy and encouragement from the support my wife Lyn provided. *Lyn, thank you for listening to me and giving me your honest feedback along the way. I love the conversations we share about story lines, characters, book covers, etc... I'm looking forward to working on the next book with you!*

www.ingramcontent.com/pod-product-compliance
Lightning Source LLC
LaVergne TN
LVHW091615070526
838199LV00044B/809